D0385220

By S. N. Behrman

Novels

THE WORCESTER ACCOUNT
PORTRAIT OF MAX
THE SUSPENDED DRAWING ROOM
DUVEEN

Plays

THE SECOND MAN
SERENA BLANDISH
BIOGRAPHY
BRIEF MOMENT
METEOR
RAIN FROM HEAVEN
END OF SUMMER
AMPHITRYON 38 (Adapted from the French of Giraudoux)
WINE OF CHOICE
NO TIME FOR COMEDY
THE PIRATE
JANE
JACOBOWSKY AND THE COLONEL (with Franz Werfel)
DUNNIGAN'S DAUGHTER
I KNOW MY LOVE (From Auprès de ma Blonde)
FANNY (with Joshua Logan)
THE COLD WIND AND THE WARM
LORD PENGO
BUT FOR WHOM CHARLIE

By S. N. Behrman

Books

DUVEEN

THE WORCESTER ACCOUNT

PORTRAIT OF MAX

THE SUSPENDED DRAWING ROOM

THE BURNING GLASS (*A Novel*)

Plays

THE SECOND MAN

SERENA BLANDISH

METEOR

BRIEF MOMENT

BIOGRAPHY

RAIN FROM HEAVEN

END OF SUMMER

AMPHITRYON 38 (*adapted from the French of Giraudoux*)

WINE OF CHOICE

NO TIME FOR COMEDY

THE TALLEY METHOD

THE PIRATE

JACOBOWSKY AND THE COLONEL (*with Franz Werfel*)

DUNNIGAN'S DAUGHTER

JANE (*from Somerset Maugham*)

I KNOW MY LOVE (*from Achard*)

FANNY (*with Joshua Logan*)

THE COLD WIND AND THE WARM

LORD PENGO

BUT FOR WHOM CHARLIE

The Burning Glass

The Morality Plays

The Burning Glass

by S. N. BEHRMAN

A Novel

LITTLE, BROWN AND COMPANY *Boston Toronto*

LIBRARY OF CONGRESS CATALOG CARD NO. 68–17266

FIRST EDITION

We are grateful for the permission of the publishers, Faber and Faber Ltd. and
Harcourt, Brace & World, Inc., to quote lines from "Gerontion" and from "The
Love Song of J. Alfred Prufrock" from *Collected Poems 1909–1962* by T. S. Eliot.
Also for the permission of Brandt & Brandt to quote "Churchbells" from *Pencil in
the Air* by Samuel Hoffenstein.

*Published simultaneously in Canada
by Little, Brown & Company (Canada) Limited*

PRINTED IN THE UNITED STATES OF AMERICA

For Brigitta and Goddard

I have not striven, in this book, for strict chronological accuracy of world events. I have tried rather to convey the atmosphere of the time. Some of the characters in *The Burning Glass* are fictional, the rest are dead, with some obvious exceptions.

The powers by which bodies operate are entirely unknown.

DAVID HUME

1
Salzburg

1. The Verandah

"Goyim nachus!" said Kaetchen.

He and Stanley Grant were on the boat deck of the *Normandie* watching Varina Lawson shooting, with merciless accuracy, at a spray of revolving clay ducks swung out over the rail. The last duck shattered, Varina turned to them. Grant couldn't help smiling. At the same time he was embarrassed and a little shocked at Kaetchen's lapse into Yiddish patois. He hoped that Varina hadn't overheard. She hadn't but she saw Grant smiling.

"What's funny?"

"Something Kaetchen said."

Varina twined her arm through Kaetchen's.

"Let me in on it."

"You tell her, Stanley," said Kaetchen.

"How can you explain a thing like that?"

"It's very simple," said Kaetchen.

The three of them walked to the main lounge where they sat down to tea. Varina was tall, gray-eyed, perfectly tweeded, a beguiling scar on her forehead. She had a low, tender, husky voice, a slow, drawling way of speaking.

"Tell me, darling, what was it that you said funny? Were you making fun of me?"

"Only generically."

"Now, Kaetchen, don't be cryptic. You know I'm simpleminded. It's wasted on me."

Kaetchen was the nickname by which he was known to his circle. His name was Alexander Löwe. But, many years before, his friend Stephanie von Arnim had said: "I simply can't call you Löwe. You don't look a bit like a lion with that adorable nose of yours. You look more like a kitten. I shall call you Kaetchen." And indeed, with his short, flat-surfaced nose, Löwe did look kittenish. The nickname stuck. From that moment none of his friends called him anything else. Kaetchen's voice never rose; his sentences were uninflected by emphasis. He purred.

Kaetchen, who knew that Grant was embarrassed and wished to drop the subject, determined to get him over this embarrassment.

"Stanley," he said, "you are a playwright. You make your living by dialogue. Tell Varina."

Grant didn't exactly care for the assignment but he undertook it. How could he convey to this innocent alien the nuances of Yiddish argot? He was annoyed with Kaetchen for having employed it.

"Well . . ." he began and stopped, baffled.

Löwe knew what Grant was going through and he was enjoying himself. Grant had become his protégé, his pupil, and he must teach him to be less self-conscious in a mixed society.

"Speak up, Stanley," he said. "Varina's on our side."

Varina leaped to the bait.

"Is it something Jewish? Then do tell it. Do!"

She conveyed that anything Jewish must be delectable. It was the summer of 1937 and the Jewish question had been given acrid stimulus by the goings-on in Germany. Grant plunged in.

"It was while you were shooting at the ducks . . ."

"Yes?" urged Varina, avid for still another insight into the arcana of her favorite race.

"You see," said Grant, "there are certain diversions, certain ways of life — blood sports for instance — safaris in Africa . . . that we're shut out from — that we don't — "

Grant bogged down.

"I can't make it, Kaetchen."

Kaetchen took over.

"Stanley's got the wrong approach. It's not that we are denied these precincts. It's that we can't understand the impulse to enter them. Stanley mentioned safaris — the idea that people should voluntarily endure God-knows-what hardships and untold expense for the pleasure of shooting an elephant or a tiger seems funny to us. While you were shooting the clay ducks, a Yiddish expression popped into my mind, that's all. I said: 'Goyim nachus!' "

"What does it mean, darling? I long to know."

"Nachus means pleasure, pride and pleasure. The expression connotes a mild bewilderment at the curious diversions from which gentiles derive pleasure."

"I love it," said Varina. "Teach it to me. Say it for me!"

Löwe repeated and Varina echoed until she had it pat.

"Next time I see Father in that ridiculous red coat and all those noisy foxhounds, I'll use it on *him!*"

Löwe smiled. He covered Varina's hand with his.

"I wish you wouldn't," he said. "Things are bad enough now!"

They were joined by Mary Kennicott and Ian Leith, the younger son of a ducal English family. Leith was tall, graceful, immensely attractive. He had wavy chestnut hair, keen blue eyes and an indolent manner. Mrs. Kennicott was the heiress, in her own right, to one of the great American fortunes. Her husband was heir to another. Mary Kennicott, fortyish, thinnish, was dark, with sad eyes. There was a downward curve to her mouth. Löwe introduced Grant to Leith and Mary. It was the first day out.

Mrs. Kennicott greeted Grant warmly.

"I am so glad to meet you. Kaetchen has been promising for a long time to produce you. You're on your way to Stephanie's, aren't you? I'm so pleased. Did you know I've taken half of her castle?"

"Yes," said Grant, "Kaetchen told me."

"You mustn't think of leaving till I come. I'll be there in two weeks. I'll give a party for you."

"Well," said Grant, "if Stephanie will let me stay that long . . ."

"I have never known," said Löwe, "an actress to kick out a playwright — not while he's writing a play for her."

"It's rather hard for me," said Ian, "to think of Stephanie as an actress. Can an aristocrat really be an actress?"

"She's a beautiful actress," said Grant.

Löwe admonished Ian. "Be careful what you say about Stephanie. My young friend is madly in love with her."

"Naturally. Who isn't! It's just that I can't imagine her an actress. The great actresses usually come from the gutter, don't they? Rachel and Sarah . . . ? But tell me, her accent — won't that be a handicap?"

"I'll make it an asset," said Grant, who had been worrying about precisely that.

"How?"

Grant was cagey.

"Somehow."

"That means that perhaps you don't know," said Ian, with a disarming smile.

"In any case," he went on, "Stephanie's in her castle right this minute studying with an English coach. She's picking up cockney like mad!"

Everybody laughed except Grant.

Ian went on. He had just returned from Hollywood where he'd been an extra in a film being shot there about Charles Stewart Parnell. He described the marvel of the set: exactly one half of the House of Commons reproduced perfectly, down to the last doorknob.

"The casting director just glanced at me," he said, "and there I was, a full-fledged M.P. So easy! No campaigning! You remember, Kaetchen, hearing me speak in the Midlands?"

He explained to the others.

"Kaetchen went down with my mother to hear me campaign. I won you both over, didn't I? Unfortunately, neither you nor my mother could vote in the Midlands. Humiliating defeat. Well, I couldn't make it at home but I made it in Hollywood. And do you know, I was paid twenty dollars a day, twice what I'd have got had I made it in England. Isn't it absurd? I think of starting a crusade! A living wage for M.P.'s. What about a letter to *The Times*? Haven't I a point? If half a House of Commons in Hollywood can pay its members twenty dollars a day, surely the whole one in Westminster should do as well? What do you think, Kaetchen, shall I agitate?"

Before Löwe could answer, René Wolfsohn, the most popular playwright in France, bore down upon them. Löwe introduced him to Mary Kennicott as the notorious French duelist. This referred to a duel Wolfsohn had fought with a rival playwright over some punctilio involving a woman. Both men had missed, which enemies of each thought a pity. Wolfsohn was sixty, a tall powerful man with a head like a buffalo's. Manet had painted him in a white sailor suit when he was five. The subject that interested him most was himself and he forced-marched everyone's attention to his favorite subject. His conceit was superb, ideal, a thing of beauty. He boasted that for forty years he had earned the contempt of his friends, the intellectuals — Gide, Claudel, Valéry. It simply proved to him that he was a true homme du théâtre, unblemished by the cloven hoof of literature. His feats of amour were notorious: the most distinguished women, half his age, kept falling in love with him. He treated them brutally. It added to his réclame.

Wolfsohn accused Grant.

"I've been calling you on the telephone all morning."

"Oh, was it you? How could I know? I don't answer the telephone."

"That is the sign of a weak man!"

Grant felt embarrassed. Actually, he was afraid of Wolfsohn's calls. Wolfsohn had been after Grant for months to collaborate with him on a play. He was very fertile in play ideas; he seemed to have a new one every day. He called them subjects. "I have a subject for you," he would say.

"Didn't you," Ian asked Wolfsohn, "once write a play about anti-Semitism?"

Grant's heart sank. Here it was again! *The* subject! *Was* there no other subject?

"I wrote the *first* play about anti-Semitism in France. The first scene is in the Jockey Club. Brilliant conception. All the members sitting around in evening clothes. They find out that a Jew has gotten in by mistake. It was a succès de scandale, that play — the talk of Paris. No one else would have had the audacity." He broke off, meditating his genius. "When I think," he said, "when I think . . ."

Everyone waited to hear the momentous thought. But Wolfsohn was lost in self-revery.

Kaetchen roused him.

"What do you think, René?" he asked.

"When I think of the masterpieces I might have written if my main interest in life hadn't been women! But it was amusing — what happened to me last week. I had a rendezvous in my rooms at midnight with a young lady who shall be nameless." He knew perfectly well that they all, except possibly Grant, knew who his current mistress was, but it was an easy fling at chivalry. "I dined on Long Island and met a ravishing lady at dinner. I devoted the evening to pursuit — needless to say successful. But I had forgotten all about my midnight date. I didn't get back to my rooms till three in the morning. There she was — she'd fallen asleep on the chaise longue in the parlor. My entrance woke her. She looked up at me with hatred and said: 'I don't know why I bother with you. You are old — you are ugly — and you are LATE!' "

Wolfsohn joined in the laughter with a good humor that made him irresistible.

"Why don't you write your reminiscences?" said Ian. "*The Women Who Have Loved Me.*"

"Because," said Wolfsohn, "I'm just at the beginning. The list wouldn't be definitive."

Ian uncoiled himself from his chair. "I've got to toddle off for a snooze," he said. "What with the going-away party and all that nonsense, I got no sleep at all last night."

"Why don't we all dine together?" said Mary. "It would be such fun."

Everybody agreed.

"I'll arrange it with the steward. Nine all right? Lovely."

"Let everybody telephone everybody," said Ian.

Varina and Ian strolled off.

Wolfsohn had been somewhat nicked by Ian.

"What do you see in that fellow?" he asked Mrs. Kennicott.

"Oh, he's enchanting. Don't you think so? The light touch."

After a moment of relapsed gaiety, Wolfsohn and Mrs. Kennicott left too.

Grant was relieved to find himself alone with his mentor. He relaxed from the strain of keeping his end up in company. He settled down pleasurably to savor the delights of the mop-up operation. This was traditional now between him and Löwe. The latter immersed him in glittering society and, after the dip, filled him in.

Grant was twenty-eight, Löwe fifty-six. Grant had been introduced to Löwe during his seemingly hopeless, lonely days in New York by a theatrical producer who had rejected his play. Löwe's passion was the theater. In his youth he had been a journalist in Vienna; he had come to New York as theatrical correspondent for a Viennese newspaper. By the time Grant met him, he had become Chef du Cabinet for the prestigious theatrical impresario of Central Europe, Rudolph Stohl. Just as Grant had met everybody through Löwe, so Löwe had met everybody through his strategic position with Stohl. Löwe had read Grant's play and liked it, but had not been able, for a long time, to persuade anyone else to like it. Grant was having a hard time finding a job. Penniless and prospectless, he used to wake up every morning with an acute, psychic pain in the pit of his stomach. It made getting up a fearsome and unnecessary procedure. He developed a slogan which he used to repeat to himself in the early morning hours: "It's better on your feet." Sometimes it was.

Grant confided to Löwe this daily hazard.

"That is the neurotic's privilege," Löwe had said, as if to assure Grant that he was not usurping a prerogative that was not rightfully his. In this exiguous time Löwe invited Grant to his stammtisch at the Colony Restaurant, where he had met the elegant, the distinguished and the beautiful, but he felt dreadfully self-conscious and out of place. He refused Löwe's subsequent invitations. He preferred to sit with him in his single room at the Ambassador. Grant couldn't get enough of Löwe's stories of the ghetto in which he had been brought up in Czernowitz, Galicia. In Löwe's room hung four watercolors of Czernowitz which Grant found fascinating. Czernowitz was more colorful than Xenia, Ohio, where Grant came from. "Yes," Löwe said, "colorful it was, but the reputation of the town for venality was so widespread that citizens of Czernowitz, when they traveled, pretended to have come from somewhere else." Löwe himself soared above such petty dissimulation. He had his cards printed:

ALEXANDER LÖWE
aus Czernowitz

Löwe told Grant about having lunch, in later days, with the redoubtable German general, von Seeckt.

"Do you know Czernowitz?" Löwe had asked.

"Know it! I took it three times."

After his play opened Grant got rid of those fearsome early mornings. He gave up his wretched room and moved to the Ambassador to be near Löwe. He now accepted Löwe's invitations. Through him he had met Stephanie von Arnim, whom he was now on the way to visit.

Through him he had met, as it is said, "everybody"; that is, the people whom one would not ordinarily meet. Paradoxically, the term was highly selective.

Löwe was short, rotund, dark-complexioned, bald in front. He dressed soberly, in well-cut lounge suits with vests. He wore invariable blue polka-dot bow ties. His head was big, out of proportion to the rest of him. His face was broad and plump, with a short, flat-surfaced nose. What illuminated his personality were his eyes. Grant occasionally felt — was it his imagination? — that he caught a look of pain in his friend's eyes. He felt it right this minute. Löwe was a chain smoker. As Grant looked at him now through the wreaths of cigarette smoke, the expression he caught in Löwe's eyes was poignant, lonely. It struck him that while he had always spilled his troubles to Löwe, he had never, really, asked him an intimate question about himself. Had he ever been in love? Was he in love now? Of course there was that English beauty with whom he corresponded and whom he was on the way to see now, but she was happily married. Someone had said that Lady Monica was Löwe's platonic mistress. Was he a lover-at-large, surrounded as he was by the beauty of the world? He was entangled with the most glamorous lives — did he have one of his own? Was he, with his multifarious involvements, fighting a running battle against loneliness? For the first time, intuition lit for Grant the basis of their relationship. Löwe was islanded in a lake of beauty but, after all, solitary. In Grant he had picked up a fellow stowaway to keep him company on the paradisaical island.

Löwe lit another cigarette.

"Well," he said, "what are your impressions?"

This was sheer courtesy. Löwe knew perfectly well that he would provide the impressions.

"I'm crazy about Varina. She's just wonderful. She's got everything."

Löwe said nothing. He allowed the pinwheel of adolescent enthusiasm to sputter out.

"And Mrs. Kennicott is very nice. Something sad about her, isn't there?"

"Her husband is insane," said Löwe, as if to account, at least partially, for Mary Kennicott's sadness.

Kaetchen enlarged.

"Mary is a bride actually, though she was married fifteen years ago. One of the most highly publicized of American marriages. The prince and princess of two great American families. Within a year the bridegroom developed alarming symptoms. He is now confined in his estate in Santa Barbara."

"Do you know him?"

"Of course. I was at the wedding. Wyman Kennicott is a delightful man. Mary spends six months of the year with him. I go to stay with them. In his lucid periods Wyman is as engaging as ever."

"What a terrible tragedy!"

"It has its comic aspects. The Kennicotts are great music lovers. Wyman engaged the San Francisco Symphony to give a concert in the drawing room of their house in Santa Barbara. It's bigger than this lounge. There we were, several hundred of us in white ties, waiting for the concert to begin. The conductor was on the platform and the full orchestra. I was sitting with Mary. Wyman hadn't appeared and the conductor was waiting for a signal from her. A bit nervous, wondering what was holding Wyman up, Mary nodded to the conductor. He gave the down beat for the Overture to *Der Freischütz*. Just at that moment Wyman appeared. He walked quietly down the aisle and took his seat beside us. He was stark naked. The audience was well-bred and pretended not to notice. Happily, the conductor's back was turned, but some of the musicians played off key. When the conductor turned to take his bow at the end, he almost dropped his baton."

"What happened then?"

"He is such a dear, that Wyman, so docile. Mary persuaded him that he was tired and had better go back to his room. She took him upstairs. She told me later that once he got there he dressed full fig in evening clothes and sat down to listen to his favorite record of *Don Giovanni*."

"Is there any hope for him?"

"None whatever. Mary showed me a letter he sent her to the boat. Enchanting. He tells her she must go to Italy and look for a certain view on the Apennine road which he saw on an early tour. He describes it exactly and beautifully. It is very sad. However, as a wise friend of mine says: 'There are very few calamities in life in which the possession of money is not a considerable mitigation.' "

"What is the mitigation here?"

"Mary has opened a clinic in San Diego for the study of mental diseases. She has great energy, you know, fragile though she appears. She is determined to shed light on the dark mystery of her husband's illness. She got hold of a brilliant young psychiatrist with whom she has fallen madly in love. She put him in charge of her clinic. Between science and love, Mary is occupied."

"Do you know him, the psychiatrist?"

"Not yet. He is coming to Stephanie's castle to stay — in Mary's half, that is. So you'll meet him."

"The number of people you know and the strange situations!"

"If you know people at all," said Löwe drily, "you are bound to encounter strange situations!"

Löwe took out his old-fashioned watch in a heavy gold case which he carried in the vest pocket of his lounge suit.

"It's time for *my* nap," he said.

"Please, Kaetchen, don't go yet. Stephanie — tell me — is she really hard up?"

"The endearing thing about your sweetheart is that she soars above the facts of life. She simply doesn't realize that the grandeur in which she lived in Berlin when her father was alive is over, done with. I've kept her going by devices. Fortunately, she still has some paintings left from her father's house in Grünewald. She brought a Rembrandt — one of those rabbis — rolled up like wallpaper and got it through customs as a family portrait. That helped for a while but she's so improvident she supports everybody who writes her a begging letter."

"You seem to criticize her for being generous."

"I criticize her for being improvident. It's a burden on her friends."

"On you, you mean."

"On me chiefly. This arrangement I've managed to make with Mary to take over half of the castle is a life saver. The castle was falling to pieces. Mary spent over three hundred thousand dollars to do up her half. To go to Mary's side from Stephanie's is like walking from the eighteenth century into the twentieth. You should see Stephanie's half. You will, of course. You'll be staying in it and I pity you."

Stephanie's lovely face was before Grant. It gave him a painful happiness just to talk about her.

"Kaetchen?"

"Well?"

"Stephanie — ?"

"Well?"

"Is she Jewish?"

"Half, which in present circumstances is more than enough."

Löwe started to get up.

"Don't go yet. There's so much I want to know — "

"Well?"

"Tell me about Ian Leith?"

"As you see, charming, delightful, almost illegally attractive."

"Why does he have to play extras in Hollywood? Isn't he awfully rich?"

"Penniless. Not a farthing."

"But I don't understand — that great family — all those famous houses!"

"He's a younger son. Haven't you heard of the law of primogeniture?"

"Are they so literal about it?"

"Quite literal. His father, besides, is pathologically stingy."

Grant was bewildered. It didn't make sense to him.

"In Xenia," he said, "though our parents had nothing, the younger sons got the better part of it."

"So in Czernowitz. But you see, my dear Stanley, both in Czernowitz and in Xenia we follow the Biblical tradition, the partiality to Benjamin. But Ian has an intermittent occupation. He can fall back on it when he wants to."

"What's that?"

"Clyde Vesper's secretary."

"Who's Clyde Vesper?"

"The son of a great shipping family. Vastly rich. Very distinguished. First-rate archaeologist. He's financed several important expeditions. Goes himself moreover. One of the most amusing men I know."

"Is Ian a suitable secretary for an archaeologist?"

"With Vesper's tastes — yes. He is — as he will himself enthusiastically tell you — a corrupter of youth."

Grant was shocked.

"You mean — "

"Exactly."

"Then Ian is — ?"

"Off and on. I'm sure he'll go back to Vesper. Vesper plays a cat and mouse game with him. Poor Ian — between Varina and Vesper — "

"Varina!"

"Oh yes, she's very much in love with Ian."

Homosexuality was a new field for Grant. In Xenia, Ohio, he and his companions had been obsessed by girls.

"But I don't understand — Varina? Doesn't she know?"

"Of course she knows."

"Well then, what good is he to her, Ian?"

Löwe sighed. Savant of the great world, he undertook the education of a talented yokel.

"My dear Stanley," he said, "fellows like Ian, they do both. Besides, they make wonderful husbands. They divest marriage of neurosis."

He got up.

"Well, I have to have my nap. See you at dinner. Work on your play. It may get you Stephanie in the end. And, if you don't get her, you'll have the play."

He started to go but turned back. "But if you take my advice, you'll marry that nice girl you introduced me to. What's her name?"

"Eileen Cavanaugh."

"Yes, obviously the poor misguided creature adores you. She's just right for you. You'll be much better off with her, I assure you."

When Grant got back to his cabin on the sun deck he was in a turmoil. His room steward was brushing his dinner jacket and hanging it. Grant greeted him and thanked him, a little incredulous that a Frenchman and a stranger should be taking such trouble over him. On the desk was an engraved invitation from the captain inviting him for lunch in his cabin the next day. How courteous of the two Frenchmen to put themselves out so for a recent nonentity from Xenia, Ohio. Grant then moved out to the verandah. Several of Kaetchen's friends, whom he had entertained the night before, had exclaimed with envy that he should have a verandah when they didn't. Five years ago, in Xenia, Grant, hopeless and helpless, had contemplated a future which was a corridor of despair. And now he was in a verandah cabin on the *Normandie* with selected Frenchmen at his service. It was all because of the accident that he had written a comedy which, after a tortuous history, was now a dazzling success in New York and was going to be produced in London.

But the years in Xenia had not fallen away from Grant; neither the poverty, nor the ghetto grayness, nor the self-doubt. Grant had an uncle who, when he was told by Grant's father that his nephew was "writing," said briskly: "I wouldn't give you a five-cent nickel for the whole business!" The accident had already produced a sum in excess of that, but Grant couldn't help sharing his uncle's skepticism. Was it a fluke? Wasn't it a fluke? Could he repeat the performance? What would happen if he couldn't? And there was another thing. Grant was comfortable alone with Löwe, but he was not comfortable in the great world to which Löwe had introduced him, especially the feminine part of it. He felt awkward, odd-looking, unattractive. He was tall and gangling. He suffered from a mild recurrent acne about which he was sensitive. He was self-conscious about his hats. No matter what hats he bought — and he bought them at Dobbs — the shape of his head was such that they never rested easily on it. With Stephanie — up to a point — it was easier. She was an actress and they had the theater in common. Stephanie had been appearing in a modernized version of the *Medea* tragedy. Grant saw it — at least Stephanie's scenes — every night. She was sweet to him. She referred to playwrights as "poets." She hoped that Grant would become her poet as Euripides was now. Grant had tried poetry at college but had learned very quickly that it was not his métier.

Grant began to change into his dinner jacket. His thoughts were in a whirl. He began to be depressed. What was he doing here — with a verandah — in the middle of the Atlantic? What was he doing with Kaetchen's set? How would he survive in it? How could he possibly compete with Ian who was so attractive, so experienced, so dextrous at doing both? How? Why? What?

A page boy arrived with a radiogram. The telephone rang.

"Damn!" thought Grant. "Wolfsohn."

For a moment he wasn't going to answer but then he thought he must demonstrate that he was not a weak man. It was Varina. She was low, she said. She felt like talking to him. Would he take a turn around the deck with her? Grant said he felt low too and would like nothing better. Varina said she'd pick him up. Grant tore open the radiogram.

MISS YOU FIERCELY. PENELOPE

Eileen! Since their affair had started, she had been reading up feverishly on Greek mythology, on everything. She studied to educate herself up to him, Grant, who knew himself to be, in spite of his Harvard degree, uneducated. He was troubled and somewhat annoyed by Eileen's telegram. He felt weighted with guilt. The cable made him uneasy. That was an equivocal situation too!

He heard Varina calling him through the partly open door. He stuffed Eileen's cable into his pocket and admitted her. He was thrilled afresh by her loveliness. He loved her low, throaty voice, her gray eyes, the scar on her forehead.

"You look very nice in your dinner jacket. But your tie . . ."

"I've never learned to do a bow properly. It drives me crazy."

"Let me try."

She undid his tie and made a beautiful bow.

"There!" she said. "I do it for Ian all the time. He says I have a knack."

Her eye caught a book on the dresser: Count Kessler's life of Walter Rathenau.

"What was — or is — Rathenau?" asked Varina without curiosity.

"Was. He was foreign minister of Germany after the First World War. He was murdered. Stephanie's first love."

"Are you reading up on Stephanie's loves, darling?"

Grant smiled.

"As far as they are recorded."

"I am seething with jealousy. Of Stephanie — of your verandah."

She walked out on it. Grant followed. They stood for a moment, looking over the rail. The great ship was plowing imperturbably through an uneventful sea.

"If you like it, I'll switch cabins with you. I'd love to. Please. Take this. I'll take yours."

"I wouldn't think of it. You deserve the verandah."

"Why do I deserve it?"

"Because you're a genius and I am nothing at all."

Grant felt like anything but a genius. He was floundering in a writer's block and was convinced, at this point, that his one success had been a fluke. But he didn't pursue the point.

Varina broke the silence.

"Isn't it funny," she said. "I feel like confiding in you."

"Do."

"You're very sympathetic. And I feel you understand a lot though you don't say much. Usually, I tell Kaetchen everything. But I'm afraid to tell him this. I don't think I'd be afraid to tell you. I need advice actually."

Grant's heart sank a bit. Would he be used eternally by girls as a confidant? That is Löwe's role, he thought, and he didn't want Löwe's role.

"But Kaetchen's so much more experienced than I. I've had very little. Surely he can advise you better?"

"Afraid to be burdened?"

"Oh, no, not at all." He stopped for a moment. "I'd do anything for you, Varina. Anything in the world."

She looked at him. Grant thought her eyes the most beautiful and moving in the world.

"I would do anything in the world for you. I love you, Stanley. You have the most wonderful face of all of them."

Why had she said that? Did she guess that he needed reassurance about his looks? She looked at him tenderly.

"Darling. You're blushing. How dear of you! Shall we take a turn around the deck?"

He followed her out of the cabin. In the corridor she said: "I won't tell you now. I'll tell you in Salzburg. So you're safe for a bit, anyway."

"I'll wait till you feel like telling me," he said. "Then I'll get Kaetchen's advice — on a hypothetical case, of course — and then I'll pass his advice on to you. Of course you could save time by just asking Kaetchen."

Varina laughed. "No matter how you squirm," she said, "I won't let you off the hook."

Walking the deck they came upon René Wolfsohn in the somewhat fading light, shooting, as if they were rival playwrights, at the revolving clay ducks.

"Goyim nachus," said Varina.

2. The Arlberg Express

No sooner had he gone through customs at Le Havre than Grant's eye was caught by a copy of *Der Stürmer*, prominently displayed on a newsstand at the pier. The cover was a gargoyle-caricature, fanged and feral, of a bearded Jew. Grant stared at it. He found himself buying it. He stood stock still, *Der Stürmer* in his hand. His thoughts had been full of Stephanie, struggling with some emergent idea for a play for Stephanie, but Dr. Goebbels's particularized message wiped his mind clean of trivia. "Why," he asked himself stupidly, "are they selling this in France? Why are they greeting tourists with it?" A dormant brain cell lit a long-since forgotten moment. In his undergraduate days at Harvard, trying out for the *Lampoon,* he had spent several afternoons in the *Lampy* office looking over old files in an effort to get the hang. He had been startled to come upon what was called the "Laski Number." Harold Laski was then an assistant professor and had taken the side of the Boston policemen who had gone on strike. Grant had later been told by a friend of Laski's that the latter claimed to have been personally responsible for the election of Calvin Coolidge to the Presidency because Coolidge, then governor of Massachusetts, had sided with the city against the policemen and against Laski and had so attained national prominence. The *Lampoon* cover was a caricature of Laski, less obscene than the one Grant held in his hand, but in the same vein. The two caricatures blurred in Grant's mind. There must be a relationship, otherwise, in the long and twisted side-alleys of memory, the same bulb wouldn't have sprung. Of course, Grant had heard of *Der Stürmer,* but here it was. A copy was in his hand. It lived up to expectations. He had crossed the ocean to be close to the enemy. In France — at the gateway to the City of Light! Why was he surprised? He knew, for example, that respectable people in places like Greenwich, Connecticut, were acting as agents for Dr. Goebbels, and were distributing his literature all over the United States. He himself had undergone a singular experience. While staying in the country house of a millionaire friend who was interested in the theater, a gentleman of great charm and good will, the

brother of his hostess had taken him aside for a confidential talk. It was
during the Roosevelt-Landon campaign. On the mistaken assumption
that Grant held the entertainment world in the palm of his hand, the
young tycoon had advised him that he'd better pivot that world to Lan-
don, otherwise what was happening in Germany might happen here.
"This is a violent country," he reminded Grant. He looked like an Ar-
row collar ad but his hard, blue eyes glinted vindictively. Why, indeed,
was he surprised?

René Wolfsohn, accompanied by a young Frenchwoman, chic and distinguished, with a slim, sensitive face, came up to him.

Wolfsohn introduced his friend. Grant hardly caught her name.

"Bedside reading?" said Wolfsohn with a glance at the magazine.

"Why are they selling this in France?" asked Grant.

"Why not? They sell it in America."

"I thought France was more civilized."

"Not about that. I've been through all that. Didn't I tell you about
my play? I took care of the whole problem in that."

Grant reflected that Wolfsohn might have taken care of it but that
he hadn't really disposed of it.

"I still think that to sell it like this — in France . . ."

"You're naïve. Don't you know that the anti-Semites and the homosexuals are the true Internationale? Freud, by the way, points out a relationship between the two cults. Shall I tell you how a friend of mine
in Paris defines the anti-Semite? 'A man who hates the Jews even more
than they deserve to be hated.' "

Wolfsohn laughed hugely at his friend's mot.

He and his companion were driving to Paris. He offered Grant a lift.
The dark young woman seconded the invitation warmly.

"René has been telling me about you — what a good time you had on
the ship. I was quite envious. Do join us!"

Grant begged off. He was taking the Arlberg that night to Salzburg
and couldn't risk missing the train.

"Ah," said Wolfsohn, "a pity! I have a beautiful subject for you."

"We hope to come to Salzburg too," said Wolfsohn's companion. "I
look forward to seeing you there."

She gave Grant her hand. Grant got an impression of warmth and
sympathy from Wolfsohn's friend. He felt like going with her. They

left. Carrying *Der Stürmer,* Grant made his way to his compartment on
the boat train.

Grant couldn't leave *Der Stürmer* alone. He immersed himself in it,
discovering what a menace he was to the human race. His German
wasn't very good but he found that personal invective is legible. For
four years now, in New York and in Hollywood, just now on the *Normandie,* it seemed to Grant that the sole topic of conversation at dinner
parties had been the Question. Whatever you started with, that's where
you ended. The preoccupation was hectic and obsessive; it swirled
around the Question in the way that sometimes a notorious and not altogether savory character, whose rise to prominence has been meteoric
and somehow mysterious, preempts all dinner table conversation. Even
in Hollywood it superseded the films as a subject. There had been that
unpleasant incident at Al Lehr's restaurant which returned now to roil
Grant. It occurred one night when Grant had dropped into Lehr's for a
bite of supper after a preview. In the vestibule he beheld a peculiar
sight. Lehr, the diminutive proprietor, a man greatly loved in the film
colony, had just knocked down Frank O'Malley, the novelist. O'Malley
had an uncanny ear for the speech of thugs. This gift had made him
famous and successful. He was agreeable enough when sober, but he
had a reputation, which he shared with others, of becoming vocally and
blatantly anti-Semitic when drunk, which he often was. Mrs. O'Malley
was helping her husband get on his feet and was steering him to the
sidewalk. Lehr explained to the crowd:

"I was helping Mrs. O'Malley on with her coat. I always do. She's a
good friend of mine. That bastard said: 'Take your Jew hand off my
wife!' I let him have it. That son-of-a-bitch is never coming into my
restaurant again."

Reading *Der Stürmer* activated in Grant a feeling of guilt he had
hitherto managed to suppress: guilt over his fastidiously selected pseudonym. Why had he changed his name? He let *Der Stürmer* fall to the
empty seat beside him. A Frenchman, sitting opposite, asked politely in
English whether he might look at it. Grant nodded. His fellow passenger thanked him and began reading it with concentration. Grant reflected that he had handed a potential enemy a lethal phial from which
he might himself presently have to suffer an injection.

Why had he done it? Why had he changed his name? He remembered now with shame his pride in concocting the pseudonym: at once aloof and rugged he had thought it. He had told himself that the fabricated name would give him freedom to improvise the masquerades of his fictions. Was that the real reason? Wasn't there, behind it, a more shameful one? Why hadn't he confined the fabricated name to his fictions and kept his own for his life. Why hadn't he been at least as defiant as Löwe was about Czernowitz? He felt a deep malaise now about this. Could he change, even now, to his right name? "Too late," he thought bitterly, "now that I am established." In his mind he put quotation marks around the word established. He was anything but established. With the cover of *Der Stürmer* burning in his mind — the man opposite was now deep in the interior of Julius Streicher's publication — and with an even deeper intensity of feeling about his own cover, Grant felt decidedly disestablished.

Impatient with himself, for distraction he got out of his valise the poems of T. S. Eliot, which he always carried with him. He knew the poems so well that reading them was like sliding on a polished groove. But some lines jumped out at him as if he were seeing them for the first time:

> *And the Jew squats on the window sill, the owner,*
> *Spawned in some estaminet of Antwerp,*
> *Blistered in Brussels, patched and peeled in London.*

A caption for the *Der Stürmer* cover! Grant had read these lines before and had not specially minded them — they were about other people — but at this moment he was hypersensitized. His eye caught another line: "There will be time to murder and create." There will indeed, he thought, be time for murder. He felt a rising anger: they are all smoothies, he thought; they are all murderers, the poet and the Greenwich tycoon. He felt himself caught up.

And then he thought of Varina and his heart melted. They were, thank God, not all like that!

That night, on the platform of the Gare du Nord, waiting for the Arlberg Express that would take him to Salzburg, Grant's morbid vaporings blew off, as if swept by a clean wind, and he walked on the train with a feeling of high excitement, even of triumph. He felt sure that he could fit for Stephanie a play idea which had tantalized him for some time. In his compartment he took out his notebook and began writing rapidly. He had a *character* he could adapt for Stephanie. He saw how. He had only to dramatize what he had himself intimately observed the summer before in Blue Hill, Maine: the story of Mrs. Frobisher, her daughter Sally and Dr. Kenneth Ogden.

In New York, a musician friend had recommended to Grant that he try Blue Hill, Maine, as a work place for the summer. Grant went and had reason to be grateful for his friend's suggestion. He got a room at the Blue Hill Inn and worked happily. The village was a beehive of aspiring instrumentalists. When he walked down the hill from the inn to the post office for mail, he heard Bach and Mozart from every window.

Where there are musicians, there are always rich people — chronologically the order is reversed — and there was a rich colony in Blue Hill, with secluded and ample houses along the bay. For some reason the place attracted oil millionaires from Cleveland, Ohio, and New Jersey. These families were unostentatious, modest and, except for musicians, exclusive. There were chamber music parties at the local hall three times a week. At one of these, Grant, always on the prowl for romance, beheld a vision: Sally Frobisher. Her father, now dead, had been a Standard Oil partner. In Xenia, Grant had often seen the Frobishers' name in the papers but it had never remotely occurred to him that he would meet one. And now, here before him, smiling at him, was Sally Frobisher. She was Grant's dream of the American Beauty rose in full flower. He fell in love with her at sight.

Sally introduced Grant to her paid companion and friend, a demure, brown-eyed girl, older than Sally, named Eileen Cavanaugh. Eileen suggested that they go swimming together the next morning. Mornings were Grant's working time, hitherto inviolate, but he forgot about that in order to see Sally again. The swim was glorious. Lying on the hot, splintered planks of the wharf after their swim, Grant exerted himself to be brilliant. He was anecdotal and funny, wreathing notorious names through his conversation. He noticed very quickly in Sally a maddening detachment. She was polite, friendly and remote; the friendliness seemed to be doled out, as if by prescription. He talked to her about the theater, which aroused interest in most people, but not in Sally. He invited her to dinner; she accepted but asked whether he'd mind if Eileen came too. They became a trio and went everywhere together and then, Grant didn't know exactly how it came about, a duo. It appeared Sally's mother was ill, she suffered from some psychic ailment; Sally would cancel their engagements at the last minute because she had to be with her mother. Grant found out very quickly that Sally was unapproachable — not merely physically but psychically. He couldn't get within a mile of her. He tried to talk to her about her mother. Even with her perfunctory replies Grant noticed that her expression changed when her mother was mentioned: she would look away as if in fear of saying something she might later regret or that would cause her, by the mere saying of it, too much pain. Her thoughts were concentrated on her mother, there was no doubt about that.

The response which Grant didn't get from Sally he got amply from Eileen. That he was an overnight wonder in the theater had made no impression at all on Sally, but to Eileen the fact that he had a play running in New York, with two famous actors in it and which people paid to see every night, made him a lord of the intellectual world. This worship amused Grant; at the same time he sopped it up. Eileen was avid for education. She questioned Grant about books and authors and Grant made fluent recommendations, mostly of weighty books which he knew only by reputation. Rolling the titles off his tongue gave him the sensation of having read them. He slipped comfortably into the niche which Eileen had so cozily furnished for him as the Man Who Knew Everything. Eileen told Grant that, in Cleveland, she practically lived in the public library. It was her other home. The minute she got back she would read all the books he had recommended. She had a busy winter ahead of her.

From Eileen, Grant found out what he wanted to know: Sally's dark family history. Her parents had been divorced. Her father had married again and died six months later. Mrs. Frobisher suffered from a serious illness; she was, in fact, dying. Dr. Ogden's ministrations, Eileen and Sally both believed, were directed toward hastening Mrs. Frobisher's end; they were sure that he was drugging her to death. Grant asked why, since Mrs. Frobisher was in any case dying, Dr. Ogden didn't simply let nature take its course. Sally was sure that Dr. Ogden had persuaded her mother to make him her heir. She had been trying frantically

to get her father's lawyer, Mr. Slater, to come from Cleveland to inter-
vene. Mr. Slater, though a rocklike family friend, found himself too
busy to come. This made Grant sure that Mr. Slater discounted the im-
aginings of the two girls as hysteria, though he didn't say this to Eileen.
But the story struck him as a dramatic possibility. When he got back to
his room that night he wrote it all down in his notebook. He determined
to get a good close look at Dr. Ogden and Mrs. Frobisher. With Eileen's
help he was sure he could contrive it.

On one of his moonlight walks with Eileen on the fir-lined road that
ran around the bay, past the villas of the summer colony, among them
the Frobishers', Grant heard himself saying:

"I'm head over heels in love with Sally, but she doesn't give a damn
for me."

"She's the most wonderful girl in the world but that's her blind spot."

The expression fell like a stone on Grant.

"She can't stand me," he said. "Why?"

"She respects you very much but she doesn't feel about you the way
I do."

Grant understood it all right but he was flattered by the implication
that if Sally didn't respond to him it must be due to some deficiency in
her emotional equipment. He kissed Eileen for putting it that way. The
intensity of her response astonished him. She was wanton. She whispered to him to take her to his room. Demure Eileen! In his room she
undressed as if a fury were after her. She was a virgin but she did everything she could to help him. The wild cries that escaped her permitted Grant the marvelous illusion that they were Sally's.

Thanks to Eileen, Grant had a voluptuous summer. Flesh, he decided, was better than fantasy. He thought it was he who had decided it
but it was flesh which had decided it. He thought it only fair to tell
Eileen that he had no intention of marrying for a very long time. (He
would have married Sally on the instant.) Eileen told him not to give
the idea of marriage another thought. She knew her place; it was wonderful luck for her just to be with him. "She thinks," thought Grant,
"that she is having an affair with Zeus!" Grant didn't really mind this
error in identity. In a letter to her mother, Eileen made the mistake of
telling her that she was seeing a friend of Sally's, a wonderful man and

a playwright named Stanley Grant. The name passed muster with Mrs. Cavanaugh but in her reply she inquired whether this Mr. Grant was a Catholic. Eileen, who suspected the dark truth, panicked. She wrote that she'd heard somewhere that Mr. Grant was a Unitarian. Mrs. Cavanaugh took a poor view. "You might as well," she snapped back in her next letter, "be a Jew as be a Unitarian!" Eileen never mentioned the celebrated Unitarian again.

Eileen fixed it so that Grant could observe Mrs. Frobisher and Dr. Ogden at close range. She got seats directly behind them at the last concert of the season. They were Sally's seats. Sally wasn't coming; she had a headache. Eileen confided to Grant that she didn't believe in the headache — it was that she couldn't bear to see her mother and the doctor together.

Studying Ogden, it was simply impossible to relate this extrovert man, with his laughing eyes and radiation of joie de vivre, with the sinister rumors relayed by Eileen. Dr. Ogden was the very picture of a Stendhal hero, with flashing dark eyes, luminous hair and an expression of rugged vivacity. He had brilliant teeth, like a film star's, and, as he laughed a lot, they were frequently visible. Grant wondered whether it wasn't dental exhibitionism that made Ogden laugh so much. Mrs. Frobisher leaned toward her companion and whispered something; Dr. Ogden's laugh rang out. In the slow movement of a Mozart quartet, Mrs. Frobisher moved closer to him; she was holding his hand. It was a kind of heliotropism: the etiolated reaching out of shadow into the sun. Grant was touched by Mrs. Frobisher. He felt that he understood her reliance on Dr. Ogden; it seemed perfectly natural, inevitable. It wasn't simply that he was good-looking; it was that he was a jetting fountain of youth. He guessed that he must be at least twenty years younger than Mrs. Frobisher. Mr. Slater, the lawyer in Cleveland, might be wonderful, but Dr. Ogden, Grant could see, was necessary. He decided to take Eileen's confidences henceforth heavily salted. He looked at Mrs. Frobisher to find a resemblance to Sally. Her cheeks were sunken and her eyes pale, but her temples, like Sally's, had shallow hollows in them.

In the interval Eileen introduced Grant to Dr. Ogden and Mrs. Frobisher. Mrs. Frobisher greeted him with wan cordiality. Sally had told her how clever he was. She stood beside Dr. Ogden, leaning against him, her arm through his, a tendril furled on an oak. Dr. Ogden was hearty. He'd seen Grant's play in New York and had greatly enjoyed it. He remembered Grant's favorite line and repeated it.

"I should so like to see it!" said Mrs. Frobisher wistfully.

"Why not?" said Dr. Ogden as if everything were possible for her. "We'll make a detour on the way back to Cleveland."

Mrs. Frobisher smiled, snapped her fingers as if to say that detours were nothing to her.

"Indeed," she said, "why not? What fun!"

Dr. Ogden grinned widely at Grant.

"You see, Mr. Grant, I've got you a customer!"

Mrs. Frobisher laughed. There was a faint flush in her cheeks. She seemed to come alive.

The interval bell rang. They moved back into the auditorium. Grant didn't tell Eileen that he liked Ogden, that he understood Mrs. Frobisher's reliance on him. It was obvious that whatever life Mrs. Frobisher had, she drew from him. He was convinced that Sally and Eileen were deluded.

In the fall Grant corresponded regularly with Eileen. Her letters continued the story of the contest between Sally, Dr. Ogden and the stalwart Mr. Slater. By this time, Grant had come to read Eileen's letters on the subject as if they were a serial story in a popular magazine. But one day, after a quick trip to the Coast, Grant found in his apartment two letters from Eileen which brought him up short. Mrs. Frobisher had been found dead in her bed by her maid. She had left a will which made Dr. Ogden her sole heir, since Sally had been amply provided for in her father's will. Mr. Slater reached heroic stature: Eileen's recounting the scene between him and Dr. Ogden — described to her by Sally — was breathless with admiration. Mr. Slater had told Dr. Ogden that he would bring charges of criminal malpractice against him unless he made handsome restitution to Sally. Apparently the autopsy had revealed certain things; Eileen didn't know exactly what they were. Whatever they were, they had induced in Dr. Ogden, in the revision of the will, an exemplary generosity toward Sally.

Eileen's second letter was even more breathless. Sally's generosity!

She was sending Eileen to New York to study. Eileen's association with Grant had made her intellectually ambitious; Sally was making it possible for her to pursue this ambition. Grant did not find this intelligence an unmixed blessing since he was, by this time, in love with Stephanie. This he told Eileen very soon after her arrival. Eileen was happy for him. Grant couldn't get rid of a sense of guilt about Eileen. He had deflowered a virgin and this was considered bad form in Xenia, unless you followed up with instant marriage. Grant tried to make up for it by taking Eileen everywhere. He introduced her to Löwe. He took her to see the play in which Stephanie was appearing and backstage to meet the star. Eileen, who was as shrewd sexually as she was devout religiously, discerned very quickly, as she listened to the endearments and shop talk between Grant and his beloved, that the latter, like Sally, had a blind spot too. For some reason which baffled her, Grant seemed to induce myopia in his sweethearts. It was mystifying and also, for her, lucky. Her heart went out in sympathy to Stanley while it counseled patience to herself. The next day Stephanie congratulated Stanley on having won the love of such a dear girl as Eileen; it was so obvious, wasn't it, that she was in love with him? Flesh superseded fantasy for the second time; Grant resumed his affair with Eileen. She demanded nothing at all but to be with him. She saw him off on the *Normandie* when he sailed to meet Stephanie.

In his compartment on the Arlberg Express, Grant was in a state of euphoria. He felt that he had the whole play cupped in his hand and a part for Stephanie. Between Stephanie and Mrs. Frobisher he discerned an analogy: both women deprived of their heritage by a sinister and uncontrollable force. Stephanie in the play would be a high-born Austrian who had married an American oil magnate whom she'd met on a business trip in Vienna. That would account for Stephanie's accent. Grant was going to set his comedy — and it would be a comedy because he had no intention of letting Mrs. Frobisher die, and in fact Sally, and not Mr. Slater, was going to stymie Dr. Ogden — on the coast of Maine, "a masculine Riviera," he had already written in a stage direction. The great stumbling block to Stephanie's career in America was her accent; Grant would now make an asset of the handicap. But then he was assailed by a worry deeper than the linguistic one. This worry struck him so sharply that he stopped writing for a few minutes and went out into the corridor to smoke a cigarette. His play would be a comedy. Was Stephanie a comedienne? Did she have a sense of humor? Never before had it occurred to him to challenge Stephanie's perfection; he had never asked himself *any* question about her; he simply worshiped her. But now a professional exigency gave him pause. He had seen Stephanie on the stage in the Greek tragedy about the Atreus family. That family was so tense and preoccupied with its darkling heritage that any trace of humor was alien to it. He worried about this at breakfast after a sleepless night. But by lunchtime he had disposed of his worry. Stephanie could do anything. He would make a comedienne of her. He would be her Pygmalion. The role of Pygmalion appealed to him.

In the early afternoon the Arlberg arrived in Salzburg. Stephanie had wired him that he would be met by her factotum, "dear Liss." Dear Liss was there, a shriveled and non-English-speaking but eager-to-please little man. Liss led him to Stephanie's wheezy car, of some foreign make.

Grant felt masterful. He was no longer afraid of being alone with Stephanie. With this play in his mind and in his notebook, he would have something to talk to her about. He was excited. It would be all right. Löwe and Varina and Mary and the rest could take their time.

3. The Crib

Liss drove Grant through a verdant, lake-beaded countryside. Little, caressive rains fell momentarily; the sun shone through them. Grant had asked Liss whether he might sit in front with him; Liss seemed honored. Grant kept putting his hand out of the open window to feel the rain on his hands; it left a fine sediment which the sun dried quickly. Portia's rains, Grant thought. In his halting German Grant inquired about Stephanie and was told that die gnädige Frau was well and awaiting him. She would have met him herself but, alas, the gnädige Frau had a headache. Der Herr Gott chose to inflict her with headaches. Liss clucked his tongue in dismay at this unjust visitation. Grant noticed that Liss, who, he imagined, could not be over forty, had a curiously wizened look. Grant asked him about the political situation. Was Austria nervous?

"He's up there," said Liss, gesturing over his shoulder.

"Where?"

"Up there. Berchtesgaden. You can see him."

Grant felt a spasm. What did Liss mean? Did he mean that "he" was actually visible? He couldn't have meant that. And yet, that's what he said. Grant asked him to stop the car. He got out and looked up to where Liss pointed.

"That's where he is. He's up there now. Up there."

Grant looked up at the aerie where "he" dwelt. It became apparent that Liss had meant only that you could see the Residence. Grant took in the outline of the building, low, compact, squarish, perched high on the mountaintop, from which its occupant could view the world that he foresaw would soon belong to him. The euphoria in which Grant had descended from the Arlberg Express evaporated quickly. He climbed back in beside Liss. Liss droned on.

"He sees everything, he knows everything. He goes there to rest and plan."

"Will he take Austria, do you think?"

Liss shook his head emphatically.

"Never. Never here."

There was something hollow in Liss's prophecy. It was bravado, not strength. The prophecy was wizened too.

The rest of Grant's journey to the castle was overcast.

They arrived finally before a vast, gray structure on the shore of an islanded lake; the castle seemed to arise from it as from a moat. It had a tower clock; it looked like a fortress. A gatekeeper, touching his cap in deference, swung open the great rusty gates. They drove into an immense graveled courtyard, like a prison compound. In front of a massive, iron-spiked door on the right, Liss stopped the car and removed Grant's luggage. Grant followed Liss inside, feeling that "he," through a telescope, was taking note of his entrance. A bobbing maid took his bags. He followed her up a creaking, uncarpeted staircase to his room.

In the room, the maid started to unpack his bags, but Grant begged her not to. She left, simpering and curtsying. Grant was longing to be alone. He sat down on a fringed, velvet-covered armchair, lit a cigarette and looked around. It was a long, oblong room and semidark. To one side he beheld an object. He stared at it. It was a bathtub. He got up to look at it, to confirm his first impression. It surely was, a zinc bathtub. It was very high and had a flat mahogany railing around its perimeter, wide enough to sit on. He wondered whether he could have it taken out but then he saw that the piping transfixed the carpet and was neatly soldered in. He guessed that he'd have to live with it and even, perhaps, take a bath in it. He turned on one of the taps; a hiccoughing, dark-brown stream trickled out. It was, moreover, lukewarm and Grant loved hot baths. He shut off the tap, feeling discouraged. The room was stuffy. He walked over to the narrow, deeply recessed window to open it. It took elbow grease but he managed it. A peculiar, unpleasant smell came through. The castle's drainage, evidently, was defective. He leaned over the recess to look at the lawn and the lake. The wall must have been five feet thick. A phrase from a modern historian popped into his head: "the architecture of fear." He must find out about the history of this fortress. From this side Berchtesgaden was not visible but it was not, in Grant's consciousness, invisible either. He tried to close the window and couldn't. He left the recess to survey the room. There was a very wide bed with a canopy, also fringed. The floor was varnished black and the varnish was flaking. There were several scatter rugs on the floor; on one of them he slipped and nearly fell. He kept slipping on those rugs; finally he rolled them up and put them into an empty room down the hall.

He looked then for a desk on which he could put his notebooks and his portable typewriter. There was one, an escritoire, with a pink shaded lamp and covered with bibelots. His first task, he knew, would be to clear off these bibelots. Against a wall stood a vast commode with a full-length mirror in the center. There would be room in that, surely. Then his eye caught a note on the escritoire, written on sheets of pale blue paper in Stephanie's familiar flourished handwriting, salient words heavily underscored in the style of Queen Victoria. The note was pinned down by a typed playscript. He devoured the note. It was entirely unpunctuated, a rush of feeling:

Darling Stanley dearest Poet It is too *wonderful you are here I can scarcely believe it I have a wretched migraine did Liss tell you but I am resting in order to be rid of it in time for dinner Everybody wants to meet you —* EVERYBODY *but I put them all off I want you to* myself *I know once people know you are here you'll be swallowed up I am resting so I will be fresh to cope with your darting mind I have just found this word in an English dictionary which I am studying day and night Isn't that clever of me?*

> *À bientôt darling your adoring*
>
> *Stephanie*

P.S. Please *read this* beautiful *play by another poet who was my dearest friend who would have loved you had he lived to know you I want to take you to Vienna to see the most* beautiful *actor in the world he was born to appear in your plays He is indifferent to me but I adore* him!!!!

In all the notes which he had received from her in New York Stephanie had been prodigal of exclamation marks. He read this one over and over. Grant tried again to close the window. The smell was really unpleasant. This time he succeeded. The evidences of poverty pleased him; they made Stephanie more accessible. He unpacked, changed and made his way downstairs to the drawing room. He felt a sense of indescribable strangeness at being here. He wanted to familiarize himself.

The drawing room was twilit too; it was a dim habitation. There were great, time-stained wavery mirrors on the walls in gilded rococo frames; the reflections from the mirrors were ectoplasmic. The grand piano, a Bechstein, was of pale gold with fluted legs. There were several Rembrandts, oils and drawings. The oils were of merchant burghers, nonrabbinical and hence not, in present circumstances, readily exportable duty-free as family portraits. These Rembrandt had executed thoughtlessly without reference to Stephanie's future needs or Löwe's eleemosynary manipulations. And everywhere, on the draped piano, on the exquisite French marquetry tables, were photographs, rhapsodically inscribed to Stephanie: great luminaries of the art world, conductors (Toscanini enshrined by himself), virtuosi, actors, composers, renowned English playwrights, Duse, Walter Rathenau. One photograph especially interested Grant. He took it to the curtained French window to look at it more closely. It was, he imagined, of Stephanie's father, looking down at his baby daughter in her crib. The crib was not the sort you saw in Xenia, Ohio. It was a miniature chariot with a canopy of creamy lace. The abundant folds of the canopy that cascaded down the sides of the crib were tucked up with great silken bows. Grant studied the late Count von Arnim. He was a portly man in a frock coat, with silk facings. His face was portly too; a small goatee sprouted on his chin. Through his pince-nez he looked down at his daughter with ineffable tenderness, with love and pride. There was a faint smile on his lips, a smile of completeness. You could see that there was nothing more he wanted of life than just to sit there watching his darling who was asleep, her fuzzy head buried in the lace-bordered pillow. Löwe had told Grant about the late Graf von Arnim. He had been a kindly and cultivated man, the head of a great banking house in a nexus affiliated with the Rothschilds. In the first days of the new regime he had been made an "honorary Jew." Under the weight of this elevation the honorary Jew had died.

There was the rustle of a dress behind him. Grant turned. It was Stephanie. He put the photograph back on the piano. She embraced him and kissed him on both cheeks.

"You're here! My poet is here! I can scarcely believe it!"

"I can't believe it either. I couldn't wait."

They embraced again. He held her close, so close that she edged, ever so slightly, away from him. Always on the qui vive for a sexual snub, Grant released her. His darting mind told him that he mustn't misinterpret her warm welcome.

"Kaetchen kept telling me you would never come. How wonderful that you did. That's what I live for really — to prove Kaetchen wrong!"

He was hung up. He took refuge in the photograph.

"It's your father, isn't it? It's you, isn't it?"

Stephanie looked at the photograph for a moment, as if to renew acquaintance with it.

"Yes. It's my father."

"He seems to be interested in you."

She smiled ruefully.

"For a long time he approved of me. Not so much when I grew up. He was the dearest, kindest man in the world."

Liss, in a white coat, brought in a tray of cocktails. They each took one. Stephanie sat beside him on the sofa. "One night he came home and told me that he was walking to his office from the restaurant when a very well-dressed man came up to him, tipped his hat and asked if he might walk with him. My father was used to being stopped by poor people — he never let anyone go away empty-handed — but this gentleman was obviously not a beggar. They walked along and chatted for a bit and then my father asked him why he had made this curious request. The man explained that his business was in difficulties, that he faced bankruptcy. 'If,' he said, 'I could be seen walking with you like this for a week or so, it would restore my credit in the city.' Isn't it sweet? Next day father took him to lunch so that they were seen together in the restaurant too. You would have loved my father. He would have loved you. He loved poets."

It was the second love, Grant reflected, that he had missed through premature deaths.

Stephanie's dining room was also candlelit and lined with veined and shadowed eighteenth-century mirrors. They converted Liss, as he moved about passing dishes, into a gnome. Stephanie, Grant thought, had the most beautiful arms and shoulders in the living world; her throat was famous for its beauty, she had no competition there. Reflected in these mirrors and in this light, Stephanie's arms and hands were like fronds of some graceful underwater plant moving in a gently pressing current. She wore a bangle bracelet with four little gold medallions on it, profiles of her heroes: Napoleon and Toscanini, Walter Rathenau and Mussolini. Grant had seen it before. Stephanie was never without it. He'd remarked on the oddity of this quartet to Löwe, who had brushed Stephanie's eccentricity aside with amiable tolerance:

"There's a farrago of nonsense in her beautiful head. You must accept the nonsense if you want the head."

Holding her wrist, Grant scrutinized the bangles.

" You seem to have a weakness for dictators."

She shot him a mischievous look.

"You mean Toscanini?"

"I understand about him. Everybody worships him."

He pointed to Mussolini.

"But why this one? Why not your home-grown one? He's much more formidable than Mussolini."

Stephanie put down her knife and fork. She was aghast. She was indignant.

"How can you say a thing like that? I am surprised at you. Don't you know that I bought this castle just to get away from that horror in Berlin? How could I go on living in the same city with that monster who is so cruel to my Jewish friends? They are the wine of life to me. Without my Jewish friends life wouldn't be worthwhile at all. My dear Mary Kennicott feels the same. *She* understands!"

Grant was flabbergasted. She had taken his poor little joke literally. It was astonishing. Evidently Stephanie didn't know that he was Jewish; she had taken him at his name. She didn't seize the facts of life; she lived in a fantasy world. Something else struck him: that for Stephanie, the Jews, although she was biologically one of them, were a race apart. She didn't feel herself one of them. For her, the persecutions were an affront, not to herself, but against her dearest friends in the world. She talked exactly like Varina! With a sinking of the heart he realized also that Stephanie wasn't strong on humor. Still, he would make a comedienne of her; he was determined. He was about to tell her about his play when she launched another offensive in order to disabuse him totally of his prejudices, to enlist him, to make him less dense, to make him understand, as Mary Kennicott understood. She showed him the profile of Walter Rathenau on her bangle.

"He was Jewish. That's why they killed him — my first love and my dearest friend, the most wonderful man who ever lived. I can't tell you . . ."

Her eyes grew misty at the recollection of her lost hero.

"Did you read the book I gave you?"

"Yes. I was fascinated. Extraordinarily many-sided, wasn't he?"

"He knew everything. The last morning of his life, on his last ride to the Foreign Office, he stopped to bring me a book. What do you think he brought me? Rilke's poems in a new edition in French. He knew I was studying French. Oh, how I wish you could have known him! You would have loved him and he would have loved you!"

The necrologue of Grant's potential admirers was growing apace.

"Now I will disillusion you. I knew that Rathenau loved my mother and that she loved him. I was frantic with jealousy. I went into Mother's clothes closet and slashed to pieces her favorite evening dress. Oh there was a scene! She told my father. I was terrified. But my father only laughed. 'Well,' he said, 'it shows that both my wife and my daughter have good taste. It's a high average!' So now you know the worst. Will you put up with me?"

She got up, put her arm through his and started to walk him to the drawing room. Before she left she gave an order to Liss, in German. She said that she was expecting a long-distance telephone call and to let her know the moment it came.

In the drawing room she sat beside him on the sofa. The curtains had been drawn. The sconced candles lit the area around them and their dim light drifted into darkness. The effect of the room was phantasmagoric. Grant felt that everything, Stephanie and he himself, were in a dream, that the whole thing was something he was dreaming.

They sat close together. She was holding his hand tightly as if she wanted to be protected from something. He felt that the distance between them was immeasurable. He wished he hadn't come. He felt that she was marking time waiting for the phone call.

"I love you, Stanley. I couldn't love you more. It's the sweetest thing, the dearest thing."

This avowal fell on Grant like a knell. He knew that he was earmarked to be a confidant. He began to play the part.

"Are you in love now?"

"Naturally. But let's not talk about it."

"Obstacles?"

"Obstacles!"

"Can't you overcome them?"

"I'm trying. But it will end badly."

They sat in silence. He knew that his love for her was ridiculous, that he had been absurd ever to entertain it. She was like a figure out of mythology. It was like being in love with a Martian.

"Tell me about your play."

"I'd rather not. I'm not good at telling stories. It'd sound complicated if I told it — all plot. But it won't be like that when I write it. It'll be simple. I'll read it to you — act by act."

"Tell me about my part."

"You play an aristocratic Viennese who marries an American businessman. The play takes place in his summer home on the coast of Maine. On the sea."

She repeated, as if mesmerized:

"On the sea . . ." She looked ahead of her dreamily.

"This makes it an advantage that you speak English with an accent."

"How clever of you, how very clever of you!"

"It's more than clever. It's extremely considerate."

She thought this over for a moment. Then she laughed. Impulsively she threw her arms about him and kissed him. It suddenly was not absurd to be in love with her. She would be in his play. He would have her to himself and, in the diapason of success, they would draw together. Her childish, heroic notions about life would dissolve in the practical exigencies of finding a suitable apartment in New York. It would be all right with them.

Liss came in, coughing behind his hand. He told his mistress that the long-distance call had come. She jumped up, said a quick good night to Grant. She felt her migraine coming back. Later, if she felt better, she would tap on his door. Would he mind that? She was gone.

Grant sat thinking. The phone call must have been from the obstacle man. However hopeless she might feel about finding happiness with him, she jumped up to get the call as if she had been charged by an electric current. The voltage was certainly high! Who was the man? Did Kaetchen know? He must; he knew everything. Should he put in a call to Kaetchen in London to find out? What was the use? What good would it do him to know? He faced the bleak fact that his case was hopeless. It was a crazy fantasy; he was idiotic to indulge it. How could he compete with the ghosts of Napoleon and Walter Rathenau, with their present incarnations, whoever they might be? How could he compete with all those photographs on the piano? He was way out of his depth. He sat in wretchedness. Out of this wretchedness he remembered that Stephanie had said that perhaps, when she felt better, she would tap on his door. He decided to return to his room and wait for her knock.

Grant's "motor coordination," he had been told at school, could do with improvement. He was clumsy. He was constantly bumping into things. He had no sense of direction whatever. In that respect, he enjoyed telling himself, he was a Mongolian idiot. Anyone else would simply have returned to his room; but in Grant's case finding his room presented a problem. He looked for Liss or the maid but there wasn't a soul around. On his way out of the drawing room he went down the hall, saw a staircase and climbed it, thinking that it must take him back to his room. It didn't. It took him into a chapel. Grant had never been in a private chapel before. In an apse scalloped in a recess in a far wall stood a wooden Madonna; a red light burning over the Madonna's head shed an eerie glow over her faded vestments. He remembered then that Stephanie had strong Catholic leanings. Is this where she went to pray for her precious friends, the Jews? Outside of the red light the chapel was in darkness. Grant felt in his pocket for matches, found some and, by matchlight, began to reconnoiter his position. He saw a heavy, nail-studded door. He went to it and pushed it open. He beheld what seemed to him the biggest room he had ever seen in his life. There were rows and rows of wooden chairs with faded scarlet cushions on them. Many of the cushions were on the floor. At one end was a stage and, above the stage, four Gothic windows, each of them at least four stories high. They admitted a pale light. Was it a theater? Did Stephanie have a private theater as well as a private chapel? Grant felt a desperate longing to be back in his room. Perhaps Stephanie was, even now, tapping at his door. He turned back, returned to the chapel and groped his way out of it. Then he went back to the drawing room and started all over again. He ultimately found the right staircase and his room. He went into it with relief.

"I must get a guide to this house," he muttered to himself. To encourage Stephanie in case she should invade, he left his door partly open. But she would not invade; he knew that. He felt anger against her. She acted as if she had no suspicion whatever that he was madly in love with her. She just held him in esteem as her poet. Even poets, Grant thought, wanted flesh; in fact it was their specialty. He felt hatred for Stephanie. He would somehow find her room, tell her he was sick of their factitious relationship and violate her. But he settled back to read the play she had left for him.

Grant couldn't concentrate; he was thinking about Stephanie in his own play. She had every quality for it: the insecurity, the self-doubt, the longing for love, the intimation of disaster. She would be marvelous in it. He would make her be marvelous in it. She would stumble over the obstacles surrounding her present infatuation and would come to his play for surcease from her pain. He had been pleased by the evidence of her poverty; now he took joy in the exigencies of her love life. He would wait it out. He would wait as a starveling waits for the death of a rich relative. Stephanie had never really had a success. The *Medea* play was a critical, not a popular success. With a real success Stephanie would be transformed. She would be caught up in adulation and would turn to him who had given it to her. She would . . .

Was there a tap on the door? He was sure there was. He ran to the door, opened it, called her name. The corridor was empty. He slammed the door shut. But he had heard a sound; he still heard it, a kind of scuffling sound. What on earth was it? He went to the window and looked down. There were figures moving about on the lawn between the castle and the lake, figures with little flashlights. The moon was fitful; when it emerged from behind a cloud he could see white slashes on the green lawn. There were about a half dozen men there, silently working. He looked at his watch. It was one o'clock. Who on earth were they, these men, and what were they doing? On his bedside table he saw a flashlight. He picked it up and left his room, determined to investigate. Before he left, he scribbled a little note to Stephanie and fixed it on his doorknob in case she should come for him. He made his way down the corridor and down the stairs to the drawing room, taking the precaution this time of noticing landmarks against his return, like a pathfinder in a forest.

Once in the drawing room he felt terror. He wanted to see what these men were doing on Stephanie's lawn at the dead of night, but he felt that he himself must be invisible. Slowly he made his way to the front hall. In the wall, beside the massive entrance door, were two tall windows, one on either side. They were blank with darkness. He put his handkerchief over his flashlight, pointed it to the floor until he reached the windows. There he switched off the flashlight. There was light from the moon. He stood on the side of one of the windows and peered out.

The men were hooded — Grant thought of the Ku Klux Klan — and were busily smearing the lawn from buckets. They had long-handled paint brushes. Shouldn't Grant wake Liss? But where was Liss? Should he go to the stairs and call up to Stephanie? He began to make out something of the appearance of the men; one, who seemed to be their leader, was tall and lithe. They all wore artisans' smocks. Suddenly the broad bands of white they were painting on the lawn joined in configuration. It was a swastika.

Grant couldn't leave his post. He stood there, watching. Six grown men had left their beds and their wives to confect this doodle on Stephanie's lawn. He watched till the design was completed; till it finally lay white in the moonlight on the disfigured lawn. The men picked up their pails and brushes and, at a gesture from the tall, lithe man, they vanished.

When they had gone Grant switched on his flashlight, counted off the landmarks on his journey back and finally made his room. He was faint; his hands were shaking. He would have given anything for a drink! He went to the window and looked out. The swastika shone in the moonlight like the belly of a dead fish.

Grant took a sleeping pill, undressed and went to bed.

They must have known, these men, that Stephanie was deeply devoted to her Jewish friends.

4. Walk in Sun and Rain

Like the English statesman who dreamt that he was addressing the House of Commons and woke up to find that it was true, Grant awoke sharply from a nightmare in which he was seeing some strange men defacing Stephanie's lawn with a swastika. It must have been four or five in the morning; it was still dark. On waking, unwinding painfully from the filaments of dream, Grant clutched at the reassuring reality of his pillow. Burrowing his face into it, he reminded himself of what he had discovered on other occasions: that reality was often more merciful than dreams. He longed for daylight to confirm this generalization; he

peeked up at the narrow recessed window, as he remembered watching
for the point of light at the end of a long black tunnel which had terrified him on a train journey when he was a child. He fell asleep again
in a mélange of foreshortened memory: listening, in the railway tunnel, to the little tinkle of Stephanie's bangle bracelet when she moved
her arm. The next time he awoke it *was* daylight. He jumped out of bed
and ran to the window for quick confirmation of the fact that the nocturnal visitation had been a dream. He saw Liss and two maids with
wire-pronged brushes and wash pails frantically scrubbing at the limed
swastika. They had erased about half of it. He dressed quickly and ran
down to the lawn. He offered to help. Liss and the maids looked terrified. They were perspiring from their labors. Liss touched his cap to
him. Without stopping his work for a minute, he rasped out in his hoarse
voice what a shame it was to do a thing like this to the gnädige Frau.
She must never see this outrage. It would upset her. The gnädige Frau
must not be upset. Would he forgive them? The moment they were
through Liss would bring him breakfast. Grant insisted on helping. One
of the maids gave him a long-handled brush and he went to work. It
took more than an hour to efface the symbol. The lawn was ruined but
the swastika was gone. How, Grant asked, would Liss explain to the
gnädige Frau the havoc on her lawn? He would say it was a blight, Liss
said. And, indeed, wasn't it? Needless to say, the noble visitor must say
nothing. Grant put his mind at rest.

At breakfast in his room Grant questioned Liss. Surely, the watcher
in the aerie who could already wreak his will on Stephanie's lawn would
descend one day and make himself the master of the rest of Austria. Liss
shook his head stoutly. Never, he said, never here. His conviction was
reassuring; it was so manifest and so sincere. The noble gentleman
must not take this incident too seriously; these were schweinehunds,
hoodlums, fanatics, no-goods, unemployeds, who put on uniforms at
night and had torchlight processions simply to give themselves importance, something to do. Grant reflected that this description might, not
so long before, have been applied to the Watcher himself. He said nothing about what he had seen during the night. When, he asked, did the
gnädige Frau have her breakfast? Liss said that his mistress seldom
rang for Kathie before noon. She never lunched.

Grant said that in that case he would prefer to have lunch by himself in Salzburg. Liss recommended the Café Bazaar. He would find other Americans there, and many prominent people. Grant said he wanted to walk. Liss suggested a walk. Grant said he'd like to go to a barbershop. Liss suggested a barbershop, very good, right in the village.

Grant settled down at the escritoire to do two hours' work, first clearing it of the little forest of bibelots. He returned to the Frobisher family and to Blue Hill with relief. Could he have a Liss-like character in it? Could he not indeed have Liss, the loyal servitor whom Mrs. Frobisher had brought with her to Maine when she married? Grant planned to set his play in the midst of the depression, when even the rich Frobishers felt insecure, and to populate their house on the masculine Riviera with her daughter's friends — young, bright, rebellious and unemployed. It was the passing of an era in America too and Liss's presence might help supply a Chekhov–*Cherry Orchard* effect. Grant leaned back in his chair; he had just written this in his notes. The phrase pleased him; it had a scientific, astrophysical sound. Grant worshiped science, especially because he was ignorant of it. He regretted not having majored in science at college. Grant was continually reproaching himself for opportunities missed and for having left inviting avenues unexplored. He read avidly in scientific books, Jeans and Eddington, with a profound sense of having wasted his life. While the phrase "the Chekhov–*Cherry Orchard* effect" pleased him, it did not fool him. It was a phrase. He was a snapper-up of unconsidered trifles — another phrase. Grant knew that he had no real culture. His memory was good and he was fluent; at college he had been able to pass examinations easily with a few days' intense cramming. He got on well with intellectuals; he entertained them with stories of the film and theater worlds, but he was sharply aware of the difference between himself and them. He took no comfort from the fact that they enjoyed his company. Stephanie, in her random way, had hit on a truth: the "darting" mind.

Moreover, as he bent to his work, the whole episode of his frustration over Sally Frobisher enveloped him and made it painful for him to continue. He stopped working. He knew that he would do no better with Stephanie than he had with Sally. To Stephanie he was no more — he would never be any more — than a "poet." Poet-at-large. It was no good. Grant wanted a more specific allocation. He couldn't work. He began to suspect the validity of the whole conception on which he was

basing his play. It was all true, it had all happened, but could he make
it seem true in the theater? Wouldn't it emerge as melodrama? On the
Arlberg Express he was sure he had it, but now the edifice crumbled.
Very depressed, he put a paperweight on his notes and went out to find
the barber, to find the Café Bazaar. He wanted to walk; he wanted to
walk it off.

The lawn was on the south side of the castle, between it and the lake.
Grant crossed the vast, gray-walled courtyard to the gate through which
Liss had driven him yesterday. The gatekeeper tipped his cap to Grant,
unlocked and swung open the heavy iron door. How, thought Grant,
had the interlopers got in during the night? Was the gatekeeper their
accomplice? The servile little man became a potential enemy. Liss was
all right, he was devoted to Stephanie, but from now on everyone Grant
passed in the street was an enemy.

It was a heavenly morning. The village was idyllic. A white-painted
church with an oblong tower chimed the hour. Belled cows grazed in the
fields. They tinkled like Stephanie's bracelet. God was in his heaven
and all was right with the world — with the exception of Grant. He
found the barbershop. The barber, a tall, lithe man in a white smock,
bowed to him, and his apprentice, a boy of seventeen wearing knicker-
bockers, blue-gray worsted stockings and buckled shoes, like an eighteenth-century page boy in a Mozart opera, doubled over in eager ser-
vility. The apprentice took his coat and hung it up. Grant sat in the
chair and asked for a haircut and shave. While cutting his hair, the barber made conversation, in which respect he was no different from American barbers. He remarked on the beauty of the morning. The noble
gentleman was an American, no? Grant admitted it and that he lived in
New York and was staying at the castle for the Festival. The barber
was tall and thin and courtly. A sudden prerecognition, an inescapable
conviction overwhelmed Grant — there was something about the barber's tall, wiry, lithe figure, the way he moved and carried himself — a
conviction that he was the leader of the little posse Grant had observed
during the night. He told himself that this was unjust, that the barber
couldn't be, and yet he was absolutely sure that he was. Grant couldn't
help it, he broached politics. What did he think, Grant inquired, would
Austria go to the observer in the aerie? In a gentle way the barber was

shocked. He shook his head emphatically: "Nimmer," he said. "Nicht hier. Nicht Oesterreich. Nimmer hier."

The barber's certitude was somewhat too emphatic. The barber knew, of course, that Grant was Jewish. He would never have told Grant what he thought. While he was being shaved, Grant thought: "He could so easily cut my throat." Grant felt an apprehension that the barber, on general principles, might do it. But why should he, so gratuitously, eliminate a customer good for the summer? Grant could see that the barber, although he might indulge in odd nocturnal diversions, was practical.

Grant tipped the barber, tipped the apprentice. They implored God to bless him and bowed him out of the neat little establishment. Nevertheless, Grant felt a certain relief when he got up from the chair; he had escaped having his throat slit at least for *this* morning. Parked at the curb as he left was a great Mercedes touring car. There was a metal swastika on the hood. A uniformed chauffeur held the door open for his passenger: a slim middle-aged major of the Wehrmacht. The officer's gloss radiated confidence. Obviously he knew that the future belonged to him. His entrance into the barbershop was a little triumphal; the barber and his apprentice knew that the future belonged to him too. The officer strode to the barber's chair as to a throne. Watching the reception from the sidewalk, Grant recalled the casual postscript to a letter shown him by an elderly, successful Jewish businessman in New York. It was a letter from a Hamburg manufacturer with whom Grant's friend had had pleasant business relations for many years. The American had been entertained at the German's home in Hamburg; Grant's friend had reciprocated in New York. The letter was typed, dictated to a secretary. It stated, with genuine regret, the Hamburger's sorrow that their business relations could no longer continue. It was a charming letter. At the end, beneath the valedictory salutation, was a postscript in the writer's own hand: "P.S. Germany cannot possibly lose the next war."

Grant walked on. He was pretty sure that the officer's conversation with the barber would have a different orientation than the barber's conversation with him. The officer's throat, he felt sure, was in no danger. Neither, he felt, was the Hamburg businessman's. He believed the prophecy in the postscript.

* * *

Grant resumed his walk through the smiling countryside. He had been instructed by Liss to take a taxi into Salzburg but he was in no hurry. He felt like walking. He stood still for a moment and looked up at the aerie, casing it as if to learn its secret. Below the mountaintop on which the holiday chancellery was perched, wreathy clouds floated upward as if to enhalo it. It was up there, that cosmic mind which had an eye for detail also, since it could encompass the desecration of Stephanie's lawn. The sun was hot. Momentarily a spindrift of rain fell; it was refreshing, a swathe of soft lace. Grant tried to imagine what was going on in the mind up there. What was it thinking? He imagined that it was not a mind at all but a will, a spiky, barbed-wire spool of will at white heat, ignited by the light disk concentrated on it, as through a burning glass of hitherto uninvented heliacal force. The life and actions of this sunburst of will were automatic, chemical. It existed to subserve itself, to project itself through space and time. It was a voltage of pure energy; it had its own insensate life; it was a private sun, isolated and therefore incommunicable with; an ultimate fixity of degree such as scientists seek for either heat or cold. A fine day, a slight breeze, the flirtations that garland the lives of commoners and kings, the delights of food and drink, the little, fine caressive rains that cease like ephemera and bear, in their brief lives, the scent of firs from the hillsides — all nothing, nonexistent to that gimlet of will — human things shriveled like moths in the shaft from the burning glass. Nothing else mattered but the immortality of that will, nothing could enter its orbit, neither the graces of earth or sky or air, nor the rustling approach of women, nor the taste or the caress of rain.

In a trance of imagining what He was thinking (Grant capitalized the pronoun in his mind, since He was a deity who would hold the world in thrall), Grant began to wonder how it came about that, at recurring intervals in the history of the world with which he was only too sketchily familiar, there periodically emerged a character who could be referred to as He and everyone in the world would know whom you meant. Stephanie's hero, Napoleon, was one such. Surely an English mother in the first decade of the nineteenth century, admonishing a recalcitrant child to behave or He would get you, knew that the identity of the He was inescapable and that the threat would have a salutary, disciplinary effect. How did it come about that these dark criminal types who came from obscurity enlisted vast loyalties and were able to luxuriate in carnage. Napoleon, Stalin, the one in Italy, and the One Up There were, with whatever variations, all of a kind. These characters move in a nimbus of charisma, a noxious gas which intoxicates them and asphyxiates millions. Grant reflected that neither England nor America had ever produced such a type before whom the whole world trembled. Could it be a question of national humor? Was it that America and England had too much humor to deify a grotesque? No wonder that galgenhumor is a German word.

Grant saw that he was passing a café and he sat outside and ordered a beer. He began to think of Stephanie's other hero, Walter Rathenau. With all his culture, with all his sensibility, as revealed in Count Kessler's biography, Grant found Rathenau unsympathetic. He had expressed this distaste to Löwe, who said: "No Jew, in 1922, should have undertaken the job of collecting war reparations from Germany." But that was exactly the point: Rathenau knew that he was Jewish, but what he really wanted to be was German. Löwe had introduced Grant to another Jewish statesman — although he was at that time decidedly without portfolio — Chaim Weizmann. In Weizmann there was no such conflict. He had a pride in being Jewish that required no assertion; as a result the English, especially their aristocrats, admired and respected him. "I always have done better with the Tories," he said. "The Tories have a tradition of sport and they have the concept of fair play, of giving the little fellow a chance." Weizmann had known poverty and Rathenau had been born to wealth and power. That made a difference. Weizmann was Russian and Rathenau was German, and that, perhaps, was the greatest difference of all. Rathenau was humorless; Weizmann had an acute sense of the comic. Of a rumor circulated by his enemies that he had been given a hundred-thousand-dollar bribe by an Arab potentate, he said: "It's too small for a bribe — too big for a tip."

Grant ordered another beer. He thought of Rathenau's last ride on the morning when he had stopped to give Stephanie Rilke's poems. He was brave. The prime minister had implored him not to go about in his open car alone. He wished him to ride in a closed car and with a guard. He knew the hatred that was abroad in Germany and that its focus was Walter Rathenau. But Rathenau would have none of it. Grant tried to recreate Rathenau's last moment. When the assassins came upon him, what was he thinking? The moment of truth! Grant had no belief in the moment of truth. He had had, himself, too many illuminations that proved, with daylight, to be tenebrous. What Rathenau must have felt was sheer panic and the wish to go on living. Can this be happening — and to me! — the last gasp of the ego. After his assassination his murderers professed to have loved Rathenau. It was the mystique of German love.

Just before he sailed Grant had seen, in the *New York Times,* a photograph of some SS men beating up a Jewish shopkeeper in Frankfurt. The shopkeeper was a spindly little man in plus fours, trying to shield his head from the descending club. Grotesquely, Grant remembered a Hollywood incident. The head of a studio for which he worked was an extraordinary character who was always making startling generalizations. Once a writer had entered his office wearing a beret. Grant made a friendly remark about the writer at which the executive barked: "Jews shouldn't wear berets." Perhaps they shouldn't wear plus fours either; evidently there were many things Jews shouldn't do, such as collecting reparations. Grant tried to still the panic — almost as acute as Rathenau's on his last morning — by the reassurance that, since he was American, he was "safe." But was not this demarcation the index of unsafety? The safety was not rooted; it derived from the most improbable of accidents, just as his being here at this moment, staring up at the aerie, was due to another accident, the flash of success. But the first accident was more basic, the act of his father's emigration from Lithuania. His parents came from Memel — "blistered in Memel." They came out of a darkness which, although he had tried, he could never penetrate. How they had made it from Memel to Xenia he never really could find out; it was certainly a most improbable journey and, as it turned out, for him, providential. Without knowing it, his father had abducted him from the Germans. Nevertheless, he felt that this survival was precarious. He remembered the scowling tycoon in Greenwich warning him that "this is a violent country." Grant began to think, with tenderness, of his father, who had died the year before. He was a simple, ineffectual, pure man, secure in the embrace of the Almighty. He was morbid on the subject of Jewish casualties in the past; he was always talking about the "rivers of blood" which had flowed in the region from which he came. He believed in being good and hoped that his son would achieve this abstract state. He believed in the Golden Rule which, he insisted, Jesus had borrowed from older and more experienced and more orthodox members of the Jewish community. Had he not headed for Xenia, Grant thought, what would be his situation at this very moment?

Grant began to think about the margins which made chivalry and civilization possible. Löwe had often teased him for being a masochist and now he settled down, with another beer, to have a really good time. How would he behave under torture? There is a point below which civilization doesn't count at all, the animal frontier-belt, the physical and neural barrier. Before you could be decent or generous or loyal, you had to have a surplus: in money, in self-belief, in life expectancy. The enjoyment of art was a dividend of surplus. To beg off a minute, a split second, from the torturer, Grant was sure he would sacrifice all the works of Beethoven and Mozart. "The saint," Rathenau had written, "derives his nourishment from the urge to life; the intellectual from the fear of death." For the moment, at least, Grant became an intellectual. There came to his mind a terrible story from some book on Zen Buddhism.

A mother is sitting by the riverside weeping, holding in her arms the body of her dead child. A stranger comes and asks: "Why do you weep?"

"I weep for the death of my beloved son."

The stranger gives her a sharp clout on the head with a stick.

"Now," he said, "I will really give you something to cry about!"

From inside the café Grant heard the music of a Strauss waltz. He remembered a Viennese comedy Löwe had sent him. It concerned a lower middle-class family living on the edge of poverty. Through the entire action of the play you heard, almost without intermission, ravishing Viennese waltzes. To this obbligato was acted out a tale of skullduggery, also without intermission: rape, robbery, infinite malice ending in murder. A play like this could of course be written about any city in the world, but without the waltzes. It was, wasn't it, the age of murder? Rathenau, Rosa Luxemburg, Liebknecht, Erzberger. But, then, hadn't every age been? Grant thought of the torturers of history, of men being drawn and quartered, of four horses being tied to the hands and feet of a culprit and whipped till they galloped away and of the spectators who watched in ecstasy. From inside the café Strauss gave way to Lehar, whom Löwe had described as a toady whose tunes beguiled the Leader to such a degree that he overlooked the solecism of Lehar's Jewish wife.

Grant caught sight of a poster announcing the coming Festival: Rudolph Stohl: *Jedermann;* Toscanini: *Fidelio.* Stephanie, he knew, couldn't wait for the arrival of her two heroes. Grant had been excited too. Now he looked at the poster morosely:

"A sheen of art," he thought, "over a swamp of murder." The shimmering crust fooled everybody: it was a gloze, a placebo, a camouflage, concealing the suppuration beneath. Why were they flocking from all over the world to this city, its streets choked with swastikaed tumbrils, for an art festival when there were issues of life and death to cope with, the One Up There to cope with?

Grant felt dizzy, as if he were going to faint. He fainted easily from the time he was in high school. He was, he knew, living a phantasmagoria, himself a puppet in it. He must see Stephanie. He must see her at once. That would drive away these morbid introspections; the sight of that pale, classically beautiful face, the music of that lovely voice. He felt himself, too, under a burning glass, shafted from a source far removed from that of the One Up There. He would, for once, surmount his inhibitions; he would abase himself before Stephanie, tell his love. She must, surely, be moved by this divestiture of pride. He gulped down the last of the beer. He realized that he hadn't had lunch yet and that he was hungry. But he wouldn't go into Salzburg; Liss must give him something to eat in the castle. He was overcome by the realization that Stephanie was a complete mystery to him. Dear as she was, she was also impenetrable. Those bangles! That hero worship! What was she about? What went on in her mind? Grant tried another exercise of the imagination: to get inside Stephanie's mind. He failed. It was like going into a dark room when you didn't know where the light switches were. He didn't know her mind but he knew his own. He must see her at once.

Grant went inside to pay his bill. He wasn't a good drinker; the three beers had made him unsteady on his feet. Inside, he caught a glimpse of himself in a mirror; his acne seemed to be in the ascendant. This sight shifted the orientation of his brooding. He gave up the idea of prostrating himself before Stephanie. It was ridiculous. He was ridiculous. He would get out of it — go home at once. He started the walk back to the castle. The sky had darkened. He looked up at the pinnacle. The clouds had moved up, enveloping it. But the battlemented cone of the retreat, with its low rooftop, was just barely visible. What was going on in the Olympian room? Some conference of generals perhaps, dominated by that strangulating voice. "He" must be working, Grant was sure, under artificial light, so much less incandescent than his own.

When he reached the castle, Liss handed him a note from Stephanie saying that she'd had to go to Vienna to see her actor friend who was ill. Grant had a miserable evening alone after dinner in the ghostly dining room. Next day came a telegram from Stephanie telling him that her friend's illness made it impossible for her to return and asking him to join her in Vienna at once. Grant worked himself up into a state of unreasonable fury; he knew it was unreasonable and that fed his fury.

He told Liss he had to go to Salzburg and would be at the Oesterreichischer Hof. He was sick of Stephanie and of himself. On the night of his arrival he went down to dinner on the porch of the hotel, very cool and pleasant, overlooking the River Salzach, at this season little more than a brook that trickled through the town. The place filled up gradually with Nazi officers and their women. Grant recognized the officer he'd seen that morning entering the barbershop. The officer met his gaze with an expression of cool contempt — or at least so Grant thought. After that, Grant took his meals in his room. For two weeks he hardly went out, working all day and far into the night; he finished the first act of his play and made a good start into the second. Sometimes at night, to get a break, he'd go out to roam the town. He sought out the old part, with its narrow, medieval streets; its tall, ancient houses converged toward each other at the top over the alleys which separated them. The passersby were drab, sullen, hostile — or so they seemed to him. He half expected them to shout "Hep — Hep" at him (Hierosolyma Est Perdita), the rallying cry for the medieval pogroms.

After two weeks he began to wrestle with the idea of going back to New York. He asked the hall porter to make him a reservation on the Arlberg. All the while he missed Stephanie terribly. He debated — hadn't he punished her enough? The phone rang while he was wrestling.

It was Stephanie, profuse in apology and reproach. She was back in the castle. Why hadn't he come to Vienna? Her friend, in his illness, had kept asking for him; they had expected him hourly. Also, there had been another admirer of Grant's in Vienna, Ian Leith. Ian was panting to see him. He must return at once — but at once.

Grant told himself that he had to go back anyway; he'd left a lot of his things in his room at the castle. He had taken only his typewriter and notebooks and toothbrush with him to Salzburg. Feeling exalted and happy — he had been missed, she missed him — he hired a car and drove back to the castle.

When he got there he found messages from Mary Kennicott and Löwe; they had just returned. He also found Stephanie with Ian.

"Well," said Ian, "the darling of the *Normandie!* Varina just couldn't stop talking about you in London. It got to be a bore. But it's lovely to see you."

"And it's nice," Grant heard himself saying, "to meet an M.P. I suppose by this time you've won over Parnell. Has he succumbed to your charm?"

"Quite the reverse. The old boy *loathes* me. In an absent-minded moment I had a thing with Kitty O'Shea. He wants Ireland to be free but not Kitty."

Stephanie hadn't the faintest idea what they were talking about but she was delighted by their rapport.

"You've made a conquest of Ian," she said. "You conquer everybody. But I'm not jealous. Not yet anyway!"

"Shall we give her reason, Stanley?"

"I'm sure you will! I'll try to behave well. Now that Ian is here, darling, you won't be bored as you are with me!"

Grant had never seen her so radiant, so happy, so beautiful. The pallor was gone. Her cheeks were flushed.

Certainty fell on him. When Stephanie told him that Ian had been in Vienna with her he'd attached no importance to it; the thing hadn't registered. It did now. It was Ian! It couldn't be and yet it was. Ian was the obstacle man.

He left them on the excuse of having to work and went to the hall to telephone Löwe. He was in an extremity. Löwe promised to meet him at the Café Bazaar in half an hour.

5. The Third Hand

In the baroque sitting room of his suite in the erstwhile palace of the Archbishop of Salzburg, Alexander Löwe aus Czernowitz sat reading the essays of Montaigne. The writings of Michel Eyquem de Montaigne were Löwe's bible. He read in them on trains and on ships, in whatever room he happened to find himself. Of all the figures in the past, the one man he would have chosen, had he the power, to resurrect would have been this former mayor of Bordeaux, the confidant of Catherine de Medici and of Henry of Navarre. It seemed to him that Montaigne was the most sensible man who had ever lived; he found identification in him, self-justification. Montaigne, he was pleased to remember, was descended from Marranos, he was half Jewish. This fact lubricated Löwe's sense of identification with his semi-ancestor. The squire of Montaigne was a sensual man but he had known how to put passion in its place, as Löwe himself had found it expedient to do. He was that rare character, a man who knew his limitations; he accepted their boundaries and was content to browse contentedly within them. So tenderly did Löwe feel toward his hero that when, in his youth, a struggling journalist in Vienna, he came upon, in Rousseau's *Confessions,* a sneer at Montaigne, a questioning of his sincerity, he took it as a personal insult. He sat down at once in his garret room and wrote a scalding feuilleton, comminating Rousseau, exalting Montaigne. Next day he took it to the offices of the Vienna Neue Freie Presse, whose literary editor happened to be Theodor Herzl. Herzl, a playwright and literary man then, who had no notion whatever that he would one day become a crusader for Zionism, asked Löwe to come back in a few days. Löwe did. Herzl was courteous and encouraging and accepted Löwe's diatribe. Because, Löwe had written, Montaigne was well-bred and reasonably happy, because he got on with people, whether they were kings or peasants, because he was utterly free of the persecution mania which bedeviled Rousseau, the latter assumed that Montaigne must be lying. In essence, Löwe had written, Rousseau was reproaching Montaigne because he wasn't as he himself was. "Indeed he wasn't," Löwe concluded fervently, "and we must thank the good Lord for it!"

It was Löwe's first and last triumph in the field of pure letters. For a few days he was given the accolade in the cafés; after that he sank back into the menial odds and ends of journalism. But, as if in gratitude to him for having given him a few days of glory, Löwe had never, since that day, let go of Montaigne. It seemed to him that, every time he read him, he discovered something new, some facet that had not been visible before. Such a quick illumination suffused him now. Montaigne was talking about marriage. Löwe read:

Connections and means have, with reason, as much weight in it, as graces and beauty, or more. We do not marry for ourselves, whatever we say; we marry just as much or more for our posterity, for our family. Therefore, I like this fashion of arranging it rather by a third hand than by our own and by the sense of others rather than by our own. How opposite is all this to the convention of love! In a good marriage, if such there be, love is dangerous; friendship should be the model.

Löwe stared at the passage. He was struck. But that was what he himself was! He was, himself, a third hand. In how many marriages, some all right, some middling, some ill-fated, had he not been the third hand. Grant, teasing him about it once, had said that he would write a sketch of him under the title: "Shadchen de Luxe." How well, Löwe felt, he and Montaigne would have got on; they would have understood each other perfectly; they might even have collaborated! He, Löwe, might well have been the third hand in Montaigne's own marriage, in the marriages of his children, of his grandchildren. No doubt about it — he could have done much for Montaigne. And, this was even more important — Montaigne could have done much for him. How would Montaigne have advised him, for example, about the new and unhappy developments with which he had immediately to cope: Varina's critical situation; about Stephanie, whose total impracticality and headlong impulses toward doom would have made even Montaigne throw his hands up, all three of them?

Löwe's meditations were interrupted by a knock on his door. It was Helmuth, the butler, to tell Löwe that he was wanted on the telephone. Löwe went down the hall to take the call. It was Grant, manifestly desperate. Löwe promised to meet him in the Café Bazaar in half an hour.

Back in his room he sighed with weariness. He felt a sinking of the heart. He did not confuse this with the chronic aberration of his physical heart about which his doctor was always warning him. This came from another source and he knew exactly whence. It felt very strange and very lonely to be here, in this palace, without Lady Monica. It was the first time it had happened. Had she been there, his tribulations, as well as her own, would have evaporated in laughter. She had the rare faculty of transmuting most happenings into the pure gold of high comedy.

He looked down ruefully at the unfinished letter he had been writing to Lady Monica. Their correspondence was unremitting; often their letters crossed. Well, he would finish the letter on his return. He had to get back in any case to get Varina's call from London. Her telegram saying that she must speak to him lay on the desk beside the unfinished letter.

Löwe went to the window and looked up at the establishment of Rudolph Stohl's nearest neighbor. Stohl had bought the palace of the late Archbishop of Salzburg many years ago. From here he directed the activities of the Salzburg Festival, which he had initiated; he couldn't have anticipated that this mountain would attract another property owner. Stohl's palace was a lavish baroque fantasy on a large scale; the neighbor's chalet was spare, functional, Spartan; it crouched on the mountaintop, ready for the spring. The Spartan looked down at the Sybarite. Between these two establishments ran the German border line. The neighbors represented oddly disparate types. "If I were Stohl," thought Löwe, "I'd pick another neighborhood." He had, indeed, suggested it to Stohl but the latter loved his palace. His only reaction to Löwe's suggestion had been to spend another fortune doing it up. He created an artificial lake which looked as real as any natural lake. Looking down at this improvisation, Löwe remembered the night, two summers ago, the gala performance of *As You Like It* which his chief had also improvised for the elect of his friends. The actors, in costume, drew up in Elizabethan barges; the gardens were lit by flambeaux; it was an evening of magic. He had sat with his English darling and her husband, a most engaging man, who was a famous international lawyer as well as a foremost scholar on the life and writings of William Blake.

He was enthralled by the pageant. He only wished, Monica's husband said, that Elizabeth I could have been there; she would have dismissed Inigo Jones and installed Rudolph Stohl. It was a triumph for the later royalty.

Indeed, Rudolph Stohl did have the manner of a benevolent monarch: simple, humorous, unaffected, perfectly natural, as if he were an ordinary human being. He simply took it for granted that his whims would be executed instantaneously, even when it was impossible to execute them, as if they were natural laws. Löwe was perfectly aware of the remark made about him by his chief to one of the other ministers in his cabinet of advisers. As he turned away from the window he could hear Stohl's voice, that musical, sex-compelling voice, saying it. An adorer of Stohl's had once confided to Löwe the effect on her of the master's voice. "He has," she said, "the sexiest voice in the world. Just talking to him on the telephone gives me an orgasm!" This is the voice Löwe heard now saying of him:

"In my discussions with Löwe he is right ninety-nine per cent of the time. On that one per cent — when I am right and he is wrong — on that one per cent I *live*."

Löwe looked at his watch. He was late. Grant must be sitting there in the Café Bazaar, stewing. Löwe enjoyed his role with Grant; dotting his oceanic naïveté with little islands of sophistication, seeding them gradually at his leisure, doling out capsules of wisdom stemming from his infinite worldly experience, the more detached since it was all vicarious. He ordered a car from Helmuth, the butler (a Nazi, Löwe was sure), and ordered Schott, the chauffeur (a Nazi, Löwe was sure), to drive him to the Café Bazaar.

Grant arrived first at the café. The place was fairly crowded; he began to walk through the series of rooms looking for Löwe. The captain came up to ask if he could help him. Grant said he had an appointment with Mr. Löwe. At that the captain opened his arms wide in a gesture of welcome. He was all smiles.

"Ah!" he exclaimed. "Mr. Löwe! Now we know the season has started! Come with me!"

Grant followed him to a corner table in the river room.

"Here," he said, "here he likes to sit. I will bring him to you."

Grant sat with his back to the window so he could watch the front entrance; he couldn't wait for Löwe to appear. Then he began to wonder how he would explain to Löwe the urgency of his call. After all, what evidence had he to support the conclusion he had come to about Stephanie and Ian? Was it not a figment of his morbid imagination, which inclined always to put the worst interpretation on things? Had not Löwe told him that Ian was in love with Varina? Löwe had not but that is how, for the moment, Grant chose to remember it. Well, one thing was sure: if his suspicion was confirmed he would go back home at once, he'd been a fool to come. With relief he saw Löwe come in from the street door. The captain greeted him, several waiters clustered around him. Löwe shook hands all around; Grant saw the smile of pleasure that lit Kaetchen's face. He had noticed before, in all of Löwe's pet restaurants, that he had a special relationship with the waiters. He greeted them as members of his household; indeed, their establishments were the only household he had.

Grant got up to greet Kaetchen. They shook hands. Löwe was in a mellow mood, carried over from his welcome by the staff. He chaffed for a moment with the waiter who had come up to take his order.

"This young man," he said in German, "doesn't know our quality. I look to you to demonstrate it."

The waiter smiled and nodded.

"Two?" he said.

Löwe nodded.

"Two."

The waiter needed no further specification. He disappeared. Kaetchen beamed at Grant.

"Well, hochstapler?"

It was a salutation with which Löwe often greeted Grant or, indeed, anyone else. It was an Austrian expression which meant, loosely, rascal or confidence man. The population of Czernowitz, Löwe often stated, consisted entirely of hochstaplers. He divided the world into two great categories: hochstaplers and würzels, literally little sausages, symbolically easy marks or suckers, the minnows that swim the seas of life for the hochstaplers to prey on.

"Well?"

"Not well. I'm in a state."

"What about?"

"Ian's with Stephanie. He seems to be installed."

"Naturally."

"I'm not crazy then?"

"That remains to be seen."

"Didn't you tell me that Ian's in love with Varina?"

"Not at all. I said that Varina's in love with Ian."

"I got a feeling — just seeing them together — that Stephanie's head over heels about him."

"Naturally."

"After what you told me — on the boat — about Ian, I wouldn't say that it's in the least naturally."

Kaetchen sighed.

"You are really terribly inexperienced."

He said it more in sorrow than in anger.

"Did you know about it — when we were on the boat?"

"Naturally."

"Then why didn't you tell me? You owed it to me to tell me. I'd not have come."

"That's why I didn't tell you. I wanted you to come."

"What for! To be made a fool of!"

"I can't quite explain it to myself — you are so callow — but I enjoy your society. Also I thought it would be good for you. To find out the facts of life for yourself. To complete your education, which I have taken in hand . . ."

Löwe permitted himself a dab of French.

"*L'Éducation non-Sentimentale.*"

The waiter came up with a vast tray: steaming cups of hot chocolate covered with mounds of whipped cream, reserves of whipped cream in sauce boats, pastries, glazed and jeweled with fruits and berries, rows of cut sandwiches. The waiter unloaded. Kaetchen fell to. Grant stared at him, miserably.

"Have some of these sandwiches. You won't get this particular brand of sausage anywhere else. Try them."

He glanced at the waiter, his hands behind his back, standing at a respectful distance, watching.

"You're not making a very good impression on the waiter. You'll hurt his feelings. Keep your end up."

Grant picked up a sandwich and took a bite. He didn't care for it very much.

"I don't believe you're in love at all. Those who are unhappily in love eat like mad. They are afflicted with kummerspeck."

"Do I have that too? What is it?"

"Kummer is anxiety, sorrow, the heartache of love. Speck is lard, bacon. It is a very compact word, pure Austrian. The idea is: when you suffer in love, you overeat. That is why so many unhappy lovers are overweight."

Grant watched as Löwe reduced the mounds before him.

"You must be terribly in love."

"Naturally. Perpetually. Try the apricot."

"In Xenia, when we're crossed in love, we don't eat at all. We die of inanition."

"You're not, luckily for you, in Xenia. I've been in Ohio, in Cleveland, and the food they give you there — what passes for food! In the richest house in Cleveland they served ices which were *bought!*"

"I'm going back tonight."

"Where to?"

"New York. I'll go up to Maine — where I belong."

"That would be foolish."

"This place is not for me. This milieu is not for me."

"Don't be narrow-minded. Widen your horizon."

"My horizon consists of Stephanie."

"What good will it do you then to transplant it to Maine? Same horizon."

There was a silence. Kaetchen ate methodically.

"Where's Varina?" said Grant. "Why didn't she come back with you?"

"That's another story. I'll tell you later."

A quartet of Nazi officers came in and were shown to a table not far from them. Grant leaned across the table and whispered to Kaetchen.

"The first night I was here — I didn't tell you — they put a great swastika on Stephanie's lawn. It took Liss and the two maids half the night to clear it off so Stephanie wouldn't know. Why shouldn't she be told the facts of life?"

"Facts don't interest Stephanie. She was born a century too late. Eighteen thirty. That's where she belongs. When Goethe published *The Sorrows of the Young Werther,* she would have joined the suicide cult encouraged by that tiresome novel. She doesn't show it, thank God, but she's more than a hundred years old."

"The age of heroes!" said Grant bitterly.

"Exactly. You're beginning to catch on."

"Ridiculous. It's really too ridiculous . . ."

"You and Stephanie? Not necessarily. Stay the course. You may win by default."

"Not me and Stephanie. Me and anybody. To indulge in private emotion! Under the hedge of that little mustache up there! How can you, how can any of us — ?"

"My dear Stanley! We all know that we are going to die, don't we? It doesn't stop us, does it, from trying to live?"

"But this is different."

"How?"

"Imminent. It's so imminent."

"I don't think so."

Grant was anxious for reassurance so that his emotional state could be justified.

"You really don't think so?"

"He'll go too far, the one up there. They always do. He'll be stopped."

"Who's going to stop him?"

"The Czechs for one. He wants to grab the Sudetenland. The Czechs are stubborn. They have a good army. They're fighters. They'll stop him."

"The Czechs . . ." Grant murmured vaguely, trying to materialize the Czechs. He didn't know much about the Czechs.

Löwe went on with quiet confidence.

"And if the Czechs don't stop him, England will. You may rely on England."

As the brightest star in his galaxy was English, Löwe was intensely Anglophile.

The Nazi officers at the next table were drinking beer and making merry.

"I can't stand it here," said Grant. "I can't stand this atmosphere. These fellows are murderers. I've got to get out of here."

"If things were going well between you and Stephanie, you wouldn't be quite so overwrought, would you?"

Grant didn't answer. He was mortified. Löwe took pity on him.

"Listen. Be sensible. You want Stephanie for your play, don't you? Finish your play. This I can tell you. Ian will never marry Stephanie. You have only to bide your time."

"What makes you so sure?"

"He wouldn't marry Varina, who will one day be very rich. Stephanie has nothing. Are you working?"

"I've got the first act done. I'm in the second."

"Good! After Ian has left the scene you'll have your play and you'll have Stephanie. Your prospects are excellent."

"Varina. She wants to marry Ian?"

"She was on the scene first. Stephanie raided."

Grant brooded.

"My prospects may be excellent. But my present is — murky."

"It'll clear up. You'll be happier when the Festival begins. Then Salzburg becomes international. True melting pot, so you'll feel quite at home. Only the food and entertainment will be better."

Löwe waved to a man who was crossing the intervening room and who was waving to him.

"Prince Hohenstein," said Löwe. "There's a hochstapler for you!"

Grant took a look at Prince Hohenstein. The prince had, Grant thought, a kind of odious good looks. He was tall and slender and managed to look elegant in lederhosen and a coat of blue wool, embroidered in dark threads and cut like a mess jacket. He carried a soft alpine hat of gray cloth with a green feather in the brim. He came up to their table, his hand outstretched. He was overjoyed to see Löwe.

"Kaetchen! How marvelous! Welcome home. Salzburg's not Salzburg without you!"

Löwe drew up an extra chair for Hohenstein. He introduced Grant as "a berühmte Schriftsteller from New York." The prince was delighted to meet Grant. He had seen his play and was enthusiastic about it. The

star was an old friend of his and she had told him about Grant. He
had, in fact, asked her to introduce him to Grant. She had promised
but, alas, well, Grant surely knew what a dizzy girl she was. Grant felt
an immediate and intense dislike for Prince Hohenstein.

"As a matter of fact," the prince went on, still addressing Grant,
"we almost met in Hollywood. I was there last spring. Were you not
there then?"

Grant admitted that he was. The prince spoke with a decided lisp.
Grant hated that too.

"What were you doing there, Nikky?" Löwe asked. "Trying to get
into films like your friend Ian?"

"I did get into films," said Nikky. "In a big way too. Right at the
top. First shot."

"Oh yes, I heard," said Löwe. "Gisele Benda."

"You know my partiality for Jewish mistresses."

"Especially when they're big stars with astronomical salaries."

"Not at all. You'd be surprised, in that way, how little an opportunist
I am. If you must know, I gave up the big star for a shopgirl, also
Jewish, with whom I almost fell in love. I got awfully bored looking at
Gisele's stills. She was always showing me her stills. Oh, Kaetchen,
look — Olga Schnitt."

He was waving to a slim, wispy lady, no longer young, who had just
entered the café. She was accompanied by a stocky young man in
lederhosen, and a jacket unadorned. Olga blew kisses at them. Kaetchen
blew back. He explained to Grant.

"She was the reigning operetta star of Central Europe. The young
man with her is Kurt Federn."

"Federn! Really! Any relation to . . . ?"

"Son."

"I devoured everything of his father's," said Grant, who was quite
excited.

"You must meet Olga," said Hohenstein. "She's the most enchanting
creature in the world." He turned to Löwe. "Madame Pompadour! Did
you see her in *Pompadour?*"

"Before you were born," said Löwe scornfully.

"And to think," said Grant, staring at Federn, "that his father wrote all those marvelous books. All those stories. All those plays. What a wonderful play *Samson* is!"

Hohenstein laughed.

"That is one play I could do without," he said. "It's about anti-Semitism and makes me blush. You know what an anti-Semite I am, Kaetchen!"

"You have the makings," said Löwe, objectively.

Hohenstein became confidential with Grant. "I say this because Kaetchen knows how I adore him. Do you know that when I lived at home and my father told me he was going to have visitors, I used to ask: 'Are there any Jews among them?' And if he said no, I wouldn't come down to dinner! But still, I must say . . ."

He was looking at Federn.

"What must you say?" said Löwe. "I know you're bound to say it."

"I like young Federn very much. He's a nice boy. But I do wish he wouldn't wear lederhosen." He explained to Grant: "It's a national costume. Somehow it annoys me to see it worn by members of your race."

Grant flushed. He remembered the berets. Another item in the sumptuary laws! He knew, if he sat there another minute, he'd hit Prince Hohenstein. He got up abruptly and left the table.

Hohenstein was astonished. He turned to Löwe.

"Did I offend him?"

"He's young. Scarcely housebroken and remember — American. From the backwoods."

"But I like him. I admire him very much. I loved his play. Did propaganda for it. Sent all my friends. How touchy all your people are! Except for you. You're the only really civilized one, I sometimes think."

His roving eye met Olga Schnitt's.

"But I must go to greet Olga. My favorite woman in the world!"

When Hohenstein arrived at Olga's table, Federn, who saw Löwe sitting alone, came up to him.

"Ah, Kurt! Happy to see you. How goes?"

Young Federn was tall, clumsy, decidedly overweight. He had a great mop of tawny hair, untidy, and pale blue eyes. There was a look of defeat in his eyes. There was an air of defeat about young Federn.

"It's wonderful to see you, Kaetchen," he said with a shy smile that made him suddenly look charming. "I've been waiting for you."

"What brings you to Salzburg?"

"I heard there was an opening for an intern in Diakonissen Haus."

"But it's a Catholic hospital."

"I know. But so they are in Vienna — most of them. You don't have to tell me it's hopeless. I know it is. But to tell you the truth, Kaetchen, things are not good with me."

"With whom are they good?" said Kaetchen cheerfully.

"I can't stand it any more at home. I must get to America. You must help me get to America."

"Perhaps it can be managed. I'll try. Does your father approve?"

"I told him I was going to ask you. He approves. He would approve, I think, to have me out of his sight."

"Come, come, Kurt! Don't exaggerate."

"He wouldn't say it — even to himself — but it is so."

He stared at Löwe. His face was flushed.

"He is even a better doctor than I will ever be. And yet with all his practice, he finds the time — to write all those books, all those plays. Still, clever as he is, he doesn't know what I know."

"What is that?"

"That one day — and sooner than he thinks — it will be all over — and for him too."

"Come, come! It's not the end of the world yet. Cheer up!"

"Please, Kaetchen. Get me to America."

"Is it to get away from the political situation or to get away from your father?"

"Both."

Löwe seemed already to be pondering ways and means.

"I've written to your father about his manuscripts. I think they might be safer with me in New York. Also, I could get a very good price for them there if he wanted to sell them. He hasn't answered. Will you mention it to him, please?"

"Certainly."

Grant came back. Löwe introduced him. Grant babbled to young Federn about his early hero worship of his father. As Grant's rhapsody mounted, young Federn's eyes seemed to cloud over. He got up and said he'd better rejoin Olga Schnitt. As he was leaving he spoke to Löwe:

"You won't forget, Kaetchen?"

"I am thinking about it," said Löwe. Federn thanked him. He took on strength from Löwe's simple statement. There was a springiness in his step as he returned to Olga's table.

And indeed Löwe was already thinking of expedients to bring Federn to New York. Perhaps his friend Dr. Binder, the fabulously successful surgeon, who was a fanatical bibliophile and collector and, besides, a power at Mount Sinai Hospital, might manage an internship there for Kurt. That might work. He would write Dr. Binder tonight. But Löwe made it a rule never to rely on a single line of strategy. Invariably he laid out several. The third hand began to throb. There was Varina — at a dead end. There was Kurt — at a dead end. Possible. Very possible. If only Kurt would spruce up a bit. He must spruce him up.

Grant broke in on his plans.

"I hated that friend of yours, Prince Hohenstein. If he'd sat here another minute I'd have hit him."

"That would have been pointless. He'd have hit you back. Look over there. You can see Olga doesn't hate him."

"He's buttering her up!" said Grant bitterly. "It's the bloody title. What snobs actresses are!"

"Especially Jewish actresses."

Grant was smouldering.

"I can't stay here. To go back to that dreary castle and watch. I'd feel like a voyeur."

"Varina will be here soon. She'll keep you company."

"In watching! You were going to tell me about Varina."

Löwe signaled the waiter and asked for more butter. The waiter brought it.

"I saw her through an abortion in London."

Grant stared at him.

"She didn't want to go through with it. She insisted on having Ian's child. Ian was in a panic. He implored Varina. She was stubborn. Ian came to me. He begged me to talk some sense into her. Where he failed, I succeeded. I persuaded her it would be a disaster for her to have a child Ian didn't want."

Löwe gave Grant a moment to absorb. He went on.

"It was rather a nuisance, you know. These things are more difficult in England than they are in America. I had to take Varina to a psychiatrist who certified her as a borderline case. It was all done quite legally — under an assumed name, of course. The awkward thing was that Varina's parents took it into their heads to come to London at just that moment. I had to improvise a fantasy for them — that Varina had accepted an invitation from some friends to go on a hiking tour in Sweden. They swallowed it."

"Poor Varina! I love Varina."

"So do I. Sentimental — like you — but very dear."

They sat in silence for a moment.

"I can't stick it. I've got to leave."

"It'll be worse in Maine. You'll be imagining things. Here — at any moment — there may be a clearing. Ian is unpredictable. You can't tell what he'll do."

"Stephanie's not for me. It's hopeless."

Kaetchen said nothing for a moment.

"Well — if you must you must."

Grant saw a look in his friend's eyes that stabbed him, a look he'd caught at fleeting moments before. Grant's departure would leave him alone on his island in the opalescent sea.

"There's another aspect of it," said Grant.

"What is it?"

"In Maine I won't have you to talk to."

"I was too modest to mention it."

He smiled at Grant. He had won his point.

"What are you doing tonight?"

"Having dinner at the castle with Stephanie. Ian'll be there, of course. Please join us. It would save my life if you would."

"Alas, I can't."

"Why not? You must!"

Löwe sighed.

"I've got to go back to *my* castle to wait for Varina's call from London."

*   *   *

Near midnight, in his room in the archbishop's palace, just before going to bed, Löwe decided to add a P.S. to the secular epistle he had just finished to Lady Monica. He sat down at the Louis XIV desk — an expensive prop from one of Rudolph Stohl's fastuous Berlin productions — to write it.

P.S. I have just had Varina's call from London. The poor child is desolate and inclined to be bitter at me for having persuaded her not to have Ian's child. She feels she should have gone through with it no matter what so that she might have had a living memento of Ian to which she could devote herself. She doesn't realize that she'd probably never have seen Ian again. To say nothing of what she'd have had to undergo with her parents. Her father would probably have cut her off. I've been through quite a lot with Lawson père. Her mother is pleasant enough, though rather colorless, but her father is a tartar. Varina has no luck. She fell in love with an engaging young friend of mine, a banker with a passion for chamber music. He is, unfortunately, Jewish. When Lawson, Sr., found out about it, there was a storm, I can tell you! It almost annihilated Varina. The old boy is violently anti-Semitic. I gave Varina your telephone number. She is a dear girl and down on her luck. Do see her. Do cheer her up. You will like her.

K.

6. 𝕿𝖍𝖊 𝕶𝖊𝖞

Back in his gloomy room at the castle, Grant, in a crosscurrent of conflicting thoughts, pushed the silly little escritoire up to the aperture of the deeply recessed window to get some light to work by. The vast house had been silent and deserted when he got back from the Café Bazaar. He tried to find Liss, who was nowhere about. He found one of the maids, who told him that Liss had taken the gnädige Frau and her other guest for a drive around the lake. The gnädige Frau had left a message for him that she would soon be back. Under his door he found a joint message from Stephanie and Ian. Stephanie's large scrawl said:

Darling we are eaten with jealousy of Kaetchen we miss you fiercely when I get back I'll knock at your door if you are busy working don't answer it yes answer it so I'll know you're there and you can send me away.

All love

Stephanie

Under which, in copper-plate handwriting, was Ian's message:

What, dear boy, has Kaetchen got that I haven't got? You'll have to tell me and I'll achieve it.

Tendresse,

Ian

The note faintly embarrassed Grant. It might have been written by a girl. None of his pals in Xenia had ever written him a note like that, for that matter no girl either.

He sat down to work but couldn't concentrate. He kept questioning whether he had done right to tell Kaetchen that he would stay on. He had yielded to a look in Kaetchen's eyes. Well, he owed it to Kaetchen to do anything he wanted. He felt tired. He stretched out on the bed, determined not to fall asleep or he might miss Stephanie's knock. Nevertheless, he fell into a half doze. The knock came. Grant jumped out of bed, ran to the door and opened it. It was Ian. He carried a bottle of champagne in his hand.

"Stephanie asked me to bring this to you. With her love. She got a bit of a headache and thought she'd better lie down. Are you terribly, terribly disappointed?"

"Not at all," said Grant. "Do come in."

Grant was pleased to discover that Stephanie could get a headache when she was with Ian too.

Ian walked in, looked around.

"What a funerary chamber! My God!"

He stared at the bathtub.

"When I go to a hotel," said Grant, "I always ask for a room with bath. Stephanie must have known that!"

"How literal can you get? This must be Liss's doing. He's an idiot. I'll see that Stephanie does better by you."

"Please don't bother. I'm used to it now."

"Are there any glasses? Let's have a party, shall we?"

Grant found some glasses. Ian poured the wine. He held up his glass. "Cheers!"

"Cheers!"

Ian's restless eyes caught sight of the manuscript on the escritoire.

"Ah!" he said. "Work in progress. New play?"

"It wants to be."

"You're the luckiest boy in the world, you know that, don't you? I envy you. I envy you madly."

Grant was astonished; Ian was so manifestly sincere. He tapped the manuscript as if it were a talisman which might bring him good luck.

"To have a métier of your own, that you can live by, that you are known for! That is independence, that is freedom! It must be delicious to be you. It must be utterly ravishing."

Grant looked at Ian. Yes, he was sincere. He meant it. He was envious. He was pathetic.

"I don't feel a bit that way," was all he could think of to say.

"Not to have to be a bloody scrounge! To be on your own! You should thank your lucky stars, dear boy. The great thing in life is to have a talent. What you're known for. I haven't got a talent for anything. Absolute zero. It's madly ungay!"

Ian lounged in an armchair. He got up, pulled up another chair and draped his long legs over that.

"I grew up on an estate of six thousand acres, in a house with a hundred rooms, nobody's ever counted how many. My baby eyes feasted on dozens of Canalettos, Guardis, Tintorettos — the whole bloody lot. My father, the duke, is pathologically stingy. The old duffer's really quite insane, you know. That's the only way you can account for him rationally at all. As if it weren't bad enough to be a younger son, His Grace imposed special penalties on me. He hated me from the beginning and I learned early to reciprocate." He smiled at Grant. "As for my older brother, His-Grace-to-be, the less said about him the better. I've got one sister. Utterly mad."

He pointed through the open window up at the aerie.

"She's got a crush on that fidget up there."

This startled Grant.

"Really?"

"Follows him about everywhere. Slave to him. We're all mad as hatters. The whole family. I wonder how I escaped. Perhaps I didn't. Do you notice any signs?"

Grant laughed. He said he hadn't noticed anything alarming. But Ian's frankness about his family astonished him. He had always understood that the English were reticent. No American would have pulled out so readily the family skeleton, to dangle its limbs before a comparative stranger. What Grant did not know was that Ian would have been equally frank with a railway porter. There was no trace of snobbery in Ian; he treated everyone exactly alike.

"What do they pay you in Hollywood?" Ian asked, without transition.

Too startled by the abruptness of the question to lie, Grant told him. Ian emitted a low whistle.

"Astronomical! Here, let me give you a dividend." He refilled Grant's glass.

"The devices to which I've been put to make do!" he said, as if, in looking back, he was surprised himself at his ingenuity.

"That Wilmerding was the hardest. She was really hell."

Ian evidently assumed that Grant knew perfectly well who the lady was, that you couldn't possibly not know Wilmerding. Nevertheless, he amplified.

"Five husbands, four of them your countrymen, and each one richer than the other. She inherited five fortunes. Vesper says only one of her husbands died a natural death and he's not sure about *him*. She took me on as a sort of secretary to run her parties for her, that sort of thing. Isn't it extraordinary, the stinginess of the rich? Do you understand it, duckie? Do you know why she fired me? Because I gave a taxi driver, who'd been standing in the rain waiting twenty minutes for the bloody bitch, an extra shilling. She said it showed that I had the wrong attitude toward her money."

Grant said that he knew of certain American millionaires who were like that.

"But at least they've earned it," said Ian. "Wilmerding's is quite literally blood money. Ask Vesper."

Again Ian assumed that Clyde Vesper was at Grant's beck and call, so that he could exchange idle gossip with him at will.

Grant was greatly taken by Ian. He found him so friendly, so easy, so frank, that he experienced the pleasurable sensation of being on a well-established footing in Ian's "set." There he was — an intimate of the homicidal Wilmerding, of the famous archaeologist Clyde Vesper. All he had to do was ring them up: "Stanley Grant speaking . . ." Also the wine, drunk at that unaccustomed hour, gave him a devil-may-care feeling. He leaned forward in his chair, having decided, in his turn, to be equally frank with Ian.

"Shall I tell you something, Ian?" he began.

"Do. I love to hear things."

"When I first met you on the boat, I envied *you*. I thought how marvelous it must be to be *you*. I thought — this young man . . ."

"Don't be deceived. My looks are deceptive. I'm much older than you think."

But Grant was not to be deterred.

"I thought — with your good looks, your address, your charm — so at home in the world — I thought surely . . ."

"Don't be taken in by all that. As you say in America — we're a dime a dozen in England. All longing to get to New York, all longing to get away from the dreary prison that is England. Not one of them who wouldn't give his right hand to be you. In turn I say, dear boy, that it must be wonderful to be you."

Grant made an effort to congratulate himself on his felicitous identity but failed. He didn't know what to say. How could he possibly tell Ian about the self-distrust in which he was continually floundering? He lacked this Englishman's gift for casual revelation.

"I don't feel that way at all," he mumbled.

"You should. You're a fool if you don't. What's your play about?"

Grant told him.

"Sounds wonderful," said Ian. "Stephanie tells me you want her to play in it. Is she good enough, do you think? I saw her in that *Medea* thing. She's good in tragedy where all you have to do is sit still and look unhappy. But isn't your play a comedy?"

Grant expressed total confidence in Stephanie.

"Let me read the play."

"I've only got the first act."

"I'd love to read that. I'll have it read by dinner."

"Certainly. Here it is."

Grant took the typescript of his first act out of the desk drawer and handed it to him.

"Couldn't you give me something in it? Anything. A bit. Don't forget — I played, with the greatest distinction, a member of Parliament in the Parnell picture. True, I was invisible — but — had they seen me — had they just seen me — they'd have been ravished."

Grant couldn't help but laugh. He found Ian irresistible.

"Trouble is," he said, "except for Stephanie, they're all Americans in the play."

"Don't give it another thought, dear boy. How well do you know Stephanie?"

The question shot out so unexpectedly that Grant was hung up.

"You know she's a crusader at heart, a reformer. The ambition of her life, you know, is to play St. Joan."

"I didn't know."

"She wants to save me from Vesper, whom she considers malevolent. He is. He's a spider. But he is also very distinguished and very amusing. She wants to make me over. Tiresome. I hop into bed with either sex. I was at Eton, you know, and studied hard — in an extracurricular way."

In Xenia High School the extracurriculum had been an obsession with girls. Grant's staggering psyche failed to embrace Eton.

"The odd thing, my dear, is that Vesper takes a very poor view of my activities. He says — meaning Stephanie — that I'm promiscuous. He's a Puritan — militant for the cause — wants to Hellenize the whole world. So you see, dear boy, I am surrounded by crusaders."

He got up. He picked up Grant's first act.

"Can't wait to read this. Can't tell you how pleased I am you're here. I'm very fond of you. Haven't quite analyzed it yet. For one thing . . . you don't seem to know how good you are. I find that most engaging. Most of my writer friends think they're much better than they are."

At the door he stopped for a moment.

"Set your mind at rest, dear boy. I won't play this sticky wicket long."

He was gone.

Grant's thoughts were in a whirl. He felt exalted. He was sure that never in his life had he met anyone as enchanting as Ian. Ian had left the champagne. He was already tipsy but he poured himself another glassful. After all, there was no reason why a member of Ian's set shouldn't drink champagne whenever he felt like it. He did not, like Ian, sip the wine; he swallowed it. He blessed Ian because of the gift he had just made him of Stephanie. He could not remember ever, perhaps not since the successful first night of his play, having felt such ascending euphoria. His hopes for Stephanie soared and soared. He sat in the dream of happiness: for himself — for Stephanie.

By the time Grant joined Stephanie and Ian in the drawing room, he was marvelously drunk. He felt worldly, secure, able to cope, released. Stephanie was wearing a black evening dress. Grant noticed a purplish welt on her upper arm. He started to ask about it but didn't. But Stephanie told him.

"Oh that," she said. "Ian beats me and I adore it."

"Really, Stephanie," said Ian, "you are indelicate."

Stephanie linked her arms through theirs as she walked them into the dining room.

"My two men," she said. "My two favorite men. How did I manage it?"

"By cunning and persistence," said Ian.

Grant's euphoria took a sharp drop. He felt homesick for Xenia. In the dining room their voices came to him as from a great distance. He looked at himself in the wavery, time-stained mirror; he saw a blur.

"Like Debussy this room, isn't it, Stanley?"

"*Afternoon of a Faun,*" Grant managed to produce.

"Not a bit. None of the sensuality. No pursuit."

"Speak for yourself," said Stephanie. "Stanley loves me." She reached out her hand and touched Grant's arm. "You do love me, don't you, darling, even if Ian doesn't?"

"I always feel underwater in this room," said Ian. "Not *Après-midi* at all. *La Mer*. Debussy's sea isn't a real sea, is it? None of the power, none of the terror. It's more a watery Everglade. Swans floating about in it at their leisure."

He turned to Stephanie.

"I see you, pet, swimming about naked in Debussy's sea. Don't you, Stanley?"

"I'd like to," said Grant, excited by the idea.

Liss served the soup in a tureen to Stephanie, who started ladling it out. From his haze Grant watched her arms and shoulders in the mirror, a choreography of grace and whiteness.

"Well, Stanley," said Ian, "I've read your first act. Very keen about it. Can't wait to read the second. First act curtain left me hanging. Fraught, isn't it?"

"Glad you think so," said Grant.

"Do you think it's nice, darling, to let Ian read your play ahead of me?"

"Ian asked for it."

"But you wouldn't let me see it. You said you wanted to finish it first. After all, I'm going to play it."

"I'm not at all sure you'll be up to it," said Ian.

It was his tone that shocked Grant. He looked at him. He'd meant it. His expression had changed. His eyes narrowed. He was vindictive. Stephanie was hurt. He wanted to protect Stephanie.

"Ian doesn't believe in me at all as an actress. But you do, don't you, darling?"

"Otherwise, would I be writing it for you?"

"We'll show Ian, won't we?"

Her voice was tremulous. There was no conviction in her defiance. For the first time Grant realized that she was unsure of herself as an actress.

"No," said Grant. "*You'll* show him."

"The play is very funny. It requires a comedienne. Not your dish at all, Stephanie. The heroine is gay and gallant. You're good in parts where you sit around feeling sorry for yourself."

Grant felt like killing Ian. What had come over him?

Stephanie was on the verge of tears.

"Well, if my poet believes in me . . ."

"It's beyond that," said Grant. "It's an article of faith."

"You're in love," said Ian.

"I am," said Grant stoutly.

Ian smiled.

"That's all right," he said. "Don't blame you a bit."

There was a silence. Stephanie broke it.

"I forgot to ask you, Stanley, didn't you ask Kaetchen to join us?"

"I did. He had to go back to wait for a telephone call from Varina."

"Dear, dear Varina. What a lovely creature she is! Of course you saw her in London, Ian?"

"Constantly."

Grant hoped, for Ian's sake, that Stephanie wouldn't pursue the subject. But she did.

"What's keeping her in London?" she asked.

"She's fallen in love."

Stephanie stopped eating.

"Are you serious? Really?"

"What's so surprising about it?"

"You know perfectly well what's surprising about it." She turned to Grant. "Bitter rivalry, you know, darling, between myself and Varina. Bitter! Bitter! If it's true, it's really a windfall for me. Don't pretend," she said to Ian, "that you don't know why it's surprising."

"Varina's turned capricious. We'll have to bear with her."

"But how wonderful for her! Who? Tell me who."

Ian winked at Stanley. Stanley didn't like it. He felt something now in Ian that was unpleasant. It wasn't the Ian who had so entranced him a few hours before.

"Clyde Vesper."

"That's not funny, Ian. It's a poor joke. Not funny at all."

"I didn't think myself it would happen. But it did. I took them to dinner. They got on like a house afire."

Stephanie's head lowered.

"If you go on with this," she mumbled, "I'll have to . . ."

Ian's voice became sharp, strident.

"This prejudice of yours against Vesper is idiotic." He put Vesper's case to Grant.

"He's a foremost scholar. He belongs to every learned society in the world. He digs madly in Ur. I don't find mummies very attractive myself but when Clyde writes about them, I read with pleasure. Varina was fascinated by him. You'll see for yourself, Stanley, as he's coming here. If he likes you, he'll take you on a dig. Would you care for that?"

Grant didn't know what to say. To go on a dig with Mr. Vesper in Ur would be somewhat of a departure from his normal routine. But he didn't have to come to grips with the new schedule because Stephanie burst out at Ian. She was livid.

"I won't have you dragging Stanley to meet Vesper."

She turned to Stanley.

"He's a monster. Ian knows it very well. Ian hates him."

"You are speaking," said Ian with mock dignity, "of the man I don't love."

He burst into laughter. There was an exaggerated, hysterical quality in his laughter.

"Do you need further demonstration, dear boy, that Stephanie is *not* a comedienne? Do you?"

What did he mean? Had it all been some kind of macabre joke? What was going on? It passed through Grant's mind that perhaps Ian was not, in spite of his protestation a little while ago, entirely free of the family taint of insanity.

Mercifully, the dinner came to an end. They went back to the drawing room. Liss served coffee and brandy.

A thunderstorm had broken out. The rain sounded like a waterfall. Ian was restless. He paced the room, a great brandy glass in his hand.

"I thought," said Grant, "that you only had light rains here."

"Oh no," said Stephanie, "we have terrible storms too."

Grant looked at her. The life had gone out of her. She sat, listless, staring into space. Ian had been flagellating her. Grant became aware of a crusade of his own: to rescue her from Ian. He wanted to embrace her, to lave her bruises — including the visible one on her arm.

Ian spoke to Grant.

"You're lucky to be American. I wish I were. God, how I hate Salzburg! It's only to see Stephanie that I come. Greater love hath no man!"

Stephanie revived a bit at this.

"Did you have an unhappy love affair here?"

"As a matter of fact I did. But that's not why. I know these people. I have an instinct. You just wait and see, that's all."

Ian's instinct had been shared by Grant.

"Nobody here seems to think that the Austrians will go that way," he said.

"They all say that, but they're lying. Don't talk to me about Austria and the Austrians. Just because they're sloppy and inefficient — all that schlämperei — people think they're ducky. Anything but! They're mean and vindictive and stupid. Stupider even than the English without the decency of the English. It's a total myth about the Austrian gemütlich-keit just as it's a total myth about the Bavarian gemütlichkeit. Believe me, when the blowup comes — and it's bound to come with that mucky Austrian masturbating up there on his mountaintop — these precious Austrians will be worse than the nasties. Just wait and see. I've lived among 'em and I know 'em."

Ian kept pacing the room. Grant felt that he was battling in some private hell.

Stephanie spoke, making an effort to sound casual.

"I told Mary Kennicott we'd look in on her after dinner. You've no idea what she's done to her side of the house. I know, Stanley, once you've seen it that you won't come back to me. Mary told me frankly that she means to abduct you. I'm terrified you won't resist."

"I'll resist all right," said true-blue Stanley.

"But Ian won't. Ian can't resist furniture. It's really astonishing what Mary has achieved!"

"I know what money can do," said Ian. He spoke to Grant.

"Did you say that Kaetchen is expecting a call from Varina?"

"Yes," said Grant.

Ian turned to Stephanie.

"Would you lend me Liss? Would he drive me to Stohl's? I want to talk to Varina too."

"In this storm!"

"I like storms. Suits my mood. Please send for Liss."

"Of course." She rang. Liss appeared.

"I won't be long. Wait up for me — both of you. I'll try to bring Kaetchen back with me."

He followed Liss out.

Grant sat beside Stephanie. He put his arm around her. She turned her Medea face to him.

"You see," she said, "I never succeed."

"I worship you. I adore you. I always will."

She squeezed his hand.

"You're sweet, sweet."

"We'll go to New York together. You'll do my play. You'll be busy. You'll be happy."

Grant felt stupid as he said it. He remembered a caricature in which a callow young man on a boat asks his girl: "Do you love me?" at a moment when she is violently seasick.

"I'll do your play — of course I will."

She said it as if it didn't matter much to her what she did. His heart sank. He let go of her. He felt helpless. He felt a flick of hatred for her.

Stephanie put her hand to her forehead.

"It's coming back," she said, "the wretched migraine. I had it before — with Ian. Did he tell you?"

Grant was sure now that she hadn't had it before; that she had simply sent Ian to him to spare herself from coming. She didn't enjoy being alone with him. He bored her; his being in love with her was a bore to her.

Grant got up.

"You should go to bed then."

"I must. I must."

Stephanie got up too.

"Will you do me a favor, darling?"

"Certainly. Anything. What?"

"I promised Mary we'd look in on her. She's longing to see you. Do go. Tell her I've got this awful . . . she knows. She'll understand."

"All right. How do I get there?"

"Through the chapel. Through the den — the theater, you know. Ian calls it my den. You can't miss it. You'll see the door to Mary's cushioned in green leather — with big brass buttons."

"All right. Haven't anything else to do anyway."

"You're the dearest creature in the world."

She embraced him, kissed him and left.

Grant sat down to reconnoiter his position. Stephanie's migraines, he reflected, contrived to make him the permanent, solitary occupant of this drawing room every evening. He looked around him bleakly: at the piano, at the photographs: a Gotha's Almanac of the arts. A vicious zig-zag of lightning lit up the aperture between the drawn curtains; it was followed by a terrific thunderclap. Grant thought of Lear on the heath; his heart went out to Lear. He felt a stab of homesickness. The wine he had drunk had made him thirsty. He would have given anything to go to the corner drugstore in Xenia for a soda. He really preferred ice cream sodas to champagne. He thought of Eileen. He'd have liked to see Eileen tonight; her friendly, affectionate, devoted brown eyes. She would be a comfort. He would have liked to see her this very minute — for consolation. At least she loved him. Well, he couldn't sit here forever. He couldn't go to his room. It would drive him crazy. Might as well go to Mary Kennicott's. If she invited him to stay on her side, he would accept. If not, he determined he would leave this lugubrious abode anyway. He would go back to the hotel in Salzburg tomorrow morning. That would be wonderful; get away from this gloaming, get into a room with a number which you could find without anxiety.

He had the foresight to go up to his room to get the flashlight. He clicked it on. Very feeble. Still, it was better than nothing. He went down again to the drawing room and scooped up all the matches he could find. Aware of his Mongoloid deficiency in sense of direction, he was fearsome of his ability, in the uncharted labyrinth of this fortress, to find that green leather door. He did remember the wrong turning he had made last time and found himself presently in the chapel. There was the Madonna with the red light over her. While he stared at this reassuring beacon, there was a tremendous thunderclap. The beacon light went out. He was in total darkness. He switched on the flashlight; the illumination it offered was ineffectual. Nevertheless, he managed to get across the chapel and into Eleonora's "den," the theater which could seat a thousand people. By the lightning flashes through the tall Gothic windows he managed to see fairly well. His thoughts ran to deserted heaths that evening; he remembered another heath in one of Hardy's novels, but the path of that groping character had been lit by fireflies, steadier than the fitful lightning on which he now depended. The flashlight was like the stick of a blind man; it forced him to move by inches, his path strewn by fallen chairs.

Beyond the opposite door was terra incognita. He came upon a hall

and a short, uncarpeted staircase. While he was climbing these stairs
the flashlight went out entirely. He threw it away and began striking
matches. For a moment he thought of backtracking and crossing the
courtyard in the rain with the hope of finding an outside entrance to
Mary's half of this intractable building. There must be an entrance to
her side! But he pushed on, made his way down a hall and down another irrational staircase. He was confronted, finally, by an iron-banded
door with a great rusty key in the lock. It was a dungeon door and it
was locked. It took a mighty effort to turn the key; it made him sweat
to do it. He put his shoulder against the door and pushed it open. He
found himself in another vast room, containing a profusion of steamer
trunks and armor: full-panoplied figures ready to go into battle or tour-
nament; there were many who had given up the fight and were lying
tenantless on the floor. He made the mistake of trying to run through
this room; he stubbed his shin against the visor of a recumbent warrior
and sprawled over him. When he got to his feet he was panting. By this
time he had given up all hope of ever finding that green leather door.
"You can't miss it," Stephanie had said. She had underestimated him.

Grant wanted to lie down and die. He blundered on, manic. And then
he felt himself treading carpet! He held a lighted match to the floor.
Mauve carpeting. He struck another and held it up. Roualt's *Christ* on
a damasked wall. He felt with his hand around the frame and pressed a
switch. An electrolier lit up over the *Christ*. Grant was pleased with
himself at his ingenuity. By the light over the picture he saw, diago-
nally across the hall, a green puffed leather door, seamed in by polished brass nail heads. To himself he muttered, in remembered schoolboy Hebrew, an incantation in praise of the Lord, uttered by the dying.

He went to the green door and opened it. Peering into the semidark-
ness before him, he saw at once that his visit was untimely. In the far
distance, at the outer penumbra of light from a single stand-lamp, he
saw two figures on a sofa. He had barged into Mary Kennicott's love
life. Hot with embarrassment, he retreated, hoping that his intrusion
had not been noticed. As he was closing the door, he heard Mary's startled voice.

"Who is it?"

"Stanley Grant. Stephanie said . . ."

"Oh! Just a minute — please — just a minute . . ."

"Excuse me. I'm sorry."

"It's all right. Be right there."

"I'll come tomorrow. Good night."

He closed the door. His heart was pounding. What a clumsy lout he was! Nothing would ever go right for him in this house. A line from a French farce popped into his head: a peeping Tom, reporting to a justifiably jealous husband, with his eye to the keyhole of a bedroom: "They are locked like letters in a monogram!"

He moved to the lighted Rouault. He had to begin the journey back. Why had he ever left Xenia?

At this moment the green door opened. Mary came to him. She was wearing a scarlet velvet dressing gown.

"My dear Stanley. So nice to see you!"

It was impossible for Mary Kennicott not to be gracious but she did wish at that moment — Grant was sure of it — that he did not exist. This wish Grant shared. He was praying that some force from above would mercifully abolish him.

"You see, Stephanie had a headache . . ."

"Poor Stephanie! I know those headaches."

Mrs. Kennicott was staring down at his hand.

"What on earth," she said, "are you doing with that key?"

Grant looked down at his hand. It was clutching the rusty key he had picked up on the way. He had been completely unaware of it. It must have weighed a pound!

"I had a hard time finding my way here. I must have . . ."

Mary felt pity for him.

"It *is* a crazy house, isn't it? All those ghostly rooms!"

"Well," he said, "I guess I'll go back. Excuse me. Good night."

He turned to go, stuffing the key into the pocket of his jacket. She took his arm.

"You mustn't think of it. Come in. I'll give you a drink."

Grant was still explaining, "You see, my flashlight went out."

Holding his arm she walked him back through the green door.

"You'd better spend the night on my side. With a good night's sleep you'll have the energy for the return trip in the morning. Besides, I want you to meet a countryman of yours."

They were back in Mrs. Kennicott's drawing room. A tall man came toward them. He smiled at Grant. He had dazzling white teeth. He reached out his hand.

"But you don't have to introduce us," he said. "We've met, haven't we, Mr. Grant?"

It was Grant's acquaintance from Blue Hill, Dr. Kenneth Ogden.

7. Three Letters

The apparition of Dr. Ogden, here of all places, had kept Grant up half the night. He had, in his notes, disposed beautifully of Ogden; he had contrived his final humiliation, his defeat, his end. What right had he to reappear now suddenly, to rise from the dead, to barge into the strong and delicate fabric of his play, ripping it apart? And, moreover, blithe, imperturbable, not in the least ended! Only yesterday, only a few hours before, Grant had brought him into the drawing room of Stephanie's Maine cottage. He had described him. Grant got out of bed, turned on the light over the escritoire and read the stage direction:

> Stephanie comes running in just ahead of Dr. Kenneth Ogden. Dr. Ogden is handsome, dark, magnetic, quiet, masterful. He is conscious of authority and gives one the sense of a strange, genius-like intuition . . .

Of course Dr. Ogden wasn't at all like that; he was hearty, extrovert, outgiving, but Grant had simply exercised his natural prerogative of re-creating Ogden into the image he wanted. What right had he to reappear and contradict Grant's stage direction? What right had he to be so calm, undamaged, in full tide of a new conquest, just as if what had happened in Blue Hill, Maine, and in Cleveland, Ohio, had never happened? For the moment Grant had used the actual names of the characters, Stephanie's, Ogden's, Sally's. He knew he'd have to change them eventually, but using the actual names made it easier for him to write the first draft. Well, Dr. Ogden's intuition *was* genius-like. It had brought him here, and at this moment, to Salzburg; his intuition **was** functioning right this minute in the twentieth-century part of Stephanie's castle. What was he trying to do anyway — spoil his play?

Grant's mind raced. Should he redo the play altogether? Shift it from Maine to Salzburg? Should he dramatize this moment? Make Stephanie the focus of Ogden's intention instead of Mary Kennicott? He discarded that idea. He wasn't, thank God, hemmed in by reality. He would stay in Maine, which he understood much better than this miasmic Salzburg, infested with glossy, uniformed Nazis. Besides, he needed Sally, his heroine's daughter, who had been onto Dr. Ogden from the beginning. He peered down at his manuscript. "I'm not at all sure I like him," Sally was saying. "He's almost too sympathetic. At the same time — he is inscrutable." No, he would stay in Maine. The audience wouldn't know that, when the occasion demanded, Dr. Ogden sometimes went abroad! Grant switched off the light over the escritoire and climbed back to bed. Once in bed, the name he would use for Dr. Ogden in the play hit him. Dr. Rice. Dr. Kenneth Rice. Grant was relieved. This Dr. Ogden could go anywhere he liked. Dr. Rice would operate in Maine.

Still his thoughts would not let him sleep. He began to think of his ridiculous entry into Mary Kennicott's drawing room clutching that abominable key. What an ass he'd made of himself! How inept and clumsy could you get? Grant writhed in self-disgust. Where was that wretched key? What had he done with it? Had he put it back into the door from which he had taken it? His return from Mary's half had been tortuous too; the first agony had not made an experienced traveler of him. He couldn't remember putting the key back into its lock. He began to worry about the whereabouts of the key. He felt on the bed table for his illuminated wristwatch. Three thirty. He got out of bed again, went to the mausoleum-like armoire and felt in his coat pocket. It was there. Flakes of rust came off it. There were no keys like that in the cottages in Maine. This key was older than the thirteen colonies. How marvelous it would be to chuck the grisly centuries and to go back home. By the time he got back into bed, Grant was acutely homesick. His mind cleared. Burrowing his head into the pillows, he reached a decision. He would go back home tomorrow. His heart lifted at the prospect. Once in New York he would leave that very evening on the boat that went through the Cape Cod Canal to Boston. In Boston, on the next evening, he would take that even lovelier boat for Rockland, Maine. And in Rockland, Maine, he would board the ineffable little steamer that stopped at all the little seaports, to disembark finally at Blue Hill. It sailed the Penobscot, the blessed river that wound, broad and narrow, between green banks. Thinking of the Penobscot, Grant unwound with it. He fell blissfully asleep.

The next afternoon, Grant, working at his desk, heard a slight cough at his shoulder. It was Liss, who walked soundlessly. Grant gave him the artifact key which he'd been using as a paperweight. As if by way of return, Liss handed Grant two letters and tiptoed out.

Grant looked at the two envelopes. He recognized at once Eileen's childish scrawl. But it was a foreign stamp. Grant peered at the postmark: Cernobbio. What on earth was Eileen doing in Italy? He looked at the second letter and he understood. It was from Sally. He knew Sally's handwriting. She had written him a note in Blue Hill once to cancel an engagement. At the sight of her handwriting, Grant's heart missed a beat. His love for her welled up. That adorable Sally, so young, so lovely, so clear and direct (alas, too direct!) — none of the penumbra of decadence that enhaloed Stephanie. He tore open the thin, lined envelope; the letter was so tightly impacted that he had to tear the envelope apart to get at it. He read:

Dear, dear Stanley,

I know that Eileen is writing you today. This letter will, I hope, reach you by the same post. Eileen does not know that I am writing you. I have not seen her letter but, knowing her as I do, what a dear and devoted creature she is, and how self-effacing, that she will not tell you the truth. I feel that I must not only for her sake, but for yours.

Eileen is far advanced in pregnancy. The doctor here (a very good and kind man) says that if all goes well, her child and yours should arrive end of August.

Had she told me in time, I might have made different arrangements but it is too late for that now. She is of course terrified that her parents will find out. They are strict Catholics and wouldn't understand this sort of thing. As it happens, I had made up my mind to live abroad for several years. Unless you choose to do something about it (I do hope you will), Eileen will stay with me. We'll settle down in Paris probably. It should be wonderful fun having a baby around.

If you decide to do nothing, Eileen need never know that you know. But I do hope that you will. She loves you so.

I love you too, dear Stanley. I do hope we will see you soon. I have never been in Salzburg. Is it fun? What an exciting time you must be having! Here it is very pretty — sweet. But very quiet. I would so love to be there during the Festival. Do you remember the concerts in Kneisel Hall? I suppose the ones in Salzburg will be on a much bigger scale — full orchestras instead of just chamber music.

Fond love,

Sally

P.S. It would be so thrilling if you invited us. If you wire, I will tell Eileen that I wrote you.

Grant stared at the letter. He felt as if an electrode had been clamped to his skull. From it, in parallel lines, dots, sharp-nailed tiny paws, kept rummaging his head. He saw an illustration: a phrenologist's head — a head with dotted lines all through it — he'd seen in a book somewhere. Was it in that course he briefly took on abnormal psychology? He picked up the letter, read it again. He concentrated on the last part. Sally wanted to come to Salzburg. A ventriloquist's dummy kept repeating this stupidly, isolating it from the attendant circumstances. Eileen's letter lay unopened.

Not only had Dr. Ogden reappeared in his play. So had Sally. What should he do? He must see Kaetchen at once. But first he must read Eileen's letter.

He opened it. A little clutter of colored snapshots of Lake Como fluttered out.

"Carissimo . . ."

Beyond that endearment Grant didn't read. How like Eileen to go Italian all of a sudden! He saw her at her desk in the hotel room, fluffing through one of those little English-Italian, Italian-English dictionaries.

He stuffed Eileen's letter into a drawer without reading it. Sally's letter he put in his jacket pocket. In a kind of somnambulism, he went out to telephone Kaetchen.

Mary Kennicott was addicted to eighteenth-century Viennese baroque. She doted on the capriccios of the architect Fischer von Erlach:

the exquisitely turned chandeliers and candlesticks in porcelain, the
curves and flourishes in plaster, the wild sunbursts in gold, the intri-
cate medallions of dynastic heraldries, the cupids, coronetted gnomes,
griffons, Medusas. Fischer von Erlach was her god, as he had been Austria's in the eighteenth century; that is, of the favored minority in
Austria which could afford him. Mary knew by heart the Belvedere
Palace in Vienna, built for Prince Eugene of Savoy by von Erlach. She
knew his other monuments too; she had made a specialty of him, she
might easily have written a monograph on von Erlach, had, indeed,
thought of doing so. Had he just waited, Fischer, for a few centuries,
waited to be Mary's contemporary, how she might have employed him,
how busy she would have kept him! She sat now with Dr. Ogden over
a marble-topped coffee table, supported by the slim convoluted body of
a faun which was an exact replica of one she had seen and fallen in love
with in Eugene's bedroom in the Belvedere. The Belvedere, alas, was
now owned by the state and nothing in it was directly purchasable. Had
it been for sale, she would have bought it outright.

Mary had been reading aloud to Dr. Ogden a letter which had arrived this morning from her husband in Santa Barbara. Wyman had
been telling Mary about a delightful visit he had had from Dr. McHale,
the renowned astronomer from UCLA:

*. . . What an altogether captivating man McHale is, so attractive, so
modest, the simplicity of greatness. One feels in him the stillness of the
endless night hours he spends up there in his astral contemplations. His
excitement over the new telescope they have built for him at Palomar
is infectious. I asked him whether looking over the vast reaches of the
universe did not make him feel insignificant. I quoted Pascal to him
who wrote:"Le silence éternel de ces espaces infinis m'effraie." Did they
not frighten him? Not at all, he said. They reassure him. He thinks of
himself as an infinitesimal segment — his words — in an evolutionary
process which has made it possible for poor creatures like himself to
bring these illimitable reaches into visibility. Humble, don't you think,
my dear, to settle for being an infinitesimal segment? I believe that
McHale is a deeply religious man. He quoted Einstein to me: "Raffiniert
ist der Herr Gott, aber Boshaft ist er nicht," which he translated
roughly as, "The Lord God is subtle but He is not malicious." Dr. Ogden — to whom please my warmest regards — will be interested, I think,
to know that McHale thinks that illnesses like mine will be cured ulti-*

mately not by psychoanalysis or psychiatrists, but by biochemistry. That is the line Dr. Ogden is taking in his clinic, isn't it? I bless Dr. Ogden's enterprise. I wish him well. Tell him, too, that if he should solve the riddle of my affliction a week or a month or a year after I am gone, I shall not reproach him for tardiness in my astral incarnation.

Mary's hand holding the letter sank to her lap. She was crying. Dr. Ogden put down his coffee cup, got up and put his arms around her. She clung to him. They left the coffee table and went to the sofa. They sat together, their hands interlocked.

"I don't suppose ever," said Mary, "not in his lifetime . . ."

"It is unlikely," said Ogden, "but not impossible. I have some extraordinarily gifted young men at the clinic. Thanks to your munificence, darling, none of the big places have any better."

Mary dabbed at her eyes.

"That exquisite sensibility of Wyman's, that awareness . . ."

"He's a wonderful man. I love him."

"It's maddening, isn't it? Some rift, some tiny rift in the brain, in the membrane . . ."

"And yet, you know, the postmortems, in cases like his, show no lesions, perfectly normal anatomically."

"What is it then, what is it . . . ?"

"That's what your staff is working on."

"If I could only contribute *something* — if only a little step — one little step . . ."

"That I think I can promise you; that is, *they* can promise you . . . I am only their director, an administrative officer, so to speak."

"Oh, you've done it all, darling. You found them all."

"I've been very careful. It's a top-grade staff. That I think I can claim."

"Will you write to Wyman? It would make him so happy to hear from you."

"Of course I will. Today."

"And so will I. I write him every day. But this time he'll have two letters!"

Dr. Ogden smiled at her.

"He certainly will!"

Mary squeezed his hand. She brightened, restored by the opulence of her husband's new prospect.

"But how odd it is — your knowing Stanley Grant! You said last night you'd tell me."

Dr. Ogden laughed.

"It is odd, I must say, his showing up here. How on earth does that peculiar bird turn up here?"

"Well, as you know, he is a playwright and Stephanie's an actress. Kaetchen brought them together, I believe. The poor boy is madly in love with her. He's writing a play for her."

"Well, I hope he's luckier with her than with a girl I knew — "

"Who was that?"

"Mrs. Frobisher's daughter. You remember. I told you about Mrs. Frobisher."

"Oh yes. Mrs. Frobisher. But you didn't tell me she had a daughter."

"Indeed she had. Sally. Entrancing creature. This Grant was madly in love with her. He bored her to death, of course. She's a clever child. She fobbed him off on her paid companion. I can't remember what her name was. Oh yes. Eileen. Eileen Cavanaugh. They were the joke of Blue Hill that summer."

"I like Stanley. Do you dislike him?"

"I didn't know him well enough to dislike him. He seems rather an ass."

"He's gauche, insecure — inferiority complex, I suppose."

"Racial," Ogden interjected, "and why not?"

"But he's talented — very talented."

"They often are."

"He's written a delightful play. He's considered to have a brilliant future."

"He'll need it!"

Mary jumped to a conclusion.

"You *don't* like him!" she said positively.

"God knows what his real name is," said Ogden. "If he had to choose a name, why didn't he find a more likely one, more convincing? And the poor boy should really do something about his acne. He'd have better luck with girls."

"Mrs. Frobisher — what was *she* like?"

"Darling — but a blackmailer."

"You're joking!"

"Not in the least. Quite literally."

Mary stared at him, wide-eyed.

"She never stopped telling me that if I left her she'd kill herself. She was so neurotic she'd have done it too. There is no more insidious blackmail than that, is there?"

"Did she hate her husband?"

"Obsessively."

"Did he deserve it?"

"Not in the least. I liked him very much. Simple, hearty fellow. She made him feel inferior because she was *cultured;* she'd read all the obvious books and knew all the obvious paintings and made a cult of music. God, the operas and concerts poor Frobisher had to listen to, the punishment he took! Oh yes. I liked George Frobisher very much."

"Did he marry again?"

"Immediately. A patient of mine — a grand girl. I was best man at their wedding. Poor fellow died six months later. He made a cult of exercise. Overdid it. Heart attack."

"Was Mrs. Frobisher in love with you?"

"She kept saying so."

"What did she die of?"

"Cancer of the womb."

"Poor thing!"

"It was tough. She was very nice in many ways. Totally self-centered. I could never beat it into her head what she was doing to *me.* God knows I tried often enough!"

"How do you mean?"

"She insisted on spending her summers in that hidebound, narrow-minded little community in Maine. And of course I had to go with her. I begged her to go abroad — offered to take her."

"She wouldn't go?" Mary was amazed that Mrs. Frobisher could pass up so throbbing an opportunity.

"Stubborn as a mule. Every time I said I had to leave her, she said she'd kill herself if I did. She put me in a very difficult position. I was very aware of the gossip about me."

"What did the silly people gossip about?"

"I must say that — from their point of view — it might have looked bad for me. I had to keep quiet, for professional reasons. The gossipers weren't inhibited at all."

"How do you mean — bad?"

"Well, here was this very rich woman manifestly dying. I knew by instinct what they must be saying, that I was just waiting for her to die — to get her money. I shouldn't be at all surprised . . ."

"What, darling?"

"In fact I am perfectly sure of it . . ."

"What?"

"That they even convinced themselves that I hastened her death."

"Oh no!"

"For all I know — even that I killed her. Drugged her to death."

"They couldn't. I'm sure you're exaggerating. They couldn't!"

"Why not? Gossip is easy. Of course I was administering drugs. Had to. She was hypersensitive to pain. Yes, I shouldn't be at all surprised if those dear people put that interpretation on it."

Mary put her hands to her ears to shut out rumor.

"What a dreadful story! I wish you hadn't told me."

"It was a very uncomfortable time for me. Do you wonder I was happy to give up private practice? I owe you, my angel, for that. I'm sorry I distressed you. It's just running into this fellow Grant — here of all places — that brought it all back to me. Well, now you forget it as I've forgotten it. Human nature is always interesting, isn't it? Let's talk of more pleasant things."

He took Mary in his arms and began to whisper to her of more pleasant things.

8. The Burning Glass

Grant got no comfort from Löwe. He had been as severe with him as his own father would have been in Xenia. He insisted that Grant assume his obligation and marry Eileen right away. Grant asked him why he couldn't arrange for Eileen to do what Varina had done. Löwe refused:

he'd been through one abortion this summer and he hadn't the vitality to undergo another. Grant must stop chasing will-o'-the-wisps. Eileen was a very nice girl, far too good for him, and if she was gullible enough to want to marry him, he must count his blessings and do it. Was he ambitious to fill the world with illegitimate children? Did he think he was Ian? Did he think he was royalty? He gave Grant no quarter.

Feeling like a convicted criminal, Grant returned to the castle. It was nearly midnight when he got back. Under the door of his room he found a note from Ian. It read:

Must see you — must. *Vesper's car is waiting to take me to Gastein. Cannot leave without seeing you. Come at once to my room, in the West Hall, next to Stephanie's. Am quite frantic. Do come at once.*

Thine,

Ian

Grant hadn't the faintest idea where the West Hall was. He had never been in Stephanie's room. He went down to the dining room and through the swinging doors into the kitchen. He found Liss there, playing checkers with the two maids. Liss piloted him to Ian's room.

Ian had run to the door to open it when he heard their footsteps in the hall. He shut the door at once when Grant came in and stood with his back against it as if he expected Grant to attempt an escape.

"I've been having a terrible time with Stephanie. She's got this demented notion of saving me from Vesper. I'm not sure Vesper isn't saving me from her. I'm soft. I might marry her out of pity. The point is she's in a terrible way. She mustn't be left alone for a minute. I count on you to spend the night here. It's jollier than your room."

"Where is she?"

Ian pointed to a door. "In there. In bed. Passed out."

"Migraine?"

"Don't be silly. Drugged. She takes this stuff." He took two phials from his pocket.

Grant swayed a bit as if he had been hit in the face.

"I've been into all of it with her doctor. The thing is I lied to her. There was no way out of it. I had to. God, Vesper'll be wondering what on earth's become of me. His car's been here for two hours."

"What did you lie to her about?"

Ian appeared to be irritated by Grant's density.

"I told her I wasn't going. I had to. I couldn't stand here arguing with her forever. She threatened. I know where she keeps the stuff and I'd stolen it. I gave her a shot to quiet her. Here's the rest."

He gave Grant the phials.

"Don't give her any more unless you have to. Unless you absolutely have to. She'll be all right for a few hours. I warn you, she's very clever, very cunning — they all are. She'll whimper. She'll beg. If necessary call her doctor. I've left his name and telephone number there on the desk. Don't leave her. Don't leave her for a minute. When she finds out I've gone, you can't tell what she'll do. If she wakes up, if she asks for me, make up some excuse. Tell her I've gone to see Kaetchen — anything. But whatever you do don't tell her I've gone to Gastein. Don't tell her the truth till after the doctor has seen her. Do you promise?"

Grant nodded.

"Don't leave her. Don't leave her for a second. Spend the night here. Promise?"

Grant nodded again. Ian rushed out.

Grant stared stupidly at the phials in his hand; he held them up to his eyes. Colorless. No labels. How did she take it? With a needle? He put the phials in the pocket of his jacket. He looked around the room. It was indeed jollier than his own, with great windows looking out on the lake. It was about five times as large for one thing, very feminine, with a tri-mirrored dressing table between two windows. Was this normally Stephanie's dressing room? Everywhere silver-framed photographs of famous faces — conductors, violinists, novelists, playwrights, actors. He found himself looking at Löwe's passive face with its sad eyes. Did Löwe know, he wondered? Probably. Everybody knew but himself, his own stupid self. He knew nothing at all of this strange world. He never would know.

He moved toward the door of Stephanie's room. Should he knock? He thought of the hours he'd spent in his room waiting for her knock that never came. Why should it? Who did he think he was? He felt an access of self-contempt at his stupidity, his vanity, his blindness, his stubborn refusal to put two and two together. Still — she was in there! Ian was out of the way. She was alone. She was accessible. He moved toward her door — a filing sucked by a magnet. He knocked several times, each time louder. He pushed the door open. The room was in darkness, save for a rose-shaded light bulb on the night table by her bed. He closed the door and took several cautious steps in the direction of the light. He made out the cavernous outlines of the bed, an enormous four-poster, hung with great folds of creamy, looped lace, a replica of the crib he had seen in the photograph. He walked to the bed. He saw Stephanie's face, a roseate glow on it from the lampshade. She was asleep, breathing heavily, a soft snore. Her face was a cameo in ivory; he had never seen it so untroubled, so unlined, so beautiful, so pure. Below her eyes there were faint shadows, blue light on snow. Except for her shoes and stockings, she was naked.

He was on his knees beside her. She stirred slightly.

"Ian?"

"Yes. Ian."

She sighed. She clung to him. He was in bed beside her. He began to lacerate the so long withheld, patrician flesh.

"Yes. Yes, darling. Teach me. Teach me."

When the first light showed through the windows, Grant got up, dressed and started to find his way back to his own room. He forgot that he'd promised Ian not to leave Stephanie alone. Once in his room, he lay down, without undressing, and fell fast asleep. He was awakened by a knock. It was Liss. The gnädige Frau wished to see him. Would the noble gentleman be so gracious? Grant looked at his wristwatch. It was nearly one o'clock. He reached into his jacket pocket for a cigarette. He came upon the phials Ian had given him the night before. He followed Liss to Stephanie's room.

Liss knocked. Stephanie's voice answered in German. Liss opened the door. Stephanie was pacing the room as if she wanted to walk through the walls. Although the sun was blazing outside, the room was in twilight; the velvet curtains had not been drawn. Was he never to see this room in the light? He saw a coffee set on a little table.

"Please," he said, "may I have a cup of coffee?"

"Oh, my darling! Certainly."

She went to pour him a cup of coffee. Her hands shook so that she couldn't manage it.

"Let me!"

He took the coffeepot from her and poured himself a cup.

"You must forgive me, darling. I am not very well."

He gulped the hot coffee. He had scarcely looked at her. Now he did. She was haggard. She couldn't stand still. She went to the windows, made as if to draw the curtains, changed her mind, resumed pacing. She was wearing an apple-green dressing gown of some filmy stuff. He remembered how she had looked in the Greek tragedy in which he had seen her; desperate, devoured. She was like that now: a maenad in an apple-green dressing gown.

"Liss says you saw Ian last night."

"I did."

"What did he tell you?"

"That you weren't well. He asked me to stay with you."

She came up to him. He was swallowing coffee.

"Why couldn't he?"

"Because he said he had to go away."

"Did he tell you where?"

"Bad Gastein. His friend's car was waiting for him."

Her voice went dead.

"He went then?"

"Yes. He went."

"He lied to me."

"Yes. He lied to you."

"Did he tell you that too?"

"Yes. He told me that too."

"Is that all he said?"

"He said he'd write to you. Call you."

"Kind of him!"

"He said you had this crazy idea of saving him from Vesper. He said he looked to Vesper — to save him from you."

He put down the coffee cup and faced her.

"I did what he asked me. I stayed with you. I slept with you."

"Was it all right?"

He took her in his arms.

"Last night you didn't know it. Now you'll know it."

"Why not?"

He saw that, with Ian gone, nothing mattered to her. He was in despair.

"I mean nothing to you."

"I love you, darling. You know that, don't you?" She spoke very fast as if she were in a telephone booth and had used up her last coin. "There's nothing in the world I wouldn't do for you. Anything. Anything you want. Any time you want to sleep with me, I'll sleep with you. Will you do something for me?"

"What do you want?"

"My medicine. Give me back my medicine. Ian stole it. I've looked everywhere. I can't find it. Did he give it to you? He must have given it to you. Stanley, darling, give it to me. It's mine. Give it to me."

"He said to call your doctor . . ."

She screamed at him. "Don't you dare call him. I loathe him. Give me back my medicine!"

He stared at her.

"If you don't, I'll never speak to you again. Darling, Stanley — I beg you!"

He took out the two phials and gave them to her. She took them and started walking him to the door.

"I must rest now. But we'll dine together, won't we? Just the two of us. Are you free? Please be free to dine with me."

"I'm free."

"You'll read your play to me."

"Yes."

He left. She slammed the door shut.

"*Carissimo*," he read and went on with Eileen's letter. She wrote a lot, sheet after sheet, in her meticulously clear childlike handwriting: how she and Sally spent their days, what an angel Sally was, how they talked and talked about him, how she had read and reread his published play till she practically knew it by heart. Grant found himself skipping. Her big news came on the last page: she was reading Dante with a trot. Sally had given her a wonderful edition, with illustrations, with the

Italian on one side and the English on the other. In this she was absorbed. She felt that there was no use reading anything else till she had
assimilated the *Inferno*. What, Grant wondered, could the *Inferno* possibly do for Eileen? Prepare her for him possibly. At the end he read:
"You are my Dante and you have the love of your eternally devoted
Beatrice."

Grant put the letter in his inside pocket beside Sally's. What a heel
Sally must think him! He must rehabilitate himself with Sally. He went
downstairs to the telephone and called for a taxi. He was somewhere
conscious that he was being led in a kind of automatism. Had not all
his life been like that? A long blunder — his alien name, the accident,
the involvement with Eileen, what he was doing right this minute —
automatism.

He asked the taxi driver to take him to the post office. He would wire
the girls to come. He would marry Eileen. He had asked for it and he
was getting it. He would do the right thing.

Anyway, he would see Sally again.

9. The Look

Löwe became very busy. He was in his element. He began treating
Grant with paternal benevolence. He congratulated him on having
whipped up the moral courage to live up to his obligation. Actually,
Grant had whipped up nothing much except himself. Löwe told Grant
he would take care of everything and he did. He arranged for a room
to be reserved for Eileen at Diakonissen Haus, a Catholic hospital,
staffed by nuns. He alerted Dr. Witte, Der Herr Primarius at the hospital, who was a friend of his. Der Herr Primarius had an excellent
nurse on tap. Löwe interviewed her and engaged her for August, still
three weeks away. She was a sturdy girl who understood English. He
had called the local rabbi, also a friend of his, to make sure that he
wouldn't be away in August. The bridegroom, he informed the rabbi,
was a famous Amerikanischer Schriftsteller, generous and affluent, who

would, he had no doubt, make a handsome gift to the welfare fund of
the Salzburg Gemeinde. In the interludes he was adding installments to
his serial letter to Lady Monica. Varina had returned. He had lunch
with her and Stephanie. It was an edgy lunch, during which he came in
for considerable criticism. It was easy for him to endure this barrage
because he appraised the combined attack on him as comic material
which might amuse Monica. Once back in his room at the palace he
added it at once to the letter already six pages long. He wrote:

*I felt exactly as if I were lunching with two widows who had been
married to the same man. I pointed out to them that Ian was quite alive,
he had simply gone to join Vesper, who was on his way to Macedonia,
for a few weeks in Bad Gastein. I pointed out that these reunions were
recurrent, that Ian and Vesper got on each other's nerves and that their
meetings invariably ended in stormy quarrels. You don't know Vesper,
do you? Next time we are in London together I will bring him to you.
He is a fascinating man, vastly cultivated, vastly rich and pathologically
stingy. He bears a banner with a strange device; he is a card-carrying
member of the Cult and, moreover, chauvinist; "the future of literature," he predicts, "will belong to homosexuality." I tell him that he sees
himself as the reincarnation of Sir Richard Burton. "Not at all," he said.
"Lady Hester Stanhope. She was much more virile." I think he would
amuse you.*

*But to Stephanie and Varina (Varina is in ecstasy about you by the
way, she says you were wonderful to her but of this I'll write you later),
to them, he is anathema. He is the "evil influence" but for whom Ian
would be the reincarnation of Sir Galahad. And, in some obscure way
— they don't say it, but it is implicit — they blame me. They imply
that I have encouraged this friendship, at least that I have not discouraged it. Merely by seeing Vesper, by finding him amusing, I have
set a bad example to Ian. I find myself an "evil influence" by proxy.
What nonsense this is about evil influence; we attract the influences
which attract us. I suppose that Iago might be called an evil influence
but actually Othello didn't need him at all. With his fathomless credulity
he'd have mucked himself up — and whomever he married too — without Iago. By the way, outside of the verbal glory, what a flimsy play
Othello is! Othello himself is really too thick-skulled for tolerance.*

*But Varina has a deeper grievance against me, passionately seconded
by Stephanie. It is that I persuaded her not to have Ian's child. When
Stephanie told her that I was arranging for Grant's girl to have his,*

*Varina's grievance was compounded. How can I explain to her the some-
what different circumstances? Coming from his environment — the respectable and fervently moral Jewish environment of Xenia, Ohio —
Grant would suffer, I am sure, from an endless sense of guilt if he abandoned Eileen. In Xenia it is considered bad form to seduce a girl and
turn your back on her if she has the bad luck to become pregnant. In
Ian's crowd it is scarcely a solecism, like forgetting to mail a postcard.
I have written you about Varina's father; I shudder to think what would
have happened had Varina gone through with it. But all Varina sees is
that Grant's girl has courage and she herself is abject, a coward. I got it,
I can tell you, from both of them — Varina gentle, of course, but
Stephanie heroic, militant, the sworn foe of "evil influence": major,
Vesper; I, minor but subtly insidious. Had my literary career, of which
you know, lasted more than forty-eight hours, I should not be struggling
now to resolve these awkward dilemmas.*

*What neither Varina nor Stephanie realizes is that there is a deeper
difficulty about Ian. The Vespers come and go. I am very fond of Ian —
as you are — but I know him very well. There is a streak of irrationality
in Ian, endemic to his family. It is submerged; he is not aware of it, it
may surface and submerge him. I suggested to him once that he put himself in the hands of a psychiatrist. "Too risky," he said. "The poor
blighter might cure me and spoil my fun!" He misapprehended my motive; I wasn't thinking of his sexual peculiarity. (Is it a peculiarity?)
What can you do with him? He makes you laugh. It's hard to be cross
with people who make you laugh. But how many people walk the earth
who are just on the verge of being crazy?*

*I have to go now to the Café Bazaar to meet Grant, who wants me to
go with him to the station to meet his enceinte bride and a friend of hers,
a Miss Frobisher. I am very fond of Stanley but he is a case too. He has
such a sense of inferiority that he feels that there must be something
wrong with Eileen or she wouldn't be in love with him. I know the girl;
she's just right for him and, somewhat sharing the code he was brought
up in, I am going to see that he does "the right thing" — arrogant
phrase, as if anybody really knew. "The right thing" is the gloss we paste
on our prejudices. The first night Grant slept at Stephanie's he saw some
hoodlums daub a swastika on her lawn. This has been a trauma to him.
He doesn't know the European tradition of anti-Semitism, that it is a
way of life here. He experienced dabs when he was a schoolboy in Xenia,
but you have to be aus Czernowitz to accept it as a fact of life, take it
in your stride. It exists, as death and disease exist. There is an illusory*

idea that psychic disturbances, prejudices, are curable, while bodily diseases are stubborn. It is an illusion: you may kill a bodily disease by arguing with a drug, but it is impossible to argue with a prejudice. Arguments against anti-Semitism only aggravate the condition because, to the anti-Semite, their source is tainted. But I feel a certain guilt about having introduced Grant into this milieu. He has no equipment to cope with it. I tell myself it's educational for him, but I suspect that my real motive is selfish — I need his companionship because I am alien to it myself. I can be as Jewish with Stanley as I am with you — incorrigible goy that you are.

I shall post this now on the way to meet the bridegroom.

Your "evil influence,"

K.

P.S. I seem to reserve P.S.'s for recommendations. As the one for Varina turned out so well, I venture another. It is for a neighbor of ours here — not the one at the Summit, but far lower, between us and the town: Thaddeus Willens, whose books you know — I have often heard you speak of them with admiration. He came to me this morning in a state of great agitation. An old friend of his here, a mediocre writer whom he has befriended, a Nazi recruit, cut him in the street. To Willens this is the beginning of the end. He is very nervous, believes the worst will happen. He says he cannot stand it here any more. He wants to go to England, which he cherishes as the enduring civilization. He has the marvelous Blake drawing of King John. He never travels without it. Your husband, I am sure, will be interested to see it. And Willens will be interested to see you. I encouraged him to go. England will calm him. You will calm him.

K.

Grant was walking along the Salzach with Varina to keep his appointment with Löwe at the Café Bazaar. Varina was subdued, sad and, in her sadness, more beautiful than ever. Grant worshiped her; he was grateful, he kept telling her, for her existence. In that she took less delight than he did. She felt herself a failure. Grant's girl, Eileen, whom she did not know, had manifested the courage which she herself lacked. This intrepid girl had not allowed her fear of her Catholic parents to deter her. She had seized her chance; Varina had muffed hers. She might have had Ian's child. She was sure that he would have looked like Ian and what more could any mother want than to have a child that looked like Ian? She might have had something to live for. What, now, had she to live for? Grant kept mumbling ineffectual condolences. She didn't mind telling Grant what she wouldn't think of telling anyone else: Ian was a marvelous lover, the most marvelous lover in the world, so marvelous that it was scarcely possible to believe that his interests were divided. And she mused on the effect that fatherhood might have had on Ian; it might have changed him altogether. He had so many and so varied talents; he needed only to coordinate them. Fatherhood might have coordinated them. Ian might even have become ambitious and, once he ceased to be a drifter, he might have become an ornament to any profession he chose to enhance. So they arrived at the Café Bazaar, where Löwe was awaiting them. Löwe ordered coffee for Varina and Grant ordered a double brandy for himself. Grant and Löwe tried to prevail on Varina to come with them to meet the Arlberg, bearing the bride-to-be and her friend Miss Frobisher. Varina refused. She thought it might be embarrassing for the bride to confront a total stranger. But she would be on call if she could be of service.

"Besides," she said, "Stanley will know what I mean — I couldn't bear it. I should be eaten with jealousy. I'm afraid it would show."

She rose to go. She smiled at Stanley.

"Courage, darling! Courage!"

She blew them a kiss and started to go. She turned back.

"Oh," she said, "I almost forgot. Mary asked me to tell you. She's giving a party on a barge — on the lake. Great preparations. Torchlit. A band from Vienna. Dr. Ogden's idea. What a pet he is, isn't he?" She spoke to Stanley. "Mary *insists* you bring your bride and her friend. Bye."

Varina left. Grant sat smouldering.

"All I need just now," he said, "is a party on a barge!"

"Good jumping-off place," said Löwe.

Grant's resentment at himself and the world in which he found himself broke out.

"All these people think about is pleasure! That's all. Pleasure!"

"What else do they have to think about?" said Löwe placidly. He looked at his watch. "But come on. It's time we were getting to the station."

Grant guzzled his brandy.

"Wait till I finish this. I need it!"

"You too, I see," said Löwe, "live for pleasure!"

On the station platform, as the Arlberg steamed in, Grant's heart was pounding. Unused to hard liquor, the stiff drink he had taken had fuddled him. He couldn't remember what Sally looked like. In his fragmented consciousness, she was a vague ectoplasm of beauty. Soon, he knew, that beauty would be defined. He saw her slender ankles and her bare tanned legs coming down the steps of the train. He knew they were Sally's. Whatever Sally wore, even the most casual, was ineluctably chic. She was wearing a plain brown linen dress with a brown leather belt and silver buckle. She kissed him on the cheek and he was aware of a haze of fragrance. He looked to see if Eileen was big, distended. She wasn't. Actually, you couldn't have told. Eileen introduced Sally to Löwe. Miss Frobisher took Kaetchen's breath away; he hadn't expected such a stunner. She was a windfall! Vistas opened up to him — the possibilities for such a prize were limitless — the third hand ached for employment. He began to chat with Sally as they moved up the platform. Grant and Eileen walked beside them. Grant heard their voices but he didn't know what they were saying. He was talking too, but he didn't know what he was saying. He heard Löwe chaffing him, heard him tell the girls that, in the interval, Stanley had become a heavy drinker. Eileen, he said, had come in the very nick of time to save Grant from dipsomania. As they got into the car he sat between Eileen and Sally. He was aware of Sally's brown bare knees and of the fragrance. As he inhaled it, he remembered the long wharf from which they used to go swimming in Blue Hill Bay and Sally, in a bathing suit, lying on her stomach on the splintery planks of the wharf, sunning.

Something happened. He was aware that something had happened. The car came to a halt. Sally was helping Eileen out of the car. Should he get out too? Löwe had jumped out from the front seat to join the two girls. He saw a bewildered look in Eileen's eyes. He looked down at the ground. She was standing in a pool of water. Löwe became commanding. He and Sally helped Eileen back into the car. With an agility unusual for him, Löwe leaped back to his seat beside the driver. He heard him speak to the driver with great authority:

"Diakonissen Haus. Schnell!"

From the hospital Löwe telephoned to Der Herr Primarius. Die Amerikanerin had been precipitate. She would need him right away.

Early next morning, Sally telephoned Grant to tell him that he was the father of a baby boy. "He leaped into the world," Sally said breathlessly, "as if he were in a hurry." Eileen was fine. She would love to see him. "She wants you to meet your son." Grant left at once for the hospital. He was admitted to Eileen's room by a girl in nurse's uniform. She was dark, almost swarthy, but had a pleasant look about her. Eileen was propped up in bed. She smiled, reached out her hand. She looked wan. Grant moved to the bedside and took her hand.

"This is Schwester," she said. The nurse bobbed her head, smiled. She had a very nice smile.

"Schwester, this is . . . my . . ."

Eileen was hung up.

Grant reached out his hand to shake Schwester's.

"Husband," he said, "father."

Eileen spoke to Schwester. "Would you please . . . is it all right, do you think? Could you bring in our son?"

Schwester nodded. She moved swiftly. She left the room.

"Bring up a chair," said Eileen. "Be comfortable."

Grant did as he was told.

"How do you feel?"

"Oh, I'm all right. It's just that . . ."

"You're worried!"

Eileen's eyes filled with tears. She brushed them away.

"Yes. I am worried. A little bit. But the doctor — he's such a wonderful man. He says it'll be all right."

"Then why worry? Take his word for it."

"He came too soon — our baby . . . He wouldn't wait."

Schwester came back, bearing, on a cushion, a tiny swaddled object. Grant looked at its face; the eyes were screwed up tight, the expression somehow truculent, defiant.

"Moment, bitte," Schwester said to Grant. He got up and gave her his chair. Schwester sat, the cushion in her lap, and began feeding the object out of an eye dropper, counting the drops of colorless liquid as she slid them between the sucked-in lips. Schwester got up bearing the cushion aloft. Eileen made some kind of gesture which Schwester understood. She was very deft; she began unswaddling her charge. Grant stared with a kind of horror at what he saw. The infant was transparent; through the membrane of skin — like some sort of invisible plastic — he could see its viscera. He stared. He beheld, in the minute coils of protoplasm, infinitesimal undulations.

He heard Eileen's voice:

"Our baby isn't finished yet."

Eileen's hand reached out. It touched the cushion. Grant turned his eyes from the baby and looked at her. It was the first time, he realized then, that he had really looked at her since her arrival yesterday. He felt that he had never seen her before at all; he had never seen this look. Her eyes were fastened on her baby. In them now Grant saw what he had never seen in them before — a look of such tenderness and sorrow that he was himself moved beyond his own understanding. Eileen's face was a pietà of love and mourning — mourning for love beheld, love taken away. She moved her body slightly toward the pitiful little object; Grant saw that she wished, helplessly, to infuse her own lifeblood, her own life essence, into her child, to strengthen the wavering thread, to quicken the faint pulsations.

He knelt by Eileen's side. He took her hands, kissed them.

"Don't worry, darling. He'll be all right. I know it."

She stroked his hands.

"Our baby doesn't cry."

"He will live. Can't you see it by the expression on his face? He is determined."

Eileen smiled at Schwester and nodded. Quickly, Schwester reswaddled her charge and bore him out. Eileen's hand was caressing Grant's head. He was still on his knees beside the bed. He buried his face in the pillow. He did not look at her for a long time. He felt that he could not bear to see again that look which mourned the swiftly passing vision of love in the tangled world.

10. Third Act

The day after Grant's baby was born Löwe invited him and Sally to dinner in a restaurant on the mountaintop overlooking the city. Grant, as the father of the first American baby to be born in Salzburg, had become an overnight celebrity in the town. When the headwaiter, an old friend of Löwe's, as all headwaiters were, received them, he handed Löwe the Salzburg newspaper and pointed to an item in it. Löwe laughed as he read it and handed the paper to Grant.

"You see, Stanley," he said, "you're famous now in Salzburg too!"

Grant stared at the paper but he didn't see.

"It describes the historic event," Löwe added as they followed the headwaiter to their table.

Grant, who was moving around in a kind of catalepsy and who, in addition, couldn't read German, kept staring stupidly at the paper through glazed eyes. He gave it back to Löwe.

"The headline says: SURPRISED WHILE ON VACATION!"

Sally smiled. Grant said nothing. He hadn't known, till this moment, that he was having a vacation. He didn't feel in the least gala.

At the table it quickly developed that Löwe and Sally had mutual acquaintances in Ohio. Löwe had been to Cleveland to beat the drum for Stohl's productions there. After the opening of *The Miracle* in Cleveland, Löwe's previous hosts had given a great party. These hosts, it turned out, were family friends of Sally's father and stepmother. They had attended that party. Sally asked whether Löwe hadn't met her father and his wife there. Löwe said that he distinctly remembered the second Mrs. Frobisher. She was a theater buff and prattled on a lot about it. Sally smiled faintly. Löwe had learned long since that it was wise not to be prematurely enthusiastic about stepmothers.

"I kept hearing about it for weeks," said Sally. "I got very tired of hearing about it. I thought they were mean not to take me. They said I was too young. But I did see the performance — at a matinee."

"Well, you'll see it again here. I'll take you. Afterwards I'll take you to supper with the professor — at the palace."

"That will be very nice," said Sally. "My parents said Professor Stohl was charming."

Grant kept hearing Stohl referred to as the professor. He wondered why. In America no matter how eminent a theater director became, he remained Mister. The Germans were more formal.

"So he is," said Löwe. "One of the most charming men in the world. He is also the greatest teacher of acting in the world. Have you any ambition to act?"

"None whatever."

"That is unusual."

"It's just that I have no talent. My school plays revealed that!"

"That is even more unusual — I mean, knowing it."

"I saw *The Miracle* from the gallery," said Grant. "I made the trip from Xenia. It's an awful play."

"It's not a play," said Löwe. "It's a spectacle. No one in the world can compare with Stohl in handling crowds."

Grant kept studying Sally. Half man, half playwright, he couldn't wait for the moment when she would confront Dr. Ogden. He wondered what she would say if he told her now, ever so casually, that her sometime antagonist was in Salzburg, that he was staying with Mary Kennicott, presumably ministering to her as he had done to her mother. How would she receive this bombshell? He remembered Eileen's letters from Cleveland: the long and lethal battle between Sally and Dr. Ogden, resolved finally by the stalwart Mr. Slater. He was athrob to tell her but he didn't. She was a strange girl. She had a secret life which absorbed her, which insulated her from passing events. Here were delights spread before her by Kaetchen; she contemplated them with detachment. What was she really thinking? Grant had never known. His mouth watered at the prospect of the meeting between Dr. Ogden and Sally — if only he were lucky enough to be present. He had a wild idea of inviting Sally to lunch and bringing Dr. Ogden without telling her. Yes, that's what he would do. He wouldn't throw away this opportunity by telling her now. He would contrive the meeting; and then he would watch it. As a dramatist he was lucky: he had his protagonists right there to act out his third act for him; he had only to observe. The excitement of this prospect drove out his personal worries — over Eileen, over his tenuously living son.

Löwe misunderstood Grant's self-communion.

"What's wrong with you, Stanley? I called Dr. Wolff. He says it's a near thing but that your son will be all right. Cheer up."

Löwe made an effort to explain Grant's self-absorption to Sally.

"For Jews," he said, "fatherhood is a serious thing. Especially for poor Jews."

Sally smiled at Grant.

"Are you poor, Stanley?"

"He was," said Löwe, "and so, with his temperament, he always will be."

At this point the waiter arrived with the great, German-written menus and handed them around. Löwe sank at once into the arcana of the menu. Sally didn't look at hers. Neither did Grant. Sally saw that Grant was unhappy and was concerned for him.

"Of course you're worried," she said. "But it'll be all right. It couldn't not be!"

Löwe, who had already picked what he wanted, was annoyed to look up and find that his guests hadn't even begun their study of what, to him, was one of the most important documents in life. For him, ordering a meal was a solemn ritual. When he invited people to a restaurant for lunch or dinner, he wished his guests would concentrate on the menu until they had decided what they wanted. They never did. They daw-dled. They chattered. He found this misapplication of energy frivolous. He couldn't stand their preoccupation with irrelevancies when there were important decisions to make. Their inattention was a dam which held everything up; one of the weaknesses of human nature, one of the few about which he was intolerant. He was even a bit edgy with Sally.

"My dear, you haven't looked at your menu. Aren't you hungry?"

"Famished," said Sally.

Löwe handed her his own menu.

"Here, order from this. I've marked it with my own recommenda-tions."

"What's tafelfleisch?" inquired Sally.

"Boiled beef. It's marvelous at Sacher in Vienna. I don't recom-mend it here."

"Why don't we have what you have, Kaetchen?" said Grant, who wasn't hungry at all.

"Oh let's!" said Sally. "I'm sure that will be splendid!"

Löwe, who had already ordered, was greatly relieved. He held up three fingers before the waiter. "Dreimal," he said.

Grant explained to Sally: "Kaetchen just can't stand it when people don't give all their attention to a menu."

"It disrupts the schedule," said Löwe. "It holds up the waiters."

"For Kaetchen," said Grant, "restaurant menus are Holy Writ. You must give them all you have."

Sally smiled at Löwe.

"I know exactly how he feels."

Löwe was delighted.

"Do you?"

"You are a gourmet, I suppose, and therefore food is your passion. I feel the way you do when I hear people whispering at concerts."

Löwe was vanquished by Sally. He was flattered by the analogy: putting his preoccupation with menus on the same level as her own with music.

"You have imagination, my dear, a sensitive imagination." He picked up her hand and kissed it. "I shall be your friend for life, your devoted friend for life."

"I will like that very much," said Sally.

Grant's eyes strayed across the room. The headwaiter was ushering in some newcomers. Grant's heart almost stopped. He felt that he was present at a miracle — Mary Kennicott and Dr. Ogden. He saw the headwaiter leading them to a remote table. He got up and made his way to them. Mary was delighted to see him; she embraced and congratulated him. Dr. Ogden joined in her congratulations. Grant told Mary that he was dining with Löwe and suggested that she join them. Mary rejected the proffered table at once.

Löwe arose to greet Mary.

"Delighted!" he said, though he wasn't entirely. He didn't like visitors at restaurant tables. But he motioned to the waiter to draw up two chairs.

Dr. Ogden saw Sally. His peerless teeth showed in a smile of pleasure.

"Sally! As I live and breathe!"

He reached out his hand, which Sally seemed not to see.

"This *is* a surprise," she said, with no air at all of being surprised. For a moment Grant thought: "She knew he was here."

The waiter brought menus which he handed to Mary and to Dr. Ogden. Mary questioned Grant about the state of things at the hospital. Löwe foresaw another delay.

"I beg you, Mary," he pleaded, "concentrate on the menu!"

Mary laughed.

"Oh, excuse me, Kaetchen, I forgot. Why can't we just have what you're having. Then the meal will have an element of surprise!"

"It has already provided that," said Ogden as he sat beside Sally. He looked at her with unconcealed delight. "I can't tell you *what* a surprise!"

Löwe made a sign to the waiter.

"Fünfmal," he said wearily.

Mary sat beside Grant.

"Well, my dear, aren't you thrilled? We were all thrilled. Stephanie asked me especially to congratulate you before she left."

"Where did she go?" asked Löwe.

"To Bad Gastein. She was feeling rather dowdy and she thought the cure might perk her up a bit."

"Good idea," said Löwe. "A cure is what she needs."

Grant was covertly watching his two characters. Mary was looking at them too. She was struck by Sally's youth and freshness. She spoke to Ogden.

"So you've found another friend from Blue Hill! Isn't it nice?"

"It's like a class reunion, isn't it, Stanley?" said Ogden. "Blue Hill, Maine, Class of 1934!"

"What did you study there?" asked Löwe.

Dr. Ogden was beaming at Sally.

"What did we study, Sally? What did we study?"

"The arts," said Sally.

"You remember, Mary," said Ogden, "my telling you about my Cleveland patient, Mrs. Frobisher?"

"Of course I do," said Mary. "Such a sad story."

"This is her daughter. Did I exaggerate?"

"You did *not* exaggerate. She is perfectly lovely."

"Thank you," said Sally. She was composed, neither pleased nor displeased, merely well-bred.

" 'Dainty rogue in porcelain,' I used to call her. I'm old-fashioned. I read Meredith. Do you remember, Sally?"

"I remember perfectly."

"It used to please you, didn't it?"

"Very much."

"Perfect!" said Mary, lavishing admiration on Sally. " 'Dainty rogue in porcelain.' Is that Meredith? But it's absolutely perfect!"

Grant's play sprang to life. A shaft of new light played on his third act. He couldn't help but admire Ogden's aplomb. *He* brought back the unhappy shade of Sally's mother. *He* flung open the door to that corridor of murky, possibly murderous, history. There came back into his mind the time when he had doubted Eileen's accounts of what was going on in Cleveland during Mrs. Frobisher's last illness, when he had thought them figments of Eileen's and Sally's morbid imaginations just as some critics think that the apparitions seen by the governess in Henry James's *Turn of the Screw* are merely morbid projections of her own frustrated love for her employer in London. And now this suspicion recurred. Surely, surely Dr. Ogden could not be so candid, so untroubled, so forthright were not the suspicions of Eileen and Sally, who were children after all, chimerical. This new aspect put Grant's mind in a whirl of dramatic possibility! Evidently, some kind of flirtation had gone on between Dr. Ogden and Sally. Sally had liked very much having Meredith's description of another heroine applied to her. According to Eileen's hysterical letters, Sally had feared and hated Dr. Ogden. And what about the big scene in the unimpeachable Mr. Slater's office when Dr. Ogden had been convinced that it would be practical for him to yield to Sally her rightful inheritance? Did Dr. Ogden call her a "dainty rogue in porcelain" in Mr. Slater's office and had she liked it even there?

One thing he knew, of one thing he felt certain. He had his last act. In his last act, *his* Kenneth Ogden would woo Sally away from her mother. He revived. He began to take a lively part in the conversation. The weight that had burdened him was sloughed off, the weight of fatherhood, of marriage, of responsibility. He saw Sally now in a new light, mysterious, lidded, inscrutable.

There was a stir in the restaurant. Necks craned. Prince Stauffer-Wernecke, the leader of the Austrian Nazi Party, had entered with four storm troopers. They were in full uniform. With hushed deference the prince and his party were escorted to their table. As he passed Löwe's table, the prince waved to him. Löwe waved back. The hum of conversation in the restaurant subsided. Everyone was staring at the Austrian leader.

"Why are these people allowed to swagger around here like this?" Mary asked. Löwe reminded her that Austria was now a German state. Mary didn't know that.

"Where's all that gemütlichkeit?" she asked.

"That's Bavarian," said Löwe. "Where Herr Schicklgruber dispenses it."

Mary was indignant.

"Just seeing these people makes me tremble for civilization," she said. Dr. Ogden addressed himself to Grant: "I don't think they'll get anywhere, do you, Stanley?"

Dr. Ogden was deferential to Grant, treating him as an authority on world affairs. In his heart Grant felt sure Ogden despised him. Ogden amplified:

"I mean — ultimately?"

"Perhaps not ultimately, but proximately. They're making many people uncomfortable — including me."

"You haven't got a thing to worry about," said Ogden. He glanced toward the prince and his storm troopers. "This sort of thing couldn't happen with us. Not possibly."

There was a moment of strained silence. Grant forebore to tell Ogden that in certain strata of American life, it already had happened. High-placed Americans had made themselves unpaid agents of Dr. Goebbels and were transmitting his suggestions for the improvement of American life all over the United States.

"It's all incredible, isn't it?" said Mary.

"It's human," said Löwe matter-of-factly.

"What do you mean by that? I'd say it's inhuman."

"Ah! An idealist!"

"You are a very cynical man!"

"I don't think so. I putter around in history. I observe the human race. That's merely a zoological classification, isn't it?"

Mary sighed.

"How lucky we are, all of us, aren't we, that we're American?"

"For the moment — yes," said Löwe.

"What an awful thing to say! How can you say a thing like that?"

"In any case," said Löwe, "we here at this table are all delightful people. There is nothing whatever wrong with *us*."

Mary laughed. She knew that Löwe didn't want to enter into a serious discussion with her, that he would consider it macabre.

"Well, whatever you say, Kaetchen, being American gives one a wonderful feeling of safety, doesn't it?"

"I always think," said Löwe, who wanted to sweep this conversation under the table, "what an odd thing it is . . . Disraeli and Karl Marx . . ."

"What about them?" said Dr. Ogden.

"Here they were in London — the two of them — for all those years — Marx working in the British Museum, Dizzy running around — and yet they never met. Wouldn't it have been interesting — isn't it too bad that they never met?"

"That Karl Marx!" said Mary with distaste. "He's responsible for everything. So unattractive, isn't he? Looks like one of those advertisements for just after you've taken something."

Grant made a mental note that someone in his play might say that. But the conversation had a depressing effect on him. Safe. Mary could feel safe. Sally could feel safe. Dr. Ogden could feel safe. But he and Löwe — could they feel safe? And even if they could, wasn't it, this safety, artificial and imposed, a form of demarcation, an arrangement, a condescension, a tip? He began to brood again. He wanted to go back to the United States right away. But then he couldn't. He had a baby in the hospital, and a bride. He was trapped.

The entrance of the prince and his party overcast Löwe's table. When they had finished eating, they rose to go. Löwe invited them all to the archbishop's palace. He wanted Sally to see it. Sally said she'd love to. In the porte cochere, waiting for Mary's car, Grant, just behind Ogden and Sally, saw Ogden lightly touch her hand. He took his hand away quickly and smiled at her. She smiled back.

Grant's spirits revived. He was even exultant. He was in a wonderful position. He would allow Ogden and Sally to play out his third act for him.

11. "Du Bist Mein Schatz"

Grant went daily to see Eileen and his child at the hospital. Most always, Sally went with him. Sally would insist on seeing the baby and usually Schwester brought him in. Grant had told Sally that the baby was transparent and wouldn't allow Schwester to unwrap him. One day Schwester showed them proudly the chart of the baby's first week of life. It showed a gain of several ounces of weight — from those injections from the eye dropper — and the graph of its evacuations. Grant was astonished; already the life cycle of this mite had started, already it had a physiological history that could be recorded. Sally would sit with them for fifteen minutes or so and then go, Grant suspected, on invented errands. She wished, without saying so, to leave Grant and Eileen alone. Leaving him alone with Eileen, Grant reflected, was a technique which Sally had perfected long ago in Blue Hill. One day, when they begged her to stay a few minutes longer, Sally said that she couldn't because Dr. Ogden was picking her up in Mary's car to take her for a drive around the lake. Eileen had been told, of course, about Dr. Ogden's presence in Salzburg. Nevertheless, at this announcement, she could scarcely conceal her astonishment. She said nothing and neither did Grant, but everything showed in Eileen's face. Sally kissed her, said she would come tomorrow and left.

"Well," said Grant, "what do you think of that?"

"Whatever Sally does is all right," said Eileen.

"Did she flirt with Ogden back there — in Blue Hill?"

"She loathed him."

"It doesn't look like it, does it? I felt it the other night — I told you — in the restaurant. There is a background there. It was obvious. He used to pay her compliments. And, moreover, she liked it. What's going on here anyway? What's Sally like? What *is* she?"

"Whatever Sally does is all right," Eileen repeated stubbornly.

"I sometimes suspected that you and Sally were indulging in hallucination. All those melodramatic letters of yours! Were they all moonshine?"

"I never wrote you a word that wasn't true."

"Well, on the basis of what you wrote me would you think that Sally would be going on drives with Dr. Ogden?"

"She has a reason."

"What reason? Do you know or are you just guessing?"

"I don't know. But I'm not guessing."

"It seems very odd to me. It doesn't make sense to me."

Eileen's brown eyes became misted over with feeling.

"When I think what Sally has done for me — the friend she's been to me. I can't tell you . . ."

"You've been a loyal friend to Sally too. You've seen her through some rough spots."

"I was hired to be her companion, not her friend. She taught me friendship. I was ignorant, you know how ignorant. I knew nothing about anything. She educated me. She . . ." Eileen couldn't go on.

"I've never seen our baby with its eyes open. He keeps them tightly shut always."

"I know."

"Why does he never open his eyes?"

"He's concentrating, I think, on keeping his poor little life going."

"He looks determined. I noticed that from the first. I think he'll keep it going."

"I pray."

"When he does open them, I hope they'll be beautiful — his eyes — like yours."

"I want him to look like you — another you."

"Oh, don't wish that on him. Don't wish acne on him."

Eileen laughed. She peered at him.

"Why, it's gone! It's almost gone. Hardly a trace of it left!"

"It comes and goes," he said grimly.

There was a silence.

"You know, dearest, you don't have to marry me. You don't love me. I'd never have let you know about the baby but Sally crossed me up. Please don't feel that you have to marry me."

"If you knew what I am — if you knew me really, what I'm capable of — you wouldn't want to marry me."

Eileen smiled. She touched his face with her palm. She smiled.

"Are you terrible?"

Grant resented her light tone on a serious topic.

"Are you very terrible?"

"I don't know myself at all — I didn't know at all what I was — till I came here."

"Do you want to confess to me? I used to go to confession and it always made me feel better."

"I haven't the courage."

"Shall I tell you the truth? I'm not curious. I don't in the least want to know."

"I'm contemptible."

Eileen dropped her light tone. She was almost sharp.

"Don't say that! I won't let you say that!"

There was a knock on the door. Schwester came back. Grant was glad to see her. He had grown to like Schwester. She was unobtrusive, silently efficient, quick, responsive, reassuring. Schwester announced tactfully that Der Herr Primarius was even now making his rounds and that perhaps it would be better . . .

Grant rose to go. He bent over Eileen and kissed her.

"I'll be in tomorrow."

"I'll be in too," said Eileen, pleased with her little joke.

"Tonight I'm going to Mary's housewarming party — big doings, supper on a barge on the lake — so I'll have lots of gossip for you."

"It sounds wonderful. Don't worry about anything. Have a good time. Have a wonderful time."

"Can I bring you anything? Is there anything you want?"

"Nothing. Just come." He turned to go. "And Stanley . . ."

"Yes, darling?"

"Don't look down on yourself."

*   *   *

Grant came to Mary's party with Löwe and Sally. Sally, in a simple black frock, was a tall-stemmed flower walking, but Grant was conscious of how dowdy he and Löwe looked. Up to this moment he had been rather complacent about his expensive, custom-made dinner jacket, but the elegance of the tall, slender young Englishmen and Austrians who were there cowed him. They wore dress costume the like of which Grant had never seen: mess jackets in pastel colors with little rows of gold buttons and beautifully knotted ties in rose, lavender and pale blue. He had never seen such exquisite and assured young men. It was a roomful of Ians! Even Dr. Ogden, who at once joined them, seemed burly and ungainly beside them. They stood about in little clumps; a modulated twittering arose from them; Grant felt that he, a mottled crow, had blundered into an aviary reserved for birds of paradise. At the grand piano, an excessively handsome young man was playing and singing from the piano score of *Der Rosenkavalier*.

Löwe whispered to Grant and Sally.

"Tetty Bolt. Marvelous stage designer. You're lucky, Stanley. I hear he's doing the sets for your play in London. He started out to be a concert pianist."

Mary came up to them. She kissed Sally, for whom she had conceived a great liking, and started walking them toward the piano.

"I want you to meet Tetty. I'm mad for him."

They joined the group around Tetty. He was singing softly, in a true and clear voice, with exact intonation. He sang both Octavian and the Marschallin in the first act. For the Marschallin he employed a falsetto, very appealing. He (she) was reassuring Octavian:

"Du bist mein Schatz . . ."

Tetty felt deeply what he was singing. It was very tender, very moving. Grant succumbed to the spell in which the others were held. He knew the opera. He had read the libretto by von Hofmannsthal, and been ravished by its elegant, lyric, rueful sophistication.

A hand took his and squeezed it. It was Varina. He squeezed her hand back. They stood together, yielding to the magic. It was a kind of mesmerism; one could have wished it to go on forever. He moved closer to Varina; why wasn't he in love with Varina, he loved her so? He looked for Sally. But she was standing with Dr. Ogden.

After the duet Tetty stopped and started to get up. But there were cries of protest. "The mirror scene! You must do the mirror scene!"

Tetty complied on the instant.

"If you hadn't asked me I should have been *furious!*" he said.

Everybody laughed. He riffled the pages of the score to the mirror scene: the Marschallin sings, *"Die Zeit das ist ein sonderbares Ding . . ."* Looking at herself in the mirror, the Marschallin visualizes the moment when she will go down the street and people will say: "There she goes — the elderly Marschallin." It was very affecting and no one was more affected than Tetty; there were tears in his eyes. Grant was looking at him. He wondered, why should the passing of time mean so much to this young man? He had so much of it left.

When he finished the mirror scene Tetty got up. Mary introduced him to Grant. Sally, Varina, Löwe and a cluster of the Olympian youths were gathered round.

"Oh! Mr. Grant! I've been longing to meet you."

Grant mumbled about how moved he had been by his rendition.

"It's my stunt, you know! But I'm wildly excited — did you know? I'm to do the sets and dresses for your play in London. I simply adore your play. It will be such fun for me. I've got my sketches. Would you like to see them?"

"I'd love to. I feel very lucky."

"It's too exciting," said Mary.

Grant felt his usual astonishment at being made such a fuss over simply because he had written a successful light comedy. He kept saying how delighted he was, how lucky he was.

"Don't be silly!" said Tetty. "I *demanded* the job. I'm very stubborn when I've set my heart on something." He turned to Mary.

"But you know that, darling? How perfectly ruthless I am when I want something?"

"I wish you'd demand something of me," said Mary wistfully.

"I will. Don't you worry. I will. You don't know the darker side of my nature. But you'll find out. You'll be *so* disillusioned!"

"I can't wait, darling. Bring on the darker side."

Tetty laughed.

"On a salver!"

"Exactly! On a salver."

Mary kissed him. Tetty waved to someone across the room and started to go. He paused for a second.

"You may tell my darling Stephanie and Ian too that I'll never forgive them — *never* — for not being here. Imagine! Preferring that dreary Gastein to us! It makes me faintly livid. It's definitely dire."

"I'm pretty bitter about it myself," said Mary.

Tetty walked away, the graceful young men following him. He moved through the room like a crown prince at his own court.

At the mention of Stephanie, Grant felt livid himself. He couldn't have borne it if she were there. He couldn't have faced her. It was bad enough without her being there.

Dr. Ogden came up to Mary.

"She's arrived," he said. "You'd better . . ."

"Oh, my God!" said Mary, looking across the room. "She's here!"

She darted off, Ogden following.

"Who is 'she'?" asked Varina.

"The Grand Duchess Marie."

They all looked. A portly middle-aged woman entered. Mary had reached the door just as the grand duchess came in. Mary floated down in a deep curtsy.

"I didn't know," said Varina in her drawling voice, "that Mary could do that! How very accomplished!"

"It's a very deep curtsy for a saleslady at Bergdorf Goodman's," observed Löwe. He explained to Grant: "That's where she works, you know."

Grant nodded. "I've seen it in the papers."

"Well, I think she deserves a very deep curtsy for being so democratic," said Sally.

Löwe let fall a little advance information.

"Mary and I went over the seating arrangement for the barge. Stanley, you'll have the grand duchess on your right and Varina on your left. What more can you want?"

"I don't want any more," said Varina. "I'm going to get chummy with the grand duchess. It would please my parents and I do so little to please them. Pilot me, Kaetchen."

Löwe complied. Grant was left alone with Sally. He had been conscious of a feeling of pleasure that Sally had been there when Tetty made such a fuss over him. Evidently Tetty's rapture had registered.

"Well, I must say, Stanley, you are in demand, aren't you? International figure! What a pity Eileen couldn't be here to see it. She'd be so proud of you. But then, she is anyway. Let's stroll about, shall we?"

Grant looked at her. Was Sally a fiend? But her expression was candid. She was sincere, delighted for Eileen, and for him too. Grant's little triumph turned to ashes.

Dr. Ogden came up to them.

"My dear Stanley," he said, "I know these lovely girls want nothing in life but to be with you. But still! I claim the priority of age. I've been wanting to talk to you ever since the other night at the restaurant."

He appealed, with an air of helplessness, to Sally.

"Won't you intercede for me, Sally? Won't you get me an audience with Stanley?"

"I can't undertake it," said Sally. "He's inaccessible. He's a celebrity."

"I know. But I don't believe Stanley is the kind of celebrity who forgets old friends."

"Well," said Sally, "queue up!"

Not till this moment had Grant known that he and Dr. Ogden were old friends. Still it would be useful to him to have a confidential chat with Ogden. He couldn't find out too much about him and Sally.

"I'd love to see you any time" he said.

Dr. Ogden showed his perfect teeth in a triumphant smile as he turned to Sally. "There! You see! I've bullied him into a date. Lunch or dinner?"

"Either one," said Grant.

"Done and done! Lunch Wednesday at the Mirabelle."

"Fine," said Grant.

Grant wanted to get outside. As he moved through the phosphorescent groups, he felt disembodied, a spar floating off from a wrecked ship. When he reached the hall he almost ran, down the stairs and through the lower hall till he came out on the lawn. He walked to the pier. There was the huge barge lit by tall flambeaux. It was a balmy, starlit night. The flame from the torches wavered in the still water; the orchestra from Vienna, installed in an improvised pavilion on the lawn, was playing waltzes, softly. At the pier a little flotilla of dinghies and motor launches was gathered to take Mary's guests to their dinners. It was a scene out of a fairy tale. What ingenuity these people expended on their diversions! Grant could not dispel a puritanic revulsion. What on earth was he doing here with grand duchesses and barges?

Grant leaned against a pier post. Scanning the dark outline of the forest horizon against the sailing clouds, he saw another light, a light fixedly burning, the light on top of the aerie. It made the light from the flambeaux on the barge seem clownish, like the glare from a carnival set up for one night. The light up there was fixed for an eternity of nights, a thousand years of nights. "He" was there and his acolytes were there. They were planning. He thought of the mite in Diakonissen Haus, marked already for the incinerating beam from the burning glass. Its eyes were always screwed up tight. What if it had opened its eyes, seen the world, despaired of it, and died? What if it had happened already? What if it was happening even now? He must get there at once to be with Eileen. He remembered her look at her baby, the look that was a transfusion of love. He belonged there, with her and the faint life he had brought into the murderous world. Eileen must know that she had an ally. Once and for all he would put a stop to his idiotic vagaries; he must clamp them into the straitjacket of custom. Since he himself was weak, at the mercy of every wind that blew, he would invoke the assumed obligation of convention to drill some sanity into him.

He found Liss, gave him a note to Mary telling her he was needed at the hospital but would return, and bribed a waiting chauffeur to take him to Diakonissen Haus.

Eileen was reading the *Inferno*. She had to cope also with a dictionary. She was astonished to see him. She let the books fall.

"Stanley! What a surprise! I thought you were at the party."

"I told Mary I wanted to look in on you. I promised to come back." He was very tense. He sat by the bed and took her hand.

"I was just thinking of you — wondering who you were flirting with. What's Stephanie wearing? Does she look marvelous?"

She had not, evidently, given her undivided attention to Dante.

"Stephanie's not there."

"Oh, so that's why . . ."

"I got worried. I got worried about the baby."

"He's fine. I'm beginning to feel hopeful."

She knocked wood on the headboard.

"Has he opened his eyes yet?"

"Don't expect miracles. Give him time. What's Sally wearing? Her taste in clothes — no matter what she puts on . . ."

"Eileen, I want you to marry me."

"What's the matter, darling? You're in a state. What's happened?"

"If you don't marry me — I'll be lost. I'll go to pieces."

"Have you had a falling out with Stephanie?"

"Please, darling, don't cross-question me."

"Is it on account of the baby you want to marry me? That you think it's your duty?"

"He's part of it, of course — part of you."

"I'll take care of him. You needn't worry about that. You see, darling — you didn't know it, did you? — I'm very vain. I want to be married for myself. I want you to be sure."

"I am sure. Why would I ask you — if I weren't sure?"

"You're so clever. I'm not up to you. You'll get famouser and famouser . . ."

"I'm torn to bits. You don't know — how wayward I am. I'm sick of it — sick of myself."

"Will it go away — the waywardness — if we're married? Mightn't it get worse? You're in some sort of mood."

"I sure am!"

"Tell me."

"Isn't it enough that I want you to marry me? What more can I say?"

"Aren't you writing your play for Stephanie?"

"What's that got to do with it?"

"Wait. Give yourself a chance. How can I marry you when I know you're in love with Stephanie? When your play gets going you'll be with her all the time. You'll patch up your quarrel. Then where will I be? It scares me."

She was light years away from the truth. If he told her the truth it would sound fantastic even to him. He couldn't. He buried his head against her shoulder. He was praying for salvation.

"Du bist mein Schatz," he whispered.

"Is that German?"

"Yes. It means you are my darling, my treasure, my love."

"Why don't you say it in Italian? Then I'd have a chance!"

She held him close to her, kissing him.

"Go back, darling. Go back to your party. Don't worry. Things will straighten themselves out — between you and Stephanie."

On the barge, Grant found himself sitting, as Löwe had promised, between the Grand Duchess Marie and Varina.

"You Americans," the grand duchess was saying, "are really fearful snobs, aren't you?"

"Are we snobs, Stanley?" said Varina. "Defend us."

The grand duchess didn't wait for Stanley's defense. She went on, good-humoredly, to explain.

"In the store where I work, the customers flock to me — men as well as women. The other salesladies are so young and attractive and I'm a plain old woman. You'd think the girls would hate me, but they don't. They're very sweet. But it's to me the customers come. And they *chat,* as if they were paying a social call. They're *so* sympathetic — the fallen grand duchess, you see — and *so* tolerant because, although I'm Russian, I'm not a Bolshevik. It's really very boring, almost as boring as it used to be at home when I *was* a grand duchess. You'll forgive me, but I don't think really I've ever encountered such snobs as you Americans."

At this moment there was a thunderclap, a jag of lightning, a sudden wind and the flambeaux went out. They were sitting in darkness. There was laughter, little cries, the scrape of chairs pushed back.

Grant looked up at the aerie. Its light burned steadily.

12. The Mustache

Salzburg began to fill up for the Festival. From all over Europe and from the two Americas music buffs came to occupy the hotel rooms and rented villas they had booked a year in advance: society leaders, luminaries of the arts, simple millionaires, abdicated kings, the wives of presidents, the widows of prime ministers. Toscanini arrived. The shop windows sprouted his photographs as they used to do of royalty. The stern, classical profile was visible everywhere. He was indeed royal and, in his own evaluation, higher. Had he not announced that he was unavailable when the King of Italy called upon him? None of the composers he played could, in their own lifetimes, have been received with anything like the rapture accorded Toscanini. The vast majority came, not to hear Mozart, Beethoven or Verdi, but to see the Maestro. He had, besides his devotion and austerity and command, the visual appeal of a great matinee idol. For the infatuated celebrants he *was* Mozart, Beethoven and Verdi — their surrogate, visible, palpable and, moreover, alive. For the ladies, even the tone-deaf ones, he was the fantasy hero of a love affair. Stephanie, in her freewheeling, independent manner, had, on one occasion, crystalized the feminine compulsion toward Toscanini. She had invited a friend to one of his concerts in New York. Just before the Maestro's entrance Stephanie's friend observed her carefully stuffing her ears with cotton. She sat, rapt, through the First Brahms. When it was over, she unstuffed and explained:

"The music distracts me. It keeps me from concentrating on *him!*"

Rudolph Stohl came and took up residence in the archiepiscopal palace. Stohl had founded the Festival. He had fallen in love with the town and conceived the idea of bringing drama and music there in the summer. The réclame of his name and his willingness to bring his own productions to Salzburg had brought his idea to life. Of later years he had found his domain occupied by Toscanini. If he felt any resentment at this preemption, he admirably suppressed it. His manners were impeccable and Toscanini went through the motions of treating him like an equal. Stohl was as much adored by ladies as Toscanini was, but, as he did not appear in public, his clientele was mostly limited to actresses who lived to be directed by him.

Grant met Dr. Ogden for lunch in the Mirabelle, an open-air restaurant where, now, it was very hard to get a table. Ogden had no trouble since he was the house guest of Mary Kennicott who had given innumerable parties there. The proprietor, Mr. Kaszner, a Hungarian, treated Dr. Ogden with almost as much deference as he treated Löwe, another inveterate patron. He personally escorted him and Stanley to their table, transmitted their orders for drinks and had a little conference about what they should eat.

"The Huhn im Topf," Dr. Ogden confided to Grant, "is marvelous here. What do you think, Mr. Kaszner?" Mr. Kaszner made a gesture to convey that the quality of the Huhn im Topf could not be expressed in words. They settled for two Huhn im Topf. There was a somewhat longer colloquy about the wine. They settled on a Riesling. Mr. Kaszner disappeared.

"Well, Stanley," said Dr. Ogden. "Kaetchen tells me you're going to be married."

"That's premature. Eileen quibbles."

"Familiar gambit. Playing hard to get."

"Eileen's not like that."

"She's the mother of your child. That should swing it."

"Not with her. She's stubborn."

"She'll succumb. Will that make you happy?"

"Happy? I don't know what that means."

Ogden laughed. He beamed at Stanley.

"Good boy! Beginning of wisdom. There is a marvelous sentence in Freud. He'd been treating hysterics. He said to a colleague: 'Much is won if we succeed in transforming hysterical misery into common unhappiness.' The trouble with our business these days is that our patients expect us to make them *happy*."

The drinks came. Ogden raised his glass to Grant.

"Cheers!"

"Cheers."

"I don't waste time. Life is too short. Tell me — do you think marriage will quench your other temptations?"

"To tell you the truth, I don't think. I seem to behave like an automaton. I don't know I'm going to do the things I do. The waves hit me."

"I understand that. I'm not like that at all. Everything I do is calculated."

Ah, thought Grant, his pose with me is going to be frankness. Aloud he said:

"Including this appointment?"

Ogden laughed. He had a very pleasant laugh, hearty but modulated.

"Certainly. I had an impulse to talk to you. My impulses serve my calculations."

The Huhn im Topf arrived. It was, they both agreed, marvelous. The wine arrived. Dr. Ogden rhapsodized about the wine. Grant, not wishing to admit that he didn't know one wine from another, murmured approving exclamations about the wine.

"I am," said Ogden, smiling at him, "out to make a friend of you."

"Why?"

"Because you're so popular. Everyone thinks the world of you. How've you managed it?"

"Perhaps it's because I'm not a threat to anybody."

Ogden laughed.

"You underrate yourself. That's a mistake."

Grant felt himself flushing. He didn't like Dr. Ogden at all. But he, too, had come for a purpose. He must stick to that purpose. He had his own way of getting back at Dr. Ogden!

"I know your opinion of me. It's based on nonsense. I know you've swallowed whole all those rumors in Blue Hill about me and Sally's mother. I mean to disabuse you of that prejudice. We should be allies. We have something in common."

"What's that?"

"We've both of us had no luck with the one girl we really want. We're both of us madly in love with Sally."

Grant stared at him. What sort of gambit was this? But he felt a kind of triumph. His pulses throbbed.

Aloud he said:

"I can't really feel sorry for you. You don't seem neglected. First Mrs. Frobisher. Now Mrs. Kennicott."

"The only women who've ever been attracted to me are those who have been defeated by life. They're losing the struggle, they expect me to bring them back. Tedious job. Impossible hours. Inconceivable monotony."

"Mary too?"

"She's worse than Sally's mother. Mary was on the verge when I met her. Suicidal. Sally's mother had a disease she could cling to. Mary was

in a vacuum. Nothing to cling to. Well, I gave her a mission. To find a
cure for the incurable."

"Do you know her husband?"

"Oh yes. Charming man. But he has the half-baked look in his eyes
of a man who's never had to make his own living. Still, in his lucid intervals, you couldn't meet a more delightful man."

"And in the others?"

"Then he's not one of us."

Dr. Ogden sipped the wine appreciatively.

"I suppose you had an austere upbringing."

"Yes. I did."

"My parents were agnostic, so I've never had a moment of guilt
about anything."

"You're lucky."

"And I suppose with you the religious thing is all intertwined with
the racial thing. Must be particularly bothersome just now. The thing
about the Jews is that — en masse — they lack charm. That's why
they're not popular."

Grant felt that the collar of his shirt was too tight. He ran his finger around the inside of it to loosen it. But he kept his voice even.

"Does Kaetchen lack charm?"

"I said — en masse."

There was a moment's silence. Grant kept struggling with his collar.

"Have I offended you?"

"Not at all."

"You're hypersensitive. All minorities are. My father wasn't a religious maniac but in a way he was worse. Poverty-stricken intellectual.
He was so bloody high-minded. Thoreau was his God. He rammed Thoreau down my throat till I regurgitated him. He'd quote him: 'Poverty
is life near the bone where it is sweetest.' He sure kept us close to the
bone all right, but I escaped it."

"No hand-sawn cabins for you."

Ogden smiled.

"I don't mind telling you, Stanley, I'm quite well off."

"And I know where you got it," said Stanley to himself. He wanted
to say it out loud but lacked the courage.

Ogden knew what he was thinking.

"And I was quite well off by the time I met Sally's mother."

"Large practice, I suppose."

"I worked my way through high school and through a jerkwater medical school. Put up my shingle in Cleveland. Nose and throat. Tonsillectomies. I got as far as you could go with tonsils. One day I gave up tonsillectomy for the soul! I discovered that the poor have tonsils but only the rich have souls."

Grant's hand reached reflexively for the pad in his jacket pocket. But he controlled himself. It wouldn't do to let Ogden catch him taking notes. He would remember that remark and give it to *his* Ogden.

"The truth is, Dr. Ogden . . ."

"Drop the 'Doctor.' You're not my patient. Kenneth is my name. Call me Ken. I'm not much of a doctor anyway."

"You're the head of Mary's clinic."

"I am. I've got some first-rate men there. Whizzes. That's what I *am* good at. Digging up scientific talent. What I really am, dear Stanley, is an administrator."

He winked at Grant. That wink won Stanley over. He felt a sneaking liking for Ogden.

"What's the truth you were going to tell me? Tell the doctor."

"That I've been bewildered, off base, since I came here. I don't understand anything at all — about myself — or anyone else. Stephanie baffles me completely."

"A masochist. On the lookout for what will make her suffer."

"Is that it?"

"Part of it."

"Stephanie and Ian. Isn't that strange?"

"Not at all. Very common. Most of the fellers you met at Mary's party the other night were pansies. They're attractive and charming and the girls love them. Those that are double-gaited often make very good husbands — especially for older women."

Grant was wistful.

"So many and so glamorous. We seem to be a minority. Are *we* abnormal?"

Ogden laughed.

"No, we're not abnormal. We may come to it but not yet. There'll be a cure one day for these fellows and it won't come from us. It'll come from the biochemists, that's what my fellows are at the clinic. It'll be a pity. It'll be a much duller world without them. I'll hate to see them go."

Grant looked at his wristwatch.

"I think I'd better be going," he said. "I've got to get back to work." He couldn't wait to get back to his room. He wanted to put down what Ogden had said about switching from tonsillectomy to the soul. There was so much he wanted to do to his play.

"Oh, wait a bit. I've asked Sally to join us. She'll be along any minute."

Grant felt a pang of jealousy.

"You see a lot of Sally," he said.

"It's you she wanted to see. She was on her way to visit Eileen. She wanted to report."

"I really have to go."

"Surely the masterpiece can wait a few minutes. She's an extraordinary girl, that Sally. Very deep. Remarkably clever. Really precocious. I've never known anyone like her."

"You seem to be very good friends."

"She hates me. She thinks I murdered her mother. Perhaps you'll tell her the truth?"

"Do I know the truth?"

Ogden laughed.

"Sure you do. I just told you. I kept her mother alive. I gave her something to live for. And at what cost to me!"

"Haven't you revealed your occupational hazards to Sally?"

"We don't discuss it. It would be much better to come from you. You see! I told you my impulses were calculated. Now you know why I wanted to see you. I want your help with Sally."

Stanley stared at him. He really didn't know what to make of this man. Ogden was aware of his effect.

"You'll find few men as candid as I am. But don't think I'm discouraged. I'd welcome your help but I think I can do without it."

"Evidently!"

"Sally hates me but that's not discouraging, is it? Hatred is intensity of feeling. I'm on her mind. She thinks about me all the time, she — "

Ogden jumped up.

"Here she is!" he said happily. "Our girl!"

Sally, in a lavender dirndl, walked up to them. Her arms were bare. She looked like a shepherdess in a Watteau, a shepherdess with a private income who took on sheep as a hobby. She took Grant's breath away. She kissed him on the cheek. She nodded to Ogden, scarcely looking at him.

"I've just seen Eileen," she said to Grant. "And the baby. Both flourishing."

"Thank you," said Grant. He got up. "I'm afraid I've got to get back to work."

"Surely," said Ogden, "you can take fifteen minutes."

"No," said Sally, "let him go. Work comes first."

Grant left. Was she impatient to be left alone with Ogden? He stood on the sidewalk and hailed a cab. He couldn't make head nor tail of anything. In the cab he took the pad out of his jacket pocket and wrote down Ogden's remark, "The poor have tonsils but only the rich have souls." That would get a laugh, Grant was sure. He would rewrite Dr. Ogden from the beginning: a compulsive gambler of the emotions, tantalized incessantly to see how far he could go, a vulgar romantic, a cheapjack of diabolism. He would have one of the unemployed young fellows hovering about Sally in the play say all this about him. Give it to that young firebrand the Catholic Communist. But what was Sally? Was she a nymphomaniac? Had she been jealous of her mother, had she contrived to take her mother's lover to herself? It was awful having these thoughts, but he was having them. He felt lost in this world — homesick. He thought again of that little boat winding its slow way between the green banks of the Penobscot. If his baby lived, he would take him and Eileen . . .

The cab was tooling its way beside the Salzach. Turning the corner from a side street he saw a tall figure in the uniform of a storm trooper walking with a girl. There was something familiar about the set of his shoulders. It was his barber. Grant had been to him almost every day since his first morning's walk in the village. The girl had her arm through his. She looked up, smiling at her tall companion. It was Schwester.

Grant forgot about his play. He forgot about Sally and Dr. Ogden.

He sat in terror. He had brought into being a frail life who had, unasking, been hurtled into a world that would soon be controlled by the vast armaments of the Mustache. For the moment, this sin drove out his other sins.

13. The Knock

By the time Grant got back to his room at the castle, his encounter with Dr. Ogden, the appearance of Sally, made him realize that he would have to revise his play from the beginning. He would begin by writing a third act and then rewrite the first two acts to live up to it. In his excitement he forgot about the Mustache, about his child, about Eileen. That was another undiscovered country! Eileen, apparently, was not a softie; she had standards of her own. But he couldn't stop thinking of Ogden: that strange and magnetic personality, seemingly so candid, actually impenetrable. What on earth was Ogden thinking of? And Sally — what on earth was she thinking of? It was inconceivable, wasn't it, that she was tempted, like the heroine of a Greek tragedy, to have a liaison with her mother's murderer? Sally was as far as possible from being a classical Greek heroine; she was an American Beauty rose. Was Ogden really thinking of throwing over Mary, the clinic, the fortune, the very likely succession to her ailing husband? Could it be that he was really in love with Sally? How much did Mary know? Did she suspect anything? She was bound to find out sooner or later. Didn't it make her wonder that Ogden was seeing so much of Sally? His own treatment, his own first version, lying there on the table, was far too bleak, "on the line," unsubtle. His hand reached into his jacket pocket for his note pad; he read Ogden's remark about giving up tonsillectomies for the soul: "The poor have tonsils but only the rich have souls." He would give that to his Dr. Ogden right away; he knew just where. But it went beyond that. What on earth was Ogden going to do? Evidently Sally had promised him nothing yet. He had said that he and Sally never talked about the past, about her mother, about the scenes in Cleveland with Mr. Slater. What then did they talk about? Of course, he was waiting to see how far he could get with Sally, what the prospect was, before extricating himself from Mary. He tried to put himself into Ogden's shoes, he tried to *be* Ogden. What would he do if he were Ogden? Suddenly he saw what Ogden *might* do. He saw! This vision drove him to his work table. He didn't care what the actual Dr. Ogden would do, but he knew what *his* Dr. Ogden would do. He began to write at breakneck pace, starting with a stage direction:

ACT THREE

At Rise: Living room of Leonie Frobisher's summer cottage in Blue Hill, Maine. Late afternoon. Dr. Kenneth Ogden, in tweed jacket and slacks, is sitting in front of the fireplace smoking a cigar. He is in deep thought. He gets up frowning, pondering deeply. Suddenly an idea strikes him. The impact is so powerful that it stops him in his walk. The frown disappears; he almost smiles. He is so seized by the sudden emergence of this idea that he resumes his walk, this time in excitement. He stamps out his cigar in an ashtray. He is like a man with a mystic illumination; he is carried away by his idea; by its boldness, its megalomania. He is exalted. Then he is seized by impatience; he cannot wait for his idea to be executed. He walks to the glassed-in verandah at the back. He calls.

KENNETH: Leonie! Leonie!

Now he must bring Leonie in. He read his original stage direction for her, on her first appearance. He had described Stephanie and given her an accent. He crossed all this out vindictively. He had decided already that he must get an American actress for the part. Moreover, he knew who! He wrote the new stage direction, with such tensity and at such speed as if to lay forever the ghost of Stephanie:

Leonie Frobisher comes in, running a little, breathless, like a young girl. As she has a daughter of twenty-one, Leonie must be herself well over forty but, at the moment, she might be sixteen. She is slim, girlish, in a young and quivering ecstacy of living and anticipation. For Leonie, her daughter is an agreeable phenomenon whom she does not especially relate to herself biologically — a lovely apparition who hovers intermittently in the wild garden of her life. There is something, for all her gaiety, heartbreaking about Leonie, something childish and childlike — an acceptance of people instantly and uncritically at the best of their own valuation. She is impulsive and warmhearted and generous to a fault. Her own fragile and exquisite loveliness she offers to the world half shyly, tentatively, bearing it like a cup of precious liquid of which not a drop must be spilled. A spirituelle amoureuse, she is repelled by the gross or the voluptuary; this is not hypocrisy — it is, in Leonie, a more serious defect than that. In the world in which she moves hypocrisy is a social lubricant, but this myopia — alas for Leonie! — springs from a congenital and temperamental inability to face anything but the pleasantest and the most immediately appealing and the most flattering aspects of things — in life and in her own character. At this moment, though, she is the loveliest fabrication of nature, happy in the summer sun and loving all the world, with particular emphasis on Dr. Kenneth Ogden.

LEONIE: Darling! Have I kept you waiting? It's this dress! It's new! I put it on for you. Like it? (*She twirls around for Ogden. He watches her. She comes up to him*) Don't you like it?

KENNETH: It's lovely. Whatever you put on.

LEONIE (*Peers at him*): Kenneth. What is it?

KENNETH: You're perceptive.

LEONIE: You look as if you had something on your mind.

KENNETH (*Rallying her*): Instead of vacuous — as usual?

LEONIE (*Laughs, a little tinkling laugh*): Darling! There's always so much in your mind. And there's nothing whatever in mine. What can I do about it? Sally's so serious, interested in causes, intellectual. Sally's always telling me to improve my mind. There's nothing much to improve. But I have my own vanity. It's quite different.

KENNETH: What's your vanity?

LEONIE: I leave the big issues to the professional altruists. I just do what I can toward making those around me happy. That's *my* vanity!

KENNETH: You do a good deal.

LEONIE (*Tenderly, dotes on him*): If I make you happy — it's all I ask.

KENNETH (*After a moment*): Leonie. I have to talk to you. I have decided — to be completely honest with you. You deserve no less.

LEONIE (*A bit sobered*): Oh, dear! Whenever anybody tells me they're going to be honest with me — I tremble. Be honest, if you must. Be as honest as you like — but don't hurt my feelings!

KENNETH: I feel like a man on a great height, irresistibly tempted to jump over. The fact is, Leonie . . .

LEONIE (*Clutched by terror at last — she is pitiful*): I can't stand it, Ken!

KENNETH: I have fallen in love. Madly. There is no other way. I have to tell you.

LEONIE (*In a strained voice*): Is it anyone I know? I'd prefer it to be — someone I don't know.

KENNETH: It is someone you know.

LEONIE (*Instinctively puts her hands to her ears to shut out the horrid sound*): Don't tell me. I'd rather not know.

KENNETH: Unfortunately — I must tell you.

LEONIE (*Sits, bracing herself*): Who is it?

KENNETH: Sally.

LEONIE (*Stupefied*): My Sally?

KENNETH: Your Sally.

KENNETH (*Reads her thoughts*): Say it. I've said it to myself. I've questioned my sanity myself.

LEONIE: Sally's a child.

KENNETH: She is exactly twelve years younger than I am. That's not an unbridgeable gap. Is it?

LEONIE (*After a moment*): Is Sally in love with you?

KENNETH: I haven't the faintest idea. I haven't asked her. I've never said a word to her. But she is attracted by me. I know that. I can't be mistaken about that.

LEONIE: Why didn't you wait then — to tell me — till you did ask her? (*Her voice rises*) Perhaps she'd have told you — that you were deluded. Then you wouldn't have had to tell me. That's all I would ask — not to know. Why couldn't you have waited?

KENNETH: Sally distrusts me. Just as I know that she is attracted, I know that too. Her friends distrust me. They think I am a charlatan. They think I am mercenary. (*Humorously*) To tell you the truth, darling, until this inexplicable thing happened to me —I half agreed with them.
    (*Leonie's head sinks. She presses the scarf she is wearing to her face*)

LEONIE: I didn't think you could be so . . .

KENNETH: I didn't think so either. I am really amused by myself. I have always made a fetish of discipline, of restraint. I've had to. You don't know what I've had to pull myself up from, what my origins were. And now, after all these years of control, I have succumbed to an inconsistency. I've had to revise my whole notion of myself. Sally is the youth I've never had, the security I've never had, the home I have longed for. (*Leonie, her face in her scarf, merely shakes her head. Kenneth goes on*) It is the first time I have ever yielded to an impractical temptation. And I have always been eminently practical.

LEONIE (*In a strangulated voice*): Why did you have to tell me before — before . . . ?

KENNETH: Before I told Sally? Before I found out from Sally? So I could come to her with clean hands. So that I could tell her that I've burned my bridges behind me. So that I could come to her with nothing to offer except my feeling for her. To show her that on the chance — on the minimal chance — that she might love me, I have given everything up: an assured future, the clinic, you, everything.
   (*Leonie gets up, starts pacing the room, clinging to anger as to a lifeline*)

LEONIE: To persuade her of your disinterestedness!

KENNETH: Exactly.

LEONIE: Hateful! You're hateful.

KENNETH (*Sadly*): You say this at a moment when, for the first time in my life, I think, my heart is full of love. And for you too.

LEONIE: And I suppose you feel — that if you fail with Sally . . .

KENNETH: I won't fail.

LEONIE: But if you do, I suppose you feel — that you'll get me back . . .

KENNETH (*Drily*): I'd try.

LEONIE (*Faces him*): I'd kill myself first.

KENNETH: But that's where I came in! I saved you from that. Remember?

LEONIE: Yes. You saved me from that. Only to destroy me. (*She is trembling*) Now I will. Now I am alone and I will.

KENNETH: Don't stoop to blackmail, darling. You're better than that.

LEONIE: I'll go to Sally. I'll tell her what you are. *I'll* tell her.

KENNETH: That might be even better.

LEONIE (*She changes. She thinks suddenly that this is a bad dream*): Kenneth. I beg you — don't do this. Sally will be horrified. Darling, I beg you — you must see — that it's insane.

It flashed through Grant's mind as he was writing that perhaps he would make Sally Leonie's stepdaughter, her husband's daughter by an earlier marriage. He would think about that. But, just now, he was writing Kenneth's reply to Leonie.

KENNETH: Because I am forthright you think me insane.

LEONIE: But Sally is in love — with that nice boy she's been seeing, Will Talbot.

KENNETH: (*This stirs Kenneth up; he is no longer suave. He is jealous*): That's how little you understand her. That puking little unemployed nobody with his half-baked Socialist ideas. When I hear the chatter of Sally's friends it makes me sick. While they prate of cooperative commonwealths, the strong man takes power and rides over their backs, which is all their backs are fit for. Never has the opportunity for the individual career been so exalted. So . . . (*He makes a wide gesture*) horizontal. House painters and minor journalists become dictators of great nations. (*He becomes less tense, smiles, makes a gesture of modest self-assertion indicating the room as part of his conquest*) Look what I have already done, unaided, alone. From an impossible distance I have come to you. I have come to Sally. What might we not do together — Sally and I?

LEONIE: Sally's different. Sally's idealistic. You don't want the same things.

KENNETH: She will. I am endlessly romantic, Leonie. And endlessly realistic. I am quite simple really, as Sally is. I just want everything.

LEONIE (*Walks away from him*): And you don't care how you get it!

KENNETH: Don't be moralistic, Leonie — I beg you. I am directly in the tradition of your own marauding ancestors. You don't know about them but I do. They pass now for pioneers — actually they fell on the true pioneers and wrested what they had away from them by sheer, brutal . . .

There was a knock on the door. Grant thought he'd heard a knock but ignored it. It was repeated, more insistently. In a rage at being interrupted, without letting go his pen, he shouted, "COME IN!" The door opened. It was Stephanie.

"Darling! I interrupted the poet while he's working! Can you forgive me?"

It darted through Grant's mind as he rose to embrace her that this knock, so little ago, would have been for him the be-all and end-all of his existence. He saw that Stephanie expected of him an ecstasy of reunion and he acted up to it. He led her inside.

"But, darling! How marvelous to see you! When did you get back?"

"Half an hour ago. You're the first person I wanted to see."

"You look wonderful."

"Do I? Do you think I do?"

He stared at her. There was something different about her. She had, Grant thought, a somewhat chastened look, the pure lines of her face, her shining dark eyes — she looked, somehow, enhaloed. Had Stephanie gone in for sainthood?

He led her to a chair.

"Did Ian come back with you?"

"No. I left him in Gastein. That's all over with. That's all behind me."

He scanned her face.

"You look different somehow."

"I *am* different. I've turned over a new leaf. I'm glad it shows."

"You'll have to tell me all about it."

"I will. Who can I tell if not you? And Eileen? And your child? How are they?"

"It was a narrow squeak — for the baby, I mean — but I think he's going to be all right. Dr. Witte is keeping them in the hospital for another two weeks. Just to make sure. But it's all right. Kaetchen's looking for an apartment — for Eileen and the baby."

"Why don't they come here? I'd love it. Please. How wonderful it would be to have a baby — *your* baby — in this gloomy house!"

"It's sweet of you. I don't know whether . . ."

"I'll ask Eileen myself. I'll make her come. She must come!"

"I'm sure she'd love to," said Grant, who was privately dismayed by the idea.

"But it's so dark in here and that silly bathtub! I could kill Liss for putting you in here. What a terrible room! I'll put you next to me. Ian's room. Wouldn't you like that?"

"Thank you, darling. I'm used to this now. It's only a few more weeks anyway."

There was a silence. Grant looked longingly at his manuscript. Stephanie caught the look.

"I long to read your play. May I read it?"

"I'm rewriting it."

"But Ian says the first act is done. Let me read that. I'll begin to study it, to memorize it — right away."

"I'm revising that too. In fact, I'll have to rewrite it. I've got a new idea on it."

"How wonderful! How exciting! It doesn't matter. I know it will be beautiful. And you'll see! I'll work hard. You'll be pleased with me. I promise. I'll think of nothing else. I can't tell you what it means to me. I can't tell how grateful I am to you for giving me this to cling to. It will save me!"

She was on the verge of tears.

"Darling, one thing I want to tell you. It might worry you, so I want to tell you. You know my bad habits. I have no secrets from my poet. I want to tell you, solemnly and sincerely. I want to tell you, I have given them up, all those habits. You need have no worry, not a shred of worry. You will have no trouble with me, no trouble at all, when I come to do your play."

"I hope you won't be too saintly. How will I live up to you?"

She laughed, threw her arms around him and kissed him.

"Don't worry, darling. I'll be saintly in moderation."

"Not fanatical?"

"Not fanatical."

She started again to go and again turned back.

"And, darling, oh yes, I almost forgot. The Maestro has given me two seats for the opening of *Fidelio*. Will you go with me? That is, if Eileen is still in the hospital."

"She will be."

"You'll come with me then?"

"I'd love to."

"That's heavenly. I'd rather go with you than anyone in the world."

She was gone. Grant felt at sixes and sevens. Damn it, he'd lost the thread on his work. Where was he? Where had he left off? And Stephanie's sudden conversion of his play into a lifeline! Was he committed? He was always getting himself committed! How could he get out of it? Kaetchen. He would have to resort to Kaetchen. But Kaetchen wanted Stephanie to do his play. Grant had, indeed, begged for Kaetchen's intercession. He looked down at his manuscript. He couldn't twist it back now to suit Stephanie. Dr. Ogden was saying to Leonie: "I am directly in the tradition of your own marauding ancestors." That meant the Ohio oil dynasty. He couldn't possibly graft Stephanie's German accent onto the Ohio Frobishers. What should he have done? Told Stephanie right out that she couldn't have the part. That would have been too cruel. Just as she had turned over a new leaf! No, he couldn't have done that.

Disconsolate, he sat down again at his desk. He stared at his manuscript. It seemed dull to him now. He couldn't pick it up again. The élan was gone. Damn! Why on earth had Stephanie chosen just this moment to knock at his door? Well, he might as well go to the hospital to see Eileen. He would tell her she needn't worry about Stephanie, that he had decided on another actress for the part.

No doubt about it. Life was complicated. Life was difficult. Was it because he was himself complicated? Was it because he himself didn't have the courage to be what he was?

14. Mary Kennicott

Löwe, Varina, Grant and Stephanie were having early dinner in the delectable Mirabelle before the opening performance of *Fidelio* at the Festspielhaus. The air in the restaurant — as indeed in the entire town — was electric. Only Löwe was imperturbable and even bored. He was frank to admit that he could live very well without opera; the fact that he could so well do without it convinced him that the rhapsodizing of others about it was an affectation. Stephanie and Varina pretended to be dismayed by his attitude, so familiar to them.

"What a pity," said Stephanie, "to waste a ticket on Kaetchen when so many people would sell their souls to get one."

"I'll gladly give mine up," said Löwe. "Find me a soul to save!"

Stephanie admonished Grant.

"Don't believe a word he says, Stanley darling. He's as excited as any of us. Nothing in the world would induce him to give up his ticket."

"Have it your own way," said Löwe equably. "I've slept through many *Fidelio*'s. I'll sleep through this one. I can use the rest, I can tell you. I've been up half the night with Stohl getting ready for Saturday's performance of *Everyman*. I detest *Everyman*. I've always hated it."

"It's an allegory, isn't it?" said Grant.

"That doesn't make it any better."

"It's Rudolph's war-horse," put in Stephanie. "He has to trot it out. People expect it."

"What does it say?" said Löwe. "That when you die you have to give up everything. Who doesn't know that? Why a play about death? It's not our realm. Life is our realm. One has nothing to do with the other. Trying to imagine, even, what death is like, is an act of life. You may imagine till you're blue in the face and you'll not get closer. Death is totally uninteresting except for the effect its inevitability has upon the living. No. I detest this play."

A little silence fell upon the four. Löwe had spoken with a fervor unusual for him. Suddenly, in this canopied and glittering restaurant, Grant found himself remembering his early horror of death when he was a child in Xenia. After he had gone to bed he would hear his father in the next room mournfully intoning his night prayer, a Hebrew prayer which was an effort to fend off a possible visit during the night of the dreaded Malach H'Amovis, the Angel of Death. Grant had been so terrified at the possibility of this angel summoning him while he was asleep that he used to clutch the posts of the brass bed to resist the pull of the invader. He permitted himself a fantasy: the Malach H'Amovis, gaunt, hooded, faceless, coming into this restaurant, strolling about noiselessly among the ranks of tables, silently tapping, making reservations. He looked at Kaetchen. His heart sank. Löwe was pale, his skin sallow, only his dark eyes alive. He felt a sting of apprehension for Löwe. He had spoken with unusual intensity. Was Löwe himself in the grip of this fear? Was he unwell? Was he ravaged by some illness of which he spoke to nobody? Fear for Kaetchen clutched at Grant's heart.

"What would you think," drawled Varina, "if *I* were to go to Gastein? Have a try at dethroning Vesper? A quite disinterested journey — to salvage Ian for our sex?"

"Why not?" said Kaetchen, his equanimity restored by being called upon for advice in the realm of which he was the acknowledged master.

"Why not? The Fifth Crusade."

Stephanie turned to Varina.

"No, darling," she said. "Don't go. Nothing can be done. Vesper is too clever. Too malign."

"Why malign?" asked Löwe.

"Oh, but you don't know," protested Stephanie, "you don't know Vesper!"

"I do know him," said Löwe. "I know him very well and I like him very much. I enjoy his company no end. He has been propelled by nature in a certain way and he follows his nature, just as Stanley and I follow ours — or try to! — and just as you and Varina follow yours. Are we malign? Are you malign? It's simple nonsense."

"I never thought of it that way," said Varina thoughtfully. "I believe there's an answer to it but I just can't think what it should be. Can you, Stanley?"

"No," said Grant, "I can't."

"Still," Varina insisted, "I think Ian should be saved."

"Try," said Löwe. "By all means try. Join the relay. When you come back, Stephanie can take another turn. Keep the relay going. Olympic game."

"I'll never go there again," said Stephanie. "I never want to see Ian again."

She turned to Grant for confirmation.

"*You* know that, don't you, Stanley?"

Grant was embarrassed by this direct allusion to Stephanie's vow to him, that she would abandon delights henceforth and devote herself exclusively to her career. He was no longer comfortable with Stephanie. He could not suppress the shame he felt about her; he tried to forget the incident that caused it, but he couldn't, although he told himself over and over that Stephanie herself must have forgotten it. And now she was reminding him of a commitment he had made which it might be very difficult for him to meet. He brooded. He kept swallowing the wine which the waiters kept supplying. Through a haze he heard Löwe announcing that it was time to go.

Not only did Grant find himself at the core of European culture but at the core of the Festspielhaus as well, sitting beside Stephanie in the center of the second row in the orchestra, directly opposite the door under the stage through which Toscanini was presently to make his entrance. Some members of the orchestra were already in their chairs, twanging or softly tootling their instruments. They were early as yet, the house was only half full, the two seats on the other side of Grant were still unoccupied. A loud buzzing of conversation rose to the ceiling like a beehive in swarm. As he had never heard *Fidelio* and had no notion of what it was about, Grant busied himself with reading the scenario of the story in the leaflet program provided by an usher. Stephanie was chatting with a friend who sat the other side of her. But Grant found that reading the program scenario was a chore beyond his capacity. It was written in pidgin English, in strange, boneless Germanic sentences often without predicates and with the verbs coming so late that you had, by the time you reached them, forgotten what the subject was. First, he got into a deep tangle with the overtures. There were four, he deduced; three entitled *Leonore* and one *Fidelio*. He read the numbers and then was told that these numberings were incorrect. "From the original performance Number two redacted was, so he is therefore correctly Number one. This so-call Number one for Prague performance redacted was but this came off never. In the copyist's hand were the score and parts but by Beethoven corrected were and only after the composer's death." Was Beethoven a revenant? "For the second revision the overture was intended but was not ready." Grant's mind reeled. He decided to let the program narrator have his own way with the overtures and settled down to try to assimilate the story. Here he got into deeper trouble. He couldn't make head nor tail of it: "The story consists in Florestan a Spaniard nobleman from Spain who, from the sinister Pizarro is put in the prison but Rocco the jailer is with Marcellina the jailer's daughter in love until he meets Fidelio who is the wife of Florestan secretly in the prison inserted and truly Eleonora." Grant studied and studied but he couldn't cope. It just couldn't be made out. Suddenly he was aware of a great stir in the house; the buzzing changed its character. It became sibilant, murmurous, ecstatic. He looked up from his studies. Coming toward him, to occupy the two empty seats beside him, were the newly married Duke and Duchess of Windsor. The duke sat next to him.

The theater was now full and the eyes of the audience converged on the bridal couple. For Grant it wasn't necessary to stare; he had only to take them in out of the corner of his eye. The duchess was beautifully composed, seemingly unaware of being the focus of attention. Her chic was an enameled glaze, encasing and protecting her. Enclosed in its lacquer she sat cool, tranquil, comfortable. The duke, far less composed, seemingly a bit edgy, without the thin but durable carapace which protected his wife, looked flurried, uncomfortable. He shifted about in his chair, then he sought refuge in the program; he buried himself in it. Grant covertly watched him while he undertook the printed journey through the mazes of Florestan's prison life. "He doesn't know what he's in for!" Grant thought gleefully. He saw the duke bend to his task with Teutonic concentration. He held the program somewhat closer to his eyes. His eyebrows came together; furrows of anxiety showed in his forehead. There was a scatter of applause; Toscanini was making his entrance. The duke and duchess had somewhat deflated the excitement of the Maestro's appearance, but the Maestro was intent on other things, he paid no attention, he scarcely nodded, turned his back on everybody and entered, after a sharp rap with his stick, into close communion with Beethoven. Grant was fascinated by the curve of the Maestro's cheek; it was a line of great strength and beauty. Grant thought that he had never seen a cheekline like that, so grave, so ominous, so sculptural. The house lights dimmed as the Maestro beat down for the first bars of one of the overtures. Grant looked at the duke on his left. He hadn't lifted his eyes from the program. In the half-light from the stage he was deep in it, determined to unravel its mysteries. By this time the duke's forehead was corrugated with a fine network of wrinkles, furrows of despair and persistence. Grant felt pity for him. He felt like whispering: "Dear duke, give up! Acknowledge defeat. I've tried it and it's no good. Toscanini is before you and the opera is about to reveal itself. Attend to them; perhaps you'll get something from *them!*" But of course he didn't, he couldn't. But what a pity it was, what a waste it was! For a long time the duke never looked up from his program at all. All during the evening he kept taking furtive glances at it, to chart him through the macabre and lowering tides surging on the stage.

Four rows behind Grant and the newlyweds sat Mary Kennicott with Dr. Ogden, Sally and young Federn. Mary Kennicott didn't have to study the program to find out what *Fidelio* was about. She knew it, both the score and the libretto, by heart. As the lights dimmed, she closed her eyes merely to listen. She remembered the last time she'd heard it; she and Wyman on their honeymoon had traveled to Zurich to hear Bruno Walter conduct it. It was after that performance, in their hotel suite, that Wyman had first undergone some manifestations of his illness. She had, it seemed to her, been listening to *Fidelio* all her life. Many years before she had read a book by an English scientist and music lover, John W. N. Sullivan, called *Beethoven: His Spiritual Development*. She had written, from her parents' house in Boston, an ecstatic letter to the author and had received from him a sympathetic reply. They had exchanged a few letters. She thought now of Beethoven's isolation, of his suffering, of his poverty, of his affliction, of his lovelessness, of his superhuman and heartbreaking strength, as described by this author. However, the Englishman had written slightingly of *Fidelio* and Mary, in one of her letters, had argued with him about this. "The string quartet," Sullivan had written, "is the most sincere form of musical expression, as the opera is the least. Beethoven wrote one opera, not one of his most successful works, and that at a time when his creative activity, through its very activity and abundance, was not perfectly discriminating." Mary had written passionately, expressing her disagreement with this judgment — "the only flaw," she had written, "in your beautiful book." The author had written back tolerantly, wondering whether his correspondent's feeling about *Fidelio* was not subjective, "programmatic." Mary remembered this now. Her feeling was indeed subjective. She could never watch the scene in which Florestan is buried in the pit without thinking of the pit in which her husband himself was intermittently buried.

The music was so familiar to Mary that it permeated and deepened her introspections. To her parents' and grandparents' house on Commonwealth Avenue, the Brahmins of the intellectual and artistic world had come: her grandmother used to tell her of sitting next to Mr. Longfellow at dinner and his amusing remarks. The photographs of William and Henry James were in the drawing room, affectionately inscribed to her father and mother. A dark and shy young girl, she was thrilled when Santayana told her that he was attracted by the "luminosity" of her face. She lived on this compliment for weeks. She studied her face to read luminosity into it. She had a crush on Santayana. But she came to observe that he had an extraordinary knack of advancing and withdrawing simultaneously. Mary grew up surrounded by distinction, but this only accentuated her shyness. She was always conscious that she was too thin. She was angular. She grew up envying roundness. She had been resigned to spinsterhood when she met Wyman. It was a miracle . . . they suited each other perfectly. Their discovery of each other was the discovery of the world. He shared her passion for music. They played duets together. They invited a chamber music quartet to spend a month with them at the summer home of her parents on the North Shore. They would decide in a moment to go to Stuttgart or Bayreuth or Hamburg or Edinburgh to hear a concert or an opera or to see an art exhibition. When the dread affliction struck Wyman, it seemed like a rebuke to them for having been so happy. They had made a pact. It had been Mary's idea. If he could be cured, well and good. If not, she would not survive him. In one of his depressed states he had attempted suicide. She had prevented it in time. It was after that they had made their pact.

She had, in a sense, made a pact with Dr. Ogden also. She had never expressed it, but it had been in her mind. He was so healthy, so authoritative, so extrovert, that it seemed to her somehow that illness could not exist in his presence. He — and the clinic she had founded under his direction — were her last chance and Wyman's last chance. But from the blight of her life with Wyman love had sprouted anew; she had a strongly sensual nature in conflict with her Puritan heritage — and Wyman had encouraged her not to remain celibate. She had, she knew now, deceived herself. She had been aware long since that the stratagem she had employed, the fiction that Ogden would save Wyman, was hollow. She had employed a lover, that's what it came down to. She no longer believed in Ogden as a healer. He was so magnetic, so confident, she had shared his sense of his own omnipotence. He would plumb the secret that was at the heart of Wyman's malady. But, she realized it now as she listened to Leonore's lovely aria in which she yearns for her imprisoned husband — imprisoned in as dark a pit as Wyman's — she had long since ceased to believe in Ogden as the liberator of her husband. She didn't even think he cared very much. He had turned over the research to others. He was, he himself had admitted it and was proud of it, an "administrator." He had no part, really, in the work that was being done by the doctors on his staff. She had met them all: they were keen, they were assiduous, they were dedicated. But they did not inspire the belief she had at first had in Ogden. When she spoke to them they were smilingly pessimistic. The enemy was elusive. They never gave her the sense that they could counter his elusiveness.

She looked for a moment at Sally. How lovely she was, how cool. What was she feeling? You couldn't tell, you could never tell. She began to think of Mrs. Frobisher, of Sally's mother. She felt a strong identification with her. Mrs. Frobisher must have felt that in Dr. Ogden she had met a savior who would stanch the growth of the dark flower that was blossoming to kill her. It was her own life she had entrusted to Ogden; that was all right, that was hers to confide, but she had confided Wyman's. She was contemptible. She was obsessed. Whose life did she want to save, Wyman's or her own? Wyman had encouraged her belief in Ogden. He seemed to share it. Was it not a ruse, this confidence, to give her the courage to strip herself of guilt and to get from Ogden possibly the life that had been denied her with him? Mrs. Frobisher had not loved her husband and had been clear about whom she did love. But she loved Wyman. Her heart ached for Wyman. She had agreed to their pact in holy sincerity. Around the margin of her thoughts she beheld Leonora, she saw Toscanini's stick inditing the curve of her voice as Leonora promised, if she could not save Florestan from the grave, to prepare to follow him into it. Mary made up her mind. She would leave at once for California to join Wyman. The fun they had together in what Wyman humorously referred to as his "outside days" would go on: the jokes, talks of books and music, listening to records. She would never risk again, however, importing an orchestra to give a concert in their drawing room. Perhaps she might risk a string quartet. Yes, that might be managed.

She had employed a lover. She had never said it to herself so brutally before. Was he not free then to seek other employment? She thought of Varina. She thought of Stephanie. They were both demonized by desire. She stole a look at Sally. She was not obsessed. She was calm. She was inscrutable. She was cool. She would never be carried away. She leaned back in her seat conscious of relief at her decision to go back to Wyman. It was lustral. She would tell Ogden right away. She would tell him after the supper party she was giving at the castle, after everyone had gone. She would leave tomorrow. What would be the effect on Ogden? Would he offer a token resistance? The lustral moment passed. Questions nagged her. How much had Sally to do with her decision? Ogden had told her that he was fond of Sally in an avuncular way and that he was determined to rid Sally's mind of the prejudice, even the hatred, that she felt for him because she stubbornly clung to the belief that he had destroyed her mother and, moreover, for materialistic reasons. Mary was too proud and too withdrawn to question this, even to the point of comment that Sally, considering that she hated Ogden, was nevertheless willing to spend considerable time with the object of her hatred. She couldn't stoop to that, even disguised as banter. In her misery she was conscious of pity for Stephanie and Varina. She loved them. They were both doomed somehow. And she herself, was she not doomed? She thought of it without fear; even with consolation.

Across the rows between them she saw Grant lean toward Stephanie and whisper something to her. He was a strange creature, that Grant. Immature. He would always be immature, gauche, self-conscious, over-eager to please. Still, that was rather a nice trait. She thought that perhaps Grant found it fatiguing to live up to his reputation for cleverness. It was a strain on him, poor boy. But he was saved by his talent. Was talent enough to save you? She supposed that it depended on how much the possessor believed in it. Beethoven was saved by his conviction of genius. He was saved. For what was he saved? Without his genius he would have married a bar maid or a prostitute, got drunk, been happy as the great multitude counts happiness. In her compassion for Stephanie and Varina, she included Beethoven. He was part of the unending sorrow of the world.

And yet, between herself and her two friends, she differentiated. They were all three obsessed, of course, but *their* obsessions, Stephanie's and Varina's, were unfathomable to her. The fact that they were in love with Ian, whose sexual interests were divided, had always been incomprehensible to her. She had so many dear friends of Ian's persuasion, she loved to be with them, they were heavenly company, but the idea of being in love with them, of going to bed with them, was beyond her imagination.

The first act, she knew, would be over in a minute. In a lapse of mercy, the jailer, at Leonora's insistence, had permitted the prisoners to go out for a few minutes into the sun and air. It was like that, just like that when Wyman emerged from his prison into the air and sun of

his "outside days." She felt the clouded joy that swept the prisoners.
As she watches the prisoners in their melancholy diversion, Marcellina,
the jailer's daughter, sings:

> *Wir eilen so zum Sonnenlicht,*
> *Und scheiden traurig wieder.*
> *Die andern murmeln nieder;*
> *Hier wohnt die Lust, die Freude nicht.*

How true, thought Mary. No joy ever again. The curtains began to
close. Looking across she saw Ogden's hand close over Sally's, just for
a second. She felt a pulse in the wound. How very true!

Mary apologized to her companions for not going out in the intermission. It would be too hectic. Sally begged particularly but Mary was
stubborn.

The melee in the restaurant-bar was ferocious. The babble rose in
sharp thunder. It was as if the audience had itself been locked in Beethoven's prison and, moreover, condemned to silence, and now this
dammed-up silence took its revenge in a cacophony of released gossip.
Ravenously, the crowd fell on the recovered power of speech as if it
were food. Their private lives and thoughts had been arbitrarily put in
abeyance and now they pounded explosively to resume them. Indeed,
those who were able to get to the counter where würstel-brot and drinks
were served stanched their hunger silently. But between the counter
and the exit doors there was a dense crowd; those who had made a more
leisurely exit had no chance whatever of getting to it.

Grant and Stephanie walked out behind the duke and duchess, for
whom a lane was made by the gaping onlookers as if invisible velvet
ropes were following in their wake. But the progress of the little procession was royally slow. By the time it reached the restaurant room it
was packed solid. Grant and Stephanie were in despair of finding Kaetchen or Mary or Varina or Sally or anybody. Stephanie, finally, caught
sight of Löwe.

"There's Kaetchen," she cried. "He's with Lady Bellamine."

In the reading room of the Xenia Public Library, Grant had read the
memoirs of this fabulous lady. He suddenly remembered. He had been
quite shocked by her candor: that the wife of a prime minister should
have been so frank — and in print — about the agonies of giving birth.

In her pain, Lady Bellamine had written, she had clung piteously to her obstetrician. "Dear doctor," she had pleaded, "don't leave me. Please don't leave me. Stay this night with me and, I promise you, I'll stay with you any night you like!"

It had really startled Grant. A prime minister's wife! He tried to imagine Mrs. Calvin Coolidge saying a thing like that and failed.

When they finally reached them, Lady Bellamine embraced Stephanie. Kaetchen introduced Grant with the information that he was having a play done in London next season and that the sets were being designed by Tetty Bolt. Lady Bellamine was entranced. Grant told her that he in turn had been entranced by her memoirs. She took his hand in hers, and gazed into his eyes.

"You haven't *read* them. You haven't really read them!"

"But I have. Every word of both volumes. In the library of Xenia, Ohio."

As Lady Bellamine still seemed faintly incredulous Grant repeated the childbirth story and admitted that he had been shocked. Stephanie, Kaetchen and Varina laughed.

"And didn't you also say, somewhere in those lovely books, that you didn't really have a face — just two profiles stuck together?"

Lady Bellamine threw her arms around Grant and kissed him. She was overcome with pleasure. It was obvious that her literary accomplishment — just at being read — meant more to her than any marginal glories she might have achieved. Grant liked that.

"You must let me know," she said, her hand on Grant's arm, "the moment you come to London. The very instant. I'll give a party for your first night. Tetty is my nearest and dearest. He'll be there too."

Lady Bellamine waved to someone.

They looked. The duke and duchess were chatting cozily with a Nazi officer in a resplendent uniform and with a striking brunette in white satin. After a moment Grant recognized the officer. It was Prince Stauffer-Wernecke. Grant felt a sudden diminution of the euphoria that had been buoying him up. Vague rumors about the duke's sympathies came to him. "The Cliveden set." He didn't know precisely what it was or who belonged to it. The duke's sympathies, he'd heard, were with the One Up There, in the aerie. Damn! Could one never get away from it?

Lady Bellamine was telling a story.

"I take a poor view, you know," she said with a tilt of her head toward the duke and duchess. "A very poor view. Do you know the favorite story in London now?"

Grant shook his head.

"Some bricklayers are working on a building under a foreman. Suddenly one of them throws down his tools and sits apart in a sulk. 'What's the matter, Tom?' the foreman asks. 'Sorry, boss,' says Tom. I can't work without the woman I love.' "

René Wolfsohn, his buffalo head high above the crowd, came up to them with the dark girl Grant had met at Le Havre.

"Ah, René," said Lady Bellamine looking up at him, "how is it up there?"

The dark girl shook hands with Grant and gave him again the warm smile with which she had greeted him at the landing. Everybody knew her, so her name was not mentioned.

"It's so nice to see you again," she said to Grant.

The intermission gong struck. Grant felt again what he had felt at Le Havre: that he didn't want to be separated from Wolfsohn's friend. Nevertheless, Stephanie took his arm and started to pilot him back.

"I want to see you," Wolfsohn shouted after Grant. "I have a subject!"

After the bedlam of the intermission the darkened theater was restful. Grant found himself sitting again beside Prince Stauffer-Wernecke's friends. That is what the Windsors had become to him. Though he had been welcomed so cordially by the brilliant widow of a prime minister, Grant was again, abruptly, ill at ease, deflated, fearful. The spurious exultation with which he had entered the theater had evaporated entirely. The unseen power of the Mustache in the aerie had descended to crush him. Grant stole a look at the duke. He was back at his program study, his brow furrowed, trying to pick up the story, presumably, where he had left off. Toscanini reappeared, his medallioned face tense and set, conveying somehow that the applause which greeted him was an affront. It was as if he knew that the audience had picked up its private life during the intermission and that he resented its presence. The recitative with which the second act began was not calculated to cheer Grant up. Florestan is sitting on a stone; he is chained to the wall. Grant was able to make out, in his somewhat improved German, the burden of Florestan's thoughts. They matched his own. "Terrible darkness . . . terrible silence . . . the darkness of the tomb." For the second time that evening Grant found himself remembering the tenement in Xenia and his father's night prayer, the hooded figure. The dread angel was back, the one he had absurdly seen stalking the restaurant tables at dinner. Surely this was morbid. He was an American. He was safe. He could get out of this cursed place any time he wanted.

Presently, Leonora and the jailer come in and begin to dig Florestan's grave. The Master Grave Digger, Grant reflected, was up there, just across the border, planning to dig many graves. Grant was furious with himself. The glamorous couple beside him had become potential enemies. Simply because of rumors about them which possibly had no basis in fact. Simply because he had seen them chatting amiably with Prince Stauffer-Wernecke. The duke leaned over to whisper something to his bride. Instinctively, Grant bent his head toward them with an impulse to eavesdrop. It was ridiculous. He felt like a spy in enemy country.

He rebelled. Was this the only norm of judgment — the attitude of the entire race toward the One Up There? Yes, it was. For him it was. Grant remembered a Yiddish play he had seen in Cleveland in which there was a very funny character at whom the audience, including himself, had roared with laughter. No matter what came up, no matter what any of the other characters said about anything, this little old man had an invariable and automatic response. His son-in-law read aloud an item from a newspaper: there had been a terrible earthquake in Bolivia. His father-in-law asks his stock question: "Is it good for Jews?"

Grant asked himself: was he getting to be like that? He sat in agony, eviscerating himself.

On the stage the opera was drawing to a close. The merciful Governor comes in. He frees Florestan. He and Leonora are united. From the grave Florestan is brought back to life. After all the inhumanities, the opera ends in a jubilee of thanksgiving for mercy.

But Grant was not comforted. The One Up There, he felt, would not be merciful.

On the way back to the castle in Mary's car, Sally insisted on sitting in front beside the driver. Mary, Dr. Ogden and young Federn sat in the back. Mary thought: "She insists on sitting in front because she fears that what there is between her and Ogden might become too manifest." Mary dismissed it as a morbid thought but, nevertheless, it persisted. Had she not seen Ogden's hand on Sally's in the Festspielhaus? She couldn't bear it. She couldn't. Anyway she would be out of it tomorrow. Tomorrow she would be on her way back to Wyman.

In front, where she was sitting beside the open window, the soft air came in, laving Sally's forehead and ruffling her hair. She was calm. She was triumphant. She felt a quiet power. She had achieved exactly what she wanted. Ogden's letter was securely in her purse. Sally had thought things out carefully and had come to a decision. She was ready, now, at last, to talk to Mary. There would be a great many people at the party: Mary, seemingly, had invited everyone in Salzburg, including Toscanini, but Sally was sure that she could contrive to see Mary alone. She would tell her. She would tell her tonight. Under pretext of finding her lipstick, she opened her purse, just to make sure. Yes, there it was, Ogden's letter. Her mind raced. The others would not be coming till very late. Stephanie, she was sure, would be going backstage to congratulate the Maestro and would be taking Varina and Kaetchen with her. Maybe, then, it would be better to talk to Mary before the party. Yes, that might be best. She would talk to Mary right away.

In back, chatting with Ogden and Federn about the opera, Mary brooded. When should she tell Ogden that she was leaving tomorrow? Late — late — after everyone had gone. What if he volunteered to come with her? He wouldn't. Of course he wouldn't. But if he did — wouldn't it show that she was indeed morbid, that her imagination had run away with her? At the thought of this possibility her heart almost stopped. But it was absurd. It couldn't be. She couldn't be wrong. It was stupid of her to indulge such hopes. She was sure. He might make a show of token resistance but, she thought bitterly, he would succumb, very gracefully and with appropriate melancholy, to the inevitable. If she had to go, she had to go.

As they came into Mary's drawing room, Redding, her English butler, handed her a cable.

"From my husband," said Mary. "He's very bitter at my hearing *Fidelio* without him."

"I'm dying of thirst," said Ogden. "I couldn't get within a mile of that bloody bar!"

"Redding will provide," said Mary. "Sally, come with me."

She led Sally into the small salon filled with the improvisations of Fischer von Erlach. As Sally followed her, her heart beat fast. Should she tell her now? Why not tell her now? She would. Perfect moment. But she held off, savoring the sense of power the impending revelation gave her, power still unexercised. She titivated herself for a moment before a mirror, cupid and gorgon and sunburst framed, a lake surrounded by fantasies in gold. Reflected in the mirror she saw Mary opening her husband's cable. She heard a deep intake of breath, a gasp. She turned quickly. Mary had sunk to a sofa, the cable in her hand, staring at it, her lips pressed tight. Sally went to her swiftly.

"Darling! What is it?"

Mary gave Sally the cable. Sally read:

DEAREST AND ONLY WHEN YOU RECEIVE THIS I SHALL BE FREED LIKE FLORESTAN. YOU TOO. CONCLUSION OF UN- DULY OUTSIDE DAY. WILL YOU THINK I AM A SPOILSPORT? PLEASE DON'T. HOW WAS TOSCANINI? WAS HE AS GOOD AS MY CHERISHED BRUNO? I WILL NEVER BELIEVE IT. ALL MY LOVE AND FOREVER IF THERE IS SUCH A THING. WYMAN

Sally looked at Mary. She was staring into space.

"I don't understand it," said Sally.

"Wyman is dead," said Mary.

Sally took Mary's hand. It was cold. She chafed it.

Redding came in.

"Your guests are arriving, madame," he announced.

"Thank you, Redding. I'll be right there."

Redding went out.

"Oh, but you mustn't," said Sally. "I'll take care of it. I'll just go out and . . ."

"Thank you, dear. But I don't want anyone to know. Not tonight. Except Kaetchen. If you get the chance — tell Kaetchen."

Mary got up. She smiled faintly at Sally.

"Will you be a darling? Will you help me — to receive?"

Sally followed Mary into the hall.

15. The Somnambulists

In the next few days Löwe found himself unusually busy. He saw Mary,
Dr. Ogden and Sally off to America. That decision had been arrived at
very quickly, overnight, after Wyman's cable. Mary had explained to
Löwe that she had found Sally unusually sympathetic from the beginning; Sally had been with her when Wyman's cable arrived, had stayed
up most of the night with her, been an angel of quiet understanding.
Mary had begged her to go with her to California and Sally had consented. Was not this sufficient evidence of her loyalty, her quality, her
genius for friendship? Löwe agreed; he never quarreled with a fait
accompli. Rudolph Stohl's distinguished coterie was arriving by train
and car from all over Europe. Löwe had to meet them, greet them, arrange for their reception at a series of lunches and dinners at the palace. He rested briefly from these labors by meeting Grant for afternoon
coffee at the Café Bazaar. They chatted about the sudden departure of
the odd trio for Santa Barbara. Löwe was not nearly as startled by the
hegira to California as Grant was. To Löwe the behavior of his friends
was always unpredictable. He noted it with the detachment of an eth-
nologist who observes the sexual habits of an aboriginal tribe. This
didn't mean that Löwe wasn't attached to his friends; he was; he loved
them as scientists who spend a long time in a Kaffir village often fall in
love with the natives.

"By the way," said Löwe after they had exhausted the subject of the
departed trio, "your son's name is Amos. I thought you ought to know.
Amos Grant. Not bad."

Löwe got the reaction he hoped for. Grant was incredulous, startled.

"How did that happen? How does he come to be Amos?"

"My favorite prophet."

"*Your* favorite! I never heard of him."

"He's an adorable prophet. Eileen is delighted. She's reading up on Amos."

"In Hebrew, I suppose!" said Grant bitterly.

Löwe chuckled.

"No. In English. I lent her books on the prophets. She's deep in them. Of course you wouldn't be interested. You're anti-Semitic."

It was a favorite accusation of Löwe's. It annoyed Grant.

"Don't you think I might have been consulted?"

"There was no time. When the baby was born I called the American embassy in Vienna to register his birth. They asked what his name was. I said Amos Grant. Just popped into my head. As you never heard of your son's namesake Eileen will tell you all about him. The more she reads the more she loves Amos the elder. She's given up Dante. She's all out now for Jewish history."

Grant resented this also.

"I know. To you she's a figure of fun!"

Löwe answered with an emphasis unusual for him.

"You're quite wrong. You couldn't be more wrong. I think she's far too good for you."

"That's what she thinks. She turned me down, you know. And why, do you think? On account of Stephanie! Can you imagine? I told her Stephanie wasn't the least bit interested in me. 'That's not the point,' she said. 'The point is that you are interested in her.' And she sticks to it. She has a code of her own. Moreover, it's spiky!"

"Her data may be wrong but her instinct is sound."

"Then why on earth are you urging this on me?"

"Because I'm hoping that marriage will rid you of the adolescent nonsense you're stuffed with. Besides which, you have an obligation to your . . . Varina!"

Löwe got up. Varina was there; they hadn't seen her approach.

Varina was agitated. Löwe drew up a chair for her.

"I've been looking everywhere for you. I've been desperate to find you."

"What's happened?"

"Ian. Vesper is dead. He died mysteriously in the night. They're holding Ian."

"How do you know?"

Varina took a sheet of blue writing paper from her purse.

"Here. Read this. From Stephanie."

Löwe took the sheet and read it. Then he read it aloud to Grant.

"Darling most dreadful news. Ian is in awful trouble. I'm going to him. Vesper died and those awful people are accusing Ian. Tell Kaetchen right away. I'll let you know. Stephanie."

"Lovers' quarrel probably," said Löwe.

Varina was not amused.

"Don't be flippant, Kaetchen. This is serious. This may be . . . I saw Ian the other day. He scared me."

"When did you see him?"

"I drove over day before yesterday."

"Why did he scare you?"

"I don't know. I can't tell you exactly. He was different. His eyes were different. He'd changed."

"Did you see Vesper?"

"No. I asked to see him. But Ian wasn't seeing Vesper."

"What was he doing there then?"

"Drinking."

There was a moment's silence. Löwe said:

"Why didn't you go with Stephanie?"

"She didn't ask me. I guess . . . I guess she wanted to be the heroine, all by herself."

It was the first time, it struck Grant, that he'd ever heard from Varina an overtone of the invidious.

Varina put her hand on Löwe's arm.

"Please, Kaetchen! Come with me to Gastein."

"I can't. It's the worst possible moment for me. I can find out by telephone what I'd find out if I went. Excuse me."

He left the table. Grant and Varina looked at each other.

"Isn't it? — " Varina made a helpless gesture.

"Poor Stephanie! And she was going to turn over a new leaf."

"What?"

"She told me she was going to give up Ian, leave all that behind her — devote herself to her career. She told me she was never going to see Ian again."

"But who could possibly have foretold a thing like this! She *had* to go. I wish it had been me."

"Why don't you go now?"

"I'd be too late — as usual."

Löwe returned.

"I spoke to the judge in Gastein. Ian was the last person seen with Vesper. They're holding him for questioning. There are some incriminating circumstances. Nothing alarming. They're waiting for the results of the autopsy."

Varina hid her face in her hands. Löwe went on.

"He promised to call me back. Don't worry. If necessary I'll go with you to Gastein."

"If anything dreadful should happen to Ian, I don't think I could . . ."

Varina got up, her face averted, and left as abruptly as she had come.

She had left Stephanie's note on the table. Löwe picked it up and studied it. He folded it and put it in his pocket. The episode would make an interesting item to add to his letter to Monica.

"Ghastly, isn't it?" said Grant. "What did your friend in Gastein really say?"

Löwe did not answer.

"Well," he said. "Stephanie's got her wish at last. She's gotten Ian away from Vesper."

He looked at Grant. His eyes were grave.

"It would have been better," he said, "better for Varina, better for Stephanie, if it had been Vesper who survived."

All the next day, Grant underwent a crise of nervousness over the ordeal ahead of him that evening. He had been summoned, through Löwe, to appear at Stohl's archbishop's palace: Stohl was giving a party for him and had invited some artists and writers from Vienna to share the privilege. The list, rattled off by Löwe, made his head swim. It had given him a sleepless night and destroyed his day. Among those who would be present was Ludwig Born, "a greater poet even," according to Löwe, "than he is a novelist." Grant had never read a word of his. To prepare him, Löwe gave Grant one of Born's novels, in English. Reading it got Grant through the day. He was fascinated by it; it was a superb novel. He would have given his soul to have been able to write a novel like that but, having finished it, the terror of the evening ahead intensified. Why should a man of Born's stature, a genuine creative force, waste his time meeting a one-shot arriviste from Xenia, Ohio? It was grotesque. It was absurd. He felt, compared to those who were coming, ignorant and uncultured. He was totally inadequate to face such a barrage of talent. He wished he were dead.

Nevertheless, at 8:30 he rang the bell at the front door of the archbishopric. A white-jacketed butler showed him into a small reception room. He would, the butler said, inform Herr Löwe that his guest was here. It dawned on Grant that this little room was exquisitely furnished. Each object had the assured look of a museum piece. There was a curved, shimmering desk. Grant knew nothing whatever about styles or periods of furniture nor did he care much. But he couldn't fail to see that this desk was a triumph of the cabinetmaker's art; he had never seen such a desk. He examined it more closely. Inset in the glowing, fluted panel above the desk was a small painting of a burgher in period costume. There was something familiar in the burgher's face. Grant peered at him; he had seen this worthy somewhere. Where? Could it have been in some textbook he had muddled through in Professor Haskins's omnibus course, History One? Löwe came in.

"Ah! Hochstapler. Good evening!"

"Who is this?"

"Martin Luther."

"I knew I knew him!" said Grant in triumph. "Who painted it?"

"Cranach the Elder. It was Stohl's idea to have it set into that desk. The desk's not bad on its own, is it? But the professor likes to improve on things."

Grant was reminded of the gaps in his culture.

"Gosh, Kaetchen," he moaned, "I'm an ignorant bastard."

"That won't keep you from writing successful plays."

"Is Cranach famous?"

"To art lovers, yes. Personally I can do without him."

"I never heard of him till this minute. I didn't even know there were two of them."

"Well, now you know. Does it make you feel better?"

"No use, Kaetchen. I'm a fish out of water here."

"You always will be. You are a waterless fish."

"Shall I tell you something? If you promise not to tell anybody . . ."

"If your secret is tantalizing, I'll make no such promise."

"I don't know the difference between baroque and rococo."

"Your secret is safe with me."

"What the hell *is* the difference?"

"I've been told many times but I never listened. But you'll meet a man tonight who will tell you."

"Who's that?"

"Sigmund Alt. Author of a famous book — *The Cultural History of Europe.*"

"Oh, God!"

Löwe laughed.

"He's easy. Relax. Only eight at dinner."

"And after dinner?"

"The deluge."

Grant was in despair. He groaned.

"Why did I ever leave Maine?"

"On account of your great love. Remember?"

"I can't face it! Please, Kaetchen, get me out of it. Say I'm ill. Anything."

"Don't be childish. You're the guest of honor. People don't chuck on Rudolph Stohl."

He walked Grant down the hall and up stairs.

"I'll show you Stohl's library. Lady Bellamine says it's the most beautiful room in Europe."

"Baroque or rococo?"

"Take your choice."

"I mean to get drunk."

"Laudable ambition. Well — how do you like our little library?"

It was a very long room paneled in some dark shimmering wood. Around it ran a balcony with a delicately columned railing of the same dark wood. The balcony was capriciously curved; it had shallow, random undulations in it; it ran around the room like a wayward stream. Behind the balustrade were the bookshelves, glassed in, the fronts crisscrossed with slender, pale silver lattices. The light from the immense, many-pronged procelain chandelier reflected on the mellow wood of the balcony railings like moonlight on dark water.

"It's adequate," said Grant, determined not to be overwhelmed.

"A great many of these objects are props from the professor's productions. He considers that anything that's good enough for his productions is good enough for his home. That chandelier, for instance. Ah! Klaus! Let me present the guest of honor. Young, isn't he, to be a guest of honor? Mr. Grant — Klaus Wolff."

Klaus Wolff was a wispy little man, with sad eyes.

"Mr. Wolff," said Löwe, "is one of the most polished stylists in Germany. He is, alas, a drama critic. — But he writes so beautifully that we enjoy being assassinated."

Klaus Wolff shrank from this praise.

"Please, Kaetchen!" he begged.

"Stanley is an ignorant American. If I don't tell him, he won't know."

A waiter brought drinks. Grant grabbed one and gulped it.

Löwe got up and walked to meet a couple who had just come in.

Klaus smiled shyly at Grant.

"The Ludwig Borns."

Grant beheld a statuesque blonde lady, in an elaborately flounced evening gown of black lace, very décolleté. She walked with the sweep of an empress; she gave the effect of mowing down space. In her wake trotted a cherubic little man: a dreadnaught piloting a tug. Löwe made the introductions. They settled down to more drinks. Frau Born sized up Grant with cool appraisal; she stared at him as if deciding whether it was worthwhile to put him on her list. But her husband was instantly likable; his eyes twinkled behind his glasses; he was a pet. Grant plunged in at once to tell him how captivated he had been by his novel, implying that he had known it for years and that he welcomed this chance to let his dammed-up enthusiasm overflow.

"There is one scene in it," said Grant, "that I couldn't get over. It is so funny and so sad."

"Ah! So?" said Born. "What scene?"

"It's the scene where these two students — who had been friends as undergraduates — meet at the class reunion. They're both failures — both starving. They take a walk. They're dreaming of food; they begin to improvise meals and then suddenly they get into a violent argument about capers. One loves capers; the other hates them. He resents the existence of capers. They part enemies. It's just marvelous. It makes you cry."

Born grinned with pleasure.

"You hear, liebchen, he liked the caper scene," he informed his wife as if she hadn't heard it. Grant noticed that her cold, appraising eyes warmed.

"You must come to our new home in Vienna," she said. "Black marble and white marble."

A tremendously tall, enormously fat man joined them, but he moved lightly.

"Mr. Sigmund Alt," said Löwe. "He will tell you what you long to know."

Alt shook hands with Grant.

"Naturally," he said, "as I am omniscient. I'll tell you even more when I've had a drink."

Löwe embarrassed Grant by saying:

"Our American friend doesn't know the difference between baroque and rococo. I said you might be able to tell him."

"Buy my book," said Alt, "thereby doubling its sale. Then you'll find out that I don't know. Nobody knows."

Born challenged Alt, his eyes twinkling.

"Ah, but you define baroque as 'the last craving for illusion.' How can you venture into definition when you don't know what you're defining?"

"As no one really knows, I can't be contradicted."

Grant stole a look at his wristwatch. It was getting on to ten o'clock. He was famished. Did they never serve dinner in this house? Where on earth was the host?

Born, who noticed everything, noticed this covert look.

"One always waits for Stohl," he said.

As if on cue, the professor joined them. He greeted his friends, lifted Frau Born's hand and kissed it. He was of medium height, compactly built and had the easy manner of a king whose throne is secure. His voice, somewhat high-pitched, had an agreeable resonance. He was presented to Grant.

The professor wasn't in the least professorial. Grant thought it was

the alivest face he had ever seen, the face of a high comedian. Stohl
gave an impression of indefatigable gaiety; his dark blue eyes were on
the qui vive for laughter. Stohl greeted Grant warmly. Grant said that
the mere announcement in a New York paper that he might do his play
in Berlin had raised his standing on Broadway.

"I like the play very much. I may even do it!"

"That would be *too* much. If you'll just keep announcing it!"

Stohl laughed. So did the others. Stohl was all mobility, held in leash.
He held the little circle in leash. In Born, Alt and Klaus Wolff he had
a special audience and it was obvious that he had been saving a tidbit
for them.

"A few nights ago there were many people here I did not know. It
sometimes happens — my good Löwe imposes it on me. This room was
crowded. In a far corner there — under the balcony — I noticed a tall,
distinguished man — elderly but elegant, extremely elegant. He was
standing quite alone, drinking glass after glass of champagne. I asked
several people — nobody knew who he was. I was curious. I decided to
speak to him. From his great height he gave me a condescending look
through this."

Stohl screwed up one eye and fixed in it an imaginary monocle. His
face took on a vapid expression; his features slumped bonelessly; his
shoulders bent forward; he conveyed acutely the impression of a tall
man stooping over to greet a smaller one. Grant remembered what
someone had said to him once about Henry Irving when he asked
whether Irving was tall: "He was tall when he wanted to be!" From his
great height Stohl peered at each of them through his monocle.

"He wasn't in the least interested in me. Didn't ask who I was — I
doubt whether he knew. He talked about himself. He was a baron —
something unpronounceable in Hungarian. He told me about his youth,
about his parents, about their power and money and their palaces. He
had been, in his youth, very brilliant, everyone had had the highest expectations of him. I began to be bored and was going to leave him when,
suddenly, he redeemed himself. He took my arm and held me. He sum-
marized himself with grandeur:

"You know," he said. "I was once — a FUTURE PRIME MINISTER!"

Stohl couldn't have expected more than he got in the way of a reaction. Born, when he had caught his breath, said that it was the saddest biography he had ever heard. Grant managed to insert:

"That's what they'll say about me when I'm old. He had a play announced once by Rudolph Stohl."

Stohl took his arm.

"Ah! But you are prime minister already!"

Frau Stohl appeared. She was tall, with ash-blonde hair, grave, stolid, the bone structure of her face so strongly marked as to seem almost skeletonized. She looked like a religieuse of peasant origin in a Dürer engraving. She mumbled an apology for having no English. Grant apologized for having no German. They all went in to dinner.

The atmosphere of the dining room and the decoration of the table were ceremonial. Though he had never been to one, Grant thought that it must be like a state dinner. He sat at the host's right; Frau Stohl was at his right. The place of honor opposite Stohl was given to Frau Born. Grant hoped that the dinner would provide an interval in which he could recoup his forces. But Stohl asked him how he was spending his time in Salzburg.

"He had a baby," said Löwe.

"Ah," said Stohl, "this I know. But in the evenings?"

Grant said that he'd enjoyed himself last evening at the Festspielhaus watching the Duke of Windsor's frantic efforts to absorb the story of *Fidelio* from the eccentric narration in the program. This caught on at once. Grant embroidered. He told how he had tried himself to dredge the story from the program and given up; how he had wished to alleviate the duke's suffering and just didn't know how to go about it. Stohl roared with laughter; so did Born and the cultural historian. Even Klaus Wolff smiled a sad smile. Löwe beamed with avuncular pride; his protégé was making good in a big way; he felt justified in his sponsorship. After Grant finished there was a buzz: there was something sadistic in their glee over the duke's agony, from which Grant deduced that perhaps the rumors about his sympathies must be true.

"It serves him right," said Alt. "He should be condemned, the dear duke, to go to *Fidelio* every night. I know the littérateur of the Festspielhaus. His German is the German of *Mein Kampf*, so I can imagine

what his English is. I must get hold of that program. I have many
friends in Vienna who deserve to have it!"

Among the friends to whom Alt said he would send the scenario was
an anti-Semitic colleague of his, who had, in fact, said something amusing to him the other day in the café they both frequented in Vienna:

"Ah, you Jews," Alt's friend had said, "you control the press, you
control the bourse and now, with Freud, you control the unconscious!"

Alt launched into a diatribe about Stohl's neighbor to the effect that
the worst sin committed by him was the corruption of the German language. Stohl put a warning finger to his lips.

"Berchta," he said, "has many ears."

Grant asked who Berchta might be.

The historian explained:

In Salzburg legend the residence of Stohl's neighbor had been named
after Berchta, a wicked fairy who dwelt in the crags of the Hoher Göll
Mountain just above. This fairy had an unappeasable grudge against
the human race: to vent her spite, she kept Berchtesgaden blanketed in
thunderstorms.

Stohl shook his head. He wanted Alt to keep quiet.

"Does Berchta understand English too?"

"Her ears are bilingual," said Stohl.

Grant divined that talk of wicked fairies, with contemporary analo-
gies, must not be indulged in before the waiters.

Stohl undertook to give the conversation a neutral turn. He asked
Grant about American novelists, playwrights and painters. Grant mus-
tered what he knew. There was great curiosity about George Gershwin,
who had died a few months before at the age of thirty-nine. He was
mourned by these people. Alt had met him in Vienna and had heard
him play the piano. It was a unique and exciting experience, he said, to
hear Gershwin play. He rhapsodized about Gershwin:

"And such a lovable man, so good-looking, so unaffected, modest
and simple. He was an authentic genius. It is a terrible loss. There is
no telling what he might have done."

Stohl was relieved that the conversation had switched from Berchta
to Gershwin.

*   *   *

Grant braced himself for the ordeal still ahead of him, meeting the dozen or so writers and artists whom Stohl had invited for after dinner. Löwe walked him back to the library. There were about a dozen men there. He found himself, Löwe by his side, at the head of a receiving line. Löwe introduced the dozen one by one; Grant heard a succession of names and the titles of works which the names had written: "the author of *Bambi* . . . the scenarist of the film . . . the composer of the operetta . . . the librettist of . . . the poet who . . ." The names drifted by, Grant couldn't seize them. The group crowded around him, asking him questions — about the New York theater, about Hollywood. Their eyes were hungry and thirsty, filled with wonder and longing. It was as if, simply by virtue of being American, he were omniscient and omnipotent, beyond mortality. Not only was he immortal, but he was enhaloed by the effulgence of the most cherishable success in the world, American success. Evidently, for them, one American success was worth a whole library of European. He had noticed this here, from the beginning. Grant felt shame at being here, that he was a fraud, bogus. He felt himself unbelievably vulgar, a blatant showpiece. He felt like saying to them: "Look, my friends and colleagues, look. I have had one accidental success in the New York theater. This accident may never be repeated. I am not, as each of you is, a writer at all. I've just manipulated, once, the trick of playwriting. I am not, as you are, distinguished. I am not educated. Until a few hours ago I'd never heard of Cranach. I didn't even know there were two Cranachs. I have no languages. I am afraid to speak the little German I know because, if I did, it would sound dangerously like Yiddish."

But he didn't say any of this. He managed to answer a question from one of the screenwriters, translated for him by Kaetchen, about who would be the most reliable agent in New York to represent his work in Hollywood. Grant offered to give this petitioner's work to his own agent in New York. The screenwriter moved forward to wring Grant's hand in gratitude. Grant looked appealingly at Kaetchen, who piloted him away.

Stohl and his dinner guests had come back, minus the ladies. Löwe sat Grant next to Klaus Wolff, who gave him a welcoming smile. Stohl said:

"You are lucky, my dear Mr. Grant, that Klaus doesn't practice his profession in New York. You would suffer from him as he has often made me suffer. Looks innocent, doesn't he? You are quite mistaken. Vitriol. But he dispenses it in bottles so beautifully carved that I forgive him. In fact, when he's not criticizing, I love him."

Wolff shrank.

A silence fell on the room. Grant caught his breath. Waiters trailed rainbows of liqueurs among the guests. Grant looked down the length of the room, softly lit, cozy as the inside of a walnut shell. "Surely," Grant thought, "the witch Berchta couldn't enter this room." Stohl's library was an exquisite conceit of civilization, safe. The guests had settled themselves on chairs or on sofas in the islets of mellow light. Everybody was having drinks. Everybody was at peace.

It was by this time past midnight. Stohl motioned to the captain of the waiters. He apologized for keeping him and his men up so late. The captain bowed and retired.

When the captain left, Stohl explained. His voice was calm, unhurried; he had the air of giving a group of actors general instructions at the first reading of a play.

"I had to caution Sigmund not to be too explicit before the waiters. He" — he made an upward gesture with his hand — "knows everything that goes on in this house: Mrs. Franklin D. Roosevelt was here this afternoon for tea. He knows it. He knows exactly when she arrived. He probably knows what our conversation was. He knows that you are all here tonight; the histories and affiliations of all of you. Therefore, as well as one can, one must be careful."

Grant asked how He knew.

"Because," said Stohl with a faint smile, "almost everyone on my staff is on his staff."

Stohl said this equably, with even a suggestion of admiration for the efficiency of his neighbor. But the little speech put a spell on the room.

Born said:

"This morning, at the performance of Verdi's *Requiem,* I saw Schuschnigg in a box. I watched him. He was listening very attentively, reverently. He didn't miss a note."

"No wonder," said Alt, "it must have occurred to him that he was listening to his own."

"Yes," said Born. "It is possible. He is a good Catholic. He looked worn. He looked desperate."

"He *is* desperate," said Alt. "No matter which way he turns, he will be crushed. There is no way out for him. The wings of this fly will be torn off by his compatriot up there — Berchta's godchild."

"I am not quite so defeatist," said Löwe. "Schuschnigg still has cards to play. He has allies. France, England, Italy. They pledged — at the Stresa Conference."

Klaus Wolff looked at Löwe. It was the first time Grant had heard him say anything.

"They will do nothing," he said. "There will be a European war and the Nazis will win it."

"I don't agree with you," said Löwe. "I don't agree with you at all. First, I don't think there will be a war. He will overreach himself and he will be stopped."

"He overreached himself last year," said Wolff softly. "In the Rhineland. Did anyone stop him?"

Löwe held his ground.

"There will be no war. You will see."

"Yes, my dear Kaetchen," said Wolff. "You will see."

Everybody sat in silence. Through this silence came the voice of the cultural historian. His vast bulk leaned forward in his chair. He was staring at Grant. His voice — sharp, penetrating, a little falsetto — was aimed at Grant.

"How do you write? Do you use pencils?"

"No," said Grant. "Usually with a fountain pen. Then I transcribe to the typewriter."

"I write with pencils. I love my pencils. I love to sharpen them. Long thin points. Then I lay them out before me: a long row of pencils — of equal length."

Grant didn't know what to say. Was the art historian drunk? What was the matter with him? They all listened, breathless.

The historian heaved himself up from his chair. He brandished his fist at the ceiling. His voice had the effect of a scream.

"If he so much as touches one of my pencils — do you hear? — I will not tolerate it. I will jump out of the window."

He sank back in his chair, exhausted. Stohl got up, went to the serving table, filled a small brandy glass and brought it to the giant, who nodded thanks and swallowed the brandy without a word. Stohl then excused himself; he had to rehearse in the morning.

By this time, Grant was so hazed with drink that the room swam before him. The others were looming apparitions, heads, hands, shoulders, gargoyle faces, grotesque, macabre. *They were sitting there!* Ghosts sipping liqueurs. They would sit there eternally while the hooded angel from the flat in Xenia moved among them, hovered over them, tapping their shoulders. Behind the exquisitely carved balcony rails Grant thought he saw a white-jacketed figure lurking, peering through the rails. He knew he wasn't seeing it and yet he did. They sat there. He felt like screaming at them: "Get up! Don't sit here! Get out!" They were all in a somnambulism and so was he. He ought to get up himself, to flee, but he knew he wouldn't. He was held in a vise, powerless, like the rest of them. It was a wakeful dream, a dream in which you see disasters descending — avalanches, fanged teeth, creeping, nameless forces, the clawed hand of death — and yet you do nothing. You know you will be eviscerated but you do nothing. These people were like effigies in a waxworks. He was himself a waxwork. He must get out into the air. He stood up. Born spoke to him. "You are going?"

"Yes," said Grant. "I feel rather tired. I've had a bit too much to drink."

"I'll see you to your car."

"Thank you very much."

Grant followed Born out of the room and downstairs to the porte cochere. They waited for Grant's car, which he had hired for the evening.

"I have wished to speak to you," said Born, "to ask of you a very great favor."

"Anything. I'll be happy to . . ."

"It concerns Klaus Wolff. He is a very shy man. He doesn't make an impression. But, my dear friend, I assure you, he is a beautiful writer. Very witty. He is our leading dramatic critic, but also he writes sketches and short stories. He is full of invention."

"I am sure. He's very appealing. Sad face, hasn't he?"

"He is bereft. His wife, to whom he was deeply devoted, died of cancer in Paris a few months ago. He is alone. I don't think he can go on much longer in Berlin. This is what I wished to speak. If you could possibly recommend Klaus for Hollywood? It would be a blessing and I can assure you he would not disappoint you."

"I'll be glad to do it. I'll do everything I can. I promise."

Grant's car drew up. Born took Grant's hand and pressed it fervently.

"I felt in you this kind of man."

"You may count on me. I'd love to do it."

They made a lunch appointment. Born stood waving to him as Grant moved off in the car.

He leaned back in the seat and lit a cigarette. It was heaven to feel the fresh air. A swastikaed Mercedes full of officers whizzed by. Grant's chauffeur wafted a furtive salute, half looking round at Grant to see whether he was being observed.

On his desk in his room at the castle Grant found an express letter. He looked at the postmark: Bad Gastein. He tore the envelope open. It was an unpunctuated letter from Stephanie. He read:

Darling beloved poet Ian and I are married we wanted you to be the first to know don't tell anyone except Kaetchen Ian adores you as much as I do we wanted you to know before anyone you will laugh when I tell you how it happened in the detent house with uniforms looking on the police officer insisted to kiss the bride!!!! We are wildly happy and long to see you our troubles will soon be over after all the agony thank God. Is your play finished I long to read it Ian is as excited about my doing it as I am I live for that what a moment it will be when I embrace you our difficulties are still hanging they are stupid as I am all our love and longing kisses kisses

Eternally your

Stephanie

Grant stared at the letter. That damned promise he had made! Would he never hear the end of it? He opened a desk drawer to put the letter away. Lying there, in the drawer, he saw more of Stephanie's scrawly handwriting; the blue sheets of her welcoming letter the night he had arrived in this room.

Grant went to bed. He fell asleep only to find himself again in the bewitching library at the archbishop's palace. He was a somnambulist in a crowd of somnambulists. They were all walking blindly into a pit. The pit was alive with cobras. He was the only one who seemed to be aware of the pit. He screamed out a warning to the rest. But his scream was soundless.

He screamed louder but he couldn't make it *sound*. They went on walking, he with them. He kept screaming. He realized that no matter how loud he screamed nothing was audible. His desperation mounted till the cobra heads darted up to seize him . . .

Next morning Liss handed Grant a cable. It was from Hollywood, offering him a contract to do a film. He went to the post office and sent a cable accepting. Then he went to the hospital to see Eileen. He found her reading *Prophecy and the Prophets in the Old Testament,* a book which Kaetchen had given her. She let go of the prophets and held him, long and close. He told her that Stephanie was married. From the hospital, Grant telephoned to Löwe. Everything was all right between him and Eileen. He asked him to find an apartment for himself, Eileen, Schwester and the baby where they could stay until he left for Hollywood. Löwe had anticipated him: he had his eye on a nice apartment, on the Salzach, belonging to a biologist who had to go to Berlin for a time. He also had a rabbi on tap, alerted to marry him to Eileen. Löwe was as gratified as if he had just come into a handsome inheritance.

16. Varina

Varina, drawing on her stockings in her hotel bedroom after a fitful night, reflected with detachment that her legs were very good. They were, in fact, perfect. And yet, she was forced to admit, they had done very little for her. They never would. Facing this ultimate, she gave up dressing. What, actually, was there to dress *for?* A temptation that had beckoned to her often beckoned to her now, even more invitingly than it had ever done before. Why not? She could think of no good reason why not. She stood before the full-length mirror, turned half around to see that the seams of her stockings were aligned, and tucked in her garters. Her gray eyes looked back at her from the mirror. Her chestnut hair fell down to her naked shoulders; she contemplated the scar on her forehead. She remembered the day of the riding accident; she had cried and cried, sure that her looks would be ruined. But it had turned out all right. Her mother had told her that the scar was piquant. "It adds something," she had said. Even now, Varina had to agree with her mother. Yes, it did add something. But, alas, not enough. Her legs were perfect, her body was perfect, her looks were certainly not disagreeable and, yet, there was something wrong. There was something deeply wrong. What was it?

It seemed to her that she had sought an answer to this wearisome question ever since she could remember. She lit a cigarette, took a swallow of coffee from the tray the waiter had left on the table and without bothering to finish dressing, sat in an armchair by the window looking out over the copper-colored Salzach. The little river was undernourished; it was so famished for water that its pebbly ribs showed. It was already very hot. The Salzburg paper, which the waiter had also left on the breakfast tray blazoned the headline: SAHARE HITZ BRENNT.

What was it? . . .

Hitherto, as her failures mounted and compounded, she had hit on various theories to account for them. She now hit on a new one, a plausible one. She was a coward. She had no courage, no strength of character. She was passive. Invariably, she did the wrong thing. Yes, that was it, surely that was it. She had never before felt so clearly that she had probed to the heart of the mystery. Since she could not change, since she knew that it was not in her nature to change, since, in any case, it was too late to change, why should she go to the bother of continuing her existence? Why should she go on living? It was really too much of a chore. She could not go on endlessly performing it. She wouldn't. She knew how to stop. She had the means in the cabinet in her bathroom.

It was not merely the news she had received from Kaetchen that Ian and Stephanie were married. It was not merely the angry letter she had received from her father summoning her to join him and her mother in London to go to the duchess's for a shoot in Scotland. No, it was neither of these things. Oddly enough, even more, it was Grant's invitation to attend, next week, his wedding to Eileen. That, somehow, pinpointed her contempt for herself in the most vivid way. This darling, ignorant, simpleminded, impoverished girl Eileen really had courage, the courage which she herself lacked. With no prospects at all, with no hope at all, with nothing in the world between her and destitution but Sally's kindness, Eileen had gone through with it. She had had her child. She, Varina, had killed hers. Eileen's parents would have been as wrathful as her own. But Eileen had followed her own bent. She had the courage of her instinct. She wanted a child of Grant's and she had it, come what may. She wasn't afraid of her parents nor of anyone. It was not that Varina felt that if she'd had Ian's child she might have induced him to marry her instead of Stephanie. It wasn't that at all. Even Stephanie was more courageous than she. She married Ian under dark circumstances. Would she have done it? She doubted it. She would have thought: "Supposing Ian is really guilty, that he murdered Vesper?" No, she'd never have done it. She'd had her chance and thrown it away. That was the thing. Had she had her child, she would have done something positive for once, given herself something to live for, a gonfalon on which to blazon her rebellion and defiance of her parents, a repository for her love.

It had been the same with her first great love, Eugene Rosenthal. He was a banker, good-looking, rich, cultivated, patron of a chamber music ensemble, an artist manqué. Of course, married, with three children. She had fallen in love with him and he with her. His wife was a delightful creature, a musician herself, a friend of Varina's. Kaetchen had been her confidant in this affair. He took a poor view.

"Aren't there enough unmarried men in the world? There's young Warburton, very eligible, who adores you."

Kaetchen had brought in young Warburton as a placebo. Warburton had very much wanted to marry Varina. Varina's parents were delighted. Young Warburton was exactly their dish. He was the perfect antidote for Varina's disease: a pathological preference for Jews. The trouble with young Warburton was that he was, indeed, very young. He would, Varina thought, even when he was middle-aged, always be "young Warburton." He would never grow up. He was callow.

With Eugene, too, she had been cowardly. Perhaps not as cowardly as Eugene, who vacillated, who was always on the verge of throwing everything over for her, but not quite. She could have pushed him over

the edge but she withheld. Her reason to herself that she didn't was that
he must be utterly clear himself, but that wasn't the real reason. She
saw that now, this minute, looking out over the gravelly river gleaming
dull under the blazing sun. The real reason was that she herself was
afraid. There was one moment when Rosenthal had said she must go
away with him; they must do something final and spectacular, they
must take the irrevocable step, confront themselves with a fait accompli. She refused. She knew that he was desperate, trying to supple-
ment his own timidities with a bold act, bolder than he was. She knew
that he would wake up one morning reproaching himself for having
abandoned his wife and children whom he adored, for having made a
shambles of his life. He would miss the Friday-night chamber music
parties in his beautiful house.

Varina's parents had found out about this affair with Rosenthal.
They were aghast. *Their* daughter, their lavishly nurtured darling, having an affair with a married man and, moreover, Jewish. This was what
hurt. The first delinquency they might have overlooked. The second
was unspeakable.

They bundled Varina off to London, where Kaetchen introduced her
to Ian Leith.

Her father's letter was on the table. She glanced at it. "I hate to tear
you away from your Jewish friends but I confess that I am at the end
of my patience with you. If it were not for your mother . . ." She
knew it all. This time her father threatened, unless she joined them at
once, to cut off her allowance. He had never threatened that before.
She felt sorry for her father; he had, she thought, missed so much in
life; he had no awareness of its true delights, the delights of art, for example. Eternal golf, eternal fishing and hunting, eternal fury at the ero-
sions of the world he believed in. The spectacle of his country being
led to the dogs by FDR made him apoplectic; his rages were so violent that his wife feared he would have a heart attack. He couldn't have
hated the traitor to his class more if he were Jewish; in fact, he persuaded himself that FDR *was* Jewish. That made it simple; it made it
possible for him to loathe the commander-in-chief of his Army and Navy
with no diminution of patriotism. It legitimatized his hate. The Jews
were an obsession with Mr. Lawson; their existence roiled him. It was

his burning glass. Varina knew that, together with other like-minded friends, he was sending the literature of Goebbels all over the United States. Still, she was sorry for him. She also hated him. The poor man was unlucky! Why had he been burdened with her? Why couldn't destiny have allotted him a more suitable daughter?

Varina pondered. It was very tempting — the solution. It had the virtue of simplicity. A hot tub and then to sink, without feeling anything much, beneath the waters of the little sea. She smiled. She wouldn't *need* an allowance.

The telephone rang. It was Kaetchen. In her indolent, drawling voice, she told him about her father's letter. She brought it to the telephone and read him the sentence about dragging her away from her Jewish friends. Kaetchen chuckled. She sounded to him — it was her controlled intention — quite as usual. She did not mention that she was toying with an alternative possibility. She had done so once in London and he had talked her out of it. His advice now was crisp and authoritarian. She must comply with her father's request at once. She must wire her father that she was leaving that afternoon on the Arlberg. He would get her reservation and pick up the ticket. The duchess he knew very well. He praised her to the skies. She was delightful, gay and humorous. As for the duke, he was unobtrusive; he seldom left his gun collection. The duchess, moreover, liked to surround herself with attractive young men. There would be diversion there. Kaetchen didn't give her a chance to say anything. He would meet her at the station with the ticket. He hung up.

"Well," said Varina to herself, "that seems to be that! I guess I'd better go. Passive again. True to form!"

She sat on the edge of the bed, thinking. There was still that other possibility about which, of course, she could say nothing to Kaetchen. About her only secret from him! Had she hinted a breath of it, he would have come running. She was sorry, almost, that he had called. Still — for how long would she go on being cowardly? She had only to run the tub. But Kaetchen would be buying a ticket for her on the Arlberg. She smiled. He would be stuck with the ticket. No, she couldn't do that to Kaetchen. Not today. He would mourn. In all the world — Kaetchen would mourn. Some other time. There would be many occasions. It was a comfort to know that she had a resource. The knowledge was companionable.

Slowly, Varina resumed dressing. She applied lipstick carefully in front of the mirror. She gave herself a final look, thought she passed muster. She went down to the lobby and sent a cable to her father to tell him that she was leaving that afternoon on the Arlberg.

Varina was late getting to the station. Kaetchen had begun to worry that she wouldn't make it. He walked her down the long platform to her car on the wagon-lit. He had taken care of everything, tipped the porters, who knew him well. He had bought her flowers and magazines to while away the time on the journey. They were both quite breathless; it was almost time for the train to move.

Varina was so sorry she would have to miss the Grants' wedding. She asked Kaetchen to give them her love; she would cable them from London. Kaetchen assured her that he would take care of all that. He, in turn, asked that his love be given to the duke and duchess. He also asked her to telephone Lady Monica in London. Varina promised.

"Any messages to my father?" said Varina, standing on the steps of the train.

Kaetchen laughed. "Tell him I'm thinking seriously of becoming a Roman Catholic."

"That's no good," said Varina. "He hates Catholics too!"

The train began to move slowly. Kaetchen walked along beside it.

"Write me about everything. Write me about the shoot."

"Oh, naturally, the shoot."

She cupped her hands around her mouth.

"Goyim nachus!" she funneled down to him.

17. Wedding Day

On the morning of his wedding day, Grant was sitting in the Bieder-meiered study of the flat Löwe had found for him, working on his play. Schwester, wearing dark glasses, came in with a cable. He asked Schwester how Amos was.

"He sleeps," said Schwester.

Grant smiled.

"Does he ever do anything else?" he asked.

"It is good for him to sleep," said Schwester as she closed the door carefully behind her. She had been instructed by Eileen that things must be kept quiet around the Master.

Schwester had confided to Eileen the reason for the dark glasses. She had developed a fierce and possessive passion for the infant Amos. She felt that she had brought him — as indeed she had — from non-life to life. When Eileen asked her to come to America with them, she had promptly consented. But when she announced this plan to her occasional sweetheart, the barber, he had given her a black eye. Of this black eye she was ashamed and she did not want Grant to see it. It was not, she explained to Eileen, that the barber was exclusively in love with her. He had, Schwester knew — and it had been the cause of many quarrels and separations between them — many girls. It was because of Amos's blood strain. The barber considered it a betrayal for Schwester to nurture a contaminated blood strain. Schwester's sacrifice endeared her to Grant. At the age of five weeks, Grant reflected, Amos had already precipitated an international crisis. He created international crises simply by existing — like the disputed sons of royalty. No doubt about it, Amos was precocious!

Grant opened the cable. It was from Sally in Santa Barbara. It read:

MY DARLING TWO KENNETH AND MARY JOIN ME IN CON-GRATULATION AND BLESSING. ALL HAPPINESS. ALL JOY. WE WILL BE WAITING FOR YOUR ARRIVAL WITH OPEN ARMS. ALL LOVE. SALLY

Grant sat staring at the cable. He felt trembly suddenly. Somehow, the cable brought to the forefront of his mind the fact that he was actually getting married, that he was resigning himself to a lifetime of domesticity. The future was closed. The rampant romanticism of his fantasies, the dabs and sallies of his absurd love-probings must come to an end. But wasn't that a good thing? It certainly was a good thing. He was emerging from prolonged adolescence into maturity. Precisely what maturity was he didn't know. It was a much-bandied-about word but what did it mean? Was it a synonym for renunciation and how did one know when one had achieved it? He began to pace the room. Was it just seeing Sally's name on the cable? He tried to steady himself. He was now, for the first time, settled, coherent. He would devote himself to his work, to planning for Amos. Amos tugged at his heart. How gallant this mite was to persist in living! He slept; he was in abeyance, gathering reserves for the struggle. Grant would oversee his education; he would see to it that Amos's would not be scrappy as his own had been. He would see to it that Amos did not waste himself on a shallow, literary education. The best brains now went into science; he would see to it that Amos would be contemporary and not, as he himself was, vestigial. He was lucky to have ended up with Eileen. Just what he needed, all the qualities he himself lacked: she was placid, steady, concentrated, finite. And she loved him. It was a cushion on which he could repose. He was, he told himself, happy. Perhaps that was going a bit too far. He was content. Yes, that was perhaps more exact. Wasn't that better? Better than anything. Bored with the maelstrom of his thoughts, he turned to the task in hand, to write a scene between Sally and his Dr. Ogden to follow the one he had written between Dr. Ogden and Sally's mother.

He itched with the mystery of Sally. She was Eileen's best friend. They corresponded with each other incessantly. Hardly a day passed that he did not see a letter from Sally in the hall. He had been tempted to open one to see what on earth she and Eileen corresponded so busily about. This temptation he had, of course, resisted. He would ask Eileen what Sally had written her about. He always got a perfunctory reply.

"Oh, just nothing," Eileen would say. "She just writes about how Mary is taking it being a widow, and like that." Whenever he asked about how Sally was taking it, she clammed up. He felt a sudden anger

against Eileen. Of course she didn't know the real reason he was so curious about Sally. She had known that he had been in love with Sally.
Did she think that this was the reason for his curiosity? Did she think
that he was still in love with her? Well, he would tell her that his interest had nothing to do with what he had felt for Sally. He would tell her
why he wanted to know, why he must know. He would, goddamnit,
break the carapace of Eileen's reticence about Sally. He would break it
or know the reason why!

In an unanticipated fury he started out of the room. In the hall, just
as she was leaving, he ran into Naomi.

Naomi was the nineteen-year-old daughter of the rabbi alerted by
Kaetchen to marry the Grants. He had brought them to the rabbi's
house to discuss arrangements for the ceremony which was to be performed in the rabbi's apartment. Naomi had great dark eyes, pale olive
skin, black hair braided in thick strands. Her hair was somewhat untidy, strands of it kept coming down on her forehead and she brushed
them off with quick gestures. She was mercurial, she gave the effect,
even when standing still, of darting about; she seemed perpetually in a
kind of dance and it was so with her speech, which came in little bursts.
She spoke English well, with a soft accent. There was a quicksilver intelligence in her expression, in what she said, full of surprising and humorous perceptions. She reminded Grant, when he first met her, of the
French lady he had met twice with René Wolfsohn. The latter was
older, of course, but she and Naomi had the same quality of quick sympathy, of intelligence at once warm and acute. Grant had a crush on
Naomi, that's what he called it, a euphemism for an emotion he did not
think it dignified to entertain. It was, he reflected ruefully, a useful
cushion-word. Had he been younger and freer he could have adored
Naomi. But, then, he had felt the same way about Wolfsohn's girl,
whose name he didn't even know. The two merged in his mind; they
appeared so woven in his fantasies. He had wanted to ask Eileen to invite Naomi to their flat for a meal but Eileen had anticipated him. She
also had taken to Naomi and had engaged her to teach her Jewish history. Eileen had abandoned her Dante studies in favor of Jewish history,
Jewish theology, Jewish everything. She meant to study Hebrew and was
shocked to find that Grant didn't know any. She meant to make up for
his ignorance. Her child, after all, was named for a Hebrew prophet.

She had, therefore, to trace her infant's genealogy, become familiar with the spiritual lineaments of his namesake. She became about this as avid as a heraldist on the scent for quarterings. Dante was left to shift for himself.

Grant asked Naomi where she was running to. She was indeed running. Grant took her bare arm and held her. With her free hand Naomi fluffed back some vagrant hair. She puffed up at it with a big breath to teach it its place. She was wearing a dark blue dirndl with a white blouse. She was barelegged. Grant took in her slim brown legs. Naomi was breathless, perhaps from the ardors of explaining to Eileen about the Rechabites and to make clear to her that *her* Amos was not one of them.

"Stay and come to the wedding with us. Kaetchen is picking us up."

"Oh, I couldn't. I have to help Mother. I have to change."

"Why change? You're lovely in this."

"This!"

Naomi took the sides of her wide skirt, spread them out for a moment, then let them fall back again.

"Oh, no. I couldn't possibly. My parents would be horrified. It's an OCCASION after all. Is it not? I have to go!"

She was gone. Grant looked after her, half smiling, and walked back down the hall to Eileen's room. Eileen wasn't there. He called out to her. Her voice answered from the baby's room:

"Just a minute."

Two chairs were drawn up before a big, heavy table in front of the window where, presumably, Eileen had been taking her lesson. Grant went to the table and looked at the books scattered about, books lent by Kaetchen: Sir G. A. Smith: *The Twelve Prophets* (when Eileen went at a thing, Grant thought, she didn't do it by halves); *Prophecy and the Prophets in the Old Testament; Harper's Commentary;* J. E. McFayden: *A Cry for Justice* (had Amos cried for justice?). Some of the books were open; in the margins he saw scribbled notes in Eileen's eager handwriting. He was trying to decipher one of Eileen's notes when she came in. She put her arms around him and kissed him.

"Oh, darling, Amos is so wonderful!"

Grant nodded at the literature.

"Which one?"

Eileen was stymied for an instant.

"Oh, I see what you mean." She laughed. "He's wonderful too. They're both wonderful. But you know — that one," she pointed to the books, "is so *interesting!* Naomi makes him so *interesting.* You wouldn't believe, darling, what that child *knows!* If we ever have a daughter, I'd want her to be like Naomi."

"Not like Sally?"

She was startled at this. She stared at him.

"What a funny thing to say!"

"Look, darling! Once and for all you've got to come clean with me about Sally!"

He was looking into her eyes, dead serious. Eileen was a little frightened.

"Every time I ask about Sally you put me off. When I ask if I might read one of her letters you act as if it were a secret document. What is this fantastic reticence of yours about Sally?"

"Do we have to talk about Sally now? Just now?"

"Yes. We do!"

"Are you still in love with Sally? I always knew it."

"Oh, my God!"

Grant sat down, his head in his hands.

Eileen went on, in a faltering voice.

"You know everything I have — everything I am — everything I know — I owe to Sally. Even — even you — I owe to Sally."

"You can't go on all your life being grateful. You can't make a career of gratitude. It's servile."

He got up, took her in his arms. She was, he saw, on the verge of tears.

"Darling, it's my fault. My fault really. Because I've never told you why I keep asking about Sally. I don't like to talk about my work before I've finished it. It's a kind of superstition. I've been secretive too. Just as secretive as you've been. You think — my constant prodding about Sally — you think it's idle curiosity, morbid, gossip-mongering. It isn't. I really have to know. It's important for me to know."

"Why?"

"Because I'm writing about her, that's why."

She stared at him, incredulous, horrified.

"That's what my play is about. It's about Sally — about Ogden and Sally's mother."

Eileen continued to stare, as if it were an enormity too great to take in.

"Well," he said, "what's wrong with it?" His voice rose. "Why do you look like that? Is it, perhaps, a forbidden subject?"

"Please, Stanley, please don't."

This was something new! Censorship! Censorship at home! He didn't trust himself to say anything. Eileen went on.

"Please, darling! Please! You have so many ideas. You're so creative! Please, darling, write something else!"

Grant saw red. His hand reached for one of the books on the table. He felt like throwing a prophet at Eileen. He knew that if he stayed in the room another second, he would hit her. He walked out quickly and banged the door behind him.

An hour later, Kaetchen picked them up in a hired car to drive them to the wedding. He saw at once that something was wrong; Eileen was pale; it was obvious that she had been crying. Grant was smouldering. "Write something else." How could he be marrying a woman capable of saying that? Kaetchen took the tension between bride and groom in his stride, quiet and cajoling.

"Why did you have to pick just this morning to quarrel?" he said, resting back comfortably between Grant and Eileen. "Why didn't you wait till you are safely married, when it would be perfectly natural?"

Neither of them smiled. Grant held on tightly to his grievance; that little query of Eileen's was branded in his psyche.

Kaetchen, not a bit discouraged by the heavy silence, went on unperturbed.

"I have news for you of another marriage. Stephanie and Ian. Yes, I'm just back from Gastein. Well, this sensational announcement doesn't seem to have created the impression I expected. But doesn't it reassure you? If those two could get married, why not you two? Compared to them you are a normal couple. It was very amusing. Stephanie is exalted. You know her stage ambition has always been to play Jeanne d'Arc. Now, in Gastein, she's playing Jeanne. She feels heroic. She married a man under lock and key, held for a grave charge. And, do you

know, it's having an effect. It may save Ian. They think, these snobbish
police, if this lady, a von, with such a distinguished ancestry, marries
this man, he must be innocent. Surely such a noble lady wouldn't marry
an accused man if there were even a possibility of his being guilty! They
just don't know Stephanie! No doubt it will save Ian. Don't you think
it's amusing?"

If Eileen and Grant thought it amusing they gave no sign.

They had arrived at their destination in one of the narrow, medieval
streets of Salzburg.

Eileen, without moving, found speech at last. Her voice was dry.

"Kaetchen! Tell Stanley he doesn't have to go through with it. It's
not too late. We can turn back right now!"

"I have no intention," said Kaetchen, as if Grant were somewhere
else, "of transmitting an absurd offer like that. You will have to find
yourself another emissary."

Eileen then spoke directly to Grant.

"You don't have to, darling! I mean it. You don't have to! Kaetchen. Ask the driver to take us back."

Without a word, Grant got out of the car and held the door open for
Eileen and Kaetchen to follow him.

Naomi and her parents received them. Naomi had changed into a
dark, flowered dress. She wore black pumps and stockings. She had
made an effort to look dignified but she still gave the impression of
wanting to dance, possibly back into her dirndl. Her parents were a lilli-
putian couple, exactly the same height, a pair of elderly marionettes,
perfectly matched. The rabbi wore a modest black beard; he was vola-
tile and humorous; Grant could see from whom Naomi had inherited
her mercurial quality. Her mother was rotund, spoke not a word of
English, smiled and nodded no matter what was said and conveyed an
impression of general amiability. A velvet canopy had been set up in a
corner of the small living room. In the dining room beyond the table was
set for tea and cakes. The flat was rather dark but shining with tidiness.

Naomi and Eileen embraced. Eileen essayed a little joke about not
having seen Naomi for such a long time. The rabbi treated Grant with
great respect. Grant had noticed on his earlier visit a difference be-

tween the rabbi's reaction to him and that of the German writers he had met. These were deferential (sometimes with an overtone of contempt) because of his glittering, pecuniary American success. But the rabbi's attitude amused and even touched him. Simply by virtue of being a Schriftsteller, a playwright, the rabbi regarded him as a spiritual leader. "As you are a Schriftsteller," the rabbi had said on Grant's earlier visit, "you are yourself a prophet. And you know," he had reminded Grant with a smile, "that is a Jewish specialty — prophecy!"

The rabbi looked forward to seeing Grant's play when Stohl produced it in Germany. Grant thought of his play, a sex-comedy, and he hoped devoutly the rabbi would never see it. If he did, Grant was sure, the rabbi would be less inclined to rank him among the prophets.

"Shall we talk a little?" the rabbi asked. "Or," he smiled at Eileen, "are you impatient?"

"Oh, let's talk a little," said Eileen, who was fighting for composure. They all sat down.

"I suppose you know," Kaetchen said to Eileen, "that your son can never be President of the United States."

"Why not?" demanded Naomi.

"Because he was born in Salzburg. That's the law in America. To be President you have to be born there."

"I think it's a very silly law," said Naomi.

"I wish there were such a law in Germany!" said the rabbi with a wry smile. There was a moment's silence.

"Maybe," said Eileen, "by the time Amos is grown up, they'll have changed the law."

"It's very unlikely," said Kaetchen. "But don't worry about it. There are so many better-paying jobs in America."

"By the way," said Grant, addressing Kaetchen, "as long as you were naming our baby, why did you have to name him after a minor prophet? Why didn't you name him after a major one — Isaiah, say, or Jeremiah?"

The rabbi took issue with this.

"Oh, but Mr. Grant, excuse me! There are no major prophets nor minor ones. This is a matter of reputation. Prophecy is a gift, a quality, a vision. And in this, Amos has no peer. In purity. In purity of vision. He was, you know, the earliest of the prophets."

"What did he stand for?" asked Eileen, who liked things in categories.

"Social righteousness. He was a herdsman, a gatherer of sycamore fruit. He was modest. He told the Lord that he had no gift for prophecy, that he was a simple farmer. But the Lord overcame his scruples. The Lord insisted."

"The Lord's confidence was justified then?" said Grant.

The rabbi looked at him and smiled.

"Yes," he said, "it was justified. The Lord had reason to be proud of him." It was obvious that the rabbi was proud too. He talked about the prophet with affectionate intimacy as of a favorite uncle.

"There is a lovely remark of his," the rabbi went on, "which is, I think, fitting for this occasion."

Eileen leaned forward eagerly.

"What is it, Rabbi?"

" 'Can two walk together, except they be agreed?' "

Eileen's eyes filled with tears.

"That's beautiful," she said. "Stanley, isn't that beautiful?"

"Yes," said Grant. "It is."

"Well," said the rabbi, "perhaps we'd better begin." He smiled at them. "I have to put on my official costume for the occasion."

He got up and went into another room.

Grant looked at Eileen. Her eyes were wet. His abrasive thoughts about her softened. She was very good, very dear, loving. He reached out and took her hand. They sat holding hands. "Write something else." Well, it was a clumsy remark. But how could Eileen be expected to know what his play meant to him, how he was agonizing over it, how tough it was? To her writing was a kind of hobby. Subjects could be picked up at random, like choosing a fruit or a breakfast food from an array in a supermarket. And she was absorbed in higher things. Dante. Jewish history. Was Eileen a highbrow? A wicked definition of the highbrow passed through his mind. In loyalty to Eileen he rejected it. Was it that she was humorless? Poor Eileen! He felt sorry for anyone who had no humor; they were blinded in some way. Well, he would supply it for both of them. He began to feel protective about Eileen. He would shield her, even from the animadversions of his own inner voice.

He looked at Naomi. She was looking at him. She smiled at him, as if to give him courage. He kept looking at her. Surely, there wasn't in the world a more beguiling creature than Naomi! In that bright face were intelligence, quick humor, awareness. Inescapably, the face of René Wolfsohn's French friend merged with Naomi's: they were the same, they were sisters in beauty, in understanding, in shimmering vitality. Should he, at this moment, be marrying, not Eileen, but, and/or Naomi-the-French-girl?

The rabbi returned wearing a white silk skullcap and an enveloping prayer shawl of silk with gold tassels. Everybody stood up. The rabbi draped around Grant's shoulders a lesser shawl, like a scarf, and gave him a black skullcap to put on. They ranged themselves under the canopy, Grant and Eileen on either side of the rabbi. The rabbi opened his prayer book.

"The service I am going to read you," he said, "is in Hebrew. The words you will hear are five thousand years old. For five thousand years they have been spoken to unite in marriage the generations of your ancestors."

He read the service, slowly and clearly. Grant noticed that the lips of the rabbi's wife moved as her husband intoned. She had heard these words so many times. She knew them by heart. Grant remembered the looks of the blocked Hebrew words he had studied when he was a child in Xenia. His father would have known what the rabbi was saying. When his father had been married in Memel — "blistered in Memel" — he had understood these words. Still, the rhythm, the cadence, the faint cantillation revived early memories: restive hours in the Xenia synagogue on the Day of Atonement, his father pacing his room at night invoking protection against the Dark Angel. He had been cradled in this language and yet he couldn't understand a word of it. But the sound, the resonance, the cut the words made in the silence, were deeply evocative. What could they mean to Eileen? Her ancestors had been married in Latin. He stole a look at her. No, she was all attention, her mouth partly open, drinking in the rabbi's recital as if it were from her abandoned God, Dante.

The rabbi brought Grant a glass tumbler wrapped in a napkin. He explained: he must crush the glass with his heel, to symbolize the destruction of the Temple in Jerusalem by the Romans. Grant couldn't help thinking that the rite was grotesquely antiquarian. Contemporary structures were in danger; they were surrounded by an enemy more vindictive than the Romans. He had been reading about synagogues and graveyards vandalized in Germany. A tidal wave was moving toward them and no one to put a finger in the dike. He felt again the terror he had experienced in Stohl's library. But he did as he was told. He crushed.

And then it was over. He embraced Eileen and whispered "I love you" into her ear. Everybody kissed everybody. He found himself kissing Naomi. He held her close. He felt sudden fear for her. What would happen to this enchanting creature under the shadow of the aerie? How could he leave her, unprotected, under the spiky hedge of the Mustache? What if he asked her father to let her go to America with them, where she would be safe? How delicious it would be to travel with Naomi, to show her the wonders of the USA!

They were all marshaled into the dining room for tea, wine and cakes. The rabbi, divested of his accoutrements, toasted the bride and groom. They toasted each other. Grant got a laugh by his little speech to Kaetchen. In this instance, he said, the Shadchen de Luxe had lowered his social standards. There was warmth and gaiety in the little dining room. They toasted peace on earth and good will to men. They wished happiness for each other and for everybody else. Jocularly, Grant proposed to Naomi's parents the wish he had felt a few minutes before, when he held Naomi in his arms, that they let him take her to Hollywood, where he would arrange to get her a screen test. There was a mania for Biblical pictures. Naomi could play Ruth. She was meant by God to play Ruth. Kaetchen explained the proposal to the rabbi's wife in German. She laughed, nodded hearty agreement to the plan.

The party broke up. The Grants were leaving the next day. The rabbi thanked Grant for his generous gift to the Gemeinde, for the poor of Salzburg. They looked forward to reunion. Naomi said Amos must come, when he was grown, to visit his birthplace. This wish Amos's father fervently echoed. He held Naomi's hand in farewell. He knew that he would never see her again.

In the car on the way back, Kaetchen broke the silence.

"Well," he said, "are you happy, at least?"

Grant smiled but didn't say anything. By way of answer Eileen moved a bit closer to her husband. Her face was flushed, her eyes misted. Grant thought she looked beautiful. He had never seen her look like that.

They arrived at the Grants' apartment house and said good-bye on the sidewalk. Kaetchen would be busy with Stohl's affairs and would be unable to go to the station tomorrow to see them off. Grant had taken a house in Beverly Hills. They insisted he come and stay with them. He promised. Eileen kissed him:

"Good-bye, dearest Kaetchen. Thank you for everything."

Schwester opened the door of their flat for them, bobbed and congratulated them. Amos had given her no trouble at all, she reported. They went at once into the baby's room. Amos was in foetal position; on his knees with his head buried in the pillow, fast asleep. Grant wondered how he breathed. They stood in silence, looking at him. Eileen's hand passed over the light fuzz on the infant's head without touching it. Grant looked at her. He saw in her eyes the same look he had seen in the hospital, when the minor prophet had been transparent. Thank God, he was no longer transparent! Grant put his arm around Eileen's shoulder. She looked at him, the same look she had given her baby. They stood in silence, holding each other close. This, after all, Grant thought, is all that matters. The rest, the absurd dalliances of his imagination, were unspeakably trivial. This was the thing. This was all.

Eileen's eyes, shining with love, were on his. Not to wake Amos, she whispered in his ear:

"God bless the three of us."

18. The Recording Angel

Grant had taken two adjoining compartments on the Arlberg Express to Paris, one for Schwester and the baby, one for himself and Eileen. Eileen was in Amos's compartment now, in conference with Schwester. Grant sat at the glass-topped shelf table in his cubicle. He had cleared off the travel folders and resort advertisements and substituted his notebook. He was on his third Scotch and soda. The rhythm of the train was lulling; he stared out of the window in a half doze. The landscape was mountainous and very pretty: multicolored, cozy chalets nestling confidingly under clumps of trees; long, narrow bridal-veil green and white waterfalls edged in spindrift that caught rainbows. The crystal-line ice-iridescence that spumed from the waterfalls seemed to Grant ef-fluvial; it gave off a double glitter that was menacing, mephitic. This picture-book prettiness reminded him for some reason of Schwester's erstwhile boyfriend the barber. That barber epitomized this country to him; he hated it; he was happy to be leaving it. Its beguilements were mantraps. He thought of the nightmarish evening in Stohl's library. Were they sitting there still? What were they waiting for? To be noosed by these wire-thin waterfalls? Grant knew he was drunk. He poured himself another Scotch — the last, he told himself — with an illogical conviction that it would sober him up.

He tried to reconstruct the two months that had elapsed since he had boarded this train in Paris. Could he have known, could he have fore-seen, that he would return on it a married man, a father? Had such an inconceivable fantasy occurred to him then, the bride would have been Stephanie. But this emotion was now so remote that he couldn't be-lieve in its actuality. It was as impossible to bring it back as the pain of a headache or a toothache of a year ago. You remembered it the way you remembered a historical date, a fact, a dead fact. You could re-member attendant circumstances — Stephanie saying matter-of-factly: "Was it all right?" She had said it, that was a dead fact. Even the shame he had felt was gone; he remembered it as you might remember a misadventure you had been told about that had happened to some-body else.

The present moment even — was it capturable? It wasn't, not really. He was waiting. He was waiting for something to happen, for some mo-ment, some reality he could capture, that would revivify him, that he could *experience*. Just now he was marking time. The seconds, the min-utes, passed him by like the trees and the houses and the waterfalls out-side the window.

In the next room was a stranger to whom he was married. He tried to figure her out and failed. She was mysterious. She had some IDEAL in her head and the realization of this appeared to be the essence of her existence. He thought of her enthusiasms since he had known her. First it was Greek mythology, then Dante and now, believe it or not, it was Jewish theology, the Hebrew ethic. Her mind was a lazy Susan which accepted what was put on it. Eileen had had a strict Catholic upbringing; was she really a religieuse? That was it, Grant thought. She should have been a nun. Too bad the Jews didn't have convents, she might have become a Jewish Mother Superior. Grant had to smile. He had explained to Eileen that she must say nothing to anybody in Hollywood about the fact that he was working on a play. He had explained to her that his contract required him to work for the film company exclusively. Eileen had been shocked by this. This was not, she had protested, ethical. It was not honest. Why didn't he wait, resume his play after his contract with the studio had terminated? Grant had temporized. It was a white lie, he said; everybody in Hollywood did it. But for Eileen there were no white lies. There were just lies.

"I have evidently," he had said to her, "married the Recording Angel."

She had kissed him, as if he had paid her a compliment.

To save acrimonious discussion he had also told her that he had dropped the play about Sally and her mother and Ogden and was working on a new idea that had hit him. For this renunciation she had been grateful. She loved him for that. She would never forget it. It occurred to Grant that Eileen loved him in a vacuum. She lived for abstractions in a cloud of abstractions. She admired him and was proud of him for being a writer, but what kind of writer he was or was trying to be she had no notion of, nor was she curious. Large concepts beckoned her, not intimacies, subtleties, gradations. She knew the difference between black and white but to the merging colorations of the spectrum she was impervious. She was color-blind. How easily she had believed he had given up one play and switched to another. All he'd had to do, evidently, was to amble from the avocado counter to the grapefruit counter in the market. How could she be made to realize the importance of this play to him, that a playwright's second play was more important to him than the first? Did he have staying power or was he a one-shot? At twenty-nine Grant lived in terror of declension.

Still he felt a rush of tender feeling for Eileen. She was really so dear — and quite funny, although he wouldn't have wanted anyone else to laugh at her; he would have resented that. She was a child, who had been accosted in the dark by the ogre of culture; she had been raped by culture. It was, moreover, his doing. He had been the rapist of that virginal mind. He had done it by sending her in profusion all those highbrow books — Frazer and Burckhardt — and she had plowed through them in a touching effort to levitate herself to the plateau which she mistakenly supposed him to inhabit. Most of the books he'd sent her he hadn't read himself; he knew what they stood for and how the contributions they had made were regarded but that was about all; in the milieu in which he moved people read little more than current novels. How could he possibly expect her to understand these things, or the subtle and maddening problems presented by his work and the fierce competitiveness of his métier? It was unreasonable. He would have to teach her. It would be amusing, wouldn't it, to teach her, to indoctrinate her in the actualities of life, with its halftones and com- promises and complexities? He would have to do it, he saw, slowly, gradually. He would have to be patient. But what fun! To transmute the nun into a woman of the world, to show her that you couldn't sur- vive by ethical maxims. He had to initiate her into the twilight zone of compromise. He had to teach her not to probe the motives of conduct too deeply, not to hunt them out of their lairs into the light of day. He had to undo a fixed code.

He looked at his notebook. He found himself confronted with the eternal query: "Sally? Motive? Define Sally. Get Sally."

He leaned back against the compartment wall, passing his hand over his face as if dry-washing it. That Sally! The enigma of Sally! The most desirable girl in the world, surely. Thinking back on the summer he met her he began to feel resentment. She had used him. She had fobbed off Eileen on him in order to get the leisure and the privacy to . . . Of course! How stupid he had been not to see it before. So simple, so clear, so all-embracing, so obvious. The invisibility of the obvious — that's why he hadn't seen it before. He leaned over his note- book and began writing at breakneck speed. The illumination he had just been blinded by revealed everything — not only for his play but the mystery of Eileen's secretiveness. Of course! Of course!

What he saw was that Eileen had been Sally's go-between, her co- conspirator, her accomplice. Didn't that clear up everything? No wonder she wouldn't talk about Sally. She was ashamed of what she had done, must keep it secret at all costs. She had been the intermediary between Sally and Ogden. No wonder she had been upset when Grant told her he was writing a play about this unsavory collusion. No wonder she had begged him to give it up. No wonder she had said: "Write something else." No wonder she had been so relieved and almost tearfully grateful when he had told her he was giving up the play. Well, he wouldn't give it up. He was, in fact, now able to finish it. Another dimension. Another character. Eileen! Yes, he would introduce Eileen. Oh, he would disguise her so that she would never recognize herself; he would make the go-between much older, a spinster schoolteacher who had made a pet of Sally. And what if she did recognize herself! Serve her damn well right! He resented them both — Eileen *and* Sally. He had served as a cover for them beneath which Ogden and Sally could carry on their unholy affair. "Is it ethical?" That was what Eileen had asked him when he told her that he was going to write his play on studio time. Well, was what she had done ethical? She was not so noble then, Eileen. Not by half. She was Mrs. Tartuffe!

Grant was bent over his notebook, giving vent, in a burst of creative fury, to his newly found grievance against Sally and against Eileen. Mrs. Tartuffe, blissfully unaware, pushed the door open, came to him, put her arms around him and kissed him. She was radiant with happiness, fragrant.

"Come and say good night to Amos, darling. He's the most wonderful traveler. He's in a wonderful mood. Come in and see. Have you been working well, darling? Come!"

Somewhat unsteadily, Grant got up and followed Eileen into the corridor and into the next compartment. The berths were made up; Amos was bedded in the lower one. Schwester was sitting beside him bent over him. Amos was exploring her face with his fingers.

"Here's Daddy come to say good night to you," said Eileen.

Amos stared at Grant wonderingly. His eyes were large and blue.

"He has blue eyes," said Grant. "Where does he get those from?"

"They will change," said Schwester.

Schwester got up from the berth to make room for Grant. Grant sat beside his son.

"How does she know they will change?"

"She knows. They're often blue in the beginning."

Amos continued to stare at his father. It was a look neither hostile nor friendly, simple query. He began to explore his father's face.

"I don't think he likes my looks," said Grant. "Well, neither do I!" Eileen laughed.

"He's just getting acquainted. After all, he hasn't seen much of you, has he? Schwester and I have monopolized him, haven't we?"

She smiled at Schwester.

"Shall we give Mr. Grant more time with him, Schwester? Does he deserve it, do you think?"

"Why not?" said Schwester.

Amos continued his unblinking stare. He made a face which looked like a smile. Eileen was delighted.

"Is he laughing with me or at me?" Grant inquired.

"He knows you're funny," said Eileen. "He knows you write comedies."

"That's more than I know," said Grant.

Outside in the corridor, the dinner bell rang for the first sitting in the dining car.

"We must go in to dinner, darling."

"What about Schwester?"

"She's on the second."

Grant followed Eileen out of the compartment. They shook themselves down the lurching corridor to the restaurant car. Once seated Grant ordered a Scotch and soda.

The waiter brought a tray of hors d'oeuvres but Grant didn't take any.

"Do take some, darling. They're delicious."

"This'll do me. It's nourishing."

"You seem to drink an awful lot. You usedn't to, did you? In Blue Hill, even in New York, I don't remember that you drank much."

"I'm celebrating."

"What?"

"A discovery."

"What about?"

"If you want me to tell you, I'll tell you. You won't enjoy it much."

She looked at him, startled.

"Are you angry about something? Have I done anything?"

"I am angry at myself. At my stupidity."

"Tell me what I've done."

"It was silly of me to keep asking you to help me on my play. To keep dunning you — about Sally, about Ogden. It was stupid of me — when the truth is so obvious."

"But you've given up this play."

"I have not. On the contrary — I now see my way clear to finish it."

"But you told me you'd given it up."

"I lied. I never had any intention of giving it up."

"Why? Why did you lie?"

"To spare ourselves nasty scenes, such as we had on our wedding morning."

"But you didn't have to lie. You could have told me. You're the master of your own life, aren't you? You can do what you like. Why do you have to lie — in order to do what you like?"

"There are many varieties of lying. One way is by keeping quiet — in order to conceal a lie."

Eileen stopped eating. There were tears in her eyes. "She cries easily," Grant thought, with a certain vindictiveness.

"It's an easy way to get the last word — by crying."

"It just seems terrible to me — to start our marriage with a lie."

Grant was irritated.

"There is also — as I just pointed out — the lie of silence."

"I don't know what you mean."

"Working in there just now, I saw the whole thing. You were the go-between — in Maine and in Cleveland — between Sally and Dr. Ogden. Sally's mother engaged you, didn't she, to be Sally's companion? You betrayed poor Mrs. Frobisher. Is that honest? To use your own favorite word — is that ethical?"

She brushed her eyes. She gave him a clear look, as if she were seeing him for the first time. He met her gaze truculently. While he was looking at her he knew, utterly, that the theory he had concocted was false. Then why didn't she deny it? The fact that she didn't drove him crazy. He heard himself saying the opposite of what he knew to be true.

"Your silence — your avoiding it — only proves that what I am accusing you of is true."

He was bitterly disappointed. He had wanted his accusation to be true, to have a justifiable grievance.

"If we are going to lie to each other — if we are going to evade each other with lies — then there is no use — is there really — any use . . . ?"

She broke off. She tried to make a show of eating. She gave it up.

"If that's the way it's going to be — it's a flop then, isn't it — our marriage?"

She looked at him again. Her eyes were tragic, contemplating the ruins. He felt pity for her; he was moved by her. At the same time he resented her for toppling his theory, for extinguishing his illumination and, moreover, without a word of denial.

"The truth is, my dearest, you are totally unrealistic. You haven't an inkling about the facts of life."

"It's what the rabbi said — it's what your own prophet said . . ."

"I don't feel possessive about our prophets!"

"Don't you remember? He said, the prophet Amos said: 'Can two walk together, except they be agreed?' "

"I'm not religious, darling."

"You believe in God, don't you?"

"Not in the least. The very mention of the word revolts me. By your own standard — God is extremely unethical."

The vehemence of his blasphemy terrified her. She looked at him, frightened. She clung to a spar.

"You don't mean that. You've been drinking. Otherwise you wouldn't . . ."

"Drinking has nothing to do with it. I tell you, darling, you're unrealistic. You won't face facts."

The dinner bell rang for the second sitting. It was a relief.

Back in his compartment with his notebook Grant was convinced that Eileen had not been an accomplice between Sally and Ogden. But what difference did that make as far as his play was concerned? He was a creator, wasn't he? He would create his own facts. They would become facts simply by virtue of his having stated them in his fiction. The theory he had evolved made sense. He could make an audience believe it. Life might be senseless but a play mustn't be. He went on scribbling until, through the partition, he heard that Schwester had come back. He undressed and got into his pajamas. He poured himself another drink and lay down on the made-up lower berth waiting for Eileen. He remodeled his grievance against her, building it up, nursing it. She was stubborn, mulishly stubborn. He would pulverize that stubbornness. He had never been up against anyone like her. He had thought he understood her; he hadn't in the least. Simple and devoted, unquestioning and loyal: that is how he had pigeonholed her. She was, it turned out, full of ambiguities; her loyalty was divided, between himself and some absurd and chimerical ideal she waved about like a banner. She was a fanatic for First Principles. She had no seconds, no thirds. She was a primitive. It was extraordinary — her behavior at dinner. She hadn't even bothered to deny his allegation against her. All she clung to was the fact that he had lied. How deftly she had converted him, the plaintiff, into the accused! She was, beyond words, tactless. "Write something else." Tactlessness certainly couldn't go beyond that. As his grievance against her mounted, so did his desire for her. What the devil was she doing inside there anyway? Schwester was back, the baby was all right, what was holding her up, why the devil didn't she come in? She was stubborn, all right; he would break that stubbornness. He was infuriated by her not coming in. He called her name and rapped on the wall of the compartment. The noise of the train, he realized, blanketed that out. He had never before so wanted her; she had become acridly desirable to him. He would break that stubbornness.

Eileen came in and began methodically to fit the chain lock into its slot. He got up and seized her.

"Just let me finish this."

He didn't let her finish it. As she submitted to him she laughed — an infuriating little laugh.

The little laugh said: "Why so ferocious — when you have nothing to conquer?"

But he did have something to conquer. He knew that if he didn't, her existence would be a threat to his own.

The next afternoon, in Paris, the Grants and Schwester boarded the boat train for Le Havre to catch the *Normandie*. "No verandah this time," Grant thought grimly when he saw the proud majesty of the liner looming up over the pier. As they walked to the passport office he saw again *Der Stürmer* on sale at a newsstand. He took in the cover.

Later edition; same theme. Mr. Streicher had, evidently, only one string to his bow. He kept twanging it. It was a female this time — a whorehouse madame — luring guileless Aryans into her lair. She was so repulsive she couldn't have done much business, Grant thought. Suddenly he remembered Naomi, slim, spritelike, Ariel in *The Tempest*. He felt a throb of anxiety for Naomi. He should have taken her away.

Grant didn't buy *Der Stürmer* this time, but he saw that several of his fellow passengers did. For boat-deck reading, he imagined.

2
Hollywood — New York

19. At Romanoff's

No sooner were the Grants and Schwester settled in their Spanish-Gothic villa on Coldwater Canyon in Beverly Hills than Eileen received word that her mother was gravely ill in Cleveland. Grant made a half-hearted offer to accompany her, but Eileen wouldn't hear of it. He must stay so that he could report to her on Amos. She trusted Schwester but it would reassure her more than anything to hear from him that everything was all right. She knew that he had to report to the studio. She wouldn't even let him drive her to the airport. Sally would do that. Sally had left Santa Barbara and was in town at the Beverly Wilshire. He must be nice to Sally. He must take her to dinner and introduce her to his glamorous friends in the film colony. She left, promising to telephone from Cleveland. Grant did as he was told. He telephoned Sally and invited her to dinner that night at Romanoff's.

At eight o'clock, in considerable excitement, Grant passed through the great doors of Mike Romanoff's restaurant, the meetingplace of the Hollywood elite. The massive and portentous front door was flanked by Imperial seals, embossed in bronze: truculent eagles, spouting sheaves of crossed spears, topped by the jewel-infested Czarist crown. It was Mike Romanoff's little tribute to his lost relatives. He found Sally waiting for him in the colonnaded circular lobby. She greeted him with cool warmth. At the same moment, the proprietor himself, the legendary Mike, came up to welcome Grant. Mike was diminutive, jaunty, impeccably dressed. He spoke approximate English in a gravelly bass. For a member of a dour and taciturn family, he was remarkably jolly. Grant told Mike that on a barge on a Salzburg lake, he had sat next to his aunt, the Grand Duchess Marie. He included Sally in this reminiscence. Sally nodded, yes, she remembered very well. But Mike did not respond with any family feeling. Perhaps he didn't like his aunt. Or perhaps she had just missed being his aunt.

The headwaiter, a pal of Grant's, showed them to their table. Grant felt happy. He was on home ground. For once, he felt free and easy with Sally; he chattered in his most amusing vein. But he had the feeling, which he always got from Sally, that she was thinking of something else. Fortunately, at that moment Hugo Stift came up to say hello to Grant. This was a windfall. Grant was delighted; he adored Stift and was flattered. Stift was the wittiest director in Hollywood and Sally must be impressed at the warmth of his greeting. He introduced Sally and insisted that he sit with them for a minute. Grant drew up a chair for him. Stift sat by Sally. Stift was little, Sally was tall. He beamed up approvingly at her. He sized her up at once: a "society girl."

Stift was swarthy; he had smooth, jet black hair, slicked down over his forehead, and great brown eyes, warm and lively. He smoked a huge cigar and spoke with a heavy German accent. His r's rolled out like heavy artillery. He took Sally in, more and more approving. He was used to taking girls in, imagining how they would look on the screen.

"You live here?"

"No," said Sally. "Just a visitor."

"You come to make a screen test?"

"Not at all."

Stift was delighted at the surprising absence in Sally of ambition.

"Torrific!" He addressed Stanley. "A girl so photogenique and don't want a screen test! Torrific!"

"Miss Frobisher," Grant explained, "is a civilian."

"So?"

Stift edged his chair up a little closer to Sally's. He smiled up at her; Sally smiled back.

"You're relieved, aren't you?" she said. "It must be tiresome for you — all those girls wanting screen tests."

"I would like," he said roguishly, "to have a severre friendship wiz you."

Sally was amused.

"I'd love it," she said. "The severer the better!"

Stift took his cigar out of his mouth. He spoke to Grant as if Sally weren't there.

"But she's nice!" he said, as if that were too much for anyone to expect. "She is vorry nice!"

Grant took the compliment graciously.

"Do you think I'd waste your time on a girl who wasn't nice? Why don't you invite us to dinner?" He explained to Sally:

"Mr. Stift has a beautiful house in Brentwood."

For a moment Stift's eyes went into mourning.

"Ah, but Stanley, you don't hear? This lovely house is no longer with me. You don't hear?"

Grant explained that he'd been in Europe.

"No more. It is now with Sandra. I am now back in Beverly Wilshire."

As he sensed a routine forming, his eyes went out of mourning.

"You know how it is here — vot happens. You come to Hollywood. You stay Beverly Wilshire. You fall in love. Vonderrful! You marry. You build beautiful house. Vonderrful! Then — it all goes, the vonderrful. Divorce. Wife, natural, gets the house. You go back Beverly Wilshire. So now I am in Beverly Wilshire."

"So is Sally."

"Vonderrful! In Europe, Stanley, where you were?"

"Salzburg."

Stift's eyes widened.

"So? Salzburg. You saw then Rudolph Stohl?"

"I certainly did. He gave a party for me."

"So? And how is he? You and Stohl — that is good. You got on well together, no?"

"He's irresistible. Enormous charm."

"Ah! Charm. In this he has monopoly. Also, he is genius. He starrted me. I was actor in his company in Berlin."

"Were you? I didn't know that."

"All of us here from Germany he starrted."

Stift now edged his chair closer to Grant.

"For Stohl I am starrting here conspiracy. I want your help, Stanley. Vorry much."

"What sort of conspiracy?"

"I don't like how things look over there. Bad! Vorry bad! Not too long Stohl's theaters in Berlin will be confiscate. Kaput! Before it happens I vant he should come here. Make here a film. I spoke to Lichtman. Lichtman tells me how vonderrful business is all over the vorrld. He is amusing man, sometimes, Lichtman. 'Hugo,' he say to me, 'business is so big even the good pictures make money.' So I say to him why you don't bring here Rudolph Stohl? He makes you good picture, great picture. Vot you think, Stanley, it would be vonderrful, no?"

"It certainly would be. What did Lichtman say?"

" 'Hugo,' he say, 'you are a vorry dangerous man.' But he listened. I think I made impression."

"Of course, I'll help you any way I can."

"He thinks vorry high of you, Lichtman. Together, we make propaganda to bring Stohl here. Yes?"

Grant stole a look at Sally. Was she impressed that Lichtman thought highly of him? He thought he'd better explain.

"Mr. Lichtman," he said to Sally, "is a big tycoon here, one of the biggest."

Sally absorbed this.

"Excuse us," Stift said to Sally, "that we talk shop."

"I love conspiracies," said Sally.

Grant questioned Stift.

"What could Stohl do here?"

Stift made a gesture embracing the universe.

"Anything! Anything in the vorrld. Shakespeare! Why not Shakespeare? After all, he is playwright too. So many millions they make why not invest, for vunce, in Shakespeare? They should let Stohl make what he has already made so marvelous in Europe. *Midsummer Night's Dream*. Why not? *Danton's Tod*. Why not? It could shine out, light up entirre industry. Perhaps, even, it transforms industry. Possible? No? Overnight, industry becomes art. They have it both ways."

Stift's enthusiasm was contagious. Grant caught it.

"It would be marvelous. I'll do everything I can. Will Stohl come, do you think?"

"Soon he will have no choice. These Gerrmans . . ."

Stift's expression darkened. He became gloomy.

"I agree with you," said Grant. "I felt it when I was there. But *they* don't seem to feel it, Stohl and the rest. Somehow, they think things will get better."

Stift shook his head.

"They are mistaken. They will not get better. They will get vorrse. But people believe what they vant believe."

For a moment Stift was silent. Then his eyes brightened. He turned to Sally.

"I remember, Miss Sally, as an example of this, how people insist to believe what they vant. During First World War I am comedian in musical comedy in Berlin. We have great patriotic second act curtain. I sing how Germany is always victorious, how we win every war, and so is inevitable we win this one. Behind me marches triumphal the chorus, half undressed, half military. Then one day is clear we are not winning, we're losing. I say to manager: 'We must get different second act curtain!' He say no this is curtain, curtain will come true. So I keep on every night singing how we win and every minute we are losing. The brave chorus marches triumphant into defeat."

A man waved to Stift from the door of the restaurant. Stift waved back. He got up, kissed Sally's hand.

"So, now I must go. It is my lawyer. He tell me how bad off I am. For this I buy him dinner. Good-bye, Miss Sally. Is vonderrful. You, Stanley, I see in studio. We lunch in commissary and make conspiracy."

He left them to join his lawyer.

"Well, Sally," Grant said, "didn't you like *him?*"

"Very much. He's sweet."

"His concern for Stohl, his loyalty . . ."

"Do you think it will succeed — the conspiracy?"

"Unlikely. It's very hard here to get them to try something new. They're doing so well with what they are doing. They think — why trifle with our luck? Still, Stift has great influence."

"So evidently have you."

Grant flushed with pleasure. So it *had* registered!

"Not compared to Hugo," he said modestly. "Do you know his pictures?"

"I think so. He did a Chevalier one, didn't he?"

Grant was let down by this. He was irritated. She was too offhand about greatness. It was as if she had said she thought, but couldn't be quite sure, that she had read *Hamlet.* He began to rhapsodize.

"But Hugo Stift is a genius! He's the only director who has a signature. You know it's a Stift picture even before it starts. I'm thinking of writing a piece on him. I'll call it 'The Touch.' I'm going to run all his films and list the things that he does that no other director would think of doing. He's a genius. A darling besides — one of the kindest men in the world."

"I liked him very much," said Sally as she studied the menu.

"Would you like to see some of his films with me — in the projection room?"

"I'm afraid I won't be here. I'm leaving tomorrow."

"For where?"

"I'm not quite sure yet."

Grant was frustrated. It was impossible to ignite Sally. She seemed immune to temptation, even of a projection room. Most girls loved to see films in projection rooms. The waiter came over and they ordered dinner. Sally didn't want wine. There was no joie de vivre in Sally.

Grant chattered on. He told anecdote after anecdote revealing the grotesqueries of life in the film colony. They were well-greased anecdotes, tried and tested. But he could see that they were wasted on Sally. As he felt himself failing, he accelerated his tempo. He knew that he was talking too much but he couldn't stop.

Finally, in the kindest way, Sally said:

"You know, Stanley, you don't have to entertain me. I don't have to be amused. I like you very much as you are, I always have."

The geyser was quenched. Grant wanted to run away. He wanted to go back to his room in Coldwater Canyon to work on his play. He would revenge himself on Sally in that. He hated her. He wanted to kill her.

A silence fell. Sally broke it.

"Eileen tells me you are very curious about me. What do you want to know? I'll tell you anything you want to know."

He looked at her, smouldering. His question came out of hatred.

"Yes," he said, "there is something I want to know."

"What is it?"

"Are you sleeping with Dr. Kenneth Ogden?"

His intention was to be brutal, but Sally answered as if he had asked her whether she had seen the last Garbo film.

"No," she said, "I'm not."

"Not ever? Did you leave him with Mary?"

"No. He's gone."

"Where to?"

"I don't know."

"What broke it up?"

"I did. I planned to do it. I did it."

He looked at her. She was spooning up ice cream. He reflected that even when she was frank, she was inscrutable.

"Well," he said, "if that's what you wanted, if that has been your mission and if you accomplished it, you must be happy."

"Happiness doesn't enter into it. It was something I had to do. Anyway, there are no victories. No complete victories."

"No?"

"Mary hates me. She hates me for freeing her. That's why I never told my mother. I struggled and struggled with the temptation to tell mother, to reveal to her what Ogden is. But there was so little time left to her. I couldn't bear it — the thought that she would die, hating me."

"So you never told her?"

"I never told her."

"But you didn't mind making Mary unhappy?"

"I told you — there are no total victories."

"Your hatred of Ogden — your desire for revenge — overrode every other consideration, didn't it?"

She met his eyes.

"Yes," she said, "it did."

Grant had ordered liqueurs. They sat sipping them.

This girl, Grant thought — this *child* — is obsessed, fanatical.

The child broke in on his reflections about her.

"You knew my mother, didn't you?"

"Yes. I met her once at a concert. Eileen introduced me."

"Did you realize — how exquisite she was?"

"She was lovely. She had the same shallow hollows in her temples that you have."

"Her mind was exquisite too. Her sensibilities were exquisite. She was not for this world. She was for another world than this."

Sally's voice dimmed off. He was touched by her. He put his hand on hers.

"Well, yes, your mother was lovely. But she's dead. Nothing can be done about that. Whatever harm Ogden did her, it's over and done with. Darling, haven't you got anything better to do than chase after Ogden?" He laughed. "Sweet, you don't want to be like Ahab and the White Whale, do you?"

"Ahab had to. I had to."

He stared at her.

"Does Ogden symbolize evil to you?"

"In a way."

"But that's just plain silly. You overestimate Ogden. You take him at his own valuation. He's just a physically magnetic, half-baked and half-educated charlatan, trying to get along the best way he knows how — through his phallus. That's what he is — a traveling salesman of the phallus. That's his banner; he waves it about. Good line. Steady demand. To symbolize him as you do is the silliest goddamn nonsense I ever heard of. How silly can you get!"

He was conscious of a pleasurable excitement in flagellating her.

"I've said most of that to myself."

"But it hasn't stopped you!"

"Would you mind taking me to your house for a few minutes? I'd like a peep at Amos."

Grant pushed his chair back.

"Certainly," he said. "Delighted."

As they left the restaurant, Stift waved to them, grinning broadly. He blew a kiss to Sally. They drove to Coldwater Canyon in a shiny Tanner Cadillac limousine which Grant had rented for the evening.

In the car they sat in silence for a while. Grant broke the silence.

"Very strange it seems to me now — this summer in Salzburg. Isn't it to you? Like a dream it seems, a chimera. Does it to you?"

"I know what you mean."

"I'm sorry you couldn't have been at my wedding. It was sweet. The rabbi and his family — the rabbi's daughter, Naomi, an enchanting creature. Like quicksilver. I wish you could have been there. I thought of you and wanted you there."

"I wish I could have been. I sent you a cable."

"I got it."

He remembered how her cable had disturbed him. He went on:

"I wonder what they're all doing? Naomi — I wonder what she's doing. I had an awful feeling, you know, all the time I was there, that they're all sitting there, immobile, frozen, waiting for the executioner. While they wait they go to plays and concerts and discuss books. Why don't they *do* something?"

"What can they do?"

"Run away. Run. Flee."

"Was Stephanie at your wedding?"

"No. She was in Bad Gastein getting Ian Leith out of jail. You know, don't you, that she married Ian?"

"Yes. Eileen wrote me."

"She married him in jail. Jeanne d'Arc act, Kaetchen says."

"You know him well, don't you, Stephanie's husband?"

"Fairly well."

"Is he the right kind of homosexual?"

"What an odd question!"

"Why?"

"Well, it's like asking — of me, for instance — whether I'm the right kind of heterosexual. Or of Ogden. You would say not — of Ogden anyway. I hope you'd do better by me. They're people, artists and imbeciles, saints and sinners, just like the rest of us."

"That's what I asked, which is Ian?"

"He's charming, very amusing and I think kind. I like him very much. But you know him. What do you think?"

"He will murder Stephanie."

Grant felt a chill. He stared at her.

"My God, Sally, you're hipped in some way. You're hipped on evil. You're an evilmonger. Are you stuck on demonism? We're not living in the Middle Ages, you know?"

"Have we advanced?"

"You ought to see a psychiatrist."

"Do you think so?"

The car crunched softly into the driveway of Grant's villa. Grant handed Sally out of the car.

"Would you ask the driver to wait for a few minutes? To drive me back to the hotel?"

"Of course."

Grant spoke to the driver and led Sally into the house. From the bottom of the stairs he called up to Schwester. Sally ran up. Schwester appeared. She bobbed to Sally. They disappeared down the hall.

Grant walked into the living room and switched on the light. It was a long, oblong room with bilious yellow walls of puckered stucco. Grant had never really looked at the room before; he did now and realized that it was ugly. He moved to the bar in the corner and poured himself a drink. He was thinking hard about Sally, analyzing Sally. Why, she was a case! He had, all this time, been in love with a nut. Of course, she believed that Ogden had killed her mother. But still . . . she hadn't told him the truth, not the whole truth, he was convinced of that. As he thought, he felt a rising fury against Sally. He too wanted revenge! Drink in hand, he began to pace the room. A curtain lifted; he saw, in clarity, still another version of the events of that summer. Why he himself had been nothing but a cog — a miserable . . . From upstairs he heard Sally saying good-bye to Schwester and her light footsteps as she came down. When she came back into the room her eyes were shining.

"Oh, Stanley, what a darling Amos is! He was asleep, of course, but I just barely touched his hand, and his fingers opened and held mine. And Schwester — how lucky you are — she's angelic. She loves it here. It's like Italy, she says. Then I found out she's never been in Italy — only postcards . . . Why, Stanley! What's the matter?"

He was staring at her. He was livid.

"I've been thinking."

"What about?"

"This summer. About what happened this summer."

"It was eventful."

Grant put his glass down on a table.

"When you came to Salzburg this summer — when you wrote me that letter?"

"Well?"

"About Eileen. That she was pregnant . . ."

"Well?"

He came close to her, stood almost touching her.

"Did you know — when you wrote that letter — that Ogden was in Salzburg?"

"I did."

"Did you know that he was living with Mary?"

"Yes. Ogden kept writing me."

"Two birds with one stone, eh? Double objective?"

"I don't see at all that one thing affects the other."

"Don't you?"

"Not in the least. I wrote you the simple facts about Eileen. You could have refused to have her come. You chose not to."

"I asked her to come because I wanted to see you!"

"That's an aberration of *yours*, isn't it? You can't really blame me for that, can you? I never encouraged you."

"You never encouraged me because you were in love with Ogden."

"If it makes you feel better to believe that — well, indulge yourself. The truth is, Stanley . . ."

He became abject, pitiful.

"Dearest Sally, I love you. I adore you, from the first moment I — "

"The truth is, dear Stanley, you're spoiled. Talented people are always spoiled."

"You knew it, didn't you, in Blue Hill — you knew it, how I longed for you."

"I did the best I could for you. I provided you . . ."

"You forced Eileen on me."

"Are you so weak?"

He was trembling with rage. He seized her by the shoulders. He held her fiercely close. He began forcing her to the sofa.

"Are you going to rape me, Stanley?"

He let her go.

"You're horrible. You're a monster. I loathe you."

"You don't. Not really. And I am very fond of you. I'm afraid I have to go now. I have to be up early to make a plane."

She started for the hall. Grant held the front door open for her.

"Good night, dear Stanley. You're lucky, you know — you'll come to see it — to have Eileen, to have Amos."

"I never want to see you again."

She smiled.

"That can be arranged. As I say, my dear, you're spoiled."

She walked to the car. The chauffeur jumped out, held the door open for her and went back to his place behind the wheel.

Through the open window Grant spoke to her.

"Why don't you face the truth about yourself? You're in love with Ogden. If you haven't slept with him, you want to. Might clear things up for you if you did."

She spoke to the chauffeur.

"One second please."

She opened her bag, took out a letter. She handed it to Grant through the window.

"Here. A letter from my beloved. I meant to show it to Mary. I never did. I didn't have to. Read it — and please, after you've read it, burn it. Good-bye, dear Stanley. Bless you."

She rolled up the window. The car moved off. Grant stood in the driveway, holding the letter in his hand. He watched the car till it disappeared.

It had become chilly. Grant was shivering. "It gets so damn cold at night here in this beastly climate," he thought. He walked back into the living room and poured himself a drink to warm up. He sat in an overstuffed chair, under a lamp, Sally's letter in his hand. He was shaking — he'd caught a chill, no doubt about it.

He read the letter.

You dirty little tease. I waited two hours for you. What are you trying to prove? Are you trying to get evidence to show Mary? Well, here it is. Show her this. I don't give a good goddamn about Mary and I thank you for getting me rid of her. It'll be a great relief to me just as it was with your mother. I despise you. And I tell you this, you phony-spiritual little bitch, honey, the next time I make a date to lay you, you'll goddamn well ask for it.

Your somewhat exercised but adoring,

Kenneth

Grant read and reread the letter. "I despise you." He had just said: "I loathe you." They were alike, he and Ogden — two of a kind. As he studied the letter, he found something admirable in it — a man strong enough to burn his bridges. Then Grant remembered — it was so long since he had worked on his play, but now he remembered that his Ogden had done what he himself had decided, in Salzburg, to make him do.

At this recollection he felt a glow of satisfaction, of reassurance. Life, he reflected, imitates art. His intuition had been sound.

He sat in the chair for a long time, transfixed, memorizing the letter. Sally had asked him to burn it. Should he burn it? He couldn't. He couldn't possibly. It was a DOCUMENT! Should he put it into his play, as Grant's favorite writer, Proust, put everything that ever happened to him into his novel?

But Sally, Sally? Her faced hovered between him and Ogden's scrawl. She was a child, an adorable child, with everything to live for. She should be playing tennis at the Yatcht Club, going to dances, falling in and out of love. Instead she was obsessed, manic, pursuing the White Whale like Ahab. She had actually thought of herself in connection with Ahab. And then another thought struck him. Eileen — Eileen and Sally. It seemed to him that he understood now what it was that held Eileen and Sally so close together, what their bond was, what it was that was at the heart of their friendship. They were both cloudstruck by abstractions, both driven in pursuit of abstractions — the abstraction of Evil, the abstraction of Good.

A sound came to him from upstairs. Amos was crying — a faint pitiful wail. What, at the moment, was Amos's obsession? Well, Grant thought, whatever it was, Schwester would allay it. He sat and sat, thinking. Was everyone obsessed, driven from cradle to grave, seeking what was not to be found? Was this the life force? Was everyone, in one way or another, in the naked interstices, between the demands of practical obligation, but at the core, under the burning glass?

He went upstairs to his study to copy Ogden's letter into his notebook.

20. Costume Jewelry

Alexander Löwe lived in two worlds, the world of the internationally famous, naturally, but he was also a kind of Haroun-al-Raschid in another world, the world of the anonymous. His specialty, of course, the cause closest to his heart, was to marry off the sons of the great Central

European men of genius. These men now, under the shadow of the Mustache, were in duress themselves, since their works were combustible. The sons were in even worse case. They bore great names and staggered under the weight of them. By marrying them off well, Löwe made it possible for them to throw off the intolerable burden of trying to emulate their elders. He had once said to a friend that by inseminating the American upper classes with the genes of genius, he was single-handedly raising the cultural level in the USA. When the friend suggested that the sons of genius did not necessarily inherit the genius, Löwe tossed it off by saying that he left that to the geneticists.

In his other world, the world of the anonymous, Löwe also gave a great deal of time and thought to relieving the privations of such of its members as were lucky enough to fall into his path. For the proprietress of a small Viennese restaurant who found her windows smashed one morning and swastikaed messages under her door, he got a job as cook with a modestly prosperous New York businessman of his acquaintance. He provided translators to publishing houses, bilingual secretaries to export and import houses, got odd jobs as waitresses, governesses, companions to the elderly and nurses for infants for all sorts of refugees who had had other backgrounds in their European lives but who were adaptable. A modest scholar who had spent his life revivifying the Etruscans became a dishwasher in Löwe's favorite New York restaurant; for a minor journalist he got a job as room clerk in his hotel, the Ambassador, where he lived in a single bedroom. He busied himself with the business of getting visas, work permits. He became a one-man adjunct, incessant and unpaid, to HIAS, the organization established to get refugees out from under the coming holocaust in Europe. He farmed out children whose parents he knew to families of the upper crust world in England, Mexico, New York and California. Löwe quietly boasted that, in this emergency, not one of his upper crust friends refused him. The great world in which he moved did not know about his other world, except when he was forced to bring it to its attention by requests for jobs, help to get visas, provide cash for crying necessities. He got money, for example, to set up Miss Dannfeld, who had worked at a jeweler's in Innsbruck, in a tiny shop on East 13th Street, where she sold costume jewelry of her own design. The costume jewelry was ugly but Löwe kept buying and buying it, sending it as Christmas presents to his effulgent ladies. They became known as Löwes even to Löwe. He would reproach one of his luncheon guests: "You're not wearing your Löwe today!" "I'll buy them," she replied, "as many as you like, but I won't wear them!" To which Löwe cited the example of his Egeria in London who had become, in some sort, an agent for Miss Dannfeld's handiwork. She not only bought it to give to her friends but blazoned it herself. When a friend teased her about its ugliness, she replied that it was to help one of Kaetchen's hapless protégées and she made her friend see, behind the vulgar configuration of the ornament, an Image of Compassion . . . Then the London ladies, too, ordered it, wore it, became compassionate.

Of course Löwe sent several dozens each right away to Eileen and to Mary in California. They now became Miss Dannfeld's salesladies. Löwes rode the bosoms of the friends of both in Beverly Hills and Santa Barbara. For a while, nourished by these stimuli, Miss Dannfeld's little boutique flourished. But it didn't, it couldn't last. The uninstructed public, who didn't know Löwe, who didn't see the Image, but saw only the costume jewelry, stayed away from Miss Dannfeld's shop and the day came when it had to close. Löwe promptly got Miss Dannfeld, a spinster of sixty, employment with another spinster of his acquaintance who was eighty and very rich. Miss Dannfeld became her companion and sat in her box every Wednesday night at the opera. Very often the older spinster felt too feeble to go and Miss Dannfeld became a patroness who was able to invite her music-loving friends to her box at the opera. Of course the first time it happened she invited Löwe. This was a mistake. He had, he explained, to undergo these tortures in Salzburg, for diplomatic reasons, but, thank God, not in this blessed New York.

The moment Löwe heard that Mary Kennicott and Dr. Ogden had come to the parting of the ways — Mary had telephoned him daily to beg him to come to Santa Barbara — his mind became active. There was an opening, there was a job vacant, there was young Federn. Who in the world was so admirably qualified to succeed Dr. Ogden as head of Mary's clinic as the brilliant young intern from Vienna? True, Federn hadn't achieved this internship yet, but that was for extraneous reasons. In the normal course of things — had his father not written a play which irritated the Catholic medical hierarchy in Vienna, were

there not a pipeline from the aerie above Salzburg transmitting preju-
dicial sentiments that made even the elder Federn insecure — his son
would even now undoubtedly be an intern in Vienna. For his present,
exiguous purpose Löwe felt justified in erasing the extraneous reasons.
He felt, too, that he could advance Federn's cause more strongly with
Mary if there were competition for his services. He telephoned his
friend Dr. Leo Binder for an appointment. Dr. Binder was, even for
him, unusually grumpy on the telephone. He wasn't feeling well, he had
terrible sinus trouble, he was seeing nobody. After setting up all these
barriers he invited Löwe to come up right away. Perhaps Löwe's gossip
might cheer him up.

Dr. Leo Binder was not only an Olympian and fantastically expensive
surgeon; he was also a manic bibliophile. The Binder collection of manuscripts and first editions was famous. He was monarch of everything
he surveyed and he surveyed the most opulent bodies in the USA. To
be operated on by Dr. Binder was like getting a decoration. He was
said to be brutal; he had a reputation for avarice and human indiffer-
ence. But a penumbra of chic surrounded those who submitted to his
virtuosity. The simple phrase "He was operated Dr. Binder" was a
Masonic password. Even when, under his ministrations, the patient died,
the survivors were consoled by the fact that their dear one had been
killed by Dr. Binder. In having supplied Dr. Binder, they had done
more than was possible; there was a necromancy in the mere procedure
which induced complacency among the bereaved.

Löwe found the necromancer, fully dressed, stretched out on a chaise
longue, with an elongated, mercurochromized toothpick stuck in each
nostril. Dr. Binder's thin, bony face was creased in suffering. In a
staccato bark he asked Löwe questions about the political situation in
Austria. Löwe gave his view, which was that the tenant of the aerie
would overreach himself and was headed for destruction. Dr. Binder
did not agree. He had many correspondents in the medical profession
in Europe. From these intelligences he gathered that it was Europe that
was headed for destruction. He became surly. There were plenty of people in this country too, he barked, who thought that the fellow in the
aerie had got hold of a good idea. Many of these had been his patients.
He had, moreover, saved many of their lives. Dr. Binder looked re-
morseful.

He brushed the distasteful subject aside.

"What'd you come for?" he snapped. Dr. Binder was shrewd. He knew that people, even Löwe, of whom, within his limitations for affection, he was fond, didn't come to see him out of love.

Löwe said he'd come to enlist his aid in behalf of a brilliant young doctor from Vienna. Dr. Binder adjusted the toothpicks in his nostrils and groaned.

"You want to get him into Mount Sinai!" said Dr. Binder accusingly, as if Mount Sinai were an illicit resort.

"Mount Sinai preferably," said Löwe.

"Impossible. Out of the question. Long waiting list now. Besieged."

He pointed to his desk covered with letters.

"You'll find twenty-thirty letters there: Berlin — Munich — all over. Impossible. Had you told me on the phone what you were coming for, I'd have saved you the trouble."

"This young man is rather special. You will like him. He is Kurt Federn, the son of . . ."

Dr. Binder pulled the toothpicks out of his nostrils. He sat up.

"Not the son of — !"

"Exactly. I told him you might be interested in the works of his father. I know you admire them."

Dr. Binder became canny. He leaned back.

"Haven't they been burned — the works of his father?"

"Not the manuscripts," said Löwe. "I have asked Kurt to bring them. The Houghton Library at Harvard is interested."

This last was an improvisation which Löwe thought privately might be worth following up.

"I want first look at them," said the doctor.

"I might arrange that," said Löwe.

"Are you in touch with this boy?"

"Naturally."

"Could you ask him — while you're about it — could he get me anything of von Hofmannsthal's?"

"Possibly. I'll find out."

"Now, Löwe, I'll tell you. Mount Sinai is practically impossible. We're overstaffed now. But, maybe I can get him in somewhere else. I'll talk to the boy. If I like him, I might even . . ."

"Yes?"

"Make him my assistant. My present one is getting married. I don't like married assistants. They interfere with my schedule."

He leaned back against the pillow, reinserted the discolored toothpicks. He was exhausted. Löwe got up. The pronged interview was over.

Back in his room at the Ambassador Löwe wrote to Federn, telling him to come to New York at once, that he had a work permit and a job in prospect for him. He would cable the money for a third-class passage, which was all he could, at the moment, manage to scrape together. He asked him to speak to his father about his manuscripts. He felt that he might dispose of them advantageously here. When he finished the letter he put in a call to Mary Kennicott at Santa Barbara. She was frantic. When was he coming? He couldn't right away, he explained, as he was waiting for his young friend from Vienna, whom surely she would remember having met in Salzburg. Mary did and warmly. She had heard *Fidelio* with him. So sympathetic! But it was terrible for her that he couldn't come right away. She was at sixes and sevens. She needed him. She needed him badly. Why didn't he bring the young man with him? Löwe said he would try but the fact was that Federn was up for a post at Mount Sinai. Still, he would try. Perhaps he could swing it. If he couldn't, he would come alone.

Between Eileen and Löwe there had developed a close rapport. She had become, in some sort, his opposite number in Hollywood. They had the refugee problem in common. Eileen had become particularly worried about Naomi. She and Naomi had kept up, since the Grants had left Salzburg, a lively correspondence. The Jewish studies which Eileen had started with Naomi in Salzburg had continued by letter; their exchange became a kind of correspondence course in Judaism. Naomi had written to Eileen, for example, about an adorable character named Moses Hess, who had written a book (which Naomi had presently sent her) called *Rome and Jerusalem*. Eileen read it with avidity. In it Hess had promulgated the idea that the Jewish problem, which since her marriage to Grant had become Eileen's problem, could only be solved by the establishment of a national home for the Jews. Hess had been the first articulate Zionist. Eileen took that on too. She began to read up on Zionism. Hess was a friend of Karl Marx, who despised him as an impractical dreamer. He was indeed a dreamer. He had married a prostitute for whom he didn't care much simply to demonstrate that all human beings must show love for each other, without distinction. The Hesses had, as a matter of fact, a happy and unclouded married life. The ex-prostitute stuck to her husband through all vicissitude and deprivation. Eileen fell in love with Moses Hess as she had fallen in love with the Hebrew prophets — the coevals of her son's ancestor. Eileen became uncomfortable when she came upon a passage in which Hess heaped contempt on his fellow Germans, who, in an attempt at protective coloration, changed their names the better to merge with the German landscape. She knew that her husband's name was not his own. She didn't know what his real name was; she didn't dare ask him.

It became increasingly a suppressed torment to Eileen that her husband — she hated to admit it, even to herself, but the realization kept nagging at her — that her husband lacked spirituality. Her mother had been a long time adying but when she finally did, Eileen returned, calm and serene, to Beverly Hills, her husband, her baby, and the Jewish problem. Grant was amazed to find her so tranquil. Her tranquility came from her certainty that she would meet her mother in heaven. What made her sad was not the separation from her mother, which was only temporary, but the fact that Grant didn't share in the least her own confidence in the reunion. Grant stated bluntly that he didn't believe in the immortality of the soul. Eileen couldn't understand how, without this belief, one could live at all. Grant had never met his mother-in-law and seemed to take it in his stride that now a meeting would never take place. It made Eileen sad.

In any case, Eileen's activities in behalf of the refugees took her mind temporarily off Grant's agnosticism. She would concentrate on that later. She knew that the task of converting Grant to his religion would take time and patience and she was prepared to expend them. She had become more Jewish than the Jews. She was constantly after the studio heads to provide jobs for Jewish writers and journalists from Central Europe. These tycoons liked Eileen. They thought it quaint, but winning, that she, a Catholic, should be so fervently enlisted in the cause of their own unfortunate coreligionists. Eileen had become a great favorite (and only slightly a figure of fun) in the film community. She

was liked even by those who didn't particularly care for Grant and
there were quite a few of those. In her salvaging efforts Eileen was incessant, tireless, so much so that she sometimes fatigued the tycoons.
Still, they received her, they listened to her. As Grant's wife — the wife
of a Name Writer — she had an automatic position of prominence in
the film colony. But Eileen didn't restrict herself to Grant's circle. She
made forays outside it. She enlisted the powerful aid of Thomas Mann,
for example, himself a refugee, though not on racial grounds.

Eileen wanted to save-at-large, but what she wanted to do most in
the world was to save Naomi. This became an obsessive idea with her.
She wanted to save Naomi's parents too but, as they weren't writers or
artists, she wasn't sure she could do anything for them, but save Naomi
she must. Until Naomi was there, in Beverly Hills, in her own sight,
beside her, she couldn't rest. As her letters to Naomi, usually so swiftly
answered, began to remain unanswered, she became increasingly worried. She sent prepaid cables. No reply. And then, one day, her heart
sank. A letter she had sent six weeks before was returned to her,
stamped with the legend, in German: "No longer at this address." Eileen felt panic. She telephoned to Löwe in New York. He must, through
his connections, find out something about Naomi. He must trace Naomi.
Löwe promised to try.

Providentially, on the very morning of Eileen's frantic call, Löwe had
a letter from Vienna from Vincent Edward Aldridge, the Third. The
third Aldridge was the only son of the second Aldridge, a distinguished
international lawyer, who had a strong penchant for Löwe. The second
Aldridge, as he didn't mind telling his friends, enjoyed Löwe's society
almost more than anyone's. Löwe had brought him to Stohl's palace in
Salzburg, where he had enjoyed himself immensely. Aldridge had helped
finance Stohl's first American tour. He loved the theater and actresses
and Löwe had given him access to both. Above all, Löwe had given him
help and council in the aggravating problems that kept coming up in
the upbringing of his son, the third Aldridge. The "boy," as his father
kept referring to him, although he was pushing thirty, wouldn't settle
down to anything. He was interested only in the arts, ballet chiefly, ballet, in fact, madly. But unless you were a choreographer or a composer
or a scene designer or a conductor or even a dancer, there was really
nothing much you could do about satisfying a passion for ballet except

to back it financially. This, the third Aldridge kept doing at the expense of the second. The latter kept imploring Löwe to find some job for the boy, something to do with the arts, he said, with a gesture indicating a vague and fathomless territory. Löwe had finally got the boy a job on a national magazine published by a friend of his with a view to his reviewing ballets. But, as the second Aldridge had decided to back no more ballets, there were no ballets to review. Löwe then suggested to the boy to write articles which he, Löwe, undertook to place for him. Young Aldridge was grateful and enthusiastic; it was, he thought, a wonderful idea. He had had many "experiences" which, he was sure, would make fascinating articles. Löwe kept asking for them but, when he came right down to it, Vincent found writing an inconvenience. When Löwe got tired of asking for a product which was not forthcoming, he felt he ought to take the third Aldridge to task. "You know, my dear Vincent," he said, "articles that are not written are seldom published." The third Aldridge adored this remark; he pronounced it "echt Kaetchen" and kept quoting it to his friends.

Such was the uneasy posture between the two Aldridges when a horrendous incident brought on a crisis. Aldridge, Sr., had a so-called "cottage" in Bar Harbor, Maine, where he spent his summers. It was a great, rambling wooden structure which had been built by the first Aldridge in the era of James G. Blaine, a fellow cottager. Aldridge loved the place; he had been brought up in it, spent his happy married life there. When his wife died, he kept it on, hoping his son would live there as happily as he had done. He usually stayed till after Labor Day, unless his practice took him to Europe, but he always managed to get in a few weeks at the Bar Harbor manse in the fall. He would then go to Boston to see his doctor for a checkup; Aldridge had a fanatical belief in Boston doctors; when he had to undergo surgery he invariably submitted to it in Massachusetts General. In the fall of 1936 he wrote, as usual, to the Ritz-Carlton Hotel in Boston for reservations. He received a letter from the management stating that they were terribly sorry but that the hotel was full up; they could not accommodate him. Now Vincent Edward Aldridge, the Second, was, quite simply, not a man for whom there were no accommodations to be had in a hotel. Furious — and bewildered — he telephoned the Ritz. He asked to speak to the manager. The manager was at first evasive and then cordial. He asked a strange question: "Am I speaking to Mr. Aldridge, the Second, or to Mr. Aldridge, the Third?" "My son hasn't been here for a month," Aldridge, Sr., said. He was exasperated. The manager hastened to assure him that his reservations would be in order. Aldridge, Sr., had an afterthought. "And what the hell difference would it make if it were my son? Isn't he good enough for your hotel?" The manager slid out from under. He said there had been a misunderstanding, that he had other calls waiting and he hoped Mr. Aldridge would be pleased with his accommodations. He would reserve his usual suite for him overlooking the Public Garden.

The incident bothered Aldridge. It bothered him exceedingly. He brooded on it on the train to Boston. He decided that he would damn well get to the bottom of it.

In Boston, after his session with his old friend the doctor, who was very pleased with his condition, Aldridge went back to the hotel. He experienced a fleeting euphoria at his doctor's good report. But the euphoria ebbed. The more he thought of the strange incident over the reservation, the refusal, then the manager's obvious relief when he found out he was talking to the father and not to the son, the more it baffled him. It had a sinister aspect, somehow. He beat about in his brain for a possible explanation. Could it be that his son was a kleptomaniac and stole the silverware from the dining room? He'd heard of eccentricities like that. He sent for the manager.

The manager, who knew that he was dealing with a VIP, was nervous. What he did not know was that he was also facing a highly skilled and subtle questioner. Yes, yes, the second Aldridge was very well pleased with his suite. He'd occupied it often before. He thanked the manager for reserving it for him, especially when the hotel was so crowded. The manager quivered. To make him less nervous, Aldridge offered him a drink. The manager refused. He offered him a cigar which the manager accepted, asking permission to reserve it for the future as he was not allowed to smoke while on duty. Aldridge then gave him three cigars to gild the managerial future. The manager was grateful and began to sidle out. He was, he explained, needed elsewhere. Aldridge wanted to keep him only for a minute. He had a slight curiosity which the manager could satisfy easily. He elicited one interesting fact: that his son had several times written for reservations in his father's name. They'd make the reservations and then find out, on the boy's arrival, that it wasn't his father at all. This amused Aldridge. He thought it very funny. Didn't the manager see how funny it was? He came up to the manager and slapped him on the shoulder. "Pretty cute, don't you think? Boy knew he'd get better reservations that way — this suite for instance." Didn't the manager think it was pretty cute? After all, not much of a forgery, was it? All the boy had to do was to change a numeral — didn't the manager see that? — otherwise their names were identical. Aldridge thought it was damned funny. He laughed aloud. Hollowly, the manager echoed his interlocutor's laughter and, perspiring, turned again, under cover of simulated hilarity, to escape. There was just one more little point on which Aldridge was curious. The little points kept coming up. By the time the successional little points were cleared up, Aldridge, in a gray voice, but with great courtesy, thanked the manager for his trouble and permitted him to depart.

In spite of the reassurances given him by his doctor, Aldridge, Sr., suddenly felt very old. He sat in an armchair looking out at the glowing autumn foliage. He did not see it. He was staring into an abyss. Finally, he got up. He put in a call to Löwe in New York and invited him to dinner this very evening in the Union Club. Löwe had an engagement. Aldridge said he must break it. Löwe said he would.

That night, in a private dining room in the Union Club, Aldridge told Löwe the story as he had finally wormed it out of the manager. He was having difficulty telling it even to Löwe, but finally he blurted it out — his son was on the hotel blacklist. The staff had been instructed on no account to give him a reservation. By getting reservations in his father's name he had eluded this boycott. Löwe was the only one in the world, Aldridge said, to whom he could tell what he was going to tell. The fact was, well, the fact was, that his son's habits were peculiar. He would leave the hotel about midnight, impeccably dressed, and return at three, four, five in the morning disheveled, sometimes all bloodied up. Sometimes he would bring strange companions with him, truck drivers, sailors. All this had been reported to the management by the lift boys. The management had decided young Aldridge's patronage wasn't good for the hotel. Aldridge put it to Löwe. What was he to do? Had Löwe been aware of the boy's proclivities?

Löwe said that of course he had. Speaking, as usual, very quietly, almost inaudibly, so that Aldridge had occasionally to cup his hand behind his ear to catch what he was saying, Löwe went on to extol the boy in measured terms. There was no young man of whom Löwe was fonder. He had immense charm, for one thing, and exquisite sensibility. He was brilliant. He hadn't quite found himself yet, but he had great promise. He took out a letter he'd had from him a few days before from a city in the Midwest where he had gone especially to see an exhibition of Houdon busts. Löwe read a sentence aloud: "You've never seen anything so lovely, dearest Kaetchen, so incredibly lovely as the marbled lace in the jabots. It's like Mozart!" Löwe put the boy's letter back in his pocket and went on. Vincent's esthetic sense was acute, extraordinarily acute, but Löwe had seen that in others. What endeared the boy to Löwe most of all, a quality he had that other esthetes didn't have, was his kindness, his sympathy. There wasn't in the world a kinder, gentler person than Vincent Edward Aldridge, the Third. When he had asked him for help once for a poor creature who was in a dreadful plight, young Aldridge's eyes had filled with tears. Löwe had had to restrain him from giving much more than he had asked for. No. Such greatness of soul was rare. Personally he, Löwe, would be proud to have a son like that. Aldridge, he said, should be proud.

Pride did not rise in Aldridge. Should he be proud of a son who is kicked out of hotels? Should he be proud of a son whose preferences . . . the father could not finish. His mind sheid away from the contemplation of these ghastly preferences.

Löwe admitted that this aspect of his son's nature was regrettable. It was sad. But it should arouse sympathy, not censure. For his part Löwe's heart went out to those so conditioned. Even though they were not sorry for themselves, Löwe was sorry for them. On numerous occasions Löwe had observed their desperation, a desperation that came from an intimation of doom.

"My boy is doomed then?" said Aldridge.

"Not at all. Not necessarily. He may get married. He probably will."

"Who on earth . . . ?"

"Some distinguished lady of the same persuasion. There are many such marriages. Very happy."

Aldridge looked at Löwe hopelessly. He wiped his forehead with a large silk handkerchief. It wasn't his idea of a happy marriage. It did not suggest St. James's, Mendelssohn, orange blossoms, rice.

Löwe went on. In the first place, such aberrations were far more widely dispersed, even in Aldridge's own circle, than Aldridge might suspect. He enumerated a list of names, not only in the arts but in science, philosophy, diplomacy and statecraft. As a patron of the arts, Aldridge should feel gratitude rather than condemnation. He asked him, for example, to contemplate Michelangelo. The latter, Löwe was sure, would have been blacklisted by the Ritz in Boston.

Aldridge didn't feel like contemplating Michelangelo; the only image that rose before him was of his dear boy, his only son and heir, his mother's darling, staggering into the Ritz lobby at five o'clock in the morning, all bloodied up. He couldn't feel pride, he could feel only revulsion and horror. Löwe saw that his friend was suffering. He looked ten years older than when he had last seen him, two weeks ago.

"But what shall I *do* with him?" he asked finally. "Shall I tell him I *know?*"

Löwe advised against that. He suggested that Aldridge send his son to Europe where ballets were frequent. Aldridge grasped at this. When he parted from Löwe, he clasped his hand and thanked him fervently. He was tremendously relieved, he said, at not having to have it out with the boy. He missed his dead wife poignantly but he was glad she hadn't lived to make the discovery that cruel fate had reserved for him. Two weeks later Aldridge and Löwe saw the third Vincent off on the *Europa*.

No sooner had Eileen hung up after telling him her hideous worry about Naomi than he returned to Vincent's letter. It was delightful and funny as always, but there was a dark note in it too. There was something new and horrid abroad in Vienna, a spirit he couldn't tolerate, a mimicry everywhere of "those nasty Germans" whom Vincent couldn't endure. He was homesick for Löwe and his other New York friends and was, as a matter of fact, thinking of coming home. Where would Löwe be? It was unthinkable, his returning only to discover that Löwe was somewhere else. Reading the letter Löwe had an inspiration. It was really an inspiration. Under the afflatus of it he began to pace the room in excitement. There was only one way to save Naomi — provided she could be found — only one way and he had hit upon it. He went back

to the telephone and called the overseas operator. He put in a call to
Aldridge, the Third, at the Hotel Imperiale in Vienna, an establishment,
he felt quite sure, more latitudinarian than the Ritz in Boston.

On Löwe's desk was the silver-framed photograph of his English love.
He picked up the photograph and looked at it long and tenderly. She
was the center of his being. He referred everything to her. If this, his
just-born little inspiration, worked out, he would have something amusing to write her. He would write her tonight, as soon as the overseas
call came in. He'd had a letter from her yesterday. It was in his pocket.
He took it out and looked at it again, though he'd already read it half
a dozen times. She had enclosed a little snapshot. It was taken in her
garden. She was wearing a working smock and a great floppy straw hat,
the vast brim of which almost covered her eyes. The smock was open
and on her blouse was pinned a Löwe. It was to show him that she wore
it even in the country. He was moved, painfully moved. He put the letter back in his pocket. The little snapshot put him in an emotional, rem-
iniscent mood. In a kind of trance, he began walking around the room,
his hands crossed behind his back. He found himself going from one to
the other of the four pastels on the walls, views of his home town:
Czernowitz. One showed the square in front of the Primaria, the City
Hall, very busy, with little tram cars, salmon colored, peasants, horses
and carts and oxen, a little group in tall, fur hats. The artist had written in pencil: *Rathaus Platz in Czernowitz*. There was a little wooden
shed where people waited for the tram cars. He remembered waiting
there as a small boy with his father. He moved to another of the pastels.
It was a funeral. The coffin, hexagonal in shape and partly covered by
a varicolored cloth, was on a plank on wheels drawn by two bullocks.
Löwe remembered. It was a young man, a contemporary of his, who
had died. The boy's father, old and bent, walked just ahead of the
bullocks, supporting himself on a long staff. Beside the coffin and behind it other mourners walked. *Begräbnis am Pruth*, the legend read.
And there was the Pruth, in the middle distance, with the unrailed
wooden bridge across it, and the cluster of white headstones in the
graveyard to which the little procession was moving and the stylized tier
of hills beyond. Löwe had known the dead boy but he now couldn't remember his face. He stood before *Alter Jüd Friedhof*, the old Jewish
cemetery. The headstones, with their faded Hebrew inscriptions, the let-

ters stark and jagged, were often surmounted by sprigs of flowers or blossoming branches. Apple blossoms, probably, Löwe thought, aware that he hadn't really looked at these pastels in a long time. The head-stones lurched every which way, toward each other and away from each other, as if in a kind of bacchanal. His parents lay in that graveyard. Löwe leant close to see if he might possibly trace them but the inscriptions were indecipherable. In any case, he didn't know Hebrew. He had known it as a child, but he had long since forgotten. Abruptly, Löwe turned away from his past to his present. This was the trick black and white kitten. Monica had sent it to him. It was inscribed: "For Kaetchen." It showed a white kitten with green eyes. But, if you turned it over, it was a black kitten with green eyes. It amused the children of his friends.

The telephone rang. At last — Vincent! But it was Varina. Löwe was delighted to hear the throaty voice and the slow drawl. He hadn't heard it in a long time. Where had she been? With her parents in Manchester, Massachusetts. She had just arrived. She had to see him. She had to see him right away. Something momentous had happened or was about to happen. She couldn't possibly tell it to him over the telephone, she had to see him to tell him and to see him alone. He invited her to dinner that evening in the Colony. No, not the Colony, there'd be too many there who would join them. He switched the invitation to Klinger's. Klinger's, Varina agreed, would be perfect.

Löwe felt himself in a kind of emotional disarray. There was only one way to find calm — to write to Monica. He was never so happy as when he was writing to Monica; he felt close to her then; it was like talking to her. He sat at the writing desk. He began by thanking her for the snapshot — how touched he had been to find her wearing the Löwe even when she was gardening. He settled into the long rhythm of his epistolary style.

The telephone rang. Resentful, he got up to answer it. This time it *was* Vincent Edward Aldridge, the Third, calling from Vienna.

21. Newsletter

Löwe became very busy; two days elapsed before he was able to continue his letter to Lady Monica. It was always so in their correspondence. Their letters were running diaries; they were constantly redating the successive entries. They each led busy lives; they began letters in the lulls and continued them in the next lulls. He would get a letter: "6 P.M. — before Covent Garden — 1 A.M. — after Covent Garden." Everything that happened to Löwe, the twists and turns of his involvements with people, were, for him, simply stuffs and textures which he appraised from the point of view of whether they were weavable for his beloved. Would they interest her? Would they entertain her? Would they provoke her? The day before he had sat down to write her, about the odd turn with Varina, the extraordinary apparition of Dr. Ogden, about Vincent's tragic cable — he had plenty really and he was fairly confident that he could hold her attention — when he felt a sharp incision of pain below his heart. He staggered to his feet, writhing, and with the familiar apprehension: Is this it then? And the letter to Monica unfinished! He swallowed one of the nitroglycerine pills he always kept by him and, when he had caught his breath, called his doctor who asked him to come at once to see him. He did. He returned. It was all right. Things were no worse. He had a reprieve. He was grateful. He could finish his letter. He would tell her everything as he always did. Except about the nitroglycerine pill; he had never said a word to Monica, nor to anyone else, about that.

It was his habit to write in the new date and the hour in red ink and to underline it in red so that Monica would be the one with him in time. He did so now and resumed the interrupted conversation.

Well, I have been busy, busier than usual. It has been since my two conversations with Vincent and Varina a few nights ago, a kind of dissolving comedy, verging on farce and tragedy. How often, don't you agree, the concerns and agonies of people, viewed from outside their frantic obsessions, emerge as farce! They suffer; we, not subject to their prejudices, can only smile. For example, Aldridge, Sr., and Varina's par-

ents — *I have had extraordinary interviews with these three parents. But that will come later. I have to begin at the beginning; as you know I am methodical. First of all about Vincent and Naomi. I take pride in this: that for once, at long last, I have arranged a completely utilitarian marriage. I know that you have teased me and scarified me in the past for marriages I have engineered, which seemed to you doomed to breakage from the start. But this time, you will have to agree, I have arranged a marriage, this world being what it is, for the soundest possible reasons, to get a visa for a bride otherwise doomed. Vincent has been an angel. He went at once to Salzburg and didn't rest till he found Naomi. Ten days before, the poor girl had taken a walk by the Salzach. She returned to her parents' flat, that cozy, sparklingly clean little flat which I described to you in my letter last summer telling you about Stanley Grant's wedding. She found her parents on the floor dead, with a swastika sign on their bodies. They were private, unofficial murders, done by unknown zealots who could not curb their impatience for the legal protocol which is sure to be coming. Vincent found Naomi living with relatives. She is, he told me (he called two days ago from Salzburg), in a cataleptic state. He asked to marry her and to bring her to me and to her devoted friend, Eileen. She showed no interest. She had, Vincent said, died too. Fortunately, Naomi's aunt and uncle saw Vincent's advent as a kind of miracle, a kind of intervention from Heaven. They were married yesterday. I got this morning a cable from Vincent. They are on the Queen Mary. I shall greet the bride and groom on Tuesday morning, the 28th.*

Vincent asked me on the telephone to inform his father. So I did. You will find, buried in the early pages of this letter, a complete account of my dinner with Vincent's father. When I told Aldridge, Sr., that his son would probably marry, I did not think the sacrament would take place quite so soon. Since you know that I am a frustrated dramatist I will set down the conversation exactly as it took place; it will give me the illusion that I'm writing a play. Alas, I could never have invented such a dialogue.

    Löwe: Congratulations! I've just heard from your son. He is married.
    Aldridge: I don't believe it. For God's sake! To whom?
    Löwe: A lovely young girl whom I know. Vincent asked me to tell you.
    Aldridge: You say you know her? What's her name?
    Löwe: Naomi Aldridge.
    Aldridge (apoplectic): I mean her maiden name.
    Löwe: I have to tell you — I really can't remember.

Aldridge: I thought you knew her! Is she one of THOSE?

For a moment I didn't know what he meant by "one of THOSE."
Then I remembered my prophecy (so mistaken) in the Union Club and
I quickly reassured him.

"Not at all," I said, "perfectly normal. You will be delighted with her,
I assure you."

"What's her name again — her first name?"

"Naomi."

"What kind of a name is that?" There was a pause, then a horrid con-
viction. "Is she Jewish?"

"Yes," I said, "she is."

"I knew there was a catch in it!"

He hung up. A half hour later he called up to apologize for being rude.
His apology was a continuation of his rudeness. He keeps forgetting, he
said, that I am Jewish because I'm so different. I'm quite used to this.
Most of my elegant friends talk about Jews before me as if I were not
one. It slips their minds. But do you see what I mean when I say that
even tragic events are edged in comedy? The farce I reserve for Varina.
I had to intercede with her parents over a surprising matrimonial caprice
of their daughter's. That I did not enjoy. Varina's father tests even my
tolerance. Vincent told me once that when Lawson, Sr., was airing him-
self one day on his favorite topic, a crony of his teased him for seemingly
making an exception of me. "Oh," he said, "Löwe's all right. He's a white
Jew." I don't really deserve this exception. It has to be faced that my
complexion is quite dark. Lawson's color blind.

The intelligence which Varina had to convey to me in the privacy of
Klinger's (this restaurant would amuse you and I will take you there
when next you come: a vast caravansery in fake-Bavarian and ersatz
gemütlichkeit) was that she has fallen in love with, and is trying to per-
suade to marry her, the hochstapler of the hochstaplers, Dr. Kenneth
Ogden. He is superb, you know, really superb, a Cagliostro of the New
Science, Arch Pontiff of the Couch — but then you know him and know
all about him. What was it you said to me about him once, that he is
every other inch a gentleman, or was that about someone else?

I have managed to keep Varina on the right side of her parents by
main strength. Last summer in London it was a near thing, as you know.
Later when she was in the slough of despond over Ian, I made her join
them in Scotland. Well, here she was at Klinger's, lovely as ever, her
voice as musical and deliberate as ever, her gray eyes, like deep water, as
still as ever. She gives every effect of being strong and in control but she

is heartbreakingly fragile. She found herself sitting next to Ogden one afternoon in Radio City! In that dim vastness these two molecules were magnetized. Since then Ogden has been rushing her. She has been trying, she told me, to persuade him to marry her. I advised, as strongly as I could, against it; so, she told me, had Ogden. Ogden joined us for coffee. I must say that, in a rather revolting way, he is very amusing. He is the most uninhibited man I've ever met. He begged me to save him from Varina; he adores her so he fears to be enslaved. On the other hand, didn't I think that Varina should try a heterosexual for once? By showing Varina that the so-called normals could make love too, he feels that he has struck a blow for the heteros against the homos. Varina loved it all. He has such abundant animal magnetism that he makes the most outrageous suggestions sound natural. Along the way he was funny about Grant. He said that Grant would really like to be like him but that he lacks the concentration. (Something in it too; I'll come to Grant later.) He'd heard that Varina's parents were terrors. What did I think? Would Varina's parents cut her off if he married her? If that were so he really couldn't risk it; he had enough for himself but he couldn't afford to keep Varina in the style to which she was accustomed. Etc. Etc. It ended by my promising to break the news of their engagement to Varina's parents.

I went to see the Lawsons to break the glad news. You know, they took it surprisingly well. Their expectations of Varina were so low that Dr. Ogden seemed to them less a catastrophe than they might have supposed. They had always complained — and, quite in the tradition, to me — that Varina seemed to care for no one but Jews. I had often consoled them about Varina's specialty. They are blissfully ignorant of Varina's infatuation for Ian Leith. They don't know what, thanks to Stephanie's heroism, they have escaped. Well, they toted Ogden up: a doctor, a dubious branch, but he had headed Mary Kennicott's clinic, hadn't he? Mary was eccentric but socially impeccable. He was good-looking, Varina's mother admitted, though in a flashy, vulgar way. It went on for quite a time, adding and subtracting. But Lawson, Senior, managed to dish up a crumb of comfort for himself "Anyway," he said in a mournful summary, "he's not Jewish!" As he has put me in a special category he felt under no obligation to apologize. Mrs. Lawson appeared to be quite reconciled, but Mr. Lawson is a hard nut to crack. He's going to have Ogden's record looked into. He has, he said, ways of finding out. Private detectives, I suppose he means. I am sure one of them will go to Cleveland, who knows where else. Varina couldn't care less if her parents cut her off but I am sure Ogden would. Poor Varina! With every natural

*gift — looks and style and a warm heart — she is at sea. I tremble for
Varina. I love her dearly, as I know you do. She is defenseless, totally
without guile. The poor child chose the wrong parents. All her choices
seem to be wrong.*

Well, I have written quite enough. I have put you au courant of . . .

The telephone rang. Resignedly Löwe got up to answer it. He coped
with the subsequent conversation, adding it as he endured it, to the unfinished letter. The moment he hung up he returned to his desk. He
dipped the special pen into the little bottle of red ink and made the
notation:

AFTER TELEPHONE CALL FROM THE GRANTS:

*Just as you were on the point of getting rid of me the telephone rang.
It was the Grants from Hollywood. I spoke to both of them. Eileen is
wildly excited about the prospect of her reunion with her cherished Hebrew teacher and Talmudist, Naomi. She insists that I bring her out and
that Naomi must stay with her. Over the phone Grant was transparently
exalted by the prospect of Naomi's arrival. He's an odd one, that Grant.
A Narcissus who is repelled by his reflection (Ogden is entranced by
his). Both types can cause trouble but on the whole I'd rather deal with
megalomaniacs who are extroverted than those who are introverted,
wouldn't you? Grant is omniverous; I'm not sure he will wear well. Un-
questionably talented. He's overpolite, insincerely effusive and too eager
to live up to a reputation for brilliance. He's constantly in love with
women who belong to other people and who, even if they didn't, wouldn't
want to belong to him. He meets René Wolfsohn's girl (very distinguished and attractive she is — Grant's taste is impeccable) and is off at
once spinning romantic fantasies about her. He confessed to me the day
after his wedding that, even during the ceremony, he felt that it was
Naomi he should be marrying. At his own wedding he fell in love with
Naomi! Poor Eileen! I am afraid she will pay dearly for her Hebrew les-
sons. Grant longs to meet you. You may even like him! Stephanie writes
me she is coming to Hollywood with Ian because she expects to act in
Grant's play. She never will but Grant promised her the part. He will
promise anything to anybody; he is so anxious to be liked, however momentarily. And, with all this, he is married to one of the dearest girls in
the world. She's a rarity, really good. Of course, she's humorless and, in
many respects, quite absurd. She's a highbrow, you know, according to
a definition I once heard somewhere of the highbrow as a person edu-*

cated above his intelligence. But she hasn't a drop of malice anywhere in her. She genuinely wants to help people. She's a kind of saint, an unsubtle saint. The other day, reading the Confessions of St. Augustine, I discovered that his mother's name was Monica. Well, Eileen isn't in the least subtle, like your long-time-ago son. Perhaps it's better for saints not to be burdened by subtleties. Eileen is free.

Well, have I bored you enough? I take my chances.

All love,

Kaetchen

P.S.   The doorbell just rang. The bellboy, a wizened dwarf of sixty, has just handed me a letter from you. For once I have something more important to do than to write you.

Love,

K.

22. The Boarder

On Tuesday morning Löwe went to Pier 57 to meet the *Queen Mary*. He had three friends on board: Mr. and Mrs. Aldridge, who were traveling first class, and Kurt Federn, who was traveling third. He had invited Aldridge, Sr., but he had to go to Chicago on a business trip. He admitted that he really didn't want to see his son, that he dreaded what the interview might lead to, that his Boston doctor had cautioned him against excess of emotional strain. He asked Löwe to inform Vincent about the dismal incident in Boston and that he thought it would be better that they did not meet until he, Aldridge, Sr., had acquired some control over himself, a mastery which, he added grimly, might take a very long time. Löwe told him not to worry. He undertook to handle Vincent.

At the pier, Löwe left a message at the third-class gangway for Federn to meet him under the letter F at customs. He then went to the first-class gangway to meet the bride and groom. Presently he saw the short stocky figure of Vincent Aldridge, III. Behind him, her hand on Vincent's shoulder, he saw a wavering, emaciated figure which he did

not at once recognize as Naomi's. Vincent greeted Löwe ecstatically. He
did not look in the least like a lace-jabot man. He was short, deep-
chested, with powerful arms and shoulders. He had the body of a professional wrestler.

Löwe took Naomi in his arms. Her body trembled. Her eyes seemed
to be alone in her face. Her thin cheeks were crisscrossed with brown
splotches. Malnutrition, Löwe decided. He would take care of that. He
would take her to Voisin for dinner. His mouth watered as he thought
of what he would order for Naomi, as well as at the thought of what he
would order for himself. Naomi spoke to him in German. The gleaming
voice had gone sallow. As he held her in his arms, Löwe thought, "She
is not alive. She has smelt death." He could hardly make out what she
was whispering to him. She was asking him to thank Vincent, since she
could not, for having been so "edel" to her. She rested in Löwe's arms
as if in a cradle.

Vincent was ebulliently apologetic. He had a fluting voice. "My dear,"
he said to Löwe, "I tried everything to amuse this dear child. I trotted
out all my jokes, all my best stories — as you know, I am madly amusing — but not once, not once, could I make her laugh. It made me cry,
literally it made me cry, that I couldn't make the dear child laugh."

"Maybe it's your German," said Löwe over Naomi's shoulder.
"Maybe your jokes don't translate into German!"

"That's a canard. My German is impeccable. You've often told
me so."

They moved along in the crush toward customs.

"But Naomi tells me you've been angelic to her. She asked me to tell
you. She is grateful. So am I."

Vincent was in high spirits, cheered up, perhaps, by the knowledge
that he had done a good deed. "But what did you expect me to be?
Don't you know that my manners are exquisite? I know I look Nean-
derthal but in sensibility I am the last word. In fact, in myself, single-
handed, I am a panorama of evolution, from the primordial to the hyper-
civilized. It's quite a responsibility but I bear it lightly. It's heaven to
see you Kaetchen. Sheer heaven. How's my precious papa? Why isn't
he here?"

"He had to go to Chicago on business."

"What a relief! God's in His Heaven. All's right with the world."

He whispered, with a side glance at Naomi.

"But she breaks my heart, that child. What will you do with her? She's gone, you know. Quite gone. I had a feeling — a feeling on the boat . . ."

"What?"

"That's she's no longer one of us."

"We'll bring her back," said Löwe with quiet confidence. "But I have another friend on the boat. Kurt Federn."

"I met almost everybody in the Verandah Bar. I didn't meet any young Federn. Is he my type?"

Löwe chuckled.

"He's not in your class."

"Is he convertible? I'm pretty good, you know, at proselytizing."

"I meant economically. He traveled steerage."

"I cruised around there too. Much more fun than first class. But I didn't meet . . ."

"Well, you will now. Here he is! Naomi! Look! A surprise for you. A fellow Salzburger!"

Federn, blond and ruddy, came up to them, smiling.

"Here, Kurt, congratulate the bride. And the groom, Mr. Vincent Edward Aldridge, the Third."

Federn was bewildered. Naomi shook hands with him, without surprise.

"I think it's too maddening," said Vincent, "that we didn't meet on the boat."

"I regret," said Federn.

"Are you the son of the playwright Federn?"

"Yes."

"But I *adore* your father's works. Simply adore them. *Parallels Sometimes Cross*, I implored Balanchine to make a ballet out of that. Wouldn't Ravel have written a marvelous score for it? Divine. I've thought of Stravinsky. What would you think of Stravinsky?"

Kurt, quite at sea, expressed a high opinion of Stravinsky.

Löwe cut through these celestial plans.

"We've got to get you through customs," he said. "Later we can talk about Stravinsky."

Löwe took charge. He found that people fumbled about when there were immediate chores to do, just as they dallied with menus in restaurants. Customs proved not to be troublesome. Neither Kurt nor Naomi had more than a dufflebag apiece. Aldridge took somewhat longer. Löwe left Naomi with Federn and walked with Vincent to the letter A. While they were waiting for Vincent's bags to be brought up, Löwe told him why his father hadn't come to the boat. Vincent's eyes narrowed. His affability vanished; he became vindictive.

"He's a nasty hypocrite. He reeks with phony nostalgia for the happy days with Mother, but he was rude to Mother. He was overbearing with Mother. I've never forgiven him for that. I never will."

Löwe knew that Vincent had adored his mother. There was a colored photograph of Augustus John's painting of her on Vincent's night table. She had been very beautiful. Vincent was fond of recalling that when they went to parties together, he would stand beside her and proclaim: "Behold! Beauty and the Beast!" It amusd everybody. While the customs man prowled through his suitcases, Vincent muttered:

"I'm glad he knows. If he weren't so dense and self-centered, he'd have known long ago. I hope I never see him again. I'm moving out of his house at once. I'll take a room at the Ambassador to be near you, Kaetchen."

"But I'm going to Hollywood. I have to take Naomi. Also Kurt. I've got to see Mary Kennicott. I've got business for Stohl."

At the mention of Hollywood, Vincent was in ecstasy.

"Oh, but how marvelous! I'm at loose ends. I've always wanted to go to Hollywood. I'll go with you. What fun! What marvelous fun!"

The four of them presently found themselves in a taxi going uptown. Vincent's spirits were restored by the new prospect; he fluted along at a great rate.

"I know that I've been a washout as a bridegroom so far but continuing our honeymoon en quatre will release me. I am determined to make Naomi laugh. Just once I've got to make her laugh. Then I'll be able to say we've had a happy marriage!"

At this Naomi smiled. Vincent was triumphant. He crowed.

"You see! You see! Won't it be jolly? Imagine! The four of us traveling to California. Century to Chicago, then the Super Chief! Through the great heartland of America. All that corn. All that wheat!"

"What will you do when you get there?"

"You know everybody everywhere, Kaetchen. Perhaps you can get me a job at one of the studios."

"But you haven't written anything. You've got nothing to show."

"I'll go in for asceticism. I'll lock myself in. I'll trump up a master-piece. You'll see!"

"I've heard that before," said Löwe. But he considered. When one of his protégées needed something, he instinctively began to improvise opportunities.

"After all, they hire everybody. Why not you?"

"Why not."

"Stanley Grant may be able to do something for you."

"Stanley Grant, the playwright? Is he a friend of yours?"

Löwe nodded wearily.

"I might have known! Of course he would be! But I adore him. I adore his play. I went to see it three times. I liked it better each time. I raved about it in London. When do we leave? I just can't stand it — till we leave!"

"I thought you were going to lock yourself in."

"I'll lock myself in in Hollywood."

"The weather is far too pleasant. Still, Naomi is going to stay with the Grants. . . ."

Vincent interrupted rapturously.

"Lovely! He can't object, can he then, Grant, if I drop in to see my bride once in a while? He can't, can he?"

Löwe chuckled.

"He won't object. He's very tolerant. And his wife is a darling. She loves you already for what you've done. You have, you know, you scoundrel, in spite of yourself, performed a Mitzvah."

"What on earth's that?"

"Tell him, Kurt."

Federn interpreted.

"A good deed."

Vincent flushed with pleasure.

"Have I? Have I really? What is it again, that lovely word?"

Löwe repeated it. He was constantly expanding the vocabularies of his pet goyim. Vincent was in ecstasy.

"I love it. I'll have a little medallion made — gold — with that word

engraved on it and wear it on my lapel. My Mitzvah medal. What do
you think, Kaetchen?"

"I don't advise you to wear it in the Union Club."

"I wouldn't be caught dead in the Union Club. My father belongs to
it." He had a bright idea. "I'll wear it when we call on the Grants."

"That won't be necessary. You'll be welcomed with open arms."

Vincent blew a kiss to the world at large.

"Marvelous! Vistas open. Isn't life wonderful? Isn't it full of sur-
prises? You have married me right into the family of my favorite playwright. And with his influence, surely he can get me a job at one of
those dear studios. Surely he can, don't you think so?"

"If he really tries he might. He's very self-centered."

"Can't you induce *him* to do a Mitzvah? Can't you tempt him to out-
Mitzvah me?"

Löwe laughed. Kurt and Naomi hadn't the faintest idea of what was
going on but they smiled on general principles.

Löwe spoke to Federn.

"You, Kurt, are a miserable immigrant, here on sufferance, but do
you realize that Naomi is a full-fledged citizen of this great republic?"

Vincent reached across Löwe and put his hand on Naomi's.

"Citizen Naomi! Dear Citizen Naomi!"

"You are kind, dear sir, you are very kind."

"Don't, dear citizen, please don't, you break my heart," said Vincent.

They had arrived at the modest hotel where Löwe had reserved rooms
for Kurt and Naomi. Vincent kept the taxi. He undertook to arrange
for the reservations to California. For once, Löwe yielded a prerogative
usually exercised by himself. Vincent held the taxi door open to say a
final word to Naomi.

"Isn't it nice, sweet, that our honeymoon isn't over? On the train, I
promise — I'll make you laugh!"

The Ian Leiths had arrived in Hollywood a week before. They had
flown in from Honolulu. Eileen busied herself with scouting about for a
place for the Leiths to live. She had found them a comfortable cottage
on the beach at Santa Monica. Stephanie was enchanted with it. She
had never known the delights of living in a small house; she told the

Grants she would never live in her castle again. Grant did not point out to her that, the way things were going in Austria, the option would not be hers. The night before the arrival of the wedding party, he and Eileen had taken Ian and Stephanie to Romanoff's for dinner. They had stayed up late. The next morning he had a full-dress conference on his finished script for Molnár's *Liliom*. He was, therefore, unable to meet the train in Pasadena. Eileen invited the Leiths to tea the next afternoon to meet Löwe, the bride and groom and young Federn. Stephanie simply couldn't wait. Imagine having Kaetchen here, right here! It was too good to be true. Eileen couldn't wait to see her darling, salvaged Naomi, an impatience shared by Grant, which he concealed.

There had been a considerable change in Ian. Even Eileen remarked it. He had gained weight, the slim elegance was gone, he was somewhat paunchy. He prattled, between drinks, but his witticisms seemed to echo from a hollow skull. Marriage had not mellowed him. The diffused amiability was gone; he was surly. But Stephanie doted on him. Altogether, the arrival of the Leiths was not an unmixed blessing for Grant. Stephanie, and Ian too, assumed that she was going to act in his play. What was particularly irritating was that Eileen assumed it too. She knew that Grant had promised it to Stephanie and, to Eileen, a promise was a promise. Grant evaded. He was still working on the play and he didn't know yet how it would come out. He was uncomfortable, now, with Stephanie. Stephanie and Eileen together made him even more uncomfortable.

In the morning, driving to the studio for his conference, Grant's thoughts were quickened by the anticipation of seeing Naomi. It would be very pleasant to see Naomi again, to have that slim, quicksilver creature in his house darting about. He remembered how alluring she was — the swift gestures and movement, the lovely long-fingered hand brushing the electric hair from her forehead. He would bring her to the studio, introduce her to his friends. She would be more responsive than Sally. He would make Naomi forget her tragedy. He remembered his joke with her parents about bringing her to Hollywood for a screen test. And here she was! It was hard to believe — how strange a twist — but here she was, he would see her right after the conference! He felt impatience with his studio commitment. What was he doing at ten

o'clock in the morning, attending a bloody conference? Still, the producer, the Studio Executive, amused him. Grant was actually fond of
him.

The executive's name was Sig Salvesh and he was an extraordinary
character. Already, Grant had entertained at parties by quoting remarks
of Sig's. He did a pretty good vocal imitation too. Salvesh had a grind-
ing voice, which sounded like an instrument for crushing pebbles into
gravel. He had a wide, swarthy face, outstanding ears and a tic. Grant
knew that at the forthcoming conference he was in for some fun. The
hero of Molnár's fantasy dies in the middle and then goes to heaven. If
there was one thing Salvesh hated it was a hero who died in the middle
or anywhere. He had not bought the "property." His studio head had
bought it and he was in New York struggling with bankers. Salvesh had
undertaken to produce the *Liliom* film against his will. He had accepted
the chore in the line of duty.

They were all there in Sig's pine-paneled office: the director, his di-
rectorial assistant, the scene designer, the costume designer, and the
continuity lady who had initiated Grant into the mysteries of film con-
struction. Everybody greeted Grant warmly except Sig, who sat behind
his great desk, the finished script before him, his tic working ominously.
The director winked at Grant and Grant returned his wink, Grant was
especially fond of the director, a great hulking Italian who might have
been a model for the equestrian statue of Colleoni. He had been a ditch
digger in the Middle West and had drifted to Hollywood and become a
Name Director.

Sig got to the point quickly. He tapped the script.

"This goddamn hero dies in the middle!"

Grant said that he was willing to make small changes but that he
couldn't change that. *Liliom* was a minor classic and there was nothing
he could do about it.

In the heavy silence of this impasse the director put in an ameliora-
tive word.

"The hero of our biggest hit, *Seventh Heaven*, goes blind."

"Yes," barked Sig, "but a blind man can still go to bed!"

This was unanswerable.

The silence hung like an albatross.

The scene designer said that he had contrived an ingenious way for

Liliom to go to heaven: in trains, lovely Pullmans in which distinguished people were dining and smoking cigars. It could all be done in miniatures.

Sig was not appeased. He didn't care for funeral trains. He didn't care for funerals.

It was agonizing. Finally Salvesh gave in. He gave in with bad grace. You could see on his swarthy face that, already, he was reproaching himself for having given his consent to the manufacture of a film in which the hero dies in the middle. He asked Grant to stay after he had dismissed the others.

Grant thought: "Is he going to fire me? He can't. I've got a contract."

But Grant was wrong. Sig's purpose in asking him to stay was paternal. He liked Grant and was impressed by him.

Grant waited. Salvesh leaned toward him, stared at him.

"You know, Stanley," he shouted, "out here you ain't writin' for a lot of goddamn Hindoos!"

Grant was mystified. He probed. Salvesh had the reputation of being one of the few executives who read books. Grant discovered that he had plowed through a book on Eastern philosophy. The idea of Nirvana had impinged on him. He expatiated on it to Grant.

"Those bastards," he growled, "love death. Out here we don't care for it!"

Lesson One administered, Sig barked an invitation to lunch with him in the executive dining room. Grant accepted.

Back in his office after lunch Grant found a telephone message from Eileen to come home as soon as possible, as Löwe and the others were impatient to see him. He still had appointments with the director, the scene designer and the continuity lady. He got through these quickly. About four he walked to the parking lot across the street from the studio entrance and got into his convertible. On the way home he arranged the events of the official conference in his mind, ready to tell. He couldn't help laughing; he was, he decided, really very fond of Sig Salvesh. It would be a good story for New York! Thinking of Naomi, he pressed his foot down on the accelerator. And Löwe. It would really be fun to see Löwe. Why had he come? What was he up to? It was always amusing to trace what Löwe was up to.

Grant found Löwe in the living room with Vincent. Löwe came up to him smiling.

"Ah! Hochstapler! You look flourishing. And why not? Here," he said, presenting Aldridge, "I've brought you an infatuated admirer. Vincent Aldridge, the Third. He dotes on you. Don't disillusion him!"

Vincent, holding Grant's hand in a long and sincere grip, babbled his admiration for his play.

"I can see one thing," said Grant, smiling at Löwe, "Mr. Aldridge is very intelligent."

"Call me Vincent. Do."

"I'm Stanley."

"But, where's Eileen? Where's Naomi?"

"In the nursery, entertaining your son."

Grant made highballs. He raised his glass to Vincent.

"I have to tell you, Vincent, that I am infatuated with your wife. When I heard you'd married Naomi, I felt a pang of jealousy. I fell for her the moment I met her. Will you mind if I continue where we left off? Will you be tolerant?"

Vincent was delighted with this fantasy. He was a married man with favors to dispense!

"I'll try. I'll try so hard. But tell me, Stanley, do tell me. She's an angel, Naomi, an absolute angel, but can you make her laugh?"

"Why yes. She was always laughing."

Vincent was disconsolate.

"Then I'm a failure, a total failure. To restore my self-esteem I had taken to telling myself that Naomi, perfect as she is, has no sense of humor. Now I'm devastated. Simply devastated."

"Cheer up! Have another drink."

Grant filled his glass. Vincent stared into it moodily.

Kurt Federn joined them. Grant greeted him. Kurt made him a stiff little bow. Eileen came up with Naomi. But this couldn't be Naomi. It was someone else.

"Naomi," said Eileen.

Grant stared at Naomi while telling himself he must not stare.

"Naomi," he said. "Hello. Welcome."

He took her in his arms. She rested there, passive, whispering something, he couldn't tell what.

He had not recognized her. Her eyes were no longer her eyes. The splotched and discolored cheeks, the emaciated body on which her dress hung loosely — she was no longer Naomi. Something asked: "How did Kafka look dead?"

There was an awkward silence. Vincent crowed:

"Well, you didn't succeed either. If you, the wittiest, couldn't then why should I? I'm reassured!"

"Naomi is very tired," said Eileen. "It has all been too much for her. I'm taking her to her room to lie down."

Naomi spoke to Vincent.

"Eileen says you are going away."

"Yes," said Vincent. "I thought of going to San Francisco. I've never been there."

Naomi reached out her hand.

"So I want to say good-bye."

Vincent took her hand.

"Good-bye, my dear. I leave you in good hands. You'll be all right now."

"You have been so kind. I thank you, sir. I thank you very much."

Vincent flushed with embarrassment.

"Please, my dear — please don't mention it."

Naomi turned away and followed Eileen out of the room and upstairs.

Vincent pushed his glass across to Grant.

"Please, Stanley. I could do with another. That child . . . she really . . ."

"It was indeed extraordinarily kind of you to get her out of there. God knows what would have happened to her if you hadn't intervened."

"Oh, I'd do anything for Kaetchen."

Vincent brightened.

"I kind of like it, you know!"

"What?"

"The sensation of being a married man. I keep telling myself: 'You're a married man.' It gives me status, don't you think?"

Grant laughed.

"What are you going to San Francisco for?"

"They're having a ballet season, I hear, at the Opera House."

"Kaetchen tells me you write very well."

Vincent flushed with pleasure.

"Does he? He's never said it to me. Does he really? That's sweet of him."

Eileen returned in time to greet the Leiths; they had just come in. Stephanie and Löwe had a rapturous reunion. Vincent's eyes were riveted on Ian.

"Who's that man?" he asked Grant.

Grant told him. Ian drifted over to the bar. Grant introduced him to Vincent. He made a drink for Ian. He chattered.

"Mr. Aldridge," he said, "has just achieved the status of a married man. Ian," he informed Vincent, "is a veteran."

Grant rambled on for a bit, but he got a quick feeling of being an outsider. Vincent and Ian were sizing each other up. A scene rose to the surface of Grant's consciousness, a marvelous and unforgettable scene in the pages of his favorite writer. It was the scene observed from a hideaway, between Baron de Charlus and M. Jupien. He had exchanged places, momentarily, with the narrator in Proust. Here it was between Ian and Vincent: the tropism, the bent light of promise. He fitted them into the botanical vocabulary of pollination employed by Proust to convey the nascent foliation of desire.

They were unaware of him. He left them to join the others.

At supper, they were all very high. Even Eileen had drunk more than she usually did. It was decided that it was absurd for Vincent to be going to San Francisco. Grant promised to see whether he could get him a job at the studio. He felt that he might. Vincent was in seventh heaven. He had left his luggage in a fleabag hotel near the station. This was, everyone agreed, shameful. Vincent then confessed that his father had so cut down his allowance that he was hard put to it to keep body and soul together. Stephanie had taken to Vincent; Vincent had taken to Stephanie. By the time they sat down to supper they were fast friends. Stephanie almost wept as Vincent described his futile efforts to amuse Naomi on the boat. Vincent's immediate destiny had become, suddenly, everybody's crying concern.

Characteristically, Stephanie solved it. Forgetting, momentarily, that she no longer lived in a castle with sixty rooms, she proposed to Vin-

cent — and why not? — how stupid that it hadn't occurred to her before? — that he stay with Ian and herself at her beach house, at least
until he got settled, until Grant had got him a job at the studio.

Everybody, especially Vincent, agreed that this would be a marvelous
solution.

In a freshet of benevolence, Stephanie spoke to Ian across the table.
"Won't it be wonderful, darling, to have Vincent for a boarder?"

23. The Promised Land

It was, as Charles Dickens said in another connection, the best of times
and worst of times. In London, Thaddeus Willens, who had always considered himself a citoyen du monde, sat in furnished rooms surrounded
by the books he had brought with him and the materials he had gathered for a book he was writing about Montaigne. On the wall was
Blake's drawing of St. John with the hallucinated eyes. He had on his
desk Löwe's letter introducing him to Lady Monica. Her husband was
a specialist in Blake and Willens would have enjoyed showing the spectacular drawing to an expert. But he had been too depressed to deliver
the letter. He kept putting it off from day to day. He was, in fact, ab-
normally shy.

From London Willens watched in agony the disintegration of his
country. He was historically minded; he knew that Austria was the
linchpin of European unity: that removed, the world — at least his
world — would crash. One day he was informed of the death of his
eighty-three-year-old mother in Vienna. He did not mourn. He had
hoped to bring her abroad but it was not possible, she was too feeble.
Vienna had taken cover, rapturously, beneath the hedge of the Mustache. The old lady had suffered indignities. She was accustomed to
taking daily walks in the Ringstrasse. Her legs were weak and she used
to rest on her walks on the public benches. One day she found these
benches denied to her; they were reserved for Aryans. A few days before
she died, her doctor got her a nurse, a middle-aged woman. The only

relative she had left in Vienna was a cousin, a sixty-year-old man, himself gravely ill. He came to the house to stay so that the old lady should not die with no member of the family present. The nurse said that she was sorry but that, under the new regulations, she could not spend the night under the same room with a non-Aryan. The regulation was an antiseptic against racial defilement. Willens did not mourn. He went, instead, to commune with another eighty-three-year-old invalid who was dying in London, Sigmund Freud.

Freud was calm and strong; Willens got great sustenance from him. In the old days, Willens, with other friends, had gone to see Freud once a week. Now the two exiles picked up where they had left off. Willens found the dying man cheerful and happy. Freud took him out to show him his garden. "Have I ever had a nicer home?" he said. Willens saw again the Egyptian statuettes so familiar to him from Freud's flat in Vienna. Willens found Freud mellower, more forbearing than he had ever known him. In Vienna Freud had always been courteous but reserved; now he was warm and affectionate. Willens told Freud what had happened to his mother. Freud sympathized but Willens could see that, although what was going on at home shocked him as a humanitarian, it in no way surprised him as a thinker, since he had always denied the supremacy of culture over the instincts. Events were confirming his long-held opinion that the destructive element in the human soul was ineradicable. He took no satisfaction on being proved right! Freud had published, not long before, a book on Moses in which he said that Moses wasn't a Jew at all but an Egyptian. He was sorry about that; he regretted having published this book in the worst moment of Jewish history. "Now that everything is being taken away from them," he said, "I had to go and take their best man."

If it was the worst of times in Vienna, in Hollywood, California, in the great Gold Rush capital of a new art, it was the best of times. There, on a Sunday morning on the beach at Santa Monica, a sardonic and justly celebrated Hollywood wit, who had not read Freud's disclaimer, stood on the verandah of the beach house of a film tycoon. He looked out over the rolling Pacific and the star- and starlet-studded beach. He made a panoramic gesture embracing the spangled scene.

"Well," he said, "this is what Moses promised us!"

*   *   *

And, in truth, nothing like the phenomenon of Hollywood had happened before in the history of the world. A British diplomat, in a report to Whitehall from his consulate in Los Angeles, had described the vast, sprawling congeries of his new post as "six suburbs in search of a city."

Hollywood was a village on the edge of these suburbs. It was neither London nor Paris nor Geneva nor Rome, the historic cities to which artists and political exiles had flocked through the centuries. And yet now it was to Hollywood that there was sluiced the greatest confluence of artistic talent ever gathered in one place. For American artists the magnet of gold was imperious. For the European exiles it was a temperate and hospitable haven. Together, the two groups conspired to fabricate a product that would be displayed in the habitations of heads of state, in the mansions of millionaires, in the palaces of maharajahs. Blackened miners, returning from long days in the slag heaps of Appalachia or Merthyr Tydfil, dropped into the local film palace to watch Apollonian actors in white dinner jackets flirting with goddesses in décolleté evening gowns. They saw these gods and goddesses strolling on marble terraces, cavorting in heart-shaped swimming pools. In Greta Garbo, Hollywood had Helen of Troy. To the latter-day Helen came tributes from all over the world, a vast and endless stream of correspondence. Helen herself never saw these letters; they were processed by a staff. Grant was shown one of them. It made him wince. It was the creamiest and thickest notepaper Grant had ever seen, coroneted in heavy gold. It was from a maharani who wrote to congratulate Miss Garbo on her new film, which she had just seen in the drawing room of her palace. She felicitated Miss Garbo on having, for once, abandoned the voluptuary, decadent types she had been playing under Semitic influence and for having portrayed, at long last, a truly Nordic heroine, untainted by degenerate Semitism: Queen Christina While she was about it, she wished to throw in a word of congratulation also to the non-decadent screenwriter Stanley Grant. It was this bouquet, mistakenly thrown at him, that made Grant wince. Well, he thought, had he not had, in youth, the clairvoyance to change his name, he would have missed the blown kiss from the maharani. The letter gave Grant a moment of discomfort, but then he laughed it off, thinking that it would make a good story to tell at Romanoff's.

Grant was probably the only writer in Hollywood who had a sneaking sympathy for his bosses, the tycoons. They were at such a disadvantage. Their most vitriolic critics were the writers whom they were making rich. The writers were articulate; the tycoons, mainly, were not. These men found themselves suddenly in possession of the fifth largest industry in America. But their position was different from the industrialists in control of General Motors or U.S. Steel. They were industrialists of art. They were creating an image of America that went all over the world. The Garys, the Schwabs, the Mellons, the Rockefellers had to worry only about the antitrust laws. The film executives found themselves with the national ethos on their hands. They had become arbiters of sex, morals, general ethics, taste, decorum, religion, politics at home and abroad. Editorialists reproached them for creating a false image of America. Was it false? The films played up sex, youth, money, success. But these were what America did worship and so did the European countries the editorialists worried about. The older civilizations had other specialties, of course, and so, at our best, did we, but the Hollywood staples were our staples and their staples.

The film tycoons had bizarre origins; they came from junkyards in Maine, from the cloak and suit industry in New York. They had been Irish political hacks in New York, trombonists in vaudeville — almost without exception they emerged from the subterranea of failure and obscurity. And now, without preparation, they found themselves in control of the most vivid and penetrating art form in the world. Moreover, their new eminence made them a force in politics. They were cosseted by the great. On the ebony cerement of L. B. Mayer's semicircular desk stood three large silver-framed photographs affectionately inscribed: by a matinee-idol general, a prince of the Catholic Church, a President of the United States. The Hollywood tycoons were persona grata in the White House and in chancelleries abroad. Grant remembered what a writer had said to him not long before, that, with all their faults, he would rather work for these lowbrows than for those executives who had college educations. There were several such from the Campus at Hanover and from the Yard in Cambridge. They were at a great disadvantage. They were insufficiently primitive. The others had the common touch, very common, very saleable.

The writers presented a curious spectacle. They were stippled in ambivalence; the tycoons were not. They knew what they were doing and why they were doing it. They functioned securely in the competitive skullduggery of the capitalist system, only their venalities were publicized, in the scuttlebut of Hollywood, while the Garys and the others played it soft. They were in far less danger of being overheard! The industry gave the writers, except for a few who were clear-sighted and cynical, the illusion of creation. After all, they were only doing what Shakespeare did when he adapted Holinshed. And when their adaptations met the strict censorship of the tycoons, they had a wonderful out. Were it not for this tyrannical constriction they would be writing masterpieces. They moaned and they groaned; they squirmed in the studio straitjacket; it slipped their minds that they didn't have to be there. The highest-paid writer in Hollywood cheated the executives unmercifully and gloated over it. He was in tremendous demand (indeed he had an astonishing and tarnished facility) and he often met this demand by farming out his jobs to cronies. He ran a "School" actually, just as the overcommissioned Renaissance and Dutch painters did. Dramatists with a flop in New York, who had neither the courage nor the invention to write another play, fled to Hollywood, got their offices, swimming pools and astronomical checks and gnawed at the tycoons who were damming up their creative lives. Grant played it cool. He was amused. He had given an unproduced comedy of his to his favorite character, Sig Salvesh, in the hope that Sig might buy it. Sig sent for him after he'd read it. The script was lying on Sig's desk before him.

"Well, Sig," Grant asked, "what do you think of it?"

Sig had never barked louder.

"It's nothing," he said, glaring at Grant from behind his thick glasses, "but a lot of goddamn phonies in a penthouse!"

"He's got a point," Grant said to himself. "In his crude way he's got a point."

The tutelary genius of Hollywood was Irving Thalberg, in whose memory there is now a vast, sparsely tenanted building which bears his name. An eternal light glows in a little crypt just off the main lobby. He was a slight figure, with a dark, sallow, sensitive face. His features were delicately modeled, his voice was soft, he never raised it. Conferences, often violent and turbulent with others, with him were controlled,

modulated, even hushed, like prayer meetings. But his opinions, quietly
and casually uttered, were seized upon as Pronouncements. He was re-
vered. When he would arrive, invariably very late, at parties, a hush
would fall upon the assembly as at the appearance of a deity. It was
known that his health was precarious; he bore the burden of sustaining
on a high level the cultural image of the Industry and so his tardiness
gave his hosts reassurance: the later Thalberg came so much the more
was added to their status. Scott Fitzgerald hero-worshiped Thalberg.
The unfinished novel he left at his death, *The Last Tycoon*, is said to
be about Thalberg. If so, Fitzgerald does not remotely approach him
nor the business he represented; Fitzgerald was romantic about both.
The playwright John Van Druten came closer in one sentence. Lunching with Grant one day in the MGM commissary, they were discussing
their boss, since both were working for him at the same time. They acknowledged the genuine aspiration in Thalberg, but Van Druten was
far more aware than Fitzgerald of the coarse fabric in which this aspiration was bedded and against which it had to worm its way. "He is," said
Van Druten, "a kind of cloak-and-suit Chatterton."

Grant had a two-thirty appointment with Thalberg for a story conference and left Van Druten to keep it, although he knew that Thalberg
wouldn't keep it. You were lucky if you saw him on the same day. Still,
he felt he ought to check in. He went in to see Goldie, the blonde deity
in charge of Thalberg's appointments.

"How does it look for a two-thirty, Goldie?"

"Not so good. Better let it go till tomorrow. I'll call you."

"Thank you, darling."

Greatly relieved, Grant left the studio and walked across the road to
his car in the parking lot. It was a Cord roadster, very dashing, which
Sam Goldwyn had given him for suggesting a title for one of Sam's
films. Goldwyn had never used the title but Grant was certainly using
the Cord. He doted on it, not merely because he had got it free but
because it was so sporting. Driving it gave Grant the feeling of belonging to the jeunesse dorée, to the Long Island polo-playing set. Its
smoothness on the road made him forget his acne. He swung the Cord
out of the parking lot. The top was down, the sun was blazing. He didn't

feel like going home. He would tool along to Malibu, maybe even to Santa Barbara. He might have dinner there at the Biltmore. Maybe, on the way, he would look in on Stephanie and Ian to see how the happy couple were getting along with their boarder. He could call Eileen and tell her he had to see a preview. He felt like ruminating behind the wheel of his Cord.

Grant was driving along Santa Monica Boulevard when, out of the corner of his eye, he caught sight, on the beach, of Vincent the Third, in trunks, lying on his back furiously bicycling his thick hairy legs in the air. Grant swung the car around in front of Stephanie's cottage and got out to study the odd spectacle more closely. He watched from the road. He saw Vincent get to his feet and start running up the beach as if he were being pursued. He ran about a hundred yards, turned around and began running back again. When he came opposite to where Grant was standing, Grant hailed him. Vincent looked up, furious at being interrupted; he was evidently on schedule. But when, squinting against the sun, he recognized Grant, he was all smiles. He waved rapturously and started toward the road.

"I'll come to you!" Grant shouted and started down the steps to the beach. Vincent was standing at the bottom when Grant came down. He was panting.

"Dear boy! What a nice surprise! It's heaven to see you!"

"Nice to see you! But I interrupted you. You were furious. Are you in training for the Olympics?"

Vincent grinned.

"In training, dear boy, but not for the Olympics."

"For what then?"

"You're too young to know!"

"I thought I'd look in on Stephanie."

"She's gone to Beverly. To see your wife, as a matter of fact."

"Ian go with her?"

"Oh no. Not Ian. I don't know where he is. Some bar probably swilling. He left this morning in a monumental pet. Very agitato. Stephanie too. They're madly possessive you know, both of them. Utterly childish. Stephanie's probably crying on your wife's shoulder right this minute."

"What's Ian in a pet about?"

"Jealous. Maniacally jealous. Let's sit for a minute under one of those delicious umbrellas."

They sat. Sweat was pouring down Vincent's face, his arms and shoulders. He picked up a towel and dabbed at himself.

"I didn't know," said Grant, "that you were a maniac on exercise."

"Have to. Defense measure. Have to keep myself in shape. I keep telling Ian. But he won't listen. He's flabby, overweight. Eats too much. Drinks too much. In a crisis he'll be no good at all. He's not in condition. I'll be all right, I promise you that."

"Crisis. What crisis?"

"When he's cruising and gets beaten up, he'll be killed. I don't mean to be. He likes rough trade, you know. So do I. But in reason!"

He grinned. In spite of his heavy frame and hairy body, his face was disarmingly boyish.

"I'm sorry your little ménage isn't tranquil."

"Anything but tranquil. It's definitely torrid! I'm clearing out as soon as I can. What about that job you were going to get me at Metro?"

"You said you'd submit something that I could show."

"Did I? Well, I will. I definitely will. You see, darling . . . I don't know why it is but I feel deliciously at ease with you. I feel like telling you things. No inhibitions with you at all. I wish I could see more of you."

"Nothing easier. Call me any time. Come to lunch with me at the studio."

"I'd adore to. I'm very depressed today. I got ghastly news this morning."

"From your father?"

Vincent looked very disappointed in Grant.

"How naïve can you be?"

"Sorry."

"A dear friend — my dearest friend — I just read it in the paper this morning — a   poet — an   exquisite   poet — so   gifted — so   very gifted . . ."

"What happened to him?"

"Killed. Murdered. In a bar in Acapulco."

"Who did it?"

"Oh, they don't know. If they do know, they won't tell. It can hap-

pen any time — to anybody. You come upon some recalcitrant innocent — and he or the gang with him — does you in. But then, you're an
innocent yourself, aren't you, dear boy? I hope not *too* recalcitrant."

He looked archly at Grant.

"Are you proselytizing, Vincent? Give it up. I'm committed."

Vincent laughed.

"You're really not my type, you know."

"I'm sorry about your friend."

"Ghastly. It shook me, I can tell you. I held it up as an example to
Ian. But wasted. No use talking to Ian. He's hopeless. *So* immature. But
it won't happen to me, I promise you. That's why I'm keeping fit. Before they do me in, I'll do them in. I'm very strong."

He stared off moodily over the Pacific.

"How's my dear little wife?"

"Oh, she's all right. Eileen keeps her busy."

"How?"

"Naomi is teaching her Jewish theology."

"How quaint!"

"It is rather."

"Come into the cottage and have a drink."

Grant got up, dusting himself off.

"No. Thank you very much. I'd better be getting back to Beverly."

"Stephanie will feel awful at having missed you. But perhaps you'll
still find her at your house. Well, if you must go, I'll return to my regime."

"Forgive me for having interrupted it."

"I'm delirious you did. I'll write something and give it to you. Perhaps I'll do up one of my old things. I'd adore to lunch with you in the
studio."

"Any time. My love to Stephanie. My love to Ian."

"Oh, I don't expect Ian will be back for days. He left me in a fiend-
ish rage. So boring! Bless you, dear Stanley."

Stanley climbed up the stairs and got back into his car. On the beach
below, Vincent had resumed his running as if the dark angel were after
him.

*   *   *

The conversation with Vincent had made Grant lose his taste for driving to Santa Barbara. He turned his car around and drove back toward Hollywood. What on earth had Stephanie got herself into? He pulled his car to a stop in front of a gas station and went inside to telephone Eileen. Eileen said Stephanie had just gone. She herself was leaving to pick up a refugee writer she was bringing home to dinner. In the Cord, driving home, Grant ruminated about his extraordinary conversation with Vincent. He felt that he understood better now why, so often, the homosexual writers equate sex with death. And Ian's "monumental pet" of jealousy. Evidently they were as promiscuous, these people, as so-called normal people, as promiscuous as he himself was. Poor Ian! Grant's heart went out to him. He had always liked him. He was so amusing, self-deprecatory, rudderless. He remembered what Löwe had said about him in Salzburg: "He's desperate — they're all desperate."

As he drove into Coldwater Canyon he began to be troubled about what Stephanie had told Eileen. He hoped she'd said nothing about his promise to give her the part in his play. She'd got this damned bee in her bonnet about playing that part. Oh, God, he groaned to himself, why did I ever make that promise? But he felt easier somewhat as he remembered that he had good news for Naomi — news that would please Eileen. It might help cancel out some of her unexpressed grievances against him.

24. High Comedy Face

As Eileen was not back yet with her refugee, Grant went to the bar in his living room to mix himself a highball. He drank it meditatively, staring, with a sense of incredulity, at the dark massive furniture and the fringed stand-lamps of the Spanish living room. He was conscious of an oncoming depression, a creeping misery, a sense of unreality. By what quirk of destiny had this come to be his living room? What was he doing in it? He was waiting for Eileen to return with her refugee. Who was Eileen? She was his wife, his lifetime partner. Surely this could not be. She was a stranger to him, as he was to her. What a curious creature she was anyway. This obsession of hers with Jewish theology — it was the zeal of the convert dazzled by a new spiritual vista. She had absorbed Jewish morality neat, straight out of the Hebrew prophets of their Grand Époque, all funneled through Naomi. Eileen had become so goddamn Jewish-ethical that you couldn't talk to her! You stubbed your toe on it wherever you went with her. He was in for it, he felt sure, about his long-ago promise to Stephanie. Damn!

There was something about Eileen's fervor, even on behalf of the refugees, that made Grant uncomfortable. He was sensitive about the way she was regarded in the film colony. She was loved, she was admired but she had also become, ever so slightly, a figure of fun. Grant didn't care for it; it made him edgy. A few days before a little incident had happened which, though he laughed it off, had made him squirm. He had run into Beth Hoffenstein, the wife of his friend Sam, the poet and screenwriter. In the studio commissary Grant found himself sitting with Beth; they were waiting for Sam. Beth asked about Eileen. "I adore Eileen," she said, "but I am also, I don't mind telling you, in terror of her." Beth was smiling as she said this in anticipation of her little joke. Grant, smiling also, asked why she was in terror. "Well," said Beth, "just a few days ago she called me up and asked me whether I'd bought my Passover matzos yet. I said I hadn't. To tell you the truth, I never think about matzos, nor, I am ashamed to say, about Passover either. Eileen became quite severe with me. 'You go right down to Lattner's this afternoon and buy your Passover matzos,' she said. Of course, I said I would. I solemnly promised."

"Did you keep your promise?"

"I meant to but I didn't. It slipped my mind. But, Stanley, if you tell Eileen that I didn't, I swear I'll never speak to you again. I love Eileen and I wouldn't lose face with her for anything in the world!"

Grant reassured her. "Don't worry. I'll keep your secret. Eileen's got a thing on promises. She believes they should be kept."

They laughed. Grant thought it was funny. But just now, in retrospect, it didn't seem to him so funny. Eileen was ridiculous. She made him ridiculous. He began to fume. Even her crusade on behalf of the refugees was exaggerated, fanatical, salvationist. She had managed to bully the executives into underwriting the importation of twelve refugee writers from a list prepared largely by Löwe. It was known as "Eileen's Dozen." It consisted of Central European screenwriters, journalists, essayists. Since some of them did not know English — a fact not emphasized by Eileen — the executives found it not easy to employ them. Still, they were on nominal salaries and they picked up English quickly. When Eileen first showed Grant the typewritten list of her dozen, a name sprang out to daunt him. Klaus Wolff. It rang a bell and then he remembered. That was the critic and essayist he had met on that frozen night at Stohl's, the wispy little man with the great dark eyes. It was in his behalf that Ludwig Born had appealed to Grant when he saw him out of the castle. He had promised Born to try to get him placed in Hollywood. Then he had forgotten all about it, till he saw Wolff's name on Eileen's list. Eileen, he reflected, had kept his promise. It was Wolff whom Eileen was bringing to dinner. Did Eileen know about this broken promise? Was she bringing Wolff as a reproach to him? Grant told himself not to be morbid but it didn't stop him from being morbid.

Born, Grant remembered, had said that Wolff was inventive. Indeed, Wolff had already proven himself so. The producer with whom Eileen had placed him, a friend of the Grants, had, to his surprise and delight, gotten a good idea from Wolff on the film then in progress. He called him into his office, motioned him to a chair, grinning with pleasure:

"Why," he exclaimed, "you're a Metziah!"

Wolff had had to explain the compliment to Eileen. "A Metziah," he said, "is an unexpected bargain found in a trash heap." Eileen, when she related this incident to Grant, was brimming with pride and pleasure. The producer's little pleasantry had made a marked man of Klaus Wolff. Eileen had taken all her dozen under her wing; she busied herself with them indefatigably, found them places to live and cosseted the wives of those who were married. She played no favorites, but she couldn't help but be thrilled by Wolff. He earned the sobriquet of "Eileen's Metziah." Wolff, who was shy, modest, and with a strong sense of humor, bore his sobriquet with patience.

Grant was annoyed at having to face Eileen's Metziah at dinner. He hated himself for feeling it. He had, oddly, wanted to be alone with Eileen, to talk to her, to confess to her the turbulent crosscurrents of self-criticism that were eroding him. He wanted to tell her about his strange interview with Vincent, to find out why Stephanie had come to see her. A black mood enveloped him; he poured himself another drink. His mind fixed on a tiny incident which loomed up in his mind, magnified into a monster of accusation. It had happened with Sam Hoffenstein. Sam was widely read. He was in a dithyramb about Balzac — "the leonine novelist," Sam called him. "You've read *Old Goriot*, of course," he said to Grant. "A very long time ago," Grant said. Sam went on, roaming authoritatively and incandescently the entire Balzacian oeuvre. Presently, Grant said:

"I do remember one page in *Old Goriot*, the page in which Balzac goes on about the linguistic habits of the Parisian young bloods in 1830, how they thought it smart to add the syllables orama to everything they said. They thought it was very funny to say: 'How is your healthorama?' And do you remember, Sam, when Goriot is dying upstairs, the painter asks Rastignac: 'Well, I hear you have a little deathorama upstairs?' And isn't it odd, Sam, isn't it odd, that the young people here, right now, a century later, who've never heard of Balzac, they do the same thing. They think it's smart to add to suffixes eroo and ola to everything they say: switcheroo, Lesbola. Plus ça change, eh, Sam?"

Sam was astonished. He himself had forgotten that passage. To think that after so many years, Grant had remembered *that!* He embraced Grant; it had sealed their friendship.

Now Grant stabbed himself with a query: why had he said that? Why had he lied? Actually, and by accident, he'd read *Old Goriot* a few weeks before. He'd found a dusty copy in the attic, left behind by the previous tenant. Why had he lied? Of course! To impress Hoffenstein with his astonishing memory. And also to impress him by the aperçu which, in fact, he had added to his all-purpose notebook only a few days before. Why had he forgotten the promise he'd made to Ludwig Born? A query sprang to life in his mind: "Can it be, so-called Stanley Grant, that you are a louse?" He gulped his drink to stifle the query.

He had worked himself up, by this time, into an ecstasy of self-flagellation. There was something wrong, there was something very wrong with him. Though he had a Spanish villa and a swimming pool on Coldwater Canyon, though he was a Name Playwright, there was something wrong. He hadn't come out well. He was evasive, he was insincere, he was theatrical — anything to make an effect — he was cowardly, he was sex-swept. He pounced on extenuation. He had never been loved, that was it, he had never been loved by those he loved; he was loved by Eileen whom he did not love, and less now, he was sure, even by her. His marriage had been an act of cowardice; he had been in a twist of contrition over Amos, Sally, Stephanie. Was it that he knew instinctively which love would be disastrous for him and made for it with an infallible instinct for self-destruction? He felt a wormy sensation of shame along his arms. He felt the sensation before he was able to trace its source. From some obscure docket in his mind Stephanie's query "Was it all right?" returned to mock him. She said it as if she were inquiring about a borrowed umbrella. He felt a rage against Stephanie. He would never give her that part! For this pettiness too he was overcome with contrition.

He rebelled against his thoughts. The drink did not nullify them. Should he find Naomi and tell her the news he had for her? But he couldn't bear to see Naomi, not alone. It was hard to talk to her, she was so withdrawn. The great dark eyes were lusterless; she stared at you without saying anything. He felt reproach in her eyes. Why? At what? She couldn't have known how he felt about her in Salzburg. He remembered her darting movements, her vibrant, braided hair, that wonderful black hair which had an electric pulse when you touched it. Now it was dank and dusty and dead. He remembered how he had held her sweet, lissome body in his arms on his wedding day and kissed her and wished to take her away with him forever. What on earth was the matter with him? Was he crazy, hallucinated? Would it never stop? Another phantom moved before him: that dark, so gracious girl of René Wolfsohn's. He poured another drink. He put it down on the bar without touching it. No use. It made no sense. He would go up to see Amos.

Schwester's door, adjoining the nursery, was open, so she could hear sounds from the next room. Schwester was inside, in a rocking chair, contentedly leafing through a film magazine. Grant stopped a second to talk to her. She rose, bobbed to him.

"Everything all right, Schwester?"

"Er schlaft."

"Good. I won't wake him. Are you happy?"

Schwester remembered that she spoke English.

"Oh yes and — I didn't thank you. I didn't."

"For what?"

Schwester pointed with pride and veneration to a framed photograph on the wall.

"For him!"

It was a glossy print of Clark Gable, inscribed to Schwester. On one side of Gable was Cary Grant, on the other, Gary Cooper. Schwester stood staring at her little Valhalla, incredulous that these heroes were there in her room, and with their handwriting on the photographs to testify that they were actually aware of her existence. The three pinup boys smiled at Schwester, full of good will to her and to the universe. She smiled dreamily back at them. Grant couldn't help remembering that in Salzburg Schwester's Valhalla had consisted of a martial photograph of her barber, in full SS regalia, and with a flourished Heil to the Führer scrawled across her gallant's torso.

"It's no trouble at all," he said. "Tell me who you want and I'll get him for you."

She bobbed.

"I'll just take a peep at him," he said. "Don't worry. I won't wake him."

Schwester nodded and returned to her rocking chair and *Film Fan*. In it, she felt sure, she would find the next member of her pantheon.

Grant opened the door to Amos's room, closed it softly behind him and tiptoed over to the crib. The descendant of the prophet was indeed asleep; Grant looked down at him. He was frowning; his fists were tightly clenched; he stirred, his arms moved as if to ward off an antagonist. Grant remembered when he had first seen him. He was transparent then; his face had been a tiny sealed envelope, his eyes shut tight, they looked as if they would never open. It was miraculous, it seemed to Grant now, that Amos had ever emerged from that catalepsy. By some quirk, some unexpected beneficence of nature, that evanescent body had fought its way through, solidified. His features were clear and defined now, even assertive, even strong. He twisted from his back to his side, his fists working. Was he, Grant wondered, having a bad dream? What sinister images could be harrying this emergent consciousness? Was he running the gauntlet already? Grant was affected. He wanted to protect Amos from his pursuers. He wanted to bring these devils into the open and ward them off. He couldn't. He watched. Little sounds were audible, moans. Grant wanted to caress that flawless skin, to assure Amos that it was only a dream, that he was safe. He had to restrain an impulse to scoop him up, to bring him into the real world where the ogres would scurry.

Looking down at Amos, he remembered, and this time without embarrassment, another line from Balzac — Old Goriot's remark: "When I became a father, I understood the nature of God." Staring at his enmeshed son, Grant felt he understood that. This was all really, this was all, to cherish Amos and to free him. Amos woke up. His blue eyes were troubled and fearsome, the frown deepened. He reached up his arms. He wanted up.

Grant swung him up, held him close. It was marvelous to hold him. It was transcending.

"You're all right," he whispered. "Up — up — up."

Holding Amos close to his heart, Grant felt that it was all right with him too, that he had emerged from his own nightmare. He would turn over a new leaf. He would reform. He would tell Eileen everything. He would make a new start with her. He would now and eternally, accompany Amos on his ascent. They would make the climb together.

He took Amos downstairs. On the lawn, beside the pool, Grant swung him high up in the air. Amos loved this exercise; he chortled with delight. Amos gestured toward a great, particolored rubber centaur riding at the edge of the pool. Grant took him over to it, mounted him, and guided it along the edge. Amos looked triumphant, lordly. Eileen joined him with Klaus Wolff. Grant welcomed Klaus warmly, recalling their meeting in Salzburg.

"I didn't think that night," he said, "that next I'd see you beside a swimming pool in California."

"I owe it to this benefactress," said Wolff, his eyes on Eileen.

"Do you remember the argument — between you and Löwe? Löwe was optimistic. You were the reverse."

"Unhappily, I was right."

"Not entirely unhappily. You are here. And already, I'm told, you've made your mark."

Wolff avoided the subject. He looked at Amos, who was staring at him.

"He rides well the centaur," he said. "Chiron."

"Who he?" said Grant.

"Achilles' music teacher," said Wolff.

Schwester appeared, demanding Amos for supper. Amos was reluctant to dismount but his mother persuaded him. She transferred him to Schwester's arms. Something about Wolff appeared to fascinate Amos. He kept staring at him inquiringly. Eileen was delighted.

"He's interested in you, Klaus."

"And I in him."

Amos reached out his hand and touched the lapel of Wolff's coat. Wolff took his hand. Amos smiled at him. Wolff smiled back. Schwester went into the house with her charge.

"You've made a conquest," said Grant.

"Not so much as he. I am enslaved. But I am afraid he is doomed."

"Why?" asked Eileen, startled.

"To be an artist. Some kind of artist."

"How can you tell?"

"From his expression. From his look."

"I hope not," said Grant. "I agree with you — it is a terrible fate."

Milton, the Grants' houseboy, a good-looking Filipino, highly scented, with hair like a polished black mirror, came up with a cocktail tray and canapés. Naomi appeared. Eileen introduced her to Wolff as Mrs. Aldridge. She always introduced her so to visitors. It never failed to startle Grant.

For once, as she greeted Wolff, Naomi smiled. He was a famous and familiar figure to her, though she had never met him.

Wolff bent over Naomi's hand and kissed it.

"Of you I know much from Mrs. Grant," he said. "Her enthusiasm makes me wish to study Hebrew with you also."

Naomi flushed slightly. Grant noticed it. "Wolff has restored her circulation," he thought.

Naomi explained to Eileen.

"It is sweet of him to say this," she said, "because he is a famous name to me. We, my father and mother and I, we used to wait for his reviews of the theater from Berlin. They were always so delightful and so funny to read."

"Funny?" said Grant, smiling at Wolff, "Can a drama critic be funny?"

"I agree," said Wolff, "I quite agree. We are undertakers. We should be abolished. And so we in Germany have been — though perhaps for the wrong reasons."

They were seated by this time with their cocktails on the verandah. Naomi looked at Wolff, smiling tautly.

"Gefühlte *Fledermaus*," she said.

"I beg you, Mrs. Aldridge, I beg you, do not recall my sins. And especially now, with dear Rudolph Stohl here. I saw him last night. As enchanting as ever. Unique man." He appealed to Grant. "What is your expression — he can charm the birds off the trees?"

"That is our expression," said Grant, "but what is that cryptic remark Naomi quoted? What does it mean and what has it got to do with Stohl?"

Naomi explained. Stohl had done a production of *Fledermaus* in Berlin which Wolff had thought overopulent. He had headed his review: "Gefühlte *Fledermaus*."

When he had absorbed it, Grant thought it quite funny.

"I take it back, Mr. Wolff," he said. "Evidently, drama critics *can* be funny." He smiled at Wolff: "But you're anti-Semitic!"

Wolff returned his smile.

"Naturally."

He accompanied this admission with a mock-helpless gesture. They all laughed. Milton came in to announce dinner. Eileen herded them inside.

Presiding at her table, under the wrought-iron Spanish chandelier, Grant thought that he had never seen Eileen so animated, so handsome. Messing about with good works seemed to put a shine on Eileen. Well, he wasn't above good works himself and he thought it was a strategic moment to trot out his own.

"I have a surprise for you, Naomi," he began.

Naomi looked at him, frightened. Grant explained to Eileen and Klaus.

"I've got Naomi a job at the studio. Script girl on my picture."

Eileen was delighted.

"Really! Stanley! How wonderful! Naomi. Darling. Congratulations!"

She lifted her wine glass to toast Naomi in her new career.

Naomi stammered.

"Mr. Grant — thank you."

Naomi never called Grant by his first name.

"When will she start?" Eileen wanted to know.

"When I start. Next week."

Naomi looked anything but happy.

"But will I know how?" she asked. "What will I have to do?"

"Nothing to it," said Grant. "You have to keep the script in order — that's all. Note all the changes — from day to day. As I'll be making the changes, you'll have an inside track. You'll be working with the director. He's good, one of the best, and a very nice guy. He's coming to lunch on Saturday, so you'll meet him."

Naomi was staring at her plate.

"You're very kind," she mumbled.

"I'm happy for Naomi but it's bad news for me," said Eileen. "It'll interfere with my studies. Just as I've met that wonderful Baal Shem."

"Ah!" said Wolff, "you're in love with the Baal Shem, are you?"

"Mad for him," said Eileen, all out for a man of whose existence she had never heard till that afternoon.

"Who he?" said Grant.

"Isn't it awful," said Eileen, "that my husband knows so little about the history of his own people?"

Rummaging in his mind Grant brought forth a scrap.

"Wasn't he a member of a sect, some kind of sect?"

"The Chassidim," said Wolff.

"He was the founder," said Eileen, out of the fullness of her scholarship. "He started it."

Grant, who felt he had established some kind of rapport with Wolff, winked at him.

"It seems to me I remember a little unkempt synagogue in Xenia, Ohio," he said, "which was devoted to that sect. We rather looked down on it."

Wolff laughed but Eileen was indignant.

"That was snobbish of you!" she said.

"Not at all," said Grant. "My father thought they were too relaxed in the rival establishment. I think he said they danced there."

"Very likely," said Wolff. "It's a lively sect, you know. They believe in joy. They believe in heaven on earth. Something to be said for it, isn't there, since heaven is an earthly fabrication?"

"No heaven in heaven, eh?" said Grant.

"There was for the Greeks. They were more inventive than we. Not only did they invent heaven, they populated it."

"We invented the Garden of Eden!"

"Yes," said Wolff, "we invented sin."

"No wonder we haven't been forgiven!" said Grant.

Wolff smiled.

"We haven't retained the monopoly," he said. "The Chassidim were not ascetic, as your father was. 'Thou shalt not hide thyself from thine own flesh,' they believed."

"If I'd known that I'd have looked in on 'em," said Grant. "Although my father would have killed me if he'd found out. He was a dear man, kindness itself, but his tolerance did not extend to that poor little synagogue. Isn't it silly?"

"All religions are internecine," said Wolff. "But the anointed leader in my country may be counted on to settle *our* differences once and for all."

A silence fell for a moment. Wolff brightened. He spoke to Grant.

"But I had a very amusing experience today. I'd read an advertisement in your trade paper the *Hollywood Reporter* . . . !" He made a large gesture: "THE BIGGEST NEWSSTAND IN THE WORLD. Well, bigness attracts me and I journeyed into Los Angeles to see it. Have you seen it?"

"I never go to Los Angeles in the daytime," said Grant. "Only in the evening for plays and music."

"Well, this newsstand's worth a visit. I've never seen anything like it. Newspapers and magazines, literally, from all over the world. I fell into conversation with the proprietor, Mr. Morton Dewey. Mr. Morton Dewey promptly greeted me in Yiddish."

"You can't escape us," said Grant, "no matter what our names are."

"Mr. Dewey is delightful. He took me in on a little private joke. In his office he showed me a great pile of *Der Stürmer,* sent him gratis by

Herr Goebbels himself. He showed me a letter from the sanctum in Berlin. Dr. Goebbels addressed Mr. Dewey affectionately and suggested to him that he sell *Der Stürmer* at its regular price and that, since he himself was above remuneration, the transaction would yield Mr. Dewey a one hundred percent profit. Mr. Dewey wrote Mr. Goebbels in appreciation of this arrangement. Mr. Dewey told me that he found the paper useful for his fireplace. Isn't it amusing?"

Somehow it wasn't. Grant thought of another source Goebbels had for distribution, through the industrialists of Greenwich, Connecticut, but he said nothing.

Naomi rose, said she had a headache and begged to be excused.

"Of course, darling," said Eileen. "Go upstairs and lie down."

Naomi left.

Eileen looked stricken.

"Poor darling," she said . . .

Wolff was very concerned.

"Did something I said upset her?"

Eileen put her hand on Wolff's to reassure him.

"Oh, no, my dear," she said. "It was just the whole conversation — it all came over her, I imagine — her murdered parents. It's wonderful you got her this job, Stanley. That should be a help — a new interest."

Wolff looked at Grant.

"We must find another subject," he said. "We really must. Isn't it extraordinary how, all over the world, there is only one focus of interest — in all the chancelleries, in all the ghettos, one point of interest: what that little man with the absurd mustache will do."

Eileen got up.

"I'll just go up and see how Naomi is," she said. "I'll be back in a minute."

Eileen left them.

"Your wife is a saint," said Wolff. "She deserves the Nobel Prize — merely for existing."

He said it quietly but there was something in the way he said it, the tone, that struck Grant. Obviously, Wolff adored Eileen. It pleased him. Or was it gratitude? Grant wondered. But Wolff changed the subject.

"I've been reading the latest by your great novelist Sinclair Lewis, *It Can't Happen Here*. Have you read it?"

"No, I haven't."

"He thinks it can."

"I know he does. But I don't agree. Not that there aren't plenty who would like to see it happen. The inventors of mechanical hearts like Lindbergh, the big industrialists, Father Coughlin, plenty of others. But we're too much of a mixture here, a nation of immigrants. There are too many good people, too many decent people. It's no climate for a dictator. We wouldn't stand for it. And don't forget, my dear Klaus . . . May I call you by your first name?"

"Please."

"Though you are a drama critic . . ."

"Ex," said Wolff in extenuation.

"In your calculations about us don't forget one thing, a rather important thing. Don't forget FDR."

"We bless his name," said Wolff quietly.

"I'll tell you something which may amuse you. The source of this is unimpeachable — a friend of mine who is close to FDR, sees him very often — you know that our ambassador to Berlin has resigned?"

"I know."

"Well, FDR said to my friend, 'You know what I'd like to do? — 'I quote him literally,' my friend said — 'You know what I'd like to do to that son-of-a-bitch in Berlin — I'd like to cable him that I am nominating to our embassy there Mr. Felix Frankfurter.' "

They both stood up as Eileen returned.

"She's all right," said Eileen as she resumed her place at the table. "I gave her two aspirins. She'll be all right."

"You have no idea," said Grant to Wolff, "what an entrancing creature Naomi was when I first met her in Salzburg. All gone now."

"Her soul is the same," said Eileen.

"Well," said Grant. "Let's get away for a minute from the awful SUBJECT. We can't do anything about it anyway. I was very amused to hear from Eileen about your triumph at the studio. Tell me about it. How do you become, instantaneously, a Metziah?"

"All miracles are instantaneous," said Klaus.

Grant was struck by the quality of Wolff's voice. His voice was wispy too, but there was power behind it; it was at once feathery and penetrating, and he had a gift for comic intonation.

"But what made him pin that Metziah medal on you?"

"I assure you it was the simplest possible suggestion. But don't you see? If, out of kindness, out of charity, you engage a deaf-mute, it astonishes you, doesn't it, to find that the deaf-mute can hear, that he can speak? I have been struck by the vast posters I see everywhere — GARBO TALKS — as if she were a horse, and speech *is* remarkable in a horse. I assure you, this accolade of the kind producer was bestowed for a miniscule suggestion."

"Don't be modest, Klaus. It'll get you nowhere."

Klaus smiled. He looked at Eileen. "But I am where I want to be. I wish to be nowhere else but here."

"Dear Klaus. It is wonderful for us that you *are* here."

Wolff spoke to Grant.

"Do you remember perhaps, Mr. Grant, that evening at Stohl's, do you remember perhaps — Sigmund Alt?"

"The big man, the cultural historian?"

"Yes."

"Of course I remember him. Very amusing man. Do you remember the extraordinary harangue he delivered about his pencils — that he'd not tolerate it if anyone touched his pencils?"

"He did not tolerate it."

"What do you mean?"

"They disturbed his pencils. He jumped out of the window. Sigmund Alt is gone. I shall miss him."

"That's terrible," said Grant, "terrible."

There was a silence. Grant burst out:

"But Klaus — tell me. Why did he stay? I've been asking myself this ever since that night. I wondered it then — even while Alt was talking. I said to myself: 'Why do you stay? Why do you sit here? Why don't you take your pencils — and run away?' "

Wolff shrugged his shoulders.

"He liked Vienna. He liked his rooms. He liked his friends. Besides . . ."

"Well?"

"He did not have the good fortune — which befell me — to attract the attention of this gracious lady."

He lifted his wine glass to Eileen. Their eyes met.

"My God," thought Grant, "he's in love with Eileen!"

Eileen got up.

"Let's have our coffee in the living room."

Grant and Wolff followed her. When they were settled in the living room with brandy and coffee, Eileen began talking about Sam Hoffenstein. Klaus, she insisted, must meet him. Sam had given her the manuscript of his new poem. It was upstairs. Would Klaus care to hear it? Klaus said he'd love to. Eileen ran upstairs to get it.

"I share Eileen's passion for Sam," Grant said. "He's probably the most genuinely talented writer here."

"Ah," said Klaus. "What does he do here?"

"He hasn't the faintest idea," said Grant.

Eileen came down with the poem. It was written on a sheet of MGM stationery. Klaus asked her to read it aloud.

"No," said Eileen. "You read it, Stanley. You read much better than I do."

Grant took Hoffenstein's manuscript. He laughed.

"Interoffice memorandum."

"Is that the title of the poem?"

"No, the stationery. But it's an idea, isn't it? I am sure Sam could write a funny poem with that title. This one is called 'Churchbells.'"

Grant read it aloud.

> *When I was a little lad*
> *Sunday churchbells made me sad,*
> *Made me wish I hadn't been*
> *Born a Jew and deep in sin,*
> *For as many a Christian boy*
> *Told me with unChristly joy*
> *I had personally done*
> *A thing to blacken sky and sun,*
> *In hate and malice sacrificed*
> *His Lord and Saviour, Jesus Christ,*
> *And though, since I was barely ten,*
> *I couldn't quite remember when*
> *I had done the hellish thing,*
> *I used to hear the churchbells ring,*
> *And dogs of terror scampered blind*

> *Through Ghetto alleys of my mind,*
> *And barked in bells from Christian spires,*
> *And ran in rings round Christian fires,*
> *And crucifixes, wild of eye,*
> *On their single legs strode by.*

Milton came in. He told Eileen that the lady who had been there this afternoon wanted her on the telephone.

"Stephanie!" Eileen ran.

"You wouldn't know it from that poem," said Grant, "but Sam Hoffenstein is a very funny man. He works for a producer who can never make up his mind about anything. Last person who talks to him influences him. Sam says he's like a glass of water without the glass. Also that he's like Jekyll just as he's becoming Hyde — just at the frontier when neither one of them is anybody! Sam was asked to write some scenes for a picture about a Mongol invasion. He declined: 'I promised my mother on her deathbed,' he said loftily, 'not to write anything east of the Euphrates.' "

Klaus smiled.

"Stephanie tells me she is going to be in your play."

"Have you ever seen her on the stage?"

"Oh, yes, often."

"How is she?"

"Suffering and nobility are her specialties. She is so beautiful that when she suffers you suffer with her. She brings such conviction to nobility that when you see her you believe in nobility."

"Ever see her in comedy?"

"Ah," said Klaus indulgently, "but comedy is much more difficult."

"I wish you'd tell that to Eileen," said Grant with some bitterness.

Grant began to feel restless. He got up and went to the bar.

"Drink, Klaus?"

"Thank you, no," said Klaus. "I must be getting home to bed. I must keep my wits about me. Being a Metziah, you know, is a responsibility. I must go on providing bargains."

Grant poured a stiff one. The inspirational mood in which he had begun the evening ebbed. He felt the lick of depression.

"God, what a life!" he said, scarcely conscious that he was saying it aloud.

"Yes," said Klaus, "they are never very far away, are they, the dogs of terror?"

Grant looked at him, surprised.

"How did you know?" he said sardonically.

Klaus spread his arms in the little deprecatory gesture characteristic of him.

"My dear friend!"

"The graph of my moods," said Grant morosely, "would serve as choreography for a St. Vitus dance!"

Grant had remembered Sally in this room and her mock-invitation to him to rape her. Sally: what a screwball she, what a deluded and prideless idiot he! He was back at his old sport. Stephanie. What would Klaus say if he knew about himself and Stephanie. Why, what he had done — it was a kind of necrophilia. No different. No better.

Eileen returned.

"I told Stephanie you were here," she said to Klaus. "She sends her love."

"Thank you."

Klaus got up.

"I really must be getting home," he said. "If you could just take me to the bus . . ."

"Nonsense," said Grant. "I'll drive you home."

"We'll both take you home," said Eileen.

They dropped Klaus at a dingy little apartment bungalow in an alley off Sunset. Grant invited him to lunch with him in the MGM commissary. He wanted, he said, to show off the talking mute. Eileen promised to keep in touch. She wanted him to come to a party she meant to give for Rudolph Stohl. Grant backed his Cord out of the alley and headed it home.

"I like your friend very much," he said.

"He has a beautiful soul."

"Have you seen it?"

This remark had an unfortunate effect. Though he did not look at her, Grant was sure that she resented it. She always smouldered at his professions of agnosticism. Damn it! He hadn't intended to start off that way at all. He had intended to bare his own soul, hopefully to have it swept clean under her scrutiny.

"What did Stephanie want? I mean, just now, when she telephoned?"

"She wanted to know whether I had spoken to you yet."

"What about?"

"The part in your play."

"Oh."

"I told her I hadn't seen you alone yet but that I would."

"I've just been talking to Klaus about her. As an actress, I mean. He says she's wonderful in tragedy but that comedy is not her strong point."

"Stanley, you've simply got to give it to her. She's desperate."

"What about?"

"Her marriage. Things aren't going at all well. It was a mistake for her to have invited Vincent to stay with them."

"Anyone would have known that but Stephanie."

"She's so dear. So generous. So outgiving."

"She is all that. She seems to have every variety of sense except common. She has a mania for self-destruction. Kaetchen told me that Ian would be fatal for her. Sally said so. He'll kill her, she said."

"She loves him."

"All right. Why did she have to marry him?"

"It helped him. In Gastein when he was in trouble. It saved him."

"Did he kill Vesper?"

"No. Stephanie says no. I believe her."

"I saw Vincent this afternoon. Had quite a chat with him."

"Did you? Where?"

"On the beach. At Malibu. I was driving along, to get the cobwebs off my mind, and there I spotted Vincent. Exercising like mad! I don't think Stephanie will keep her boarder for very long."

They were stuck in traffic on Hollywood Boulevard. The audience drifting out of Grauman's Chinese Theater looked green-faced under the neons.

Grant muttered aloud.

"There's something hellish about this place."

"I don't see that it's very different from Broadway."

"New York doesn't pretend to be paradise!"

"It's all in your mind."

"That's where most things are," said Grant.

Grant propelled his car into Rodeo Drive. Here the streets were dark and quiet, smug-suburban.

Grant tried to recapture his earlier mood, when he had held Amos close to him.

"Eileen — "

"Yes, Stanley?"

"Things aren't right between us. Things aren't right — with me. I want to tell you."

"Tell me."

"I wanted to talk to you about *my* dilemma. Instead, you insist on involving me in Stephanie's."

There was bitterness in his tone, reproach.

"I know you don't love me. You never did. In a way it's my fault, our marriage. Without meaning to, I forced you. I lied to you."

"Did you? That humanizes you. It's tough work — being married to a saint."

The reconciliation scene, the dramatist reflected, was turning into a muted quarrel.

"I told you — in New York, before you sailed, that it was all right, when we were both so scared about my pregnancy. It wasn't all right. I lied to you. I didn't want you to sail under a cloud of worry. I didn't want to spoil your summer. I wanted your child. I never intended to tell you. It was Sally who told you. Still — I lied."

They drove on in silence for a few minutes. Eileen said:

"I know you're twisted and torn. I know about the women. It's your nature. You can't help it. I'm reconciled to that. I don't mind that."

"What do you mind?"

"Your dishonesty."

"My God, can't we get away from Stephanie? It's becoming an obsessive subject — like the Jews."

"It's the same."

"What on earth do you mean?"

"Because it comes down to justice. Simple justice. Your religion and mine — they're based on justice. What's going on in Germany is done by atheists. People who've turned their backs on religion."

"That's nonsense. You're ignorant of history. When I think of the horrors that have been done in the name of religion!"

"In the name. Not religion. Religion itself — yours and mine — is humane."

"Too humane perhaps to be human. To fulfill Christianity you'd have to be superhuman. People just aren't nor should they be expected to be. Result: hypocrisy. There are no Christian states though they all pretend to be. You're naïve."

"So were the early Christian Fathers. Sally says so. Sally says it's the sophisticated who've muddied things up."

"Sally?"

"Yes."

"Where is Sally?"

"She's taking instruction in a convent in Italy."

"Sally!"

"Yes. She's happy. She doesn't want what she was. She never wanted it."

The Cord crunched into the driveway of their house in Coldwater Canyon.

They tiptoed into Amos's room to see him asleep. Only the top of his head was visible over the thin blanket that covered him. One arm hung limp between the bars of his crib. Eileen's hand hovered over the blanket without touching it. They tiptoed out.

They went down to the living room. Grant poured himself a drink.

"I hope he's having nice dreams," said Grant.

"Oh, yes. He's sleeping soundly."

"When I went in to see him — before you and Klaus came — he seemed to be having a bad dream. When I picked him up, when I held him close, I thought: This is all there is in the world!"

"Darling! Of course. It *is* all there is in the world."

Eileen got up, stifled a yawn.

"Very tired. I'm going to bed."

She came over to him and kissed him.

"I can't get over what you told me about Sally."

"Yes. She's wanted that — ever since her mother died."

"Do you hear from her — from Italy?"

"Oh, yes. All the time. Very funny letters she writes too. Good night, darling. Sleep well."

"I'll stay up for a bit. Feel like working."

"Good luck."

Eileen started out of the room.

"Eileen . . ."

"Yes?"

"About Stephanie . . ."

"Well?"

"Tell her it'll be all right. She can have the part. I'll write to Bob that I've cast it."

She returned to him. Her eyes were shining.

"Bless you! Bless you! You won't be sorry. You'll see! You won't be sorry. May I tell Stephanie — it's settled?"

"Of course you can."

"I'll call her! Right away! She'll be . . ."

But she was out of the room and on the way to her telephone before she could complete the prophecy of what Stephanie would be.

Grant took his highball upstairs to his study and sat at his desk to have a look at his manuscript. But he couldn't help marveling about Eileen, about Sally. It was as if they had rediscovered, for themselves and by themselves, the simple axioms of good and evil. Modern life made these truths archaic; no one ever thought of them or expressed them, except in sermons, attended by the yokelry, and it never remotely occurred even to these, in their private lives, that these axioms might have a practical application. Oh well . . . He leafed through the pages of his play, reading Leonie's lines. Somehow, the more he read them, they were so light and glancing, he couldn't, though he tried, hear Stephanie saying them. It wasn't her temperament. Well, poor Stephanie, she was in a terrible way, and he *had* promised. Now, under the spell of Amos, out of Eileen's need — as desperate almost as Stephanie's — he'd promised twice. Well, what the hell? Bob was a wonderful director, he would dictate a performance to Stephanie. She was so beautiful, she would win the audience's sympathy. She'd be pathetic anyway. His lines and the clothes designer would do the rest. The critics, who knew so little, would think her wonderful.

As he read through the scenes between Sally and Ogden, he felt relief that Sally was in Italy and wouldn't see that he had left her, after all, a winsome ingenue, that she would not be a witness to the capitulation of verity to commerce. She had said, hadn't she, that the Sally he had was more "saleable" than the Sally who was? Damn difficult, he thought, full of pitfalls, dramatizing an actual experience. He would never do it again.

Grant took a sleeping pill and went to bed.

The next morning Grant got into his Cord and drove to the studio, to keep his deferred appointment with Thalberg. Goldie had telephoned to change his appointment to 11:30. That meant 12:30 — if he was lucky! Well, he would exchange studio scuttlebut with Goldie; he enjoyed that. In fact, Grant felt, he enjoyed everything. He was pleased with himself too about giving Stephanie the part. He felt virtuous. It would make Stephanie happy. It would show Eileen that he was a man who could keep a promise. It was a radiant morning; he drove through the streets of Belle Aire, the little hills, tree-studded, like illustrations in an illuminated Bible, the trim houses varicolored, as in the coastal towns of the Italian Riviera. It struck him again, he felt a sense of incredulity again, at the munificence of the perquisites that had accrued to him simply because he had this odd knack of writing dialogue that actors enjoyed speaking: this Cord, this astronomical salary, the vista of his play about to come on in New York, this sense of well-being, this morning.

Goldie greeted him warmly.

"How're chances, Goldie?"

"Very good. He's read your scenes. He expects you."

Grant paused for a moment before he descended the few steps leading to the anteroom to have a look around. At any hour of the day the waiting room of Thalberg's office presented a striking spectacle. The room was crowded to the last chair: Nobel Prize winners, scads of Pulitzers, great composers, famous chorcographers, scene designers, actors and actresses whose names were household words all over the world, virtuosi, poets, novelists, hacks. There was the greatest possible variety but they all had a common denominator: they wanted money. A nod of approval from Thalberg meant money. Grant had been reading a novel by Alphonse Daudet, *The Nabob,* in pursuit of an idea he thought might make a play. In this novel Daudet has a wonderful description of the

crowd of petitioners, on any morning, waiting to see the Duc de Morny.
A nod of approval from Morny meant money too.

Scanning the crowd of Thalberg petitioners, he saw a face that erased
his marginal thoughts. He knew this face — he'd seen it and yet he had
never seen it. A high comedy face, luminous, pale radiance that at any
moment — a funny remark, a funny sight, an unexpected anomaly of
character — would light into incandescence. Leonie — the perfect Leonie! He remembered. He'd seen her in films. She played secondary
parts, young-mature women who made brittle remarks. But, in black
and white, the iridescence did not register. He thought he saw her looking at him. He thought she smiled faintly. He made his way to her. A
phrase and its music sang in his mind — the phrase from *Rosenkavalier*
he'd heard in Salzburg at Mary Kennicott's party, "Du bist mein
Schatz." By the time he reached her she was smiling at him. He introduced himself. It was unnecessary. The high comedy face was breathless with recognition of the Name Playwright.

The love he had never found was here. It was all in the world that
mattered; it was all there was in the world.

25. Hof Jude

In the parlor of his suite in Mary Kennicott's mansion in Santa Barbara, Alexander Löwe aus Czernowitz sat in an early American rocker
which was somewhat too small for him, reading Montaigne on suicide.
He had been impelled to do this by the news he had received that
morning, which had greatly saddened him, of the suicide of his old
friend Thaddeus Willens. "Not all ills," the Squire of Montaigne was
saying, "are worth dying to avoid. And besides, there being so many
changes in human affairs, it is difficult to decide at what exact point we
are at the end of our hope." In this connection Montaigne adduces the
example of Josephus. He writes: "We see Josephus involved in a danger so manifest and imminent, a whole nation having risen up against
him, that reason could hold out no hope of escape. Yet being advised in

this strait by one of his friends, as he informs us, to do away with himself, it turned out well for him that he obstinately clung to hope. For Fortune, against all human reason, so changed the situation that he found himself free and unharmed."

Löwe edged himself out of the rocker and began to pace the room, his hands clasped behind his back. He sighed. He meditated deeply. It was no use, he reflected. Art, literature, even the best, had no influence whatever in modifying the lives of people. It might entertain and amuse the intelligent and, momentarily, even edify their fantasies, but in no way did it affect their conduct. Willens had, Löwe knew, intended, had even begun, to write a novel about Montaigne. He knew Montaigne by heart. Hadn't he remembered the squire's words on the subject of suicide? Why, before he did it, didn't he remember Josephus and wait for a turn in the Via Dolorosa? Löwe even felt a nuance of irritation. What right had Willens to indulge himself in this luxury? He was rich, he was famous, he had been received everywhere with honor, even with veneration. What should the poor Hollywood refugees, Eileen's Dozen, poverty-stricken, anonymous, smuggled in on sufferance, what should they do? They had infinitely more right to such self-indulgence than Willens, yet they denied themselves. Yes, Löwe was miffed with his old friend. There was a concentration camp in his mind; he couldn't escape the mephitic cloud which had shadowed him since he left Salzburg. He was a pessimist. But that, Löwe thought, was the trouble with Willens. He was too rational, too methodical. He lacked resilience. He lacked courage. He was sure that the hedge of the Mustache would ring in the whole world. Possibly it would, and yet — and yet — maybe it wouldn't. Maybe sooner or later the Mustache would be clipped. Maybe England and France would clip it — maybe even America. Yes, Willens lacked Montaigne's adaptability.

What would Montaigne have thought of it all? Löwe went on pacing, went on meditating. What would his hero have said if he were living now? What would have been his reflections about the methodical, marvelously organized incineration, of books and bodies, now going on in Germany? As he was half Jewish, he would have been proscribed. His books would have been burned and, unless he managed to escape, he himself. Montaigne would have managed, of that Löwe was sure. He would have escaped as he had escaped from the plagues and pillages that infested his own countryside during the terrible religious wars that raged around the book-lined turret of his chateau where he sought solitude and silence and insulation even from his own household. Nor would he have been greatly surprised; he would have accepted the mass murder as natural; unlike Willens he would have taken it in his stride. The phenomenon would have been familiar to him; he would have accepted it as natural human conduct. His friend Henry the Fourth, a prisoner in the Louvre on the eve of St. Bartholomew, had seen with his own eyes, through the windows of the palace, ardent Catholic women drinking the blood of freshly slaughtered Protestants.

Montaigne loved animals; he cherished and respected them. He knew that they were sane, that they were not — like his own kind — vindictive. They were sensible. They had limited objectives: for sex and sustenance. "Look to the animals," he kept saying, "look to the animals and notice what we are all here for, what we are equipped by nature to achieve: tranquility and preservation." Löwe meditated on this. Since they had no religious beliefs, animals were not murderous. Having no love of God, they had no need to slaughter each other in order to demonstrate that love. Nor did they slaughter each other over the minutiae of ideology. They were — one could not say human because that would be to slander them — but, unlike their masters and their hunters, they were peaceable. The medieval bestiaries, compared to the Chronicles, were idyllic. The bestiaries were fanciful; the Chronicles dripped blood and fire.

Löwe walked to the tall windows and stared at the long allée of eucalyptus trees with the emerald-blue shimmer of the Pacific at its end. On the Duncan Phyfe table was a letter which he had been writing to Lady Monica. Beside it was a little pile of four exquisitely bound and illustrated German books which he meant to send her. One of them, on the Minnesingers, he had inscribed: "Just to remind you of another Germany." He picked up another, *Das Kleine Buch der Tropenwunder,* a succession of butterflies and caterpillars on the branches of fruit trees and glowing bushes. The colors were miraculous, the detail microscopic, clear. Another, *Der Kleine Goldfischteich,* was devoted to fishes. They swam against pale green backgrounds, their scales rainbow-colored, their fins and tails ribbed, as if etched, but their eyes were fixed, angry, stupid, belying their shimmering bodies.

"They have the eyes of gauleiters," Löwe thought.

Then he picked up his favorite, on the Minnesingers. Here was Tannhäuser and here, Löwe's pet, Walther von der Vogelweide.

Herr Walther, in an opalescent blue-green robe, was placidly climbing a short, uncertain ladder, carrying a scroll on which he had inscribed his latest to a lady in garnet, leaning over the machicolated railing of a deciduous balcony, waiting to crown him with a wreath. Another troubadour, Herr Kristan von Hamle, approached his lady by a more ingenious method. He was in a yellow-and-crimson-striped bucket. His lady, on her balcony, was working a pulley to bring the bucket up to her. She got the leverage from a huge, crimson star, with a yellow center, working slowly each prong of the star. They were all, these love singers, royally dressed and accoutred; they were not in a frenzy, neither when they were composing their verses nor when they delivered them; their ladies received their offerings like roses, knowing they would be good, knowing what they would say. They rode on palfreys, releasing birds; they rocked in shallops on the spiraled crests of little hillocks of water, on stylized green and white waves. The horses they rode were as wondrously caparisoned as the riders. They rode, side by side, the lady holding a falcon, the gentleman holding the lady, but without insistence.

"They seem to have time on their hands," thought Löwe, "nonobsessive, pre-Freud."

He sat down at the Duncan Phyfe which, Mary had told him, had belonged to Jérôme Bonaparte. What had he been telling Monica? He read:

Poor Sally! She has accomplished nothing — less than nothing. This, I imagine she thought, was to be her last act before quitting the world, before taking the veil, to rid it of Ogden. How naïve! She had played a long cat-and-mouse game with this virtuoso of sex. Did she cherish the illusion that by frustrating and exposing him she would, to that degree, staunch the metastasis of evil in the world? I suspect that she was in love with Ogden but her religion gave her an even more powerful drive toward goodness, toward purity. So, like Isabella in Measure for Mea-

*sure, she sought escape from the sexual impulse toward an object she
loathed, to give up her life to a God whom she worships. I am told that
the order she has joined is so strict that when she receives visitors, she
can only talk to them through a grille. Poor darling! I hope that she will
never find out how farcical her maneuver was. Dr. Ogden is adroit. Dr.
Ogden is bouncing. He is in fine fettle, more active than ever, as I will
tell you . . .*

He picked up his pen to go on but he put it down again. He felt tired.
He felt the restlessness of fatigue. He sat again in the early American
rocker by the window, shifting about in it uncomfortably. In a burst of
chauvinism, Mary had furnished this suite, indeed the whole house,
early American. The early American cabinetmakers had been austere
and angular; Löwe preferred the satined curvatures in Mary's Austrian
castle and also the creations of Adam in her London house. For the first
time since he had been here — nearly a week — he began to pay attention to the portraits of two ladies hanging on the wall. One was of a
very handsome woman in eighteenth-century dress, sitting, holding a
book in her lap with her very beautiful hands, of which, obviously, she
and the artist were both conscious. Löwe walked over to the painting
and read the name-plate: *Mrs. William Bowdoin — 1748.* The artist
was Robert Feke. Löwe had never heard of him but he thought he was
not bad. Mrs. Bowdoin, whoever she was, had a very nice face and her
hands were all you could possibly expect of hands. He left Mrs. Bowdoin to get acquainted with Miss Van Buren by Thomas Eakins. She
was a totally different type from Mrs. Bowdoin. Miss Van Buren, although she had a fan in her lap, was serious, intellectual. She was lost
in thought. She had a fine forehead, a high-bridged nose, her face resting on her hand in absorption. Of what was she thinking? He would
have liked to share her thoughts. She would surely have shared them
with him had he known her. She was distinguished. She would have been
a definite addition to his stammtisch at the Colony in New York or at
the Ritz in London. Why was she a Miss? Did she never marry? Ah,
thought Löwe, had she been his contemporary he would so nicely have
employed his third hand in Miss Van Buren's behalf.

For a change, Löwe sat on an early American sofa, which Mary had
divested of the original horsehair and done up in black-and-yellow-
striped silk. It was against the wall opposite the two early American

ladies and he now sat staring at them from that vantage point. He was aware of a sense of unreality at being in this room. This had happened to him often before in the variegated rooms he occupied and it was always accompanied by the query: "Will this be the last room?" "Odd," he thought, "if it should be here, if I passed out early American!" He knew the unpredictability of the illness from which he suffered, its unceremoniousness, its abrupt summons, as boorish as the door knocks of the SS in Germany on their summary roundups of victims. His irritation with Willens returned. Why give up, voluntarily, this marvelous thing? He himself was impassioned with life, an intensity that could be felt only by those under a death sentence. Everyone was under a death sentence but unconscious of it. They did not feel that it applied to them; it was for other people. He remembered what his friend W. S. Maugham had said to him the last time he'd seen him in London. They were having dinner in Maugham's suite in the Dorchester: "You know, Kaetchen," he said, "every time I get to London after a long absence, the first thing I look at in *The Times* is the obituary columns. I know that one morning my obituary will appear in those columns, but I don't believe it!" But Löwe did believe it. He looked around the sun-flooded room. He savored this moment, this silence, the consciousness of being alive. He was aware of the minutes passing by, a silken filament slowly unwinding. He reveled in the awareness of the agility of consciousness, in the glow and versatility of his thoughts, able to command from far and near scenes, effigies, blazing gardens, lamp-lit rooms, silver and china on tablecloths. He summoned Monica, her violet eyes, the gleaming tangents of her wit, her laugh, the quickness and precision of her movements. Monica, he reflected, was both mercurial and serene. He took pleasure in the fact that he had never before had this particular thought about her, so compact.

Unwinding on the filament he saw the rooms he occupied in the archbishop's palace in Salzburg, in Mary's house in London. Every room he stayed in was like an inn to Löwe; he had been, for years, constantly en voyage. And then another room came to life, a garret room in a thatched cottage in Czernowitz. It was a long distance, that garret room, from his present quarters which he shared with Mrs. Bowdoin and Miss Van Buren. He had shared it with the three orphaned children of his aunt. Their bedroom was directly beneath the sharply an-

gled eave of the roof. As he had grown taller, he had had to move to
the door, where he could stand upright, to dress. He hoped that when
it did come, it would be in his room at the Ambassador. He loved that
room. He had lived in it for so many years. He was very fond of the
elderly Irishwoman who did for him, and Katie was very fond of him.
He knew that because she had said to one of his friends who had been
waiting for him: "Mr. Löwe" — she pronounced it Lowey — "is a very
fine gentleman, quiet and soft-spoken, a very fine gentleman indeed."
He missed his Lares and Penates, the watercolors of Czernowitz, the
littered gravestones in the Jewish cemetery, the oxen in the square, the
wooden bridge across the Pruth, the protean black and white kitten.

He must terminate this visit. He must get back to Varina who was in
desperate straits. He must provide for young Federn. The stupid boy
was living above his means emotionally; he had been foolish enough to
fall in love with Mary Kennicott. As he thought of the impasse he was
at with Federn, Löwe's mind clicked, automatically, into its accustomed
groove. Of course! Perfect! Varina! She was high and dry. Here was
young Federn, at a dead end. Two waifs. He would join the two waifs.
In their loneliness they would reach out to each other. He would take
young Federn back to New York with him. He would confide his new-
formed plan to Monica. He must resume his letter to Monica.

But he didn't. He felt lazy. He enjoyed his introspections. And just
now he was thinking thoughts which he couldn't possibly transmit to
Monica. Thoughts of dissolution. She would be pained; it would be ex-
ecrable taste. He couldn't possibly be guilty of such a solecism. He was
proud of his secretiveness, that no one in the world, except his doctor,
knew what was wrong with him. He would be mourned by Monica, by
Mary, by Stephanie, by Varina, by the Irish maid in the Ambassador.
It amused him to call the roll of his mourners. He smiled. Monica's husband would console her. Not that he wasn't fond of Löwe. He was. They
were very good friends. As Löwe knew everything in the circles in which
he moved, as his informers were numerous — and sometimes invidious
— he knew the terms in which Monica's husband had defended him to
one of his detractors. Löwe had many detractors, that he knew, and
many of them were his friends who never knew that he knew. This particular one had denounced him to Monica's husband as a parasite who
sponged on the rich. The latter had fended off the accusation with an

airy remark: "Oh, well, you know Kaetchen is an eighteenth-century character!" thereby making him immune to judgment by contemporary standards. Löwe considered both the accusation and the defense with detachment. "The old boy is well-meaning," he thought, "but wrong. I am not at all an eighteenth-century character. I shouldn't have done at all well in the eighteenth century. What I really am is a Renaissance character, a Jew of the Renaissance, a contemporary of Montaigne or even earlier. I should have fitted nicely in the fourteenth, fifteenth or sixteenth centuries. I should have been, probably, a Hof Jude, a Court Jew, advising some duke or minor princeling on his investments, just as I'm doing now for Mary Kennicott."

To get rid of these morbid introspections, he sat down again at the Duncan Phyfe to resume his letter. Conversing with her, confiding to her, he felt cozy and at ease. He read again what he had been writing her about Ogden.

Well, I was telling you about Ogden. Thinking of him just now, a line from Virgil, from my Gymnasium days, popped into my mind, after how many years! Isn't it extraordinary and mysterious, these odds and ends trapped in cells in some coil of the cortex, how they suddenly escape their traps, like puppets, summoned by who knows what ventriloquist! "Flectere si nequeo Superos, Acherenta movebo," which I bent over my desk in the Vienna schoolroom to construe as: "If I cannot bend the will of Heaven, I will cause turmoil in Hell." Ogden is like a manic racing driver who must see how close he can shave death and miss it. As you know, my narrative method is roundabout, Talmudic. You are accustomed to it and will bear with it. Thinking of Ogden, I remembered the crude, woodcut engravings in the Hagadah, the ritual handbook from which my sainted father in Czernowitz used to conduct the Passover service when I was a child. The Hagadah describes the events of the night that the Jews, led by Moses, escaped from their bondage in Egypt. How can I convey to you the magical necromantic effect of the Passover service on the imagination of a child? The strange symbolic foods. Every spring I remember it, every spring I long for it. Oh, I've been to many ersatz Passovers since, in the houses of the haute juiverie, but to get its full flavor, it must be conducted in the Orthodox ritual and by parents who believe. As the youngest I asked the thematic questions: "In what respect does this night differ from other nights of the year?" A friend of mine in Hollywood, a screenwriter, who had been living with a girl for nine years, finally married her and he received, on his wedding night, a telegram from an irreverent friend, posing this very question. Blasphemy!

There was the elaborate concealment of a bit of food; it was called the aphikoman, which was to be picked up later in the evening by the Messiah. Year after year I determined to be awake to see the Messiah's entrance and to watch how, with unerring, supernatural instinct, he would nab the aphikoman. Alas, I was never awake; I was made drowsy by the heavy sweet wine which I was allowed to sip so that I never saw the Messiah in the flesh. Does a Messiah have flesh? I never found out. But the historical illustrations in the Hagadah are before me now. (Don't think, my dear, that I have lost my thread; I am returning, in my own way, to Dr. Ogden — you know you can't hurry me!) There was an illustration showing Pharaoh in a kind of amphibious chariot, going down in the Red Sea. There he was, in a mitred crown and jewel-studded robes, sinking, sinking. I couldn't but be impressed by Pharaoh's aplomb; his expression was imperturbable, as if he were going down in a royal lift. Though he was the Enemy, I remember feeling that I must somehow communicate to him that his situation was parlous; that he was about to drown and to get his heavy clothes off so that he might have a fighting chance and swim for it. But his expression was so frozen that you couldn't communicate with him. The woodcut that fascinated me most was the one which divides the human race into four categories, the four prototypes of humanity. First there is the Good Man. He asks the four questions, as I myself had done. He is curious, he wants to know, he takes an intelligent and patriotic interest; you may count on him always to do the Right Thing. He looked, as I remember, extremely naïve, but pure. I was flattered to be in his company, to be on the way to becoming what he was. Then there is the next prototype, the neutral, the incurious, the man who just lives from day to day (vast mass of the human race). He's heard vaguely about the goings-on in Egypt but is disinclined to make the effort to capture the details. He is not hopeless, he is just ignorant, he is worth making a fight for. Then there is the simpleton (vaster mass): he is a problem; not only doesn't he know enough to ask the questions, to query the cosmos, but he wouldn't understand the answers. In any case, he wants no part of it; he is hopeless. He is what I suppose we'd call nowadays retarded. Then we come to Category Four, the Rosho, the Evil One. He is clever. He knows the questions; he knows the answers. He is all-knowing, but he is dead set against enlight-

*enment; he wants to destroy the spirit which animates the questioners
and the listeners; he wants no affirmations. He is a naysayer, a nihilist,
I remember him well; he is fashionably dressed in Oriental style,
bearded, with shining teeth, bared in a contemptuous smile. The first
time I met Dr. Ogden, I remembered my friend from the Hagadah. I
thought, "Ah-hah! Category Four!" Ogden isn't bearded and is genial
rather than dour but the gleam of his teeth is the same. Identical gleam.*

*But I must, at long last, tell you the awkward situation in which I find
myself. You will laugh, since it isn't my situation really, but Varina's,
Mary's, that of my poor young protégé Kurt Federn. But then, as you
know, I am a molecule of vicariousness, and I suppose that in some
degree I am responsible. When I left New York, and as I wrote you from
there, Varina had gotten herself engaged to the learned doctor. Her parents had always been afraid that she would marry a Jew and they accepted Ogden because at least he had spared them that catastrophe. But
Lawson père is a cautious man. He had Dr. Ogden investigated. I don't
know what the sleuths discovered but it was sufficient for him to summon
Varina and warn her that if she married Ogden he would cut her off.
Varina couldn't have cared less, but Dr. Ogden cared. As a way out of
their dilemma he suggested that perhaps Mary would give him his job
back. She might do it, he said, as she was so fond of Varina. He suggested to Varina that she call Mary to make this request of her. Varina
couldn't quite see her way clear to doing it. "Very well," said Ogden,
"I'll do it!" He did. (You are familiar with the quality known as chutz-
pah. It is supposed to be a predominantly Jewish trait, but, as usual, the
Jews are overestimated. Goyim have it in abundance.) Ogden telephoned
Mary himself — to announce his engagement to Varina. I don't know
what she said. All I know is the result; that, by the time the conversation was over, Ogden's engagement to Varina was broken and the good
doctor reinstated in his post as director of Mary's clinic. I'm very troubled about Varina. The poor darling has no luck. I don't know a dearer
nor a lovelier girl, but there it is — she has no luck. She has this damna-
ble instinct for making wrong choices in men. Fatal. Yes, the situation is
one of the most awkward I have ever been in but it stimulates my ingenuity. I will go back to New York and take Federn with me. I introduced him to Varina in Salzburg but he was shy and she was bored.
Perhaps in their common grief they will reach sympathy. The final irony
I have not yet told you: the poor boy is madly in love with Mary. For
him she is the ideal of all women. Again* Measure for Measure.:

O heavens!
Why does my blood thus muster to my heart,
Making both it unable for itself,
And dispossessing all my other parts
Of necessary fitness?

Poor Federn! He is dispossessed all right. You see how awkward my
position is. What am I to do? This is a rhetorical question. I don't ex-
pect you to advise me. I shall trust to the . . .

There was a knock on the door. It was the Chinese boy with a telegram. Löwe took it, thanked the boy, closed the door and went back to
the chair. He read the telegram. It was from Varina's father. It said:

THOUGHT WE OUGHT TO LET YOU KNOW THAT VARINA
DID AWAY WITH HERSELF EARLY THIS MORNING TO SPARE
YOU THE SHOCK OF READING IT IN THE PAPERS. KAY IS
TAKING IT HARD. WHEN DO YOU RETURN? REGARDS.
HUBERT LAWSON

He sat for a moment staring at the telegram. He felt a kind of anger.
Why hadn't she waited for him! He had told her, over the telephone
two days ago, that he would be back in a week. She hadn't waited. Several years ago in London, when she told him she saw no hope for herself, that she was thinking of doing it, he had talked her out of it. He
had teased and rallied her. He hadn't really believed she meant it. Evidently, she *had* meant it. He reflected: was everything she had done
since, the men she had fallen in love with, was it all part of a semi-
conscious plan to put herself in a position where there was nothing else
she could do? And then he began to think about *her,* Varina herself, Varina as she was, and he was overcome with sorrow. Dear Varina — the
beautiful gray eyes, that deep, slow, drawling voice. The scar on her
forehead that so belonged to her. Could he have seen her just once he
would have talked her out of it. He was sure. Now she was beyond him,
beyond everything. She and Thaddeus Willens. Why hadn't they waited
— for a turn in the road, for a rift in the clouds? Montaigne would not
have approved of either of them. The difficulty was, the pain was — he
could take it about Willens — but Varina — he could not really take it
about Varina. The world, his world, would never be the same again

without Varina. A grace was gone, a grace would be missing. Why hadn't
he left at once when she begged him? Why hadn't she waited?

The telephone rang. Löwe got up to answer. Was it Mary? Had she
heard? But it was Grant. He sounded very tense. He was too self-
absorbed to dally with salutations.

"Kaetchen! I wish you'd come to Beverly for a few days. I need you
badly. I'm up against it."

"So am I."

"You! Really? Why?"

It evidently startled Grant — the possibility that Löwe himself might
be in trouble. It violated all precedent.

"I've just had a telegram from Varina's parents. Varina's dead."

"Varina! No!"

"She killed herself."

"Oh, no, Kaetchen. No."

"Unfortunately — yes."

"I can't stand it."

"There's nothing to do."

"It's unbearable. I just can't . . ."

"I am very angry with her."

"No more Varina!"

"No more Varina. That's why I'm angry."

"I remember . . . on the *Normandie* . . ."

Löwe waited.

"She said to me — Kaetchen, I just can't stand it . . ."

"What did she say?"

"She said — I hear her voice saying it . . ."

Grant's voice broke. Löwe waited.

"Out of kindness — she said to me: 'You have the finest face of all
of them.'"

Grant was crying. He hung up.

Löwe returned to the Duncan Phyfe and sat heavily before it. Yes,
that was kind of Varina, that was like Varina. She had known that ultimately that was what Grant was worried about — his sex appeal. She
had laid a poultice to that wound. And that's what Grant remembered
of Varina. That's why he loved Varina.

He felt drowsy. He would lie down and take a nap. But he roused himself. The morbid apprehension he had felt before returned. He might not wake up. And he had not finished his letter to Monica. He pulled his chair up close to the desk and picked up his pen. He looked at the letter. He had not even finished the last sentence. He had written: "I shall trust to the . . ." What would he trust to? To the suppleness of the third hand? The third hand was powerless now; its latest reflex stillborn. Varina had rendered it impotent.

There were three quick knocks on his door, light but imperious. Mary. Löwe knew that knock and liked it. It was the knock of a very rich woman who knew that no door could possibly be closed to her. He walked to the door and opened it. She strode by him without speaking. Her mouth was screwed up tight as if she were holding in a scream. She was wearing dark, beautifully fitting slacks, a light blue shirtwaist and a cardigan of soft wool that hovered between gray and lavender. She was thin and she looked well in slacks, boyish. She picked up a cigarette from the Duncan Phyfe and lit it. She inhaled deeply, blew out the smoke and looked at Löwe as if he were her mortal enemy.

"Well, Kaetchen, are you disgusted with me?"

He had seen that tense, defiant look before. He remembered when — on the night, in this very house, when her husband had made his unconventional appearance at the concert. Without waiting for an answer to her question, she walked to the window, looked out and returned.

"I have sad news," said Löwe.

"I know. Kenneth telephoned. She did it to stop us. She won't stop us!"

Löwe, seldom shocked, was shocked.

She looked at him, tortured.

"Well, why don't you say something?"

"You're not yourself."

"No? How do you know what I am? You don't know what I am."

"Well, we've met!"

"First Sally, now Varina. Kenneth understands it. He understands it perfectly. As they couldn't have him, they didn't want me to. Varina's way is the more cowardly. To cast a shadow over us. To frighten us. Mean. Mean."

"But, darling . . ."

She did not let him finish. "I'll never forgive her for doing it. I loved her. I loved Varina. I love her now. To spite me, that's why she did it!"

"You couldn't be more mistaken," said Löwe quietly. "I stopped her doing it long ago in London — before she knew you or Ogden. It was her destiny. She had to follow it. It wasn't Ogden. It wasn't you."

Mary's voice rose.

"I've had to take it! Why couldn't she take it?"

"You're tougher than Varina."

"You *are* disgusted with me. Well, I'll have to take that too!"

"You are too tough for martyrdom also, my dear. It's not becoming to you. I rely on your taste."

She hunched her shoulders beneath her cardigan as if she were cold.

"There's only once I've been happy. Wyman wanted it for me. What else is there? Wyman wanted me to be happy."

"So do I."

She came close to him.

"Do you? Do you?"

"No, darling. I want you to be miserable. I lie awake nights — thinking how to make you miserable!"

She gave up. She threw her arms around him, held him close to her. She leant her face against his cheek. She whispered.

"Dearest Kaetchen. Don't hate me. Don't despise me. Love me. Love me."

She kissed his cheek and was out of the room.

Löwe sat again at the Duncan Phyfe. He was too disturbed to go on with his letter. He was oppressed, overcome by the irrationality in things. There was no order — no way of controlling anything even in his own little circle of the protected. He didn't feel well; he was painfully tired. He moved over to the green and yellow sofa, adjusted the pillows and lay down. He reveled in the delicious sense of forthcoming sleep. He knew that with people afflicted as he was, the tension and terror generated by nightmares could cause their hearts to fail in sleep. Sleep, he knew, was perilous, dreams dangerous. But he longed for the blessed oblivion. What matter, after all, if he didn't wake up? The thing was to sleep. The cushions were soft and cool. He dug his face into them. He slept.

26. Stammtisch

Since Klaus Wolff had no car, Eileen had fallen into the habit of picking him up every day at the studio at five o'clock and driving him home. They had also fallen into the habit of stopping at a waffleburger on the Strip for a cup of coffee. Klaus loved this waffleburger; for him it was quintessentially American, quintessentially Hollywood. He cherished it as he did other local phenomena; the idyllic "Rest Home" advertisements of the undertakers, the advertisements of the clockmakers with their enormous cardboard clocks set fixedly at three o'clock. When he asked "Why at three o'clock?" he was told that that was the hour in the morning at which Abraham Lincoln had died. One day he showed Eileen an item he had clipped from the *Los Angeles Times* showing a picture of the late Thomas Hardy. The caption beneath the photograph stated: "Thomas Hardy, author of *Tess of the D'Urbervilles* from which Ideal Films made *Vagrants of the Night*." That was about the only identification made of Hardy. He scanned the film trade papers with avidity. When he read one morning that Henry B. Walthall had played the district attorney in the film version of Dante's *Inferno,* his cup of happiness ran over. Through the long afternoon hours at the studio he longed for the moment when he and Eileen would enter the waffleburger. He felt at home in it. He loved it. Eileen too had become attached to it. They were safe there from the intrusion of the celebrated and the notorious. Sitting across from each other at one of the little unadorned wooden tables, they were relaxed, cozy. There weren't many customers at that hour and, after a few visits, they fixed on a corner table for themselves. It began to be saved for them; they were expected at it. "Our stammtisch," said Klaus in triumph as he led her to it. "But you mustn't tell Kaetchen or he'll invade. Can you imagine Kaetchen at *this* stammtisch!"

Eileen laughed. She found that with Klaus she laughed a good deal. She was smiling now as Klaus made a mock ceremonial of holding her chair for her. The waiter brought their coffee.

"There is something very wrong with you, Klaus. You know that, don't you?"

He smiled at her.

"Break it to me gently."

"You don't think I'm stupid. The only one here."

"I don't know. Perhaps if I made a point of it, I might find a companion."

She shook her head.

"High and low — you wouldn't!"

"I've had no complaints on that score among your dozen."

"Oh, well, they're — you might say — subsidized."

"Ludwig Born likes you! And he got here on his own!"

"He hardly knows me. We barely met. We just said we were glad to meet each other."

"Born is very keen. He was taken by you. He appreciated you. He told me."

"It's my charitable reputation. So *he's* charitable."

They were looking into each other's eyes over the coffee cups.

"And Frau Born? I talked much more to her. Does she like me?"

"Even Olga is tolerant."

Eileen laughed.

"But as you know," Klaus went on, "she's not interested in wives. More in husbands. Productive husbands."

"She should like Stanley then."

"She does. Very much."

"He's creative. Definitely creative."

"She has taken note of it. She wrote his name down on her place card when I sat next to her at dinner at Hugo Stift's. Olga's instinct for the creative is infallible."

"You must tell Stanley. It'll please him."

"I have told him. He *was* pleased. To be in Olga's Valhalla is no mean achievement. There have been such flaring stars in it. Her specialty."

There was a moment's silence. Their eyes never left each other's.

"They don't think I know it, but I do know it. To all these people in Stanley's world I am a figure of fun. I know that they laugh at me behind my back. Stanley's taken the trouble to tell me. But I don't mind. I don't mind a bit. Not really."

"They laugh at you to absolve themselves of guilt."

"Do you think so? Is it as deep as that? I don't think so, I think they just laugh at me because I'm so serious . . ." she laughed herself, "so *severe* with them. They laugh because I take their religion seriously. Stanley doesn't laugh. He's just irritated. I don't really understand Stanley at all. He doesn't seem to believe in anything. Why, he might just as well not be Jewish at all!"

At this Klaus laughed.

"You see!" she said in mock triumph. "You laugh at me too!"

He put his hand on hers for a moment.

"Yes," he said, "I laugh at you."

"And yet, I don't see what's funny. It must be that I have no sense of humor."

"I have another theory."

"What is it?"

"I wouldn't think of telling you. It would embarrass you."

"Anyway, I'm glad you don't think I'm stupid. I think I'm less stupid than I used to be."

"Were you?"

"You wouldn't believe it. How stupid!"

"Try to persuade me."

"When I first met Stanley, I tried to lift myself up by the bootstraps. To reach his level. I had no education at all. He knew everything. I tried to read up on Greek mythology, all those names, all those complicated family relationships. They made my poor head swim."

"Now you've journeyed from Zeus to Moses. From paganism to asceticism. Is it a crescendo? I wonder."

Eileen didn't take him up on this. She made a mental note to think it over, at leisure.

"And would you believe it? I studied Italian so I could read Dante in the original."

"I have a friend who did exactly that. He's not in the least stupid."

They sat in silence for a moment, looking at each other.

"Stanley's found a new love, you know."

"I've heard."

"Do you know her?"

"I've seen her."

"Is she beautiful?"

"I regret to say — radiant."

"Why do you regret it? I'm happy for him."

"You are unusually tolerant."

"I'm sorry for him. He has never been loved."

"Not by you?"

"Oh, yes. By me passionately. Certainly before I married him. But the sad thing about Stanley is . . ."

"Yes?"

"That whoever loves him, he is sure, can't really be much. If she were anything much, he thinks, she wouldn't love *me*."

"That *is* sad."

"What really worries me about it — what really gives me sleepless nights . . ."

His eyes questioned hers.

"Is that he'll break his promise to Stephanie. That he'll give the part in his play to this girl — what's her name?"

"Doris Linden."

"Is she a good actress?"

"She's effective on the screen. That doesn't mean in the least that she'll be good on the stage."

Eileen took hope from this.

"Really?"

"The theater requires sustained vitality. Film actresses play bits and pieces, tiny scenes. You hear people say — I've heard playwrights say it: 'Ah! If only Garbo would do my play!' No one admires Miss Garbo more than I do. She is the most aristocratic of artists. I've watched her work on the set. I am sure she would be quite inadequate on the stage. She hasn't that kind of vitality. I am sure she knows it herself and would never think of attempting it!"

"Please, Klaus. Please tell it to Stanley."

"I will if you want me to. But I must tell you — I'm not really sure of Stephanie either."

"Stohl used her."

"Never in comedy."

"Stanley promised her. He promised twice. He promised me. He promised her."

"Theatrical promises are writ in water. You know, of course, Sam

Goldwyn's immortal remark: 'A verbal promise isn't worth the paper it's written on!' "

"But if you can't trust a person's word — what can you trust?"

"It's really quite remarkable . . . in fact, it's phenomenal . . ."

She was looking at him, frowning in perplexity. She waited.

"A French writer, who is not overfond of us, said that there were two kinds of Jew; he divided us into two categories: the severe, moralistic Jew — the Hebrew — and what he calls the Carthaginian Jew, who, he says, is greedy for sensation. Now how did Stanley, the Carthaginian, come to marry you, the moralist? How did you lead him into it? You should have warned him."

"Poor Stanley, he married me in a fit of sentimentality over Amos. I knew it. I took advantage of it. I knew he didn't love me. I trapped him. I wanted Amos to have a father."

"What's Stanley's real name?"

"I never asked him. I believe he's forgotten it himself."

"It is strange. It is very strange indeed to find someone — and of all places here — who takes basic moral axioms seriously. An American professor records with startled surprise that George Orwell is like that. The professor can't get over it about Orwell. I can't get over it about you!"

"Your religion teaches it."

Klaus made a gesture of helpless resignation.

"It has taught it for so long that we have forgotten it! Just as your husband has forgotten his real name."

"It's a matter of life and death to Stephanie."

"As serious as that, you think?"

"I am sure. Yes. I know!"

"Well, I think she might get away with it. She is so lovely and so — distinguished. Yes. Stanley might manage with her."

"He must give it to her. He must. It's all I want of Stanley."

There was a little silence. The waiter brought them another cup of coffee.

"I know so little about you, Klaus — your life before you came here, your wife. Was your marriage happy?"

"Yes. It was happy. It was unclouded happiness."

Klaus took out his wallet. He extracted a snapshot from it and handed it to Eileen. Eileen studied it.

"She's lovely. Such a dear face."

"She saved my life. I was impossible when I was young. Melancholiac. Gide says sadness is a state of sin. I sinned."

"How can one help being sad — when one looks around?"

"Most sadness doesn't come from looking around. It comes from looking within. Inverted vanity. Vanity in the dumps. Self-indulgence. Why are we sad? Why are we depressed? Because we haven't done enough, because we haven't really succeeded, because we're insufficiently recognized. When I was writing reviews I used to think: 'Oh yes, very clever but why don't you write something original about which other people can be clever?' "

Eileen picked up the snapshot and looked at it again.

"How did you meet her?"

"She picked me up. She picked me up on a streetcorner in an awful section of Berlin. I was crying. Her voice — asking me why I was crying — came to me before I saw her."

"I ask you too."

"My parents died within a few days of each other. A film I had been working on, of which I had great hopes, proved a disaster. There was nothing. I had to leave my parents' house, the house in which I was born, and move to a horrid hotel in a degraded section of Berlin. I will never forget my first evening in that awful hotel room. I left it and walked. I was twenty-one — orphaned and a failure. Suddenly I couldn't go on walking. There was no place to walk *to*. So I stopped. I stopped at a streetcorner and cried. That's when Wanda spoke to me. She was simply there. For fourteen years I never cried again — not till two years ago in the Jewish cemetery in Paris where I buried her. She was very gay, you know — to the last. She had friends in Paris; she attracted everybody. She was dying of cancer. A friend of hers in the Foreign Office offered her French citizenship. She refused his offer. She said she could endure a German woman dying, but she didn't want a Frenchwoman to die."

Eileen said nothing for a few moments.

"I hope your friend . . . what's his name . . . who said that sadness is a state of sin . . ."

"He's not my friend but his name is André Gide."

"I hope you won't tell him but your story makes me sad."

Klaus smiled. "I promise. He'll never hear a word about it. I also promise not to make you sad again if I can help it. It's just that I wanted you to know the worst about me."

"I have to talk to you about Naomi. It was Naomi, you know — did I ever tell you? — it was Naomi who picked your name on the list Kaetchen sent me."

Her brown eyes were mischievous.

"She winnowed you out."

"You didn't tell me."

"Oh, she's a great fan of yours. 'He's wonderful,' she said. 'We doted — my father and I — on his reviews.' 'What a fierce name!' I said. 'Klaus, claws — Wolff, wolf.' "

"Big, bad wolf! How disappointed you must have been to encounter a sheep."

"A lamb."

"What is it about Naomi?"

"She thinks Stanley's script is very foolish. She wants to go to Palestine."

"I understand that."

"I think I do too."

"The terrible thing for Naomi is that she was there. She *saw* it. She saw her parents lying there. She hasn't the advantage which the rest of us have of limited imagination."

"I'm not sure I know what you mean."

"If our imaginations and sympathies weren't limited, we couldn't possibly live. If, for example, if I knew, right this minute, what is going on in Germany, in individual cases, I'd have to cut my throat. Luckily, I don't. One day I'll read about it. Then it will be history."

Klaus smiled.

"You can take anything from history."

"Can you?"

"Does it mean anything, for example, when you read that in Spain, in the sixteenth century, an Inquisitor burned alive three hundred heretics? Nothing at all. The dead, especially en masse, are uninteresting. It is the advantage of our limited imaginations that we do not see that masses are composed of individuals, each one with his private hell, his private universe. Numbers, you see, are no longer people."

"That's terrible."

"Young Federn, for example. He's pretty sure that his parents are dead. Or, if they are still alive, perhaps worse than that. But he doesn't *know* it. Poor Naomi. She saw it. She knows it. I understand her wanting to go to Palestine. She will feel closer to her parents there. Yes, dearest Eileen, I thrive, as the rest of us do, on my limitations. I sit here, I look at you. I am happy. Think what it would mean to them, to those others, if they could sit here with you, in this heaven, in this blessed waffleburger."

They sat for a time in silence. Eileen looked again at the snapshot.

"I don't know why — your wife — she makes me think of Naomi."

"Oh, but Wanda was robust. Full of life."

"Full of life! I can't tell you how full of life Naomi was, how adorable she was. She used to dart about. Quicksilver. Right after we were married — in her parents' little flat — I saw Stanley holding her, kissing her. I thought — I *knew* — 'It is Naomi he wants. It is Naomi he would wish to have married.' I didn't blame him either. She was beautiful."

She returned the snapshot. Klaus put it back in his wallet.

"Naomi wants me to go with her."

"Does she?"

"Are you tempted?"

"Very."

"What about Amos?"

"I would take Amos."

"To bring up Amos in the land of his ancestors?"

"Yes. I want him to grow up believing in *something*."

"Many Palestinians are atheists."

"But they must have other beliefs."

"How will Stanley feel about it?"

"Oh, he'll be relieved to have me go. But he won't like it to have Amos go. He loves Amos. He does love Amos. What do you think?"

"I think that for Naomi it might be good."

"And for me?"

"How can I encourage you — to leave a rival?"

He spoke very lightly.

"Naomi keeps pressing me."

"What do you say to her?"

"How can I tell her . . . what holds me?"

"What holds you?"

Her head lowered slightly. He saw the flush rise in her cheeks. To spare her answering, he spoke to her.

"You come to us, you know, at our lowest moment."

She lifted her head and faced him.

"Yes," she said, "I come to you."

"I thought, when I said good-bye to Wanda, that I had seen the last of goodness. I was wrong."

The restaurant was beginning to fill up. He paid the bill. They got up to go. When they left the waffleburger, they were holding hands, their fingers interlocked.

27. Stephanie

I. The Crib

Stephanie sat in the cramped living room of her cottage in Santa Monica studying her part in Grant's play. Although Grant had told her not to, since there would still be changes, she had learned it by heart. She had engaged a teacher of phonetics to perfect her English pronunciation; he had gone over every syllable of the role with her. The more she knew the part, the more impressed she was by Grant's genius. How wonderful he was, how immensely intuitive, to have divined this woman, so very much like herself, impulsively generous but misguided. But after all he had written it for her, from her. Still, when he wrote it, he hadn't known her very well and yet he did; he had, in some sort, foretold her disasters. She was in the scene of the third act where Leonie, the heroine, comes downstairs in her grandmother's wedding dress which she has just come upon in the attic, in rehearsal for her wedding — a wedding that would never take place. She let the script fall in her lap and repeated from memory Leonie's speeches. First when she is twirling around in the old-time dress for her daughter and for Kenneth to admire: Kenneth has just told her the dress is exquisite:

Isn't it? Yes. Exquisite. Can you imagine the scene? Can you imagine Granny walking down the aisle — and all the august spectators in muttonchop whiskers and Prince Alberts? We've lost something these days — a good deal. Oh, I don't mean the muttonchops — but in ceremony, I mean — in punctilio and grace . . .

And, later, when the blow falls on her, when she wonders what it is that is wrong with her:

I suppose the thing about me that is wrong is that love is really all I care about. I suppose I should have been interested in other things. Good works. Do they sustain you? But I couldn't somehow. I think when you're not in love — you're dead. Yes, that must be why I'm . . .

She glanced at the script; the stage direction read: *Her voice trailed off.* This part was made in heaven for her; she would play it beautifully. She knew how she would play it, just how. How wonderful it would be to have it every night to come to, to get away from herself, to be somebody else for those hours of performance. Somebody else and yet herself too. For she was very tired of herself; herself had disappointed her. There was something wrong with her, deeply wrong, far more wrong than there was with Leonie. And then she was assailed by fear, a paralyzing fear. Would she get it? Would she? She was unlucky; nothing, in so long, had come right for her. Why should this bleak pattern suddenly change? She got into a panic. Grant had been evasive lately; he had avoided her. But then she made an effort to allay her panic. She remembered not only that Stanley had promised her the part but that he had repeated the promise to Eileen too. Eileen had called her up joyously, expressly to reassure her.

When she thought of this her panic subsided. What a dear, kind creature Eileen was! If, in her disordered world, there was one person you could count on, it was that darling Eileen. How lucky Grant was to have her though he didn't seem to know it. He was an odd one, that Grant. Though he understood her, he understood her perfectly, otherwise he

could never have written Leonie, she didn't in the least understand him.
She was content merely to know him. He had been in love with her;
there was no doubt he had been in love with her. How clumsy he had
been about it too! It had been embarrassing. She had been at her wit's
end for devices to put him off. That, on one occasion, she had not put
him off, she had completely forgotten. Still, he was a genius even if he
didn't know anything worth knowing. How very amusing Ian had been
about him!

Ian. Where was Ian? She hadn't seen him or Vincent in two days.
She had found one of those crazy, funny notes, signed by both of them,
when she had returned from Beverly the day before:

> *Have gone to Venice, Cal., to see the Giotto frescoes and the Tintoret-
> tos. Tell your beads. We'll be back any minute.*

> Tendresse,
> Ta-Ta, Mirandola

Ta-Ta was the nickname Ian had pinned on Vincent. The letter was
in Ian's handwriting and Mirandola some silly improvisation for himself.
She looked at the note again. "Any minute!" Forty-eight hours ago. She
hadn't missed them. She had been in a swoon of adoration about the
part and how she would play it. It was quiet and peaceful in the little
house without them. She enjoyed listening to the monotonous drone of
the surf outside her front door. The silence had given her a chance to
think, to pull herself together, to indulge in reverie. When they were
there, those two, it was clamorous: they were so incessantly and boister-
ously funny, spinning out an endless web of private jokes, in an arcane
argot — wooings, involving herself, eroticism, jagged fantasies. They
were certainly funny, Vincent particularly. Vincent liked to be tapped.
He insisted on being tapped. He would stretch out his bare, muscular
forearm. "Feel my bicep, Stephanie," he would pipe. "Feel that bicep."
She would tap it; she would feel it. "Hard as iron," she would say,
"marvelous." At this Vincent would grin, complacent, as happy as if
she'd never said it before, and tell her it was no use tapping Ian as he
was gone to seed, flabby. The little exhibitions amused Ian. "He's a
muscle hoarder — dotty about 'em," he would say: " 'Admire my physical condition!' It's his oriflamme!" He was a boy, Vincent, a child on

perpetual holiday. He was good for Ian. He cheered him up. Ian could be funny too but he had a grim, dark side, a cavern to which he retired, a cavern peopled by horrid goblins from which her imagination shrank. Lately, Ian had begun to frighten her. Vincent sensed it; he had become a shield between her and Ian; he amused and soothed her. How had it all come about? What was she doing with them? The play — the play would extricate her from this. Vincent knew it; he was constantly rallying Ian about it. "I look into the crystal ball," he'd say, "and what do I see? Cinderella in New York taking bows in pimple-Stanley-three-balls' play and forlorn Ta-Ta and pretty-paunch Ian alone — alone, wandering the heath alone."

Well, actually, Vincent was right in his crazy way. That was what she was living for. They'd be better off without her and so would she. They'd need her money and they could have it. Unless, of course, Vincent became reconciled with his father but this he vowed he'd never do. Vincent was proud. His pride was precious to him. He didn't mind living on Stephanie because she was "one of the gang" and, in addition, "a duck." She was duckie. Stephanie smiled. The inheritance from her mother had dwindled. On the walls were several Rembrandt drawings, studies for several of his paintings of rabbis. The rabbis for which these drawings were studies had belonged to Stephanie; she had inherited them from her father. Kaetchen had sold them for her and on this money the three of them were now living. Vincent derived endless amusement from this as well as spending money. He crowed over it. "Two queens living off those dear, dead rabbis. Wildly chic, isn't it?"

Stephanie was at a dead end. For the first time in these last forty-eight hours she felt lonely. Where had they gone? What were they doing? The mythical artworks in Venice, Cal., must be singularly alluring. It was eight o'clock. What should she do with her evening? Should she call Eileen to find out whether she had any news? She decided against. She didn't want to be a pest. If there were news Eileen would lose no time in calling her.

She began to browse among her bibelots. Stephanie had brought with her, when she departed her half castle, a choice selection from her private pantheon; there were the autographed photographs of actors, composers, playwrights, virtuosi and her one conductor, the large, affectionately signed, silver-framed portrait-study of Toscanini. As she looked at the portrait she recalled the last time she had seen him. It was in a hospital in Philadelphia; the Maestro had been forced, for the first time in his long career, to miss a concert through illness. Stephanie had found him in a fury of rebellion against his debility. Stephanie tried to soothe him. She had read in the papers, on the train from New York, that Churchill and FDR were both ill and had been forced to cancel their appointments. "If they can be ill," she said, "surely you have a right to be ill." It was a right which Toscanini spurned. "But THEY'RE weaklings!" he shouted at her. She lifted her wrist and looked at the classic profile on her bangle. Yes, he belonged on it surely, with Walter Rathenau and Napoleon. She was less sure now about Mussolini; he hadn't seemed, lately, to be behaving very well, she'd had bad reports on him from her politically minded friends, but she decided not to remove him yet; she would give him a chance for regeneration. But Rathenau, dear Walter Rathenau! She remembered the fragrant, sunny morning in Grünewald, his last morning, when he had stopped by her house to give her Rilke's *Letters to a Young Poet* in French. It was on the table beside her now.

She opened the lovely slim book to Rathenau's inscription, a quotation from Rilke's French and a message of his own in German. It was the last thing he had ever written; it was his last communion with another human being.

Rathenau had teased her about being a hero-worshiper; he had warned her against excess of this emotion. The quotation read: "Songez combien votre âme d'enfant enviait le cercle des 'grandes personnes.' Je vois maintenant que ce cercle des grandes personnes ne vous suffit plus et que vous aspirez plus haut." Then he had written in German that he would ask her to show him this passage in the book when next he saw her. The wonderful man! This was his way of insuring that she would read the book. He needn't have worried; she had run directly to her bedroom, hugging the book close to her, and read in it till she came upon the passage Rathenau had quoted. But she had never gotten the chance to display her erudition. By the time she came upon the passage, Rathenau had been murdered.

She closed the book and sat, dreaming about the past, embraced in a warm sadness. She pulled toward her her father's photograph standing on the table beside her. There he was, the faint smile of pride on his lips, looking down at her adoringly in her lace-canopied crib. She took him in in detail: the silk-lapeled frock coat, the gold-rimmed pince-nez, the plump cheeks, the beautifully trimmed mustache and goatee, the bulging cushion of his cravat with the black opal pin stuck in the center of it. She used to fumble frantically at this pin — so he had told her when she was a little grown up — to try to uproot it from its bed, to acquire it. But what enraptured her now was the little smile as he looked down at her undefined, tiny face. For him it did not lack definition; it was, for him, his daughter's face.

She spoke to her father:

"Your daughter might have done better, mightn't she, darling?"

Stephanie believed firmly in the immortality of the soul. What would she tell her father on their next confrontation? How could she explain to him? How, indeed, as she thought back over all of it, could she explain to herself? Faced by this impending questionnaire, she brightened. She might hope to get good marks from him for at least one accomplishment: her self-willed conquest of the drug habit. She had been afraid that Grant's knowledge of this habit might legitimately prevent him giving her the part. So she had struggled, had submitted herself to a doctor, gone into a hospital, undergone the agonies of withdrawal. She was proud of that, even Kaetchen had praised her; perhaps her father would. She laughed to herself about this; stern Kaetchen, he admonished her always as if she were an erring governess. Her father, thank God, was much more indulgent.

She began to think of Varina. That was another confrontation. She would scold Varina. Why hadn't she waited? And yet she understood her impatience. Sometimes she shared it herself. She half envied Varina's courage. She had wanted to be out of it and she was out of it. But for what a silly reason. Ogden! This was mysterious to Stephanie. She had never in the least been attracted to Ogden. In fact, she had found him faintly repellent. He was so vulgarly, so crassly, so ostentatiously virile. He was so manifestly sure of himself; so obviously did he take it for granted that he was irresistible. That ever-ready smile, that ever-ready laugh. It was not a laugh; it was a guffaw. He was too sunnily extrovert; there was no penumbra around him, nothing mysterious, no halftones; in her men she preferred the crepuscular, the erratic, the cruel, the unpredictable. And yet, here were all these women mad for Ogden. Mary had taken him back. He was there now in Santa Barbara. Kaetchen had called to tell her that Mary was going to marry him. He, Kaetchen, was going to be best man. It was depressing. There was something not palatable about it. How could Varina, who had loved Ian, content herself with Ogden? Whatever you might say about Ian, he was . . .

The telephone rang. Ah, Eileen! She rushed to answer it. But it was not Eileen. It was a hard-voiced stranger who wanted to speak to Mrs. Leith. She said: "This is Mrs. Leith." The hard voice said that he was Police Lieutenant Mahoney, Fourth District, that her husband had had an accident and that she must come at once and take this address.

"Will you wait a moment please — so I can write it down?"

She picked up a pad and pencil and asked for the address. The officer gave it to her. She wrote it down. He asked her to repeat it. She did. The officer said that was correct and to waste no time. She began to stammer a question but the stranger had hung up.

What should she do? How could she get Kaetchen? Kaetchen was in Santa Barbara. How would she get there? The boys had taken her car. She rang the Santa Monica taxi service, fortunately close by. She begged for a cab right away; it was an emergency. They promised to send one. She grabbed her handbag and rushed through the kitchen and the back door so that she would be ready for the cab on Santa Monica Boulevard. As she ran out she heard the telephone ring again. But she was too frantic to go back to answer it.

The cab came very quickly. She handed the cabby the piece of paper and implored him to hurry. The cabby looked at the paper and then at her, oddly.

"That's a tough neighborhood, lady," he said. "I don't much relish going in there."

"Please. It's a matter of life and death. I'll give you a big tip. I'll give you anything you want."

"All right, lady," he said. "You're the boss. Get in."

JJ. Counterpoint

At dinner, with Eileen and Naomi, Grant was high. He talked a blue streak. Eileen was sure that Doris Linden must have been nice to him.

Grant had had, he said, a marvelous day — a fabulous lunch about
which he promised to tell them. Drinks with Ogden, Mary Kennicott
and Kaetchen. He liked Ogden very much.

"He's very amusing, Ogden. He said that the difference between him
and me is that he's a dedicated heel and that I'm a half-baked one, a
heel with a Jewish conscience. I must get over it, he said. All or nothing,
he said. Get rid of that conscience, it's vestigial, like the appendix. I
asked how to go about it. A psychoanalyst, he was sure, could turn the
trick. I asked him to recommend one. He suggested himself. He said he'd
give me a rate. I took him on. Isn't that funny?"

Grant didn't get a satisfactory response to this.

"You two are killjoys. Well, you can't depress me. I feel too good. The
Legion of Honor is nothing compared to the accolade which touched me
at lunch. Aren't you curious? Are you two in a conspiracy not to be
amused by me?"

Eileen asked what the great honor was.

"I was invited, I'll have you know, by L.B. himself, to lunch in the
executive dining room. Very few writers attain that pinnacle."

"I thought," said Eileen, "that you'd won the Pulitzer Prize or something."

Grant affected mock horror.

"The Pulitzer Prize! You have to be mediocre to get that and you
know I'm not mediocre. Or am I? There they all sat at this long table,
all the producers, all the executives. Like a conclave of the Roman Curia
and at the head of the table the Pope himself. The pasha. The pasha was
disturbed. His top janissary, his right hand, was late. 'Where is my
dear Eddie?' said L.B., unable to start on his MGM chicken soup
without his prime minister. Eddie appeared. He was in a towering rage.

" 'What's wrong, Eddie?' said L.B., alarmed.

" 'It's those goddamn arrangers. They drive me crazy. Just been listening to the trailer music for the San Francisco picture. It's all loused
up. They've got so much stuff in it I couldn't hear the goddamn melody.
I said to this bastard for Christ's sake where's the melody? He said the
way it was was counterpoint. I said: "Screw the counterpoint. Let me
hear the melody." But he wouldn't do a goddamn thing. He has to have
his counterpoint!'

"L.B. became tearful.

" 'Oh, but Eddie, my dear Eddie, do you think that *you* run the studio? Do you think that *I* run the studio? Oh, no. We don't run the studio. The arrangers — they run the studio.'

"At this L.B., who is surely one of the greatest character actors of this era, got up from his chair and knelt before Eddie. He lifted his clasped hands in prayer. His voice was rapt, votive.

" 'I go down on my knees to them. I pray to them. Please, I say, please — let me hear the melody. But no, oh no. They've got to have their counterpoint.'

"Eddie threw his napkin on the table.

" 'Well, goddamn it, either counterpoint leaves the studio or I leave the studio!' "

Eileen laughed. Naomi smiled. Grant was pleased.

"Now, I ask you, what's the Pulitzer Prize compared to that!"

"You're not eating anything," said Eileen.

"This is where my heart lies," said Grant. He poured himself another glass of wine. "By the way, I ran into Faye Salvesh today. She's giving a big party. Sig's running his latest. Wants us to come."

"I know," said Eileen, "she telephoned. I turned it down. I love Faye but not her parties."

Grant was relieved. He could now take Doris. He went on describing his studded day.

"In Thalberg's waiting room I saw Ludwig Born. He was with Arnold Schönberg. Born was taking him in to meet Thalberg. Can you imagine that? Schönberg! The most intense, penetrating eyes I've ever seen in my life. You feel that those eyes can see through walls. Skin drawn tight over his skull. Think of the immensities that go on inside that skull. And that little, marvelous roly-poly Born. I adore him."

"I hear he likes me," said Eileen.

"Why shouldn't he?"

"Well, it's nice to hear that he does."

"Who told you?"

Eileen flushed. Grant noticed it.

"Klaus Wolff."

"Oh. I believe he likes you even better. In fact, I think he's in love with you. Why don't you step out, honey? Klaus is a clever fellow. A bit dehydrated. Is he potent? I like him very much. It's a funny thing, you know. Ever since I was a kid I was drawn to these Central European writers. Budapest. Vienna. Those plays and those novels. I read 'em all. A doom-laden, amorous world. Officers from the garrison. They loved and gambled and drank themselves to death. There were no garrisons around Xenia, no rose-lit restaurants, no ballet girls to flirt with from the Opera House. God, it made my mouth water. Oh, I thought, to have been born in Budapest or Vienna. They were twin cities to me like Minneapolis and St. Paul."

He poured himself more wine. He became moody.

"Think of the books Born has written. Compared to him I'm nothing. A pygmy. A money-grubbing hack. Nothing at all."

Eileen and Naomi were silent.

"Well, you might at least have the grace to contradict me! But I know what you both think of me. I know what Naomi thinks of my script. I had the misfortune to employ a highbrow film critic for my script girl."

Eileen got up. They went into the living room. Grant went to the bar and poured himself a brandy. Naomi shrank into an armchair. Grant went to her.

"Hope you weren't offended, darling. I was only joking. It doesn't matter in the least to me, really, what you think of my script. How did things go today, on the set?"

"I made a blunder. I'm afraid I'm stupid."

"Oh well, that can happen."

"Mr. Kingdon was angry."

"Don't give it another thought. I'll fix it up with Kingdon."

"The truth is, Mr. Grant . . ."

Naomi couldn't go on. Her mouth twitched. Eileen intervened.

"Stanley. Naomi wants to tell you something."

"Why doesn't she tell me? Is she afraid of me? Am I an ogre or something? What is it, Naomi?"

"It is a terrible way to repay your kindness . . ."

"What is?"

Naomi swallowed. She wasn't looking at Grant.

"I must leave this work."

"Because of this silly mishap today?"

Naomi shook her head.

"No. Because I must go away."

"Where to?"

She couldn't say it. Eileen said it.

"Naomi wants to go to Palestine."

"Palestine!"

Naomi nodded.

"Nostalgia for the Wailing Wall?"

Naomi, her head bent, got up and left the room.

Grant wished he hadn't said it.

"It seems that I can't do anything right!"

"I want to go with her."

"To Palestine!"

"Yes."

"The second Exodus!"

"I won't let Naomi go alone."

"Well, if you want a jaunt, no reason you shouldn't have it."

"I want to take Amos."

"That, my dear, I will not let you do."

Eileen went to the window and stared out at the floodlit pool. Amos's centaur was floating serenely on it.

"Under no conditions will I allow it. And I'll tell you another thing . . ."

Eileen turned away from the window and faced him.

"Well?"

"I'll never give Stephanie that part."

"Is that your revenge? After all, it isn't Stephanie you hate. It's me you hate."

"I never meant to give it to her."

"That can scarcely be true as you wrote it for her."

"It's been an albatross around my neck. This silly promise. Okay I promised. I've changed my mind. So what? It happens all the time. Stephanie's a half amateur or she'd know it. She'd accept it. I couldn't possibly give that part to a dope addict."

"That's unfair. It's monstrous. It's a lie. You know it's a lie. Stephanie's over that. She underwent tortures to get over it. I hate you for saying that."

"She's a screwball. Decadent."

"Perhaps you are too in a profounder way."

"Marrying a pansy!"

"She loved Ian."

"And taking Vincent to live with them. She's just plain nuts."

"She's kind. She's generous. Vincent was marvelous to Naomi. I'll never forget his kindness to Naomi. Neither will she."

"All right. You win. They're the salt of the earth! But I tell you now, I'll never give Stephanie that part."

Grant looked at his wristwatch.

"I've got to go."

Eileen knew where. To meet Stephanie's successor.

"Before I go I ask a favor of you. Please call Stephanie and tell her to get this silly notion out of her head. Once and for all."

"Very well. I will."

"Do it now."

"Very well. I will."

Eileen went to the telephone and gave Stephanie's number to the operator. She waited. She put down the receiver.

"There's no answer. She must have gone out."

"Will you call her later then?"

"Yes."

"Promise?"

She nodded.

He went to her and kissed her on the cheek, his good humor restored.

"Since you promise, I know you'll do it. Not like a promise made by me, is it? Thank you. It'll be a load off my mind. Good night, darling. Have fun!"

He was gone.

The image of Stephanie rose before Eileen — that pure face, so trusting, so vulnerable, so . . . she couldn't bear to think of Stephanie. She ran upstairs and knocked at Naomi's door. Naomi let her in. She saw that Eileen was in a state.

"What's happened?"

"He asked me to call Stephanie. To tell her she can't have the part. He's decided, I'm sure, who's going to play it."

"I never believed really that he would give it to her."

"It'll break her heart. It's her only hope."

"The sooner she knows, the better. She can look for something else."

"He doesn't even have the courage to tell her himself. He makes me do it."

"You can't make a candid man out of an evasive man. He evades himself. He doesn't dare find out who he is, so he'll never know."

There was a silence.

"Naomi . . ."

"Yes?"

"I am going with you."

"Amos?"

"I'll take Amos. And Naomi . . ."

"Yes?"

"Klaus Wolff is coming with us."

"That would make me very happy for you. Has Klaus said he would come?"

"No. But he will."

Eileen went downstairs to put in another call to Stephanie. There was still no answer.

III. Taj Mahal

In the cab Stephanie was overcome by it, by desire for the drug. She had to have it. She knew a drugstore where she could get it; she hadn't thought of that resource for some time but now she remembered it. But it was far out of the way. The driver would think she was crazy. And yet, if she didn't get it, she would scream. And if she screamed, the cabby, already suspicious of her, would probably stop the cab and ask her to get out. She put her thumb in her mouth and bit at it. In her handbag was an ampoule which her doctor had given her to inject in her arm for the migraine headaches which afflicted her. She broke the cap in her handkerchief and injected the needled phial in her arm. It did no good. Scorpions gnawed at her nerve ends. She had left in her bathroom a bottle of ether. If only she had that; she would press it to her nostrils and the gnawing would go away. She would ask the driver to go back. But he was already in the city; the cab was jolting through the softly moaning, welted streets of Watts. She experienced a hallucination. The cab had stopped at an intersection. She beheld, glistering balefully in the moonlight, triple towers made, seemingly, of bits of colored glass, reds, greens, blues. She wondered; how, without the drug, could she be subject to this phantasmagoria? Could the migraine injection have caused it? It had never done so before. The driver, in his mirror, saw her staring at the triple vision. He turned his head for comment.

"Somet'n, ain't it! Some dago nut's been working at it for years. Broken Seven-Up bottles he made it outta. Stuff he picks up in the junkyards. Garbage towers, you might say." He laughed at his own witticism. "Public nuisance, if you ask me. They'd ought to tear it down and put that dago in the nut house."

It was real then. Stephanie looked at it with wonder. She forgot her state for a moment. One of the towers, the tallest of the three, was a pagoda shape, it billowed up and up. The two lesser satellites, faceted torches, spiralled up gracefully to pencil points. They made her think of something, something she had seen on her trip to the Far East with Ian. The Angkor Vat? It didn't glow like these towers. Looking at these aspiring shapes relaxed her. She kept looking at them from the rear window when the cab started again.

"Taj Mahal," she thought. "The Taj Mahal of Watts," she had a foreboding: "That is a tomb too."

The impulse to scream came back.

"How far are we, driver?"

"Two blocks. 107th. Lotus Club. Honky-tonk. No place for you, lady. Want me to take you back?"

"I don't know."

"Don't worry. I'll keep an eye on you."

As they turned the corner on 107th a hearse passed them.

She knew that Ian was in it.

There was a crowd outside the club, white and colored. Several patrol cars were parked in front of it, and an ambulance. "I don't have to go in now," she thought. She spoke to the driver.

"Follow the hearse," she said.

"You sure, lady?"

"Yes," she said. "Follow it."

The driver was by this time in front of the club. A police lieutenant, evidently waiting for her, opened the door of the cab.

"Mrs. Leith?"

Stephanie nodded.

"Come in, please."

But Stephanie had fainted.

In spite of his meticulously honed regimen of physical culture, in spite of the absence of fat and the hardness of muscle, it was Vincent who had been killed. He had been stabbed to death by the father of a Negro boy. Ian, trying to save him, had been badly beaten up. The doctor who revived Stephanie told her that her husband wasn't seriously hurt at all. No bones were broken. There might be a brain concussion but he'd have to wait a few days on that. In any case, even that was not necessarily fatal. He would take him to a hospital if she liked, but he would perhaps be better off at home. He had an ambulance waiting. He would provide a nurse though he couldn't promise that till tomorrow. There was a terrible shortage of nurses. He would come himself tomorrow, unless, of course, she preferred her regular doctor. Stephanie said she had no regular doctor and would be grateful if he would come. The doctor, who was sympathetic, then turned her over to the police lieutenant, who was also present. The police lieutenant questioned her interminably. Did she know anything about the dead man, her husband's friend? Stephanie provided his name and said that he had been her house guest. The officer wrote down Vincent's name and his father's name. He wanted Vincent's father's address. Stephanie couldn't tell him that but she said she might have it at home somewhere. At this point the doctor whispered to the lieutenant. The officer snapped his notebook shut.

"I'll come to see you tomorrow for that," he said. "I'll telephone before I come." He went out.

Stephanie thanked the doctor for his intervention. He took her out to see Ian, who was lying on a sofa in the brightly lit club office. The walls were covered by photographs of stripteasers: white, black and Malaysian. Ian was very pale, his face was bruised, he tossed around, he was talking to himself.

"I've given him sedation," said the doctor. "I assure you that with a week's care, he'll be quite himself again. I assure you."

The ambulance orderlies came in and lifted Ian off the sofa. The doc-

tor and Stephanie followed them. On the sidewalk the taxi driver spoke
to Stephanie.

"Shall I take you back, lady?"

Stephanie spoke to the doctor.

"Couldn't I go in the ambulance?"

"Of course. I'd much rather you would."

"I'm sorry," Stephanie said to the cabby. She opened her purse, took
out all the bills there were in it and handed them to the cabby.

"Oh, lady," he said, "you don't owe me all that."

He stripped off several bills and gave the rest back to her.

"Thank you very much," she said. "You've been very kind."

"Good luck, lady," he said. He touched his cap and went back to his
cab.

The doctor helped Stephanie up the few steps at the back of the
ambulance.

"You'll be very comfortable in there," he said, "beside your husband.
He'll be irrational probably but don't let that bother you. One
thing . . ."

Stephanie waited.

"He doesn't know that his friend is dead. Don't tell him. I'll tell him
when I come tomorrow. If he should ask just say that I've hospitalized
him for a few days but that he's all right."

Stephanie nodded.

The doctor smiled at her.

"I'll tell him when he's brisker. Keep your spirits up. I'll see you in
the morning."

Stephanie climbed in and sat on a jump seat beside Ian. She held his
hand. The orderly clamped down the back panel. The ambulance moved
off. Quite numb, not feeling much of anything, holding Ian's hand,
Stephanie saw the Taj Mahal again. The ambulance had stopped at the
same intersection. Vincent's tomb, not Ian's. She stared at these tall
stalks rising from this improbable soil, with their myriad-colored blossoms. She saw then that the towers were beautiful. They were a work of
art, a wild and ordered distillation of genius. She felt hero worship for
the genius who had created them. How could she meet this anonymous
man, this artist? She remembered the warning in Rilke, to aspire to

higher than hero worship. She disagreed. Whom to worship, if not artists? Tomorrow she would seek him out and kneel before him. The ambulance moved on. She clung to the towers till they disappeared. Had
she dreamt them? Had they been there? Would she find them when she
came tomorrow?

Ian began to mumble. At first she couldn't make out his mumblings,
nor did she really try — her memory of the towers transfixed them —
but gradually single words impinged on her. She realized that Ian was
talking to Vincent.

"Ta-ta — Ta-ta, are you there?"

He squeezed her hand convulsively. She heard herself saying:

"Yes. I'm here."

"Don't worry."

"I'm not worried."

"Everything will be all right."

She gave his hand an answering squeeze.

"Of course it will."

"Once she's out of the way, everything will be all right. I'll do for the
filthy bitch. Just as I did for that stingy bastard — that spider — "

She felt a chill.

"Are you there, Ta-ta?"

"Yes."

Ian was perspiring. She wiped his forehead with her handkerchief.
Ian had done it then. She had been sure, she had always been sure, that
he was innocent. There was nothing, there was nothing in the world
about which she had been right. She accepted this revelation calmly.

"She's left me everything. We'll live it up, dearest. We'll have fun.
If only — do you love me, Ta-ta?"

"Yes."

"You don't say — you don't say you love me."

"I do say it. I love you."

"Tell me again."

"I love you."

He tossed around on the narrow cot. He dislodged the blanket that
covered him. She carefully readjusted the blanket, tucking it in beneath
his shoulderblades. He fell stertorously asleep. She sat beside him, holding his hand. All she saw in the surrounding darkness was the image of

the three towers etched in her mind. It was, she felt sure, an apparition. She had never seen those towers. They would not be there when she came tomorrow. They were an illusion like everything else in the world.

When they arrived at her cottage, the orderlies jumped out, lifted the back panel and carried Ian into the house.

"Where shall we put him, ma'am?"

Stephanie opened the door to her bedroom just off the living room. There were fortunately no stairs to climb. They deposited Ian on the bed. Stephanie thanked them and they departed. The telephone rang. Stephanie went to answer it. It was Eileen. They exchanged endearments.

"Oh darling, I'm so sorry . . . we went to a movie . . . no, just Ian and I. Vincent went off somewhere . . . *Ninotchka* . . . yes, I did, but Ian hadn't seen it . . . marvelous . . . she should be very grateful to Hugo, shouldn't she, to get that performance out of her?" Then Stephanie listened for a bit.

"But darling," she said, "I never really believed I'd get it . . . of course you did everything you could . . . don't I know it? . . . but Stanley never really wanted me — I knew he didn't and after all, he's the poet, isn't he? It's his play and in these things we have to listen to the poet, don't we? Please, darling, don't give it another thought. I shan't . . . the truth is Ian isn't feeling very well . . . he's got a headache and he's such a baby when he gets a headache — he's calling me now so I can't . . . tomorrow? Of course — any time tomorrow . . . lunch . . . I'd love to . . . fine . . . I'd love to see Klaus, please bring him, please . . . Good night, darling . . . God bless."

She hung up. Actually, the news which Eileen had so dreaded giving made very little impression on Stephanie now. She had no memory of how she had longed for the part in Grant's play. It was a thing of the world and the things of the world had receded very far from her.

Ian came in. He was smouldering with anger.

"Where's the car?"

"Darling, you should be lying down. The doctor said . . ."

"I don't give a fuck what the doctor said. Where's the car?"

"You took it. Two days ago. Don't you remember? You and Vincent took it."

"That's what I need the car for. To find Vincent. Where is he?"

"He's in the hospital. Just for a few days. That nice doctor . . ."

"What hospital?"

"I don't know. The doctor didn't tell me."

"What's he doing in a hospital?"

"You were in a fight or something — in that place — the Lotus . . ."

He screamed at her.

"Get that doctor on the telephone and find out where Vincent is."

"I don't even know his name. He's coming in the morning. He'll tell you."

"I won't wait for the morning. I've got to find out what's the matter with Vincent."

"The doctor says it's nothing at all. He wants Vincent to rest for a bit. He says you should too. Please, Ian, go in and lie down."

He screamed at her.

"You're lying. You know where he is. You'd better tell me or I'll . . ."

He went to the side table by her chair and swept everything on it to the floor: her father, Rilke's *Letters to a Young Poet*. He confronted her.

"Where is he?"

"I don't know. If I knew I'd tell you."

He walked away from her. He went to the wall and stood facing it, his back to her. When he turned he had changed. His rage appeared to have ebbed. He pointed to her treasures on the floor.

"I'm sorry, darling. I'm a bit nervy, you know. I'll pick them up."

"Don't bother."

He began to walk around the room, stopping every once in a while to look at her, to see the effect he was making. His voice was gentle, little above a whisper, honeyed. He managed to produce an intonation of factitious candor.

"I dare say I'm a bit of a nuisance. I'm sorry. I love you very much, you know. Always have. My weakness. My one weakness. Well, I won't say one. It would be an exaggeration, wouldn't it, to say one? But you're the soul of patience, the soul of understanding."

He came close to her, smiling at her. She wasn't in the least frightened. She simply felt very tired. Still, she found his new manner unpleasant.

He became jocular.

"Let's turn over a new leaf, shall we? You'll help me to reform. I'll be pliable, I promise you. I'll . . ."

"Ian."

"Yes, love."

"You don't have to do it, you know."

"What, darling?" He stared at her.

"I'll do it for you. Save you the trouble."

"I beg your pardon?"

"You might not come out so well this time. As you did with Vesper."

The bruises on his face became livid. His eyes narrowed, glinted. She went on.

"It's much the simplest. Surely you see that. I'll just write a little note. That will save you all the trouble."

She got up, went to the desk, wrote a note, put it in an envelope, addressed the envelope and got up to go. He was watching her as if she were an actress on a stage. She paused to pick up the photograph of her father looking down into the crib. The fall had broken the supporting flap. She propped the photograph up against the lamp. She looked at her father and at herself. She went into her room.

Ian went to the door of her bedroom and looked in. She had gone into the bathroom. He heard the bathwater running. He went back to the desk and picked up the note she had written.

It was addressed to Eileen Grant. He read the note, in her large, scrawly handwriting with its heavy underlinings:

Dearest and darling Eileen — I'm sorry I won't be able to meet you tomorrow. I am terribly tired. I just want to sleep. Forgive me please both for the lunch date and for what I am doing. It has nothing to do with Stanley's play. It has nothing to do with Ian. *I love you darling.*

Stephanie

P.S. *My love to Kaetchen and to Klaus.*

Ian carefully put the note back in its envelope and left it there. He still heard the bathwater running. He walked into Stephanie's bedroom — their bedroom. Stephanie's dress was lying on the floor. The bathroom door was slightly open. He went in. Stephanie was lying in the tub, partly dressed. She was holding a drenched cloth to her nostrils. Her eyes were closed.

Ian sat on the edge of the tub. Stephanie's hand slipped away from the cloth. Ian held it close. When her body slipped under the water he went out. He thought perhaps he should shut off the water. He returned to shut it off. Back in the living room he had an afterthought. The police might inquire who shut the water off. He went back and turned it on again. He did not look at Stephanie. Then he left the house and stood at the curb of Santa Monica Boulevard to hail a taxi. He was determined to find Vincent.

28. Hollywood Party

The residence of Mr. and Mrs. Sig Salvesh, on a hillock in Belle Aire, was a perfect little Renaissance castle in the style of François Premier, the kind of house, Sam Hoffenstein had said, which a grand duke might build for his mistress. Nevertheless, Sig lived in it very respectably with his attractive wife Faye, who painted, and his three teen-age children. Sam Hoffenstein had also given the estate a sobriquet which it hadn't been able to shake off. Standing on the porticoed verandah, looking down the allée to the oblong emerald of the swimming pool, he had muttered in admiration: "It's a kind of Kosher Versailles, isn't it?" For Faye, pictures meant painted ones, for Sig, negatives. Faye took very little interest in her husband's handiwork. To Sig, his wife's avocation was a harmless pastime for which he was grateful because it kept her, in contrast to the wives of other producers, from airing her opinions on his product. Faye Salvesh was a dear soul, whom all of Sig's helpers and friends, the writers who kept coming in droves on the Super Chief, loved. Certainly the struggling artists who were beginning to infiltrate the film capital had reason to be grateful to her. She swam, starstruck, through all the arts except the one which her husband practiced. She wrote poetry, privately and exquisitely printed, verses which were athrob with response to love and nature. She had commissioned one of her protégés, a young artist whom she thought supremely gifted and who was certainly good-looking, to do a series of murals in pastel for the drawing room of her castle. It depicted the Salvesh family, five of them, in Renaissance costume to harmonize with the architecture of the dwelling itself. For this project, an ambitious one, she and her protégé collaborated in exhaustive research. There were long and sober debates on the exact color of Sig's doublet and hose, Faye's wimples and furbelows, the costumes of the children, two boys and a girl. They all had to be historically accurate and so they were, since they were copied meticulously from art and history books borrowed from "Research" in the studio library. It was a good library. "Get it from Research" was the printed instruction handed to writers whose assignments forced them to reanimate bygone centuries. Faye had pleaded with her collaborator not to make the family portraits realistic, merely suggestive. Sig, for example, must not be wearing glasses and on no account must he be smoking one of his inseparable cigars. The likenesses, she urged, must be no more than ever so faintly recognizable. She herself, she wished, was to look more like Isabella d'Este than herself. She had come upon Isabella in one of the research books and had fallen in love with her. The young artist found it a happy coincidence that his present patroness so miraculously resembled the earlier one.

"Do you really think so? Do you really?" Faye asked, incredulous at the windfall, but thrilled.

Under the perceptive guidance of her protégé's keener eye, Faye began, imperceptibly, to see the resemblance too. This perception merged into a sense of identification. She was, she would never have thought of saying it aloud to anyone, she was the reincarnated Isabella d'Este of Belle Aire. The role exalted her. Faye did not know it, she never could have known it, but a similar transference of personalities had occurred in faraway Boston, to a lady separated from Faye, in background, early history and social eminence, by light years, Isabella Gardner. In the latter case it was a resemblance in nomenclature; in Faye's a resemblance, pointed out by her protégé, the muralist, in looks. While Sig spent sleepless nights worrying about the next vehicle he would provide for Janet Gaynor, his wife, in a separate and dreamy bedroom, staring rapt at a watercolor of herself leaning against the violet cushions of a skiff in which she was being paddled about by a liveried boatman on Lake

Como, began to evolve another and equally thrilling transposition of personalities. She began to see her protégé, Derek Shapiro, as Isabella d'Este's protégé, Raphael.

There were about thirty guests at small tables in the Salvesh dining room. At Grant's table there were the Ludwig Borns and Kaetchen. There was an empty chair for Doris Linden, who was filming and would, therefore, be late. They were deep in discussion — as indeed, who was not — about the sad end of Stephanie von Arnim. In a few weeks the whole thing would be forgotten, but just now it was a teeming subject.

"Poor, drowned Ophelia," said Born.

Kenneth Ogden came over from his hostess's table to chat with them for a few minutes. In response to Kaetchen's question he said that Mary had undergone a crise of shyness and decided not to come at the last minute. The question was put up to him. Was it suicide? Was it murder?

"Why not give the poor guy the benefit of the doubt?" said Ogden.

"A good friend of mine," said Grant, "and of Stephanie's, said to me long ago that Ian would kill her."

"I can imagine who that good friend is," said Ogden genially, "and if it's who I think it is, she's paranoiac and I wouldn't accept her opinion about anything."

Grant was abashed.

"Sally," Ogden added, "hates men, as you and I both have reason to know."

Ogden smiled. He appeared to be in wonderful humor.

"I didn't know these boys could be so lethal," said Grant. He said it although he knew, while he was saying it, that it was a stupid remark.

"Sheer nonsense, dear playwright. There are more killers among the heterosexuals than among the pansies. Perhaps that's because there are more heterosexuals. Or are there?"

He looked from Born to Löwe as if he were unsure. Born laughed. Ogden's quizzical, probing look was very comic. "I've never been entirely sure of you, Kaetchen," he said.

Kaetchen chuckled. "I'm not sure of myself."

"In any case," said Ogden, "my best friends are pansies. I couldn't live without them."

"I thought it was Jews," said Kaetchen.

"They too," said Ogden. 'I couldn't live without them either."

"The trouble with the Jews," said Frau Born, who was a Catholic, "is that the minute I get involved with one, they begin talking about Jesus Christ to me."

Born looked guilty. He was mystical and very close to Catholicism. In Lourdes, when he was escaping from France, he had vowed that if ever he did escape, he would dedicate a book to the Saint of Lourdes. He kept his vow.

Grant was brooding. He had been brooding ever since he got the news. He had been riven with guilt. Eileen, who told him what had happened, never said a word to him about what she knew he was thinking and what she was thinking herself. He almost wished that she would accuse him so that he could defend himself.

"Still," he said, "I can't help it. I've got a terrible feeling of guilt about Stephanie."

"She absolves you, doesn't she," said Kaetchen, "in her farewell note?"

"That note might have been dictated," said Grant. "It might have been written under duress."

"Would Ian have taken the trouble to dictate a note in which she absolved you?" Ogden said. "Was he as fond of you as that?"

"She may absolve me, but I don't feel absolved. I can't help thinking: maybe if I'd given her that silly part she wouldn't have done it. I know Eileen thinks so."

"Isn't it extraordinary?" said Ogden. "In every suicide everyone is considered guilty except the one who does it. Snap out of it, Stanley. Stephanie had every reason to do what she did. I went through that about Varina. If it's any comfort to you, you and I are exactly in the same boat. Fellow culprits! Aren't we?"

"How do you mean?"

"I am blamed for Varina's death. The fact is Varina simply used me as an excuse to kill herself, to accomplish her real motive."

"What was that?" asked Löwe.

"Revenge on Mary."

There was a shocked silence. Ogden went on.

"Freud makes it clear. It's never themselves suicides want to destroy; it's always someone else. Otherwise they'd never have the gumption to do it; they are energized by the revenge motive. Kids spiting their parents. It's a classical example."

Born shook his head.

"Too simple," he said, "too simple."

"On the contrary," said Ogden, "it's very complicated."

Faye Salvesh, looking beautiful in a mauve, trailing hostess gown, her reddish brown hair parted chastely in the middle showing her classical forehead to advantage, came up and tapped Ogden on the shoulder.

"Tiens, tiens, we've lent you out long enough! I want you back. Derek wants you back. Sam H. wants you back. Hugo Stift wants you back." She smiled at the others. "You may have him later — if you are alert!"

She wavered off to her own table where Stift, Hoffenstein and the muralist were sitting.

Ogden got up to follow.

"Pre-Raphaelitish, isn't she? I'm sure Burne-Jones will drop in any minute. Don't brood, Stanley. It's unrealistic."

Frau Born seemed to be fascinated by Ogden. She hadn't taken her eyes off him. She now turned to Kaetchen.

"He is Aryan?"

"Entirely."

"That is almost too much," said Born, his eyes twinkling behind his glasses.

Olga fished in her handbag and took out a gold pencil and a card. She handed them to Grant.

"Write me down his name, please."

Grant did as he was told. He gave the card back to Olga. He knew that Born enjoyed being teased about his wife's roving eye. It made him happier in the possession of those beautiful rovers.

"Lucky for you," he said, "that Ogden's going to marry Mary Kennicott."

"Ah," said Born, "will that nullify him?"

"He is not going to marry Mary Kennicott," said Löwe, almost inaudibly.

He loved delivering world-shaking announcements in a whisper.

"What did you say?" said Grant. "Did I hear you correctly?"

"Yes," said Kaetchen.

"How do you know?"

"Because he told me. He said he'd talked Mary out of it. That's why she isn't here tonight. It was not a crise of shyness. It's a crise of disappointment."

"But for God's sake why?"

"He explained it to me. I quite understood it. He doesn't want to marry. What he cherishes above all else in the world is independence. He's always been independent. He wants to continue so."

"I'll be damned! What a strange guy!"

"From his point of view he made sense." After a reflective moment he went on. "I began to think," he said, "that perhaps I have underestimated Dr. Ogden."

Grant was irritated by this remark of Kaetchen's. He had been irritated by Ogden's giving him blanket absolution for the death of Stephanie; he resented being deprived of his guilt so summarily. Ogden had been too glib about it; there was, after all, such a thing as responsibility. Ogden *was* responsible for Varina's death, no matter what he said about it, just as he himself was responsible for Stephanie's. He didn't care what Stephanie's last letter said. That was *like* Stephanie; it was to console Eileen, to spare Eileen, that she wrote it. There was no way out of it: he *was* a heel, even if not, as Ogden had said to him the other day, a dedicated one. He was an undedicated heel, casual and sloppy, even worse. He hated Ogden almost as much as he despised himself.

Grant sank into a private inferno. He had again the feeling he had in Salzburg, that he was way out of his depth with these people, a yokel at a saturnalia. He remembered what a high-spirited girl he knew had said once of a metropolitan rustic who bored her: "He has hayseed instead of vine leaves in his hair." He applied this remark now to himself; it seemed to fit. The only nice person he knew really was Eileen and Eileen hated him — and with reason. He must not let go of Eileen; she was the only spar to which he must cling. He would never let her go to Palestine. He hoped Naomi would go. He had begun to dislike Naomi. He should never have given her that job. She despised his script. Who was she to despise his script? She was like a skeleton in his house, poring with Eileen over forgotten codes and rituals that he didn't give a damn about. With Eileen and Naomi absorbed in their endless lucubrations in Judaica, he was back in the oppressive atmosphere of his father's house in Xenia. He might just as well have never left home.

Doris Linden appeared and sat in the empty chair beside Grant. She apologized, not in the least breathlessly, for being late; she had been working since six that morning, but she looked fresh as a daisy; she had seen to that. She was gracious to the Borns. She dazzled them. She assured Born that the actress who was going to play the heroine in the film that was being made of his novel would be wonderful. She had seen her test and it was glorious. The Borns were touched by her generosity toward a fellow artist. "Don't they know," thought Grant, "that it's pure fake, that she doesn't mean a word of it?" Her quick success with the Borns annoyed him.

"He may be a great novelist and a great poet," he thought, "and he may come from Vienna, but he's a yokel too."

They were all very cozy together, except Grant. He was overcome by the conviction — and it wasn't the first time he had had it — that Doris didn't really care for him at all. It was the part in his play that she wanted. Her deepest interest, he had discovered, was clothes. She had a profound, scholar's interest in women's clothes. She herself was casually chic. She had a library on couture. She knew what women wore and how they looked in the sixteenth, seventeenth, eighteenth and nineteenth centuries. She had great volumes, beautifully illustrated, from Austria, Italy, France and Germany. Her real ambition, Grant had come to realize, was to be listed among the Ten Best-dressed Women in America. She would make it, too, Grant thought bitterly — indeed he had prophesied it to her — as soon as she appeared in his play.

Sig Salvesh was making a tour of the tables, to see that everything was all right, that his guests were having a good time. He stopped by Grant's table. He took his cigar out of his mouth long enough to kiss Doris. His tic was working furiously. Born said how eagerly he was looking forward to seeing Dante's *Inferno*.

"I switched it," said Salvesh. "Showing the Chopin picture instead."

Born was stricken with disappointment.

"Why'd you switch it, Sig?" asked Grant. "Ashamed of it?"

Salvesh grinned affectionately at Grant.

"Wise guy! It's a great picture. I switched it because it's a hot night. You can't show Dante's *Inferno* on a hot night!"

He moved on to the next table. Born was overjoyed. He asserted that Sig Salvesh was a great man.

Grant agreed.

"He is," he said. "He's terrific."

Doris had a roving eye, like Olga Born's, only Doris's eyes were gray-green. She was giving the room the once-over.

"Stanley," she said.

"Yes, darling?"

"Who is that man?"

"What man?"

"The dark man — at Faye's table."

Grant looked. Ogden was looking at Doris too. They were sizing each other up.

"His name is Ogden," said Grant. "Kenneth Ogden."

"Actor?"

"Psychoanalyst."

It was as if by mutual consent that Doris and Ogden stopped looking at each other. It was also as if by mutual consent that they would hold their look in abeyance. It was the recreation of the moment by the bar in his living room when Vincent had first beheld Ian. "Who is that man?" Vincent had asked. He remembered the Proustian reference. This time it was not Proustian but it was the same. It was exactly the same.

There was no possible way out of it: for the general good and for his private good he must get rid of Ogden. He wanted to kill Ogden. Through the alcoholic haze he saw it as a "crime of passion." It fixed him firmly into an ennobling tradition.

After dinner, the company drifted into the drawing room where the film was to be shown. There were the Salveshes on the walls in dreamy pastel: soft rose and lavender costumes, as correct as Research could make them, opalescent greens and yellows. They cavorted innocently behind hedges; the children played at bowls on sward like carpeting; the elders were gauntleted, falconed. In one panel, Sig, faintly recognizable, in doublet and hose (green and yellow) assisted Faye, easily recognizable, to dismount from her palfrey. Kaetchen, who had seen these murals before, guided the Borns along the walls. Olga was staring at them through a lorgnette. Her husband was fascinated, incredulous.

"It's like the minnesingers, isn't it?" said Kaetchen. He would have

given anything in the world to have Lady Monica there; it was just her
thing; she would have adored it. Well, he would write her about it. Faye,
looking very much the likeness of herself which was exactly the likeness
of Isabella d'Este, brought the artist up to present him to the Borns. He
was a charming and attractive and becomingly modest man. Olga transferred her piercing lorgnette from the pastels to Derek. A comment was
mandatory. Born produced it. "I have never," he said with utter sincerity, "seen anything like it before."

For Faye it was a moment of triumph.

"You see, Derek," she cried, "you won't believe me when I tell you.
Perhaps you will believe it when Mr. Born tells you!"

She exulted to the Borns:

"He is the Raphael de nos jours, but he's too modest to admit it."

The only concession to modern art in the room was a plump and rosy
Renoir nude over the fireplace. The guests seated themselves in great,
overstuffed armchairs, with little tables beside them; on the tables were
cigarettes and chocolates. Grant had disappeared. He was in the bar,
drinking and planning the perfect crime. Ogden sat with Doris, Kaetchen and the Borns. The room darkened. The Renoir lady, compliant,
descended to make way for the film. Her place was taken by the wide
screen. The room filled with a lion's roar, which also subsided, and there
was Franz Liszt, in an elegant Parisian drawing room of the eighteen
thirties, introducing Frederic Chopin to Mme. Sand. Born, whose passion was music — he was brought up on it, he lived for it, he had indeed
written a biography of Berlioz — chortled silently, with a welling inner
joy, at the picture of musicians presented in this film. They were swoon-
ing with magnanimity. Liszt was entirely self-forgetful; he had no ego
at all. All he wanted to do was to get Chopin moving. He refuses to
play; he makes Chopin do it. Mme. Sand is impressed by Chopin's performance. The moment he finishes, Liszt, with an air of "See! I told you
so!", brings him up to Mme. Sand. Mme. Sand gives Chopin the eye.

"What are your plans, Mr. Chopin?" she inquires.

Born's cup ran over. It kept running over. Later, Chopin, now firmly
established, is playing nocturnes for Mme. Sand.

"This one, George," he says as he wafts her a nocturne, "is for you."

Finally, it was over. The lights came up and so did the Renoir girl,
none the worse for her experience.

The guests crowded around the Salveshes, inundating them with congratulation. No doubt about it, Sig had produced a masterpiece. The film was tremendous, marvelous, a milestone. Sig could rest easy. In spite of the fact that it was artistic, it would make a mint. Born's remark about the panels came in handy again; he could repeat, and with sincerity, that he had never seen anything like it before. Only on one point did he quibble. When Doris, in simulated, professional ecstasy, came up to him with: "And Merle! Wasn't she marvelous, simply marvelous?" Born was forced to dissent.

"Sainte-Beuve, you know, my dear, said of Mme. Sand that she had a magnanimous soul and a perfectly enormous behind. Posteriorly, I found Miss Oberon inadequate."

Grant, having decided to buy all the whodunits he could put his hands on to limber him up for his new role as assassin, had come back for the last reel. He did not share Born's bubbling joy over the film. Neither did Frau Olga. Frau Olga took a poor view. She had been married to a great composer and she felt that the film was unrealistic.

Sig, incessantly creative, was on the scent, already, for greater triumphs. Grant was standing with the Borns. He noticed that Doris and Ogden had disappeared. Sig came up to them. He barked at Grant:

"Have you given any thought to *Crime and Punishment?*"

Grant, hazy, said, "No. Should I?"

"One thing I've decided," said Sig, taking it for granted that now Grant would begin to think about it, "we ain't going to lay it in Russia."

Born listened — transfixed.

"Where you going to lay it, Sig?"

"Vienna!"

"Why Vienna?"

"Because there's something about Russians that ain't funny!"

Born had to repress a strong impulse to hug Sig.

Sig added an envoy.

"And remember this," he admonished. "We got to end it on a note of hope for Gaynor."

The seed planted, Salvesh disappeared.

Born turned to his wife who hadn't taken in Sig's generalizations.

"Fabelhaft!"

His eyes twinkled with joy. He was disappointed that Grant wasn't as happy as he was.

"But, my dear Stanley! 'Something about Russians that ain't funny!' It's classical. Moreover — IT'S TRUE!"

Grant drove Doris home in his Cord. She kept up a steady chatter: about the film, about how wonderful Merle Oberon was, about how adorable and cozy Ludwig Born was. "He's so nice and jolly you'd never think he's a great man, would you?" As Grant was unresponsive, she inserted some remarks about his play. "Do you know something?" she said. "I take your script to my bungalow on the set. I keep it under the shooting script and when I go back between shots I read it and read it. I *study* it. When I hear George or anybody else coming, I hide it like it was contraband or something. I just love your play. I can't wait for rehearsals to begin."

Even this brought nothing from Grant. Doris had decided not to mention Kenneth, from whom she was expecting a call when she got home. Then she decided it would seem unnatural not to mention him and she did.

"Your friend, Dr. Ogden, thinks pretty well of himself, doesn't he?"

They arrived at the entrance to Château Marmont, where Doris was living.

"I have to be on the set at eight tomorrow morning. Isn't it ghastly! One reason I can't wait to do your play is that I'll be able to sleep in the morning."

She had feared that he would go upstairs with her, which would have interfered with Ogden's call.

She kissed him.

"But I'll expect you tomorrow night for dinner. Pick me up early!"

"Doris."

"Yes, darling?"

"I've changed my mind."

"About what?"

"I'm not giving you the part. I think you're wrong for it."

She was stunned. She couldn't believe he'd said it.

"You're not serious. You can't be. You've had too much to drink. Your only fault."

"I'm not drunk. I know exactly what I'm saying."

"Are you sore at me or something?"

"Not sore. Why should I be sore?"

"All those dark thoughts my genius has. I'll brush them away, whistle them away." She emitted a long, low whistle and waved her hand before his face as if exorcising an evil spirit. "Come early tomorrow. As early as you can."

"I'll call you. Good night."

"Good night, darling. Love you."

She ran inside the lobby. She had been frightened for a minute. He'd seen that. But the wave and the whistle had reassured her, even if it hadn't him. As he drove home he cursed himself. How inept he was. How uncontrolled! Couldn't he have waited till tomorrow? There wasn't a thing in the world that was right about him — nothing at all.

Then he seized on the one truth that might save him. There was one spar to which he must cling. He must win back Eileen. He must regain Eileen.

29. Father Confessor

Grant remembered that it was Schwester's night off; she had gone to a movie in Beverly. Eileen must be upstairs in Amos's room, baby-sitting. He wanted badly to see her, to confess to what he was feeling, to turn over a new leaf. He went to the bar in his living room to pour himself a drink, to fortify himself, to force some coherence into his thoughts. The constant question: what was he? What had become of him? He was a mess. He didn't fit. He wasn't genuine. In his youth he had been quite decent, aspiring. He had meant well. He always reverted, in these moments of self-abasement, to a mystical experience he had had when he was young. It was on a summer afternoon, on the deck of the little boat that plied the coast of Maine, between Rockland and Blue Hill, the first time he went there. It was that summer he had written the play, assisted the accident which had brought him to where he was standing at this moment, at the bar of a strange, gloomy Spanish living room. It had happened on the narrow deck of the chugging little steamer while he was leaning over the rail, watching the rainbowed spume in the wake of the side paddles. The afternoon was passing by in slow bliss; tiny villages nestled in the valleys of the low hills, cattle ruminated in the salt marshes, sailboats dotted the estuaries, fishermen dangled their legs from long, dark-brown wooden wharves, playing their lines, hoping for the best. The world was a glowing carpet of beauty, spread out for his delight. He felt himself to be one of God's children, given a lifetime to play in it. Nor was it his father's God, minatory, but another God entirely, companionable, sympathetic, indulgent — more like his mother! In that moment of diffused pantheism, he felt that the world was good, that life was good and that he himself was a constituent of this goodness. He remembered this now in surprise and bitterness; the subscriber to goodness was standing here now consumed by an insensate hatred of a man he hardly knew, a stranger named Kenneth Ogden. How had this alchemy, of good metal into base, come about?

His thoughts darted off in another direction. After all, this suspicion of Doris and Ogden, what was it based on? Nothing but his ghastly habit of dousing himself in the dirty waters of masochism. He had dreamed it all up; there was nothing to it. It was sheer fantasy. He started for the telephone. He would call Doris, he would apologize, he would be abject, he . . . but he stopped. No, it was not imagination. He had seen that look. He had seen them chattering in corners. The very way she had brought up Ogden's name in the car — "Your friend thinks pretty well of himself, doesn't he?" — was proof enough. Why had she felt it necessary to erect a barricade against suspicion? God's child, far removed suddenly from the ruminating cattle of the Maine salt marshes, was now obsessed by the conviction that he must kill Ogden. By doing this he would win the respect of the community. Recently a Hollywood producer, in a breach of hospitality, had shot his house guest, not fatally, but sufficiently. The producer, hitherto regarded as a milksop, had acquired status. He too could join the Guard of Honor. Trouble was, he had no gun. How could he get a gun?

Eileen walked into the room, carrying Amos.

"Stanley! I didn't know you were home. Amos couldn't sleep. He was restless." She smiled down at Amos. "He felt like walking."

Grant put down his glass and walked up to them. An extraordinary thing happened. Amos reached out his arms to Grant and began squealing in ecstasy:

"Daddy! Daddy! Daddy!"

He kept repeating the word in crescendo. It was as though he had discovered, for the first time, the capacity to speak, to articulate, to express welling delight, love. Eileen relinquished him. Grant took him in his arms and held him close. Amos's hands traveled his face.

"Daddy! Daddy! Daddy!"

"You see," said Eileen, "you are precious to him."

Everything vanished. Everything was wiped out but this warm tiny closeness. It was an instant totally experienced, a pantheism not diffused but essential. In that instant Grant felt that he shared the throb at the center of meaning. He knew everything that he needed to know. He wanted to prolong the instant. At the same time he knew that it could not be prolonged as it reached already into infinity. Eileen stood watching. Then Amos, as if himself exhausted by transfiguration, rested his head on Grant's shoulder and fell fast asleep.

They stood in silence.

"He'll sleep now," said Eileen. "I'll take him up. Schwester'll be back any minute now. Can you wait for me? I want to talk to you."

Grant nodded. He watched her carry Amos upstairs. A moment later he heard Schwester let herself in at the front door. Eileen returned.

"Well," she said, "that was quite a welcome you got! Aren't you pleased?"

"Eileen . . ."

"Yes? . . ."

"I want to begin again. With you. With him."

"It's too late."

"What do you mean?"

"Just that. I have no life with you. I never will have."

"I came back to tell you. I want to turn over a new leaf. I know I've been — well, you know what I've been. I'm not apologizing. I want to make a fresh start. I'll try. I'll try harder. I'll try."

"Are things not going well?"

He hated her for saying that. She shouldn't have said that. Goddamn her for saying that! But he must exercise self-control.

"Look. Eileen! Look. Don't dig into the past. It's dead. Let's plan for the future. Amos's. Ours."

"We've turned over so many new leaves. Haven't we? I told you the other night — the night Stephanie died — I told you then I was leaving you. You'd been drinking. It made no impression on you. But I did tell you."

"What about Amos?"

"I'm taking Amos."

He came up to her.

"You'll never take Amos. Understand that. Never."

"The little scene just now," she said quietly, "was bad luck for me. Mostly you forget all about him."

"That's where you're dead wrong. He means more to me than anything in the world. He's all that means anything to me."

He was enraged, his intentions had been so lofty.

"You say you're leaving. Where to?"

"Palestine."

"I'll be goddamned. You're not serious!"

"I told you that the other night too. Again — you didn't listen!"

"What on earth do you want to go to Palestine for?"

"I want to bring up Amos there."

"Is it Naomi's idea?"

"She is going. Yes."

"It's all right for her, I suppose. It's silly for you. As for Amos — it's ridiculous. Fantastic. Absurd."

"We don't think so."

"Who's we?"

"Klaus and I."

He stared at her.

"Klaus Wolff?"

"I love him. I want never to be away from him."

There was a silence. He stared at her.

"I should think he'd be better suited to Naomi than to you."

"I don't know what you mean by that?"

"Why marry the pupil when he can marry the teacher?"

"It's no use. There never has been. Why don't you face up to it and let us go."

"Not Amos. Never. It's the most cockeyed idea I ever heard of. Why Palestine? It's all right for them — from Germany. They have no choice. Do you think that they go because they want to?"

"I don't know. Klaus and I want to."

"My God! A Zionist too! Naomi's certainly done a job on you! You're ridiculous. This convert's zeal of yours has always been ridiculous. It's made a laughingstock of me. Wolff's an intelligent fellow. Can't he make you see how ridiculous it is?"

"Ask him."

"If you think I'm going to let you take Amos to that godforsaken disputed desert, you're crazy. You've chosen a fine moment! How're you going to get there? They're dumping shiploads of immigrants in the harbors right this minute. They're . . ."

The telephone rang. Grant answered it. It was Ogden.

"Stanley? I hope I don't disturb you."

"Not at all. I've been thinking of you. I've been planning how to kill you."

"That's healthy. Come over. We'll discuss it. I'm in Bungalow six at the Beverly Hills Hotel. Five minutes from you. I'll have a drink ready for you."

"I'll be right over."

Grant hung up. Eileen was watching him. She saw that he was far gone. She felt pity for him.

"Don't go, Stanley. What for? Go to bed. See him tomorrow if you have to. I'll call him if you like — tell him you're not coming."

"No thanks. I'm due to see Dr. Ogden. He's probably the better man. If he is — it will solve all your problems!"

Eileen was frightened. Was he going to fight Ogden? He was in poor shape. He'd be no match for Ogden.

"Don't go," she said. "Please don't go."

He went out into the hall. Then he remembered something. He ran up to his room, opened a drawer of his desk, found the letter Ogden had written to Sally which she had asked him to destroy. He put it in his pocket, ran downstairs and got into his car.

Ogden opened the door of Bungalow six to admit Stanley. He led him into the parlor. There were flowers everywhere. Ogden was wearing a magnificent Oriental dressing gown, a Christmas present from Mary. He appeared to be in wonderful spirits. His eyes glowed, his teeth shone, he radiated tremendous, controlled vitality.

"What's the matter, Stanley? You look done in. Here! Let the good doctor make you comfortable." He indicated an immense, overstuffed armchair. "What'll you have?"

"Brandy please."

"Done and done."

He gave Stanley the brandy.

"Thanks."

Ogden hovered over him for a moment like a male nurse.

"So you've been thinking about killing me. Have you got a gun?"

"Wouldn't know where to get one."

"Shall I call room service?"

"If there were no penalty for homicide," said Grant, "I'd kill you."

Ogden laughed.

"Sane point of view. Realistic. Comfort in that, don't you think, for the capital punishment boys? Let the abolitionists take heed."

"Anyway, I wouldn't know how to go about it."

"Nothing easier. Anybody can shoot anybody. That's why so many idiots do it. But it would really be very silly of you to kill me. In the first place, I'm very fond of you. It would be a terrible waste of your talents. You have a dazzling career ahead of you. Quite a distinction for me — to be bumped off by a celebrated character like you. You would only immortalize me. Wasted on me. I have no craving whatever for immortality. I haven't that kind of vanity. Quite content, dear boy, just to be mortal."

"Why did you call me?"

"Because I wanted to see you."

"What about?"

"I think you are behaving very foolishly. From your own point of view — destructively. As destructively, almost, as if you were to screw yourself up by killing me."

"How?"

"By taking the part in your play away from Doris."

"How do you know that?"

"She told me. On the telephone."

"I was right then! She called you."

"I called her. I said I would at the Salvesh's."

"I was going to call her up — to apologize — for distrusting her."

"I'm glad you didn't. Your artist's intuition was right."

"You mean that you've already . . . ?"

Ogden laughed.

"There's scarcely been time. But you are right. It is inevitable."

There was a silence. Grant was left alone with the inevitable.

"Doris is very upset. She loves your play and her part. I reassured her. I told her that when you'd recovered a bit you'd see how silly it is. I've read your play. Doris is ideal for it. She'll be stunning in it."

"How on earth did you . . . ?"

"Mary gave it to me. The copy you lent her. I was very much interested. Naturally, as I am the principal character."

Grant forgot his homicidal mission.

"How'd you like it?"

"I like it very much. You are superficial about Sally. You are superficial about me. But it's very amusing. Wittily written. It's sure to be a success. I'd gladly invest in it. By the way — I was flattered to see that you quote me."

"Do I? Where?"

"A remark I made when we lunched together in Salzburg. Didn't I say that I switched from tonsillectomies to psychoanalysis because I discovered that the poor have tonsils but that the rich have souls?"

"You did. I wrote it on a pad in the cab on the way home. I stuck it in."

"You'll owe me royalties."

"If it gets a laugh, I'll pay you. If it doesn't, I'll cut it out."

"Let's bet on it. A hundred dollars. If it gets a laugh, you'll pay me. If it doesn't, I'll pay you. You can't lose."

"All right. It's a bet."

"I'm going to your opening with Mary. I'll be very tense."

Ogden was enjoying himself. Grant found it annoying. He was even more annoyed at Ogden's criticism of superficiality, especially as Sally had made it too.

"You think I am superficial about Sally. I happen to know a lot about that."

"So do I!"

Grant reached into his breast pocket and took out Ogden's letter.

"Do you recognize your handwriting?"

"She gave you that, did she? Just like Sally. I meant for her to show it to Mary."

"She never showed it to Mary."

"Mistaken gallantry. Mind you, that note wasn't entirely calculated. I did have a thing on Sally. I was good and stuck on her. She had a thing on me too, but then, she's God-struck. Formidable rival."

"It may be petty of me but I derive satisfaction from knowing that you've had at least one failure."

"Do you call that a failure? To drive a virgin into a nunnery? It's my subtlest success. Mind you, I wouldn't want success like that too often. It would be inconvenient."

"It must be wonderful," Grant said, "to have such an exalted opinion of yourself."

"Not at all. I discovered when I was young that I was attractive to women. Since I don't care for anything but, I've devoted my life to them. I'm not in the least ambitious. I just want to have a good time. I'm about the only psychoanalyst you'll ever meet who isn't all screwed up himself. God, the cant I have to listen to!"

Grant felt like demolishing him with a riposte but the riposte failed to materialize. He asked for another brandy.

"You drink too much, but then I'm not out to reform you. Odd little trick Doris has," he said as he gave Grant the brandy, "have you noticed?"

"Trick? What trick?"

"When she's with a man she considers intellectual she has a trick of saying: 'Of course I don't know anything. I'm just a pinhead.' Actually she's extremely shrewd, very clever. While she's saying it, she thinks: 'I'd just as soon you'd think I'm a pinhead but I know that you are a goddamn fool!' Have you noticed that little trick of hers?"

Grant had noticed it; he had, in fact, been flattered by it, but he had no intention of admitting it. He sat in utter misery.

"What's the matter? Cheer up."

"I'm a mess."

"You're talented. You're successful. What more do you want? I've seen your play. It amuses people. It amused me."

"It was an accident."

"So is everything in life. Talent is an accident. Genius is an accident. Accidents are irrational. Life is irrational. Once you accept that you won't take yourself so seriously."

"If that is so, then what's the use of anything?"

"Do you call it rational when a feller named Schicklgruber can terrorize the world? But it's not the world that's bothering you. It's something closer. What is it?"

"Eileen's leaving me."

"Oh? For anybody?"

"Klaus Wolff."

"Oh? I've met him."

"They want to go to Palestine."

"Good idea. Martyrdom suits their personalities."

"They want to take Amos."

"Why not?"

"I'll never let them take Amos."

"Why not?"

"You're not a father. I couldn't expect you to understand what I feel about Amos."

"And yet Amos, too, was an accident. I know a lot about your marriage. Eileen cozened you into it. You were in a sentimental fog. Moreover, Jewish-sentimental — the densest variety there is."

"You're anti-Semitic. I've long suspected that."

"You people are awfully touchy. I had a patient in Cleveland once. Nice fellow. He had halitosis and he thought it was anti-Semitism. I changed his diet and cured him. If you're so patriotic, why did you change your name?"

Grant winced.

"Don't wince. Face up to it. You wanted to be Stanley Grant. Okay. *Be* Stanley Grant."

Ogden went to the table covered with bottles and poured himself a drink.

"But let's get it straight about Doris. She asked me to deny that there was anything between us. But I'm too fond of you to kid you. You're wounded. Why? Why are you taking the part away from Doris? Because you've discovered that she doesn't love you for yourself alone. What vanity! Why should she? Would you love her if she weren't a damn good actress and you needed her for the part? You're both after exactly the same thing. You're gifted and likable, dear boy, but you are also foolish. Cutting off your nose to spite your face. Also, you have an instinct, an infallible instinct . . ."

The telephone rang. Ogden answered it. It was Doris.

"You can't sleep? . . . didn't I tell you super-Daddy would take care of it? . . . He's right here . . . want to talk to him?"

He held the receiver for Grant. Grant took it.

"Hello, Doris . . . I'm sorry you're having a sleepless night . . . I was going to call you . . . You're the only one in the world for the part . . . Kenneth's read the play and thinks you'll be great in it. Is our dinner date okay for tomorrow? Shall I invite Kenneth? . . . Good night, darling. Get your beauty sleep. Forgive me? . . . Thanks, darling. I love you."

Grant hung up. He went back to his chair. He expected to be congratulated on his magnanimity, but Ogden simply said:

"Sorry, I can't join you tomorrow night. I'm having dinner with Mary."

"What," said Grant, "do I have an infallible instinct for?"

"For falling in love with girls you know will reject you. And you're seldom disappointed." Ogden looked at his wristwatch. He yawned.

"Two o'clock. Doctor's getting sleepy."

Grant rose to go. Ogden ushered him to the door.

"It's been good talking to you," he said. "Sometime I'd like to sample *your* conversation."

He grinned happily.

"Sorry you can't have dinner with us tomorrow night."

"So am I. I have a floating dinner date with Doris some night this week. I'll invite you."

Driving home Grant found that he no longer hated Ogden. He had, after all, saved Doris for his play. Still, he resented him. He was glib, superficial. He had evolved a philosophy of life to suit his personal indulgences.

"Spiritually," he thought, "he has no eyelids."

Grant was pleased with this reflection. He would write it down.

When he got home he switched on the light in the drawing room. He sat at the desk and wrote a note to Eileen.

Dearest and long-suffering Eileen,

I have thought things over. I will put nothing in your way. You may follow your heart's desire with my love and blessing.

Your ex-husband,
Stanley

He put the note into an envelope, without sealing it. He went upstairs and slipped it under Eileen's door. Then he went to his own room. He wasn't sleepy. He felt a strange excitement. He couldn't fathom its source. He opened his notebook to write down the phrase he had just formulated about Ogden. Then an idea for a play hit him. He began writing at top speed in his notebook. He realized then that that was the cause of his excitement. A man, in a paroxysm of jealousy, decides to kill his rival. He buys a gun. The potential murderer is a scientist, a physicist. Yes, that suited Grant because, to him, a dedicated scientist was a symbol of purity. But the victim, a glib and accomplished gigolo . . .

When Grant finished writing it was high dawn.

30. The Most Cultivated Mind in the World

Löwe had been back in his room at the Ambassador for several months. He had embarked on a new crusade: to get published a novel by a German writer, Selig Langfeld, whom he had managed, by the pulling of high-voltage wires, to smuggle into New York. The author was badly crippled: one arm had been burnt off by some freelance Brownshirts in a sportive mood. He had been beaten so badly about the head that he was nearly deaf. Nevertheless, he had managed to complete a long, epical novel, a parable of the totalitarian state, which he had begun in Europe. To support him while he was finishing this novel, Löwe had enlisted the aid of Mr. Lloyd McIlwaine, the newspaper magnate. This aid was funneled through Löwe as Mr. McIlwaine wished to remain anonymous. Löwe had persuaded his friend Ludwig Born, who had never met the novelist, to write an introduction. It was hard going to get this novel published; it was heavy, not only in weight, but in matter. Everybody turned it down; they had been turning it down for some time. But Löwe had no ear for rejections. He kept resubmitting it until finally a major publisher, worn out by attrition, accepted it. Löwe even got a modest advance for his protégé, which, for the author, was a bonanza. Born's introduction helped. In it he tried to explain the novelist's parable, his created world as a mirror analogy of the present world of Germany. He concludes his preface:

Mr. Langfeld has not only written a great novel, but also an important political work. We must recognize the enemy whom we would strike dead; and I can think of no other aid toward recognizing the German character that I would place above this myriad-figured, fantastic, and precise vision.

Löwe had arranged for the first copy to be sent him so he could have the pleasure of bringing it to the author. There it was and very handsome: on the jacket a sheaf of upthrust gleaming bayonets supporting a furled crimson flag. The novel was so long, the characters so multitudinous that the publisher had had the courtesy to include an eight-page leaflet: Alphabetical Index of Names and Explanatory Group Index. On the dedication page Löwe read his own name. He went downstairs, got a taxi and delivered the book to the author and his wife. On his return he described the scene in his letter to Monica:

It was quite affecting. I went to their one-room flat on Third Avenue. I don't suppose Langfeld can be over fifty but he looks an old man. His nice wife, about the same age, unscarified, looks like his daughter. Well, I put the book in his hand. He was trembling. There it was, his book, his child, newborn, intact. The wife, looking at it over his shoulder, wept. His life was in this book and now his life was in his hand. He held it. He read the biographical material about him on the jacket. He was enraptured by the Alphabetical Index of Names. *I felt that I had returned to them a long-lost child whom they had given up for dead. He said that now he would be able to repay me for the expenditures I had made in his behalf; I couldn't, of course, tell him who his true benefactor was. You know McIlwaine and what a generous man he is. But isn't it sad? Langfeld knows nothing whatever of this country and its book market. He thinks: 'Well, here is a book, handsome and substantial with an introduction by Ludwig Born; there will be a stampede for it.' He doesn't know, alas, that once I have bought copies to give to my friends, the sale will stop. I shan't send it to you. It would bore you as it bores me. It's the kind of heavy German allegorical style that has always bored me. I am shallow and lightsome you see, aus Czernowitz. The book cannot possibly sell. It will be remaindered. It will be forgotten. But not by poor Langfeld. Not by his wife. Born, in his introduction, speaks of a "mirror world." He will live henceforth, the poor man, in this mirror world.*

But happily, I have something more cheerful to tell you, an event about which I feel modestly triumphant, an arrival as miraculous to me as the book to poor Langfeld. Just the other day I found waiting for me a vast and battered bundle, bearing the postmarks of Vienna, Belgrade, Istanbul, Vera Cruz. The Federn manuscripts! I couldn't believe it! You know how long and vainly I have been trying to get them. Who sent them I do not know; there was no communication of any sort. But there they were, the plays and novels in Federn's handwriting. Perhaps Federn's lawyer sent them, perhaps, Kurt thinks, an Aryan assistant to his father who had read one of my begging letters. Federn himself, we are pretty sure, is dead. Well! The comedy began and I have never seen one on the stage that I enjoyed more. I telephoned Dr. Binder. He barked as usual and said that if it was young Federn I was bothering him about I might as well hang up. I said not at all, that I had other plans for young Federn, which, thanks to Dr. Binder, indeed I have. Dr. Binder went on sputtering about this and that — he hates the human race — and then I said casually that the Federn manuscripts had arrived. It was Dr. Binder who hung up! Fifteen minutes later he appeared in this room. You've never seen anything like it, how he groveled over those manuscripts. It was quite ugly to watch — like a miser drooling over his gold. The two impulses are the same, don't you think? Acquisition neat, distilled, uncorrupted by foreign matter. All collectors are a bit mad, don't you agree? Young Federn is now Dr. Binder's pro-

fessional assistant. He is also fairly well off. I can present him as a young man with a distinguished position, a future and a private income. I am about to flex the third hand in his behalf. I have a fascinating prospect for young Federn.

By this time, surely, Stanley Grant will have delivered my letter to you. You will have met him and seen his play. Did it not open last night? The play I feel pretty sure you must have liked. What about the author? I long to hear. I admire him more and more and approve of him less and less. I think the trouble with him is that he wants to be Lord Byron. As we say here: "no dice." How many young men have been misled by wishing to be Byron as older ones are deluded by thinking they are Napoleon! Those telltale busts of Napoleon in the paneled offices of so many American tycoons. They forget how much of their eminence is due to circumstances entirely fortuitous and indeed this was true of their hero's career. But they forget that Napoleon — what a Mafia organizer he would have made! — had an added something. The effect of these two traditions — Byronic and Napoleonic — on the scores of generations in the Western world would make an interesting book. Stanley's new play goes into rehearsal next week, so I suppose he'll be back any minute. Dr. Ogden and Mary Kennicott are coming for the opening. A new development — I don't think I've told you — Dr. Ogden and Grant are now the greatest friends. They are Damon and Pythias. Grant doesn't make a move without consulting the Warden of All Souls (a poor pun, forgive me). He calls him from New York daily; Dr. Ogden calls Doris, Stanley's actress, from California daily. Well, I have learned not to be surprised by anything people do. I have learned to accept things as they are. Is this wisdom or is it . . .

His doorbell rang. It was a page boy with a cable. Löwe tipped the boy and read the cable.

THANKS MESSAGE. PLAY WENT WELL. TRYING TO INDUCE MONICA TO SAIL WITH ME WEDNESDAY. SHE IS STUBBORN OTHERWISE FLAWLESS. LOVE. STANLEY. TRYING TO INDUCE STANLEY TO SHIP YOU HERE TURNAROUND QUEEN MARY. HE IS TOO OLD FOR ME BUT OTHERWISE EVERYTHING YOU SAY. TENDRESSE. MONICA

He returned to his desk smiling over Monica's message. So she agreed with him about Stanley! She saw through him! How deft, with this am-

biguous remark, to have reassured Grant that they both — he and
Monica — held him on a pinnacle of regard. Well!

He looked at his watch. He had an appointment with his doctor. He
looked down at his letter, saw the unfinished sentence. What had he been
saying? He read: "Is this wisdom or is it . . ." He wrote "fatigue?"
and left to keep his appointment.

When Emmeline Baer was nine years old, an advertent remark by a
classmate in the fashionable girls' school she attended, accusing her of
being Jewish, caused her to burst into tears. She ran home weeping to
her mother, hoping for denial. Her mother, the widow of a great German-
Jewish banker, had, for so many years, held this secret close from her
daughter. She was unable to offer solace. She had to admit that the
allegation was true but she tried to put the matter "in perspective," an
operation which she herself had never been able to perform. "Most
everyone," she said, "in one way or another, has to go through life under some handicap. Everyone has sand in the carburetor some place."
Yes, it was sad and she was sorry but it was true. But the stigma could
be eradicated. It would be eradicated. Her dear child was beautiful. She
would grow into greater beauty. There was no reason, given the circumstance of the great wealth that would accrue to her, that she would not
marry into an impeccable family of the cherished race. The inherited
stigma would be diluted and, gradually, evaporated. Meantime she
should not think about it. She should forget it. She should pretend she
had never heard it. She should do as she herself had done, eliminate it
from her consciousness. She knew, while she was saying it, that she was
lying. There was little else in her consciousness except the grain of sand
in the carburetor. Through all of Emmeline's childhood Mrs. Baer had
lived in terror of the moment when her daughter would find out. Well,
it was here and she was getting it over with. She predicted, for her
daughter, a radiant life in an uncontaminated Aryan pleasure ground.
Emmeline dried her tears and went to her room to try to concentrate on
her homework. She couldn't. The Elysian future predicted by her mother
did not comfort her. She had to live in the present, the dark present.
Henceforth she had to drag a shadow, not her own, but bequeathed to
her by insensitive ancestors.

After Emmeline left, Mrs. Baer sat for a long time in her chair, in pain and sorrow. The poor child! Why had she to be told so soon? She knew the little girl who had leveled the charge. She was quite unattractive and Mrs. Baer drew comfort from that. Nor was her family too secure financially. She drew comfort from that. But these marginal comforts did not really comfort her. Her heart ached for Emmeline. There was only one possible comfort, at least a diversion. Mrs. Baer lived in one of the last remaining private mansions on Fifth Avenue. It contained the greatest jade collection in the world, a passionate hobby of her late husband's. She went to the drawing room where the collection was housed in vitrines. There they were, the fantastic, cunning, smooth beauties. She consulted the ornate, beautifully printed catalogue which had been made of her possessions and checked them off one by one. They all said "present." They were all there, palely shimmering, unselfconscious, secure. Absorbed in this unfailing pastime, Mrs. Baer forgot.

Mrs. Baer's prediction, the future she promised Emmeline when she was nine, came true. When Emmeline was twenty-two she married Rutherford Lord, a thoroughly eligible member of an admitted family. He had been introduced to her by Kaetchen. Oddly enough Mrs. Baer liked Kaetchen because so many high-placed Aryans seemed to think well of him. Mrs. Baer was overjoyed; in her timid way so was Emmeline. Lord had been a star end at Yale and then gone into the family textile business. Rutherford drank. After the hero worship to which he was accustomed in college, the routine of the textile business was virulently dull. Emmeline was beautiful. She was dear and she would emancipate him from the textile business and from his father. He proposed to Emmeline. Before she accepted him she felt that she must bring the secret out into the open. Of course he knew about it; his parents had dilated upon it but he thought they were old fogies. He and Emmeline had a deep, long talk about it. He cheered her up. He was free of the prejudices of his parents and of his circle. He said it didn't in the least matter. He himself was secure and unassailable; he would carry her along in the strong current of his own heredity. He was glad they were having this talk; he knew it was on her mind as it had been on his. He had already coped with it and surmounted it and that was that. He exacted from Emmeline a promise that it would never be mentioned between them again. The ogre was to be hermetically sealed in a steel-lined cabinet and thrown into Long Island Sound. Their marriage was a success. Lord was charming to her. He treated her as if she were normal.

Five months later, Rutherford, driving back to Long Island from New York in the early morning after a heady party in town, ran his roadster into a telephone pole and was killed. At twenty-three Emmeline was a widow. To her mother there was an assuagement of grief. Her daughter was now Mrs. Rutherford Lord.

But Löwe's resources were seemingly endless. To his stammtisch in the Colony Restaurant he invited Emmeline and a charming young man named Worthington Platt. No young man would have been nicer than Worthington Platt. He was candid, affectionate and a historian of art, a subject he taught in a branch of the City University in Brooklyn. He lived with his widowed mother, one of the most famous women in America. When her husband — an art historian like his son — died, Mrs. Platt found herself penniless and with a ten-year-old son to bring up. She had married beneath her; it was a love match. She herself belonged to one of the most distinguished families in America, never rich but celebrated. Among her ancestors there had been statesmen, editors and one heroic mugwump uncle who had ruined himself by taking what he considered the right side in the Pullman strike of 1894. Worthington's parents had had an ideal married life; they were constantly running off to Europe to look at pictures and very often on borrowed money. It never occurred to either of them to save anything for the future. With her husband's death Mrs. Platt found the future imminent and with a load of debt in the present. But she was resourceful. She had lived all her life in the best society and there was nothing she did not know about the punctilio of correct behavior in that society. A publisher friend who owned a string of newspapers suggested to her that she write a column for one of his papers to guide the uninformed and the misinformed about just how to behave at dinner parties, wedding breakfasts and funerals. Mrs. Platt did. Within a year the debts were paid. Within two years she was famous as well as solvent. She wrote books which became the vade mecums of uncertain hostesses. She became the acknowledged social arbiter of the forty-eight states. Her mail had to be handled by a staff of secretaries. Hostesses in Spokane and Vicksburg wouldn't buy a doily without her.

Worthington adored Emmeline but he didn't really want to get married. He was perfectly happy living with his mother. But Mrs. Platt, a strong character, thought it was high time. She nagged him about it till Worthington began to devise expedients to avoid meeting her at dinner. Mrs. Platt liked Emmeline immensely. Emmeline would be perfect for him. As for Mrs. Baer, she was transported. It was a windfall of unimaginable proportions. Worthington took Emmeline to theaters, concerts and art museums but he was laggard about proposing. Until, one night, Emmeline showed him her mother's jade collection. Worthington capitulated. The wedding arrangements were supervised by Mrs. Platt. The photographs filled the fashion magazines. It was a triumph also for Mrs. Platt. Her books sold better than ever. Mrs. Baer's wedding present to Worthington was the jade collection.

Emmeline returned from the honeymoon with her mother but without Worthington. Worthington left a note for Emmeline in their suite at the Ritz in Paris saying that he couldn't, a fact which Emmeline had already discovered. He had not inherited from his mother her knack for correct behavior. He simply disappeared. Emmeline called her mother and the Paris police. Mrs. Baer went to see Mrs. Platt. Mrs. Platt was efficient. She regretted that Emmeline had notified the police. She cabled Emmeline to inform the police that her husband had returned. She must hire private detectives. He would be found; Mrs. Platt, who had long suspected that her son had recondite tastes, said grimly that she would go to Europe herself if necessary to find her son and bring him back. She calmed Mrs. Baer by her confidence and efficiency. Emmeline, alone in her suite at the Ritz, was having hysterics. Mrs. Baer left to join her. Mrs. Platt saw her off. She again reassured Mrs. Baer. The boy would have to return because he would soon run out of money. On a later visit to Paris, Mrs. Baer was startled to find, at an art dealer's where she had gone to browse, some of the most exquisite items in her jade collection. She bought them back.

This was the bruised and bewildered and insecure young woman of twenty-nine whom Kaetchen's third hand had now docketed for the brilliant young playwright, Stanley Grant.

Kaetchen had alerted Grant about Emmeline in a letter to London. He sketched briefly her matrimonial history. She had resumed her maiden name in an effort to obliterate the sad history of her two marriages. She was, Kaetchen wrote, mad about the theater. He permitted himself an ironic passage because he could not resist rallying Grant about his hypersensitivity in a certain area. ("The sensitive person," he had written to Monica in a little dissertation on Grant, "is aware of the feelings of other people; the hypersensitive is only conscious of himself.") To Grant he wrote: "You will probably, should you marry Emmeline Baer, find it a great relief not to be under the stern code of Jewish moralism as you were with your Catholic wife; Emmeline is as shy of the subject as you are." He planned Stanley's meeting with Emmeline with great care. In his matrimonial schemes Kaetchen believed in what stockbrokers call a diversified portfolio. He invited also young Federn and Liza Scherman. Liza was twenty-two, the daughter of a multimillionaire Republican who was a distinguished public servant. He was an adviser to Presidents. Liza had a clear, candid face, a clear voice and a hearty ringing laugh. She had a great sense of humor and oblong brown eyes. She had a secret life. She was a card-carrying Communist. Kaetchen was the only one in her circle who knew.

Kaetchen persuaded Federn to spruce up for the occasion. He had taken him to a tailor and to his barber who styled his unruly hair. He gave him a pep talk. He pointed out that he could now take his place in society. He was associated with a famous surgeon, he had money, he had prospects. He must improve on these prospects. He enlarged upon all of Liza Scherman's manifest advantages. He did not mention her political affiliation. He didn't believe in overloading prospects with irrelevant information. Federn promised to show up at the Colony looking tidy.

Kaetchen had engaged a suite in the Ambassador for Grant. The moment he got into it from the boat Grant put in a call to Ogden. He had written several letters to Ogden from London telling him about the play, so Ogden knew all about that. Grant asked about Mary. Mary had not been very well. It had to be faced that she was forty-five and having woman's trouble. Nevertheless, she was coming with him to Grant's opening in New York. She wouldn't miss it for anything in the world. Grant then said:

"If you believe Kaetchen, I am on the verge of marriage."

"To whom?"

"Emmeline Baer."

Ogden emitted a long, low whistle.

"Know her? Impressed?"

"I don't know her but I am impressed. At one leap, my boy, you make the Mount Everest of Jewish society."

"I am an arduous climber, you know that."

"Climb and climb but don't get married. Keep your freedom. Keep your independence. You may get tired of climbing and want to descend."

"I've done that already," said Grant. "Why shouldn't I climb for a change?"

"Of course. Keep your crampons polished. But one word from the all-wise, all-knowing. Life on the upper levels is hell, sheer hell. I've been in it. I know."

Grant was smiling. He always felt good when he was talking to Ogden.

"I'll take no step till you get here."

"How's Doris?"

"Haven't seen her yet. First reading Monday."

"Call me. Tell me how she sounds."

"I certainly will."

"She tells me she's got ants in her pants from nerves."

"She needn't. She'll be great. I'm leaving this minute for the peak of Mount Everest."

"Plant your flag there."

"Okeydoke."

"Okeydoke."

At the Colony, Grant and Emmeline Baer were both late. Kaetchen marked time with Liza and Federn. He was pleased with Federn's appearance — overweight, a bit jowly, but quite smart. Federn was in an abysmal mood. He had just heard of the Molotov-Ribbentrop pact.

"It's all over," he said. "It's the end."

"Not yet, not yet," said the disciple of Montaigne.

"I'm glad you think so," said Federn. "I wish I could."

He turned to Liza Scherman whom he had just met.

"What do you think, Miss Scherman?"

Liza turned her candid eyes to him.

"It's all right with me," she said.

Federn felt he hadn't heard correctly.

"It's all right with you?"

"Perfectly all right with me."

"Do you mean it?"

"I wouldn't say it," said Liza calmly, "if I didn't mean it!"

Federn put his napkin back on his plate. He rose.

"I'm sorry, Kaetchen. I'm very sorry. But I simply can't have lunch with anyone who can say a thing like that. She's with the murderers."

Federn left the restaurant.

Kaetchen tried to explain.

"He's a dear fellow — not quite housebroken. Lost his parents to Herr von Ribbentrop's countrymen."

"Oh," said Liza with feeling. "I'm sorry. I wouldn't have said it had I known."

But Kaetchen felt as if he were holding his third hand in a blazing fire. It shriveled. It was really ungracious of the ex-champagne salesman and Stony Pants to disrupt so willfully his carefully laid plan. Grant bumped into Federn as he was leaving. Federn, taut with anger, had not responded to his greeting. Kaetchen introduced Liza.

"What's the matter with Federn?"

"Oh," said Kaetchen, "he got a call from Dr. Binder. Had to go to the hospital. Emergency."

At this moment Miss Baer arrived. She was flurried and full of apologies for being late. Actually she had been on the verge of canceling the appointment. She was conscious that she had little conversation, that she had no equipment to face intellectual society. The strain of meeting Stanley Grant had seemed too much for her. But she had surmounted it.

Grant beheld a tall, slender, blue-eyed, olive-skinned young woman. She looked, he thought, exotic, a Coptic princess, the consort of some king in an Assyrian frieze. Grant was glad he'd come. He was glad Federn had disappeared. Liza was pretty but she was a little girl; she didn't matter. He had the occasion to himself. He felt in great fettle. He began to show off. He talked about his visit to London and the reception of his play. Emmeline began to hear a succession of fabled names. Her head swam. She kept telling herself desperately that she must keep it above water.

Grant told of going to the Savoy Grill in London with his leading man and leading lady after a disastrous dress rehearsal of his play. There, Noel Coward joined them. He was marvelous. Grant's leading lady had tried to comfort him with the theatrical cliché that a bad dress rehearsal means a triumphant opening night. Coward demurred.

"Don't you believe it," he said. "The dress rehearsal of my last play was disaster. But the opening night was worse. They booed me!"

Kaetchen laughed but Grant saw at once that he hadn't succeeded with the ladies. Emmeline was too awed at meeting a man who knew Noel Coward; Liza found these bourgeois capers tiresome. This failure only tightened Grant's resolve. He would show Miss Baer that he was no lightweight.

"My play got over all right," he said. "The notices were good but I had two major failures." Kaetchen inquired what these were.

"You remember Lady Bellamine to whom you introduced me in Salzburg?"

Kaetchen remembered.

"Well, her daughter introduced me to her husband. He writes plays, as who doesn't, but I was very keen to meet him as he was a great friend of Marcel Proust."

Kaetchen explained to the girls.

"Stanley is a great Proust fan. I don't share his enthusiasm. Proust puts me to sleep."

"Naturally," said Grant, "you read that stick-in-the-mud, Montaigne."

"Proust is perfect reading for hochstaplers," said Kaetchen kindly.

"And Montaigne for the disengaged," said Grant. That wasn't bad. Did Miss Baer get it? He went on.

"Well, I was so eager to find out about Proust from Lady Bellamine's son-in-law. But every time I approached the subject, he shunted me off. He wanted to know what they paid in Hollywood. He wanted to know how to go about getting his play filmed. I suggested that the best way would be to get it produced. He expected me to suggest a shortcut. I couldn't. He gave me a letter to another great friend of Proust's, Reynaldo Hahn, the French composer. I went to Paris to see him but he wouldn't talk about Proust either. Do you know what *he* wanted? How to go about getting a commission to do the score for a Broadway musical comedy!"

Somehow, Grant still felt that he wasn't getting over. Emmeline was stunned; Liza bored. These shenanigans were so marginal to the central, throbbing issue. Grant turned to Emmeline.

"Do you know Proust, Miss Baer?"

Emmeline, who knew by this time that she had been wrong to come, didn't know what to say. She didn't know whether Proust was alive or dead, whether Grant meant had she met him personally or had she read him. Why hadn't he asked about Tennyson?

"I'm afraid I don't," she said.

"The only one who helped me about Proust was Somerset Maugham."

At this Emmeline's cramped horizon widened. Ah! At last! She could partake! She was in! She thought Maugham the greatest writer in the world. He spoke to her. He understood her. She swallowed each novel as it appeared. Just let him ask her did she know Somerset Maugham!

"Did you see Willie?" said Kaetchen.

"Oh yes, quite a bit. He came to my opening."

"How'd he like it?"

"He said it was not bad. That, for him, is rhapsody."

"How did he help you with Proust?"

"He's a nut on Proust. He says he'd rather be bored by Proust than entertained by anybody else. He gave me a farewell lunch. I asked him whether he wanted to be remembered to anyone in New York. He said yes. To André, the barman at Pavillon. He'll tell you about Proust," he said. "He knew him well. He used to wait on him at the Ritz in Paris."

"Have you seen André?"

"No. But you can bet I will."

He turned to Miss Baer.

"As you don't know Proust," he said, "may I introduce him to you? May I send you his book?"

Miss Baer said that she'd be ever so . . . She was so dazzled that she couldn't quite express what she would be. Grant turned to Kaetchen.

"I came across an extraordinary passage just the other day in *The Cities of the Plain*."

Emmeline's heart sank again. Another author she didn't know. How could she possibly cope with erudition on this plane?

"I hadn't particularly noticed it before, but now with my wife and son in Palestine, among the dedicated Zionists, it struck me. Proust segregates Zionists with the homosexuals as two groups which arouse hostility."

At the mention of Zionists Grant noticed that Emmeline winced. He was happy to discover that he didn't have a monopoly on winces.

"I don't believe in Zionism," said Liza. "I'm dead against it. Too many small nationalities now."

"You believe in just one big nationalism, don't you, darling?" said Kaetchen.

Grant switched the conversation to Dostoevski. He had read a review of a book by Malcolm Cowley which praised him for pointing out that in *The Possessed* Dostoevski had proved himself to be a great comic writer. Grant appropriated Cowley's insight; he managed to convey that he was prepared to breast the tide of popular misconception of Dostoevski.

He looked at his watch. He decided that he could not improve his position by staying. He rose to go; he had a date with his director. He said good-bye to Miss Scherman, who extended him a limp hand, and more fervently to Emmeline. She said it had been wonderful to meet him. He said he would send her Marcel Proust. She was grateful and would write to thank him when she had read it. Grant said he wouldn't wait for that because Proust was somewhat long-winded.

When he had gone, Kaetchen questioned both his guests.

"Well?" he said.

"Surely," said Emmeline, "Mr. Grant has the most cultivated mind in the world."

"He reads a lot," said Kaetchen.

Emmeline rose to go. She thanked Kaetchen for this wonderful lunch. It had been heaven.

"I'll take you to Grant's opening," said Kaetchen.

Emmeline kissed him, begged him not to forget and left.

Kaetchen now turned to Liza for her verdict.

"He works too hard," said Liza. "He's a fake."

Kaetchen chided her.

"You belong to a rigorous cult," he said. "You have the truth in the palm of your hand. If you weren't so adorable, Liza dear, this omniscience might be irritating."

Liza, since Kaetchen was irredeemably in outer darkness, never bothered to argue with him.

"And you, my darling, pampered parasite, I couldn't love you more even if you had a glimmering of what it's all about."

She left the parasite to meet the uniformed family chauffeur who was waiting outside to drive her to a cell meeting in Brooklyn.

Kaetchen visited at a few tables to greet his friends — there was scarcely a person there he did not know — and then took a taxi to the Ambassador. In his room he thought things over. His third hand had achieved a resounding failure and a brilliant success. He felt certain that he had pulled it off grandly with Grant and Emmeline. Mrs. Baer wouldn't like it. Still, as he meant to point out to her, STANLEY GRANT wouldn't look too bad on the engraved wedding invitations. It was a bit factitious that name; it hadn't the authenticity quite of Rutherford Lord or Worthington Platt but it would serve. What a funny lunch! He called Federn to admonish him but he was out. He called Grant in his rooms upstairs to congratulate him but he was out. Then he sat at his desk to describe the event to Monica.

Emmeline Baer kept a diary. She wrote in it every night, in a schoolgirl's copybook, in her round childish hand. Her diary comforted her. It kept her company. That night she wrote:

Wonderful lunch with Kaetchen. He introduced me to his friend, the playwright Stanley Grant. Fascinating. He knows everything and everybody. He knows Noel Coward and Somerset Maugham . . .

31. Opening Night

Kaetchen had invited Dr. Ogden and Mary Kennicott to have early dinner with him and Emmeline Baer at his stammtisch in the Colony Restaurant so that they would be in good time for the opening of Grant's play. Kaetchen was distressed at the change in Mary's appearance. She had aged since he had last seen her, only six months before. Her hair had gone white; it was very becoming to her: a slim dowager, Kaetchen thought. But she was as warm and responsive as ever. She had been told by Ogden that Miss Baer was in line to marry Stanley; she knew her sad history and she made a special effort to initiate friendship with her. Emmeline was in a glow of excitement about seeing a play which emanated from the most cultivated mind in the world. Mary told her she had read it and that it was wonderful. They toasted it and its author in champagne.

"The play may be wonderful," said Ogden, "but it's a libel on me."

Mary laughed but Emmeline was startled.

"Really," she said, "what do you mean?"

"He's got me in it," said Ogden. "I'm the villain. Tell me, Miss Baer, you've just met me but I'm sure that your intuition is unerring. Do I look to you like a villain?"

Emmeline was hung up. She didn't know what to say. She was embarrassed. Mary put her hand on Emmeline's.

"My dear, don't pay any attention to what Dr. Ogden says. It's his style."

"But darling," Ogden said to Mary, "I *am* the villain. I victimize the poor heroine's mother. I try to seduce her daughter. Moreover, and this is what I really do resent, the daughter outwits me! I may sue Stanley for libel for that."

Kaetchen chuckled and Mary laughed but Emmeline was bewildered.

"But didn't Stanley make up the play?"

"Not at all," said Ogden. "He lacks the invention. I made it up for him."

Emmeline felt that she was being teased. She looked at the others for help. She spoke to Kaetchen.

"What does Dr. Ogden mean?"

"Ask him," said Kaetchen. "Corner him."

Emmeline, lit by the wine, encouraged by Mary's friendliness, liberated at being at the center of a fabulous circumstance, launched into daring and wit.

"If you made it up," she said, "then why isn't your name in the advertisements?"

Everybody was delighted by her triumphant logic.

"Good for you, my dear," said Mary.

"You've met your match, Kenneth," said Kaetchen.

"Exactly what I've always been looking for. Thank you, Miss Baer," he said, smiling at Emmeline, "for turning up in the nick of time."

Emmeline felt that she had been graduated from Vassar summa cum laude. Actually she had dropped out in her sophomore year.

"I didn't mean," said Ogden, "that I wrote the play. I'm far too busy for such mechanical tasks. I mean that I gave Stanley the whole idea."

"How?" said Emmeline.

"By existing," said Ogden. "No me. No play."

"Henry V might have said that to Shakespeare," said Kaetchen, "but I'm sure he didn't."

"Perhaps old Henry was too modest. But modesty is a weakness I haven't got. As a matter of fact," he turned to Emmeline, "Miss Baer . . . may I call you Emmeline? Stanley keeps babbling your name at me all the time. May I?"

"I wish you would."

"As a matter of fact, though I am ignored in the ads, I *am* part author. Moreover, I have a financial stake in it!"

"Did you invest?"

"I have a bet on it. With Stanley. I did write one line which Stanley stole from me. Kaetchen. Can I sue him for plagiarism?"

"That's not plagiarism," said Kaetchen, "that's quotation. You can't sue for quotation unless it's misquotation. Then it's libel."

"What's the bet?" asked Mary.

"I took Stanley to lunch in Salzburg. I told him my personal history about which, dear Emmeline, I am not reticent. I made a remark which Stanley — he told me so himself — wrote down on a pad right after he left me and stuck in his dialogue. We bet a hundred dollars. If it gets a big laugh, he pays me. If it lays an egg, I pay him. So you can understand I am very tense, more involved than any of you."

Emmeline, who didn't laugh much, laughed. So did Mary.

"It's really good for you to see people," she said. "Alone with me you've become rather dull."

"But," said Kaetchen, "outside of anxiety about your bet, aren't you concerned about how your sweetheart will be?"

"I couldn't care less. As a matter of fact I didn't want her to do this part. Risky experiment."

"If it's a flop she can always go back to pictures," said Kaetchen.

"I don't mean risky for her. Risky for me. If she's a hit, she'll be impossible. If she's a flop she'll be a bore. She'll go into mourning. I'll have to pretend I'm sorry. Actors take themselves so seriously. They're so solemn about what they refer to as their 'careers.' "

There was "stimmung" among the four of them. It generated from Ogden. Emmeline felt that she had never been so happy in her life. Never before, she felt, had she been so close to the very heart of things. Kaetchen reflected on the difference in styles between Ogden and Grant who had held forth at this same table only a little while ago. Grant had been entertaining but he worked hard at it; he used up all his reserves. Ogden was good-humored, casual, effortless. You felt that he didn't care a tinker's damn whether he was getting over or not.

They left for the theater in Emmeline's chauffered limousine.

When they were seated studying the programs, Ogden, pointing to a name in the cast, Dr. Seymour Rice, whispered to Emmeline: "That's me! Don't believe a word he says!"

The lights lowered. The play began. The curtain rose on the living room of Leonie Frothingham's cottage in Blue Hill, Maine. On the backdrop you saw the battlemented hills of the "masculine Riviera."

The play takes place during the depression of 1929. Leonie has her daughter Paula's unemployed friends staying with her, Will Dexter, Paula's boyfriend, and Dennis McCarthy, a Catholic Communist. Also staying with her is Count Boris Mirsky, son of the great Russian novelist Count Mirsky. Leonie has given him house room to enable him to write his memoirs of his father. She has also been having an affair with him, now on the wane. Paula discovers that a psychoanalyst from New York, Dr. Rice, is coming to stay also. Paula is disconcerted by this: "Where'd you find *him?*" she asks.

LEONIE

I met him at a party at Sissy Drake's. He *saved* Sissy.

PAULA

From what?

LEONIE

From that awful eye condition.

PAULA

Is he an oculist too?

LEONIE

She went to every oculist in the world — she went to Baltimore and she went to Vienna. Nobody could do a thing for her — her eyes kept blinking — twitching really in the most unaccountable way. It was an ordeal to talk to her — and of course she must have undergone agonies of embarrassment. But Dr. Rice psychoanalyzed her and completely cured her. How do you suppose? Well, he found that the seat of the trouble lay in her unconscious. It was too simple. She blinked in that awful way because actually she couldn't bear to look at her husband. So she divorced Drake and since she's married to Bill Alsop she's as normal as you or me. Now I'll take you into a little secret. I'm having Dr. Rice up to see Boris. Of course Boris mustn't know it's for him.

PAULA

What's the matter with Boris?

LEONIE

I'm not sure. I think he's working too hard.

WILL

What's he working at?

LEONIE

Don't you know? Didn't you tell him, Paula? His father's memoirs. He's the son, you know, of the great Count Mirsky!

WILL

I know.

LEONIE

I must show you the photographs of his father — a wonderful old man with a great white beard like a snowstorm — looks like Moses — a Russian Moses — and Boris is sitting on his knees — couldn't be over ten years old and wearing a fur cap and boots — boots! And they drank tea out of tall glasses with raspberry jelly in — people came from all over the world, you know, to see his father . . . !

PAULA

(*With some malice*)
Is Dr. Rice going to help you acclimate him?

LEONIE

I hope so. You and Paula will have to entertain him — you young intellectuals. Isn't it a pity I have no mind?

In spite of Klaus Wolff's skepticism about the stage viability of film actresses, it was apparent, from the beginning of Doris's first scene, that she was a discovery, a hit. The audience took her to its heart at once. She was enchanting, with her lit, eager face, the delicate self-raillery, her joy in just living, the warmth and affection she felt for those near her, and the touching insecurity about whether they felt the same affection for her. There was no doubt about what the audience felt; it cradled her in affection which flowed across the footlights. It was quite remarkable. This girl, who had no education, who came from God-knows-where, moved with grace and authority. Her diction was lapidary. She was mistress of the gradations of inflection. Her speech rippled, the arpeggios, the crescendi, the diminuendi, every syllable etched in clarity. Her timing was uncanny. She was a great comedienne, which meant that she was emotionally precise and heartbreakingly moving. There was the underlying tragic sense which can be conveyed only by the actress who understands comedy. When the curtain fell on Act One, there was no doubt about it, Doris was in.

"She won't be a bore," Kaetchen said to Ogden as they rose to go out for the intermission.

"No," said Ogden, "she'll just be impossible."

In the packed lobby the four of them found a little enclave for themselves in a corner.

"Aren't we going to see Stanley?" said Emmeline.

"Not till after the second act," said Kaetchen.

"By that time he'll owe me money," said Ogden.

"That's mean of him," said Emmeline, "to make us wait till then to congratulate him."

"Well, learned doctor," said Kaetchen, "how do you like yourself on stage?"

"Oh," said Emmeline, who was now bolder than bold, "I think the actor who plays you is wonderful."

"Very good," said Ogden, "but miscast."

Kaetchen smiled.

"He's better than you deserve," he said.

"He's saturnine," said Ogden. "Emmeline, am I saturnine?"

As Emmeline didn't know what saturnine meant, she withheld her opinion. Ogden took this to mean that she thought he might be.

"But surely you can see that I'm anything but. Don't you know now that the essence of my character is benevolence?" He tapped the program. "This actor looks like a bad lot. You know nothing good will come of him. Opportunist, shady. Whereas, dear Emmeline, I am always thinking of others. This actor's cadaverous. Am I cadaverous? If anything, as Mary keeps complaining, I am overweight."

"Indeed you are," said Mary. "If you let yourself get paunchy, you'll find the going harder."

Liza Scherman came up to them. Kaetchen presented her to Mary and Ogden.

"Well, Liza," said Kaetchen, "how do you like it?"

"About what I'd expect from your playwright friend."

"How did you like Miss Linden?"

"Oh, she's marvelous. She's heaven."

"What didn't you like?"

"That character — Paula's friend — the Catholic Communist."

"I thought he was very amusing," said Ogden. "Quite original."

"He's original all right," said Liza. "He has no counterpart in anything I know. I didn't believe for a minute that he's a Catholic and I *know* he isn't a Communist!"

She disappeared.

"Disagreeable girl," said Ogden, "pretty, but not refreshing."

The lights lowered for the second act. They returned to their seats.

"It's in this act," said Ogden, "that my fate will be decided. If that line doesn't get a laugh I shall give up authorship forever."

In Act Two the plot thickened. The audience was attentive and even amused but it was obvious that it couldn't wait for Doris to come on again. Dr. Rice, quietly authoritative, tells Leonie what is wrong with the son of the great Count Mirsky; by this time Leonie's interest has begun to swerve from the patient to the doctor:

LEONIE

Dr. Rice — I haven't seen you all day.

DR. RICE

I've been in my room slaving away at a scientific paper.

LEONIE

My house hums with creative activity. I love it. It gives me a sense of vicarious importance. What's your paper on?

DR. RICE

Shadow-neurosis.

LEONIE

Shadow-neurosis. How marvelous! What does it mean?

The last four words were a tripping scherzo. The audience laughed. It wasn't a belly laugh. It was a laugh of affectionate appreciation. Dr. Rice, a superb actor, waited for the laugh to subside before he answered.

DR. RICE

It is a sensation of nonexistence.

Kaetchen, dazzled, as the rest of the audience was, by Doris, found himself thinking of Stephanie. To the end, Stephanie had lived on the hope of playing this part. He felt pain in his heart for Stephanie; not because she was gone but because she could never have played it as

Doris was playing it. Even her beauty would have been a handicap — that grave, still, classical beauty. Doris's looks, pert, piquant, inescapably American, were perfect. Her sensibility, her culture would have been a handicap to Stephanie. Her aristocracy would have been a handicap. This simple, gum-chewing American girl had the ease and assurance of a great lady. Stephanie *was* a great lady but she could never have conveyed it as Doris did. It was mysterious. It saddened him. He thought of Stephanie up there on the stage, visualized her walk, her looks, her beautiful immobilized voice. She would have been stately. He took a crumb of comfort in the thought that she had been spared this evening. She would have failed. It would have added to the long line of her failures. Kaetchen didn't know, no one knew, the exact manner of her death. But at least she died thinking she might have done it and been good. Kaetchen hoped so.

While everyone was waiting, once Doris had left the stage, for her to come back, Dr. Ogden, with author's nerves, was waiting for the arrival of his brainchild. He had read the play and he knew exactly where it was coming: in a scene between Dr. Rice and Paula. By this time Dr. Rice knew that he could take his time with Leonie; it was Paula he was after. He has discovered that Count Mirsky is not writing a book about his father at all. He has merely been sitting in his room, nourishing his hatred of his father and of Leonie too, for supporting him and for losing interest in him. Dr. Rice fixes it so that Count Mirsky finds it expedient to chase his shadow-neurosis through other pastures. He has cleared the path to Leonie; he now attempts to clear it to Paula. At the beginning of this scene Ogden nudged Kaetchen, interrupting his thoughts of Stephanie. He whispered:

"It's coming now. Pray for me!"

Paula is fascinated by Dr. Rice. She resents it. She wants to give all her thoughts to the boy she is in love with, Will Dexter, but Dr. Rice, somehow, intrudes. She pumps him:

PAULA

What were your origins?

DR. RICE
(*Lighting a cigarette*)

Anonymous.

PAULA

What do you mean?

DR. RICE

In a foundling asylum in New England. The place lacked charm. This sounds like an unpromising beginning, but actually it was more stimulating than you might imagine. I remember as a kid of twelve going to the library at Springfield and getting down the *Dictionary of National Biography* and hunting out the bastards. Surprising how many distinguished ones there were and are. I allied myself early with the brilliant and variegated company of the illegitimate.

PAULA

You don't know who your parents were?

DR. RICE

No.

PAULA

Did you get yourself through college?

DR. RICE

And medical school.

PAULA

Did you practice medicine?

DR. RICE

For a bit. I devoted myself — when the victims would let me — to their noses and throats. It was a starveling occupation. But I gave up tonsillectomy for the soul. The poor have tonsils but only the rich have souls.

The laugh was like a thunderclap.

In the intermission they found the same enclave they had occupied after the first act. Ogden basked in triumph. Grant appeared. Without a word of greeting to anyone — he had planned it so — he took out a hundred dollar bill and gave it to Ogden. He turned to go, as if, having completed the transaction, he had no further business there.

Mary laughingly held him back and he rejoined them, one arm around Mary's shoulder, the other around Emmeline's. He was elated.

"What an idiot I was," said Kenneth, "not to have made it a thousand!"

"Biggest laugh in the show," said Grant handsomely. "Why write 'em when you can steal 'em?"

"Can't you give him program credit, Stanley?" said Mary. "Can't you say: Line 640, Act Two, by Dr. Kenneth Ogden?"

"I could, but I won't," said Stanley. He turned to Emmeline. "Enjoying yourself, honey?"

Emmeline made a helpless gesture. What she was feeling was too ineffable to be expressed in words.

"Isn't Doris marvelous!" said Grant. "Isn't she heaven!"

They all agreed. All round them they heard exclamations of delight about Doris. The audience was scarcely talking about anything else.

Ogden spoke to Emmeline.

"I want you to know, Emmeline, that this suggestion of Stanley's that I am illegitimate is a libel. I was born extremely respectably in Cleveland, Ohio. My parents believed in God and Henry Thoreau. Kaetchen, shall I sue Stanley for libel?"

"I'll be your chief witness," said Grant. "I've got to go back. I want to tell Doris how great she is."

"I don't think you have to tell her," said Ogden. "I think she suspects."

"See you all after. Doris's dressing room."

When the curtain fell on the last act there was no demand for the author but Doris received an ovation.

Grant had invited his cast of ten, two stage managers and his four guests to supper in a private dining room at the 21 Club after the show. Kaetchen begged off. He had to get his beauty sleep. He went back to his hotel room to describe the evening in his letter to Monica. Backstage was turmoil. Grant was congratulated on his play but even more for his percipience in discovering Doris. Doris herself was surrounded by wor-

shippers including Emmeline and Mary Kennicott; Grant stood with
Ogden, a two-man receiving line, ushering the acolytes on their way.
Ogden was amused and exhilarated by the whole thing but he kept up,
not too seriously, his pose of detachment. He had his moment when one
pal of Grant's said to him: "That was a hell of a funny line about the
tonsils." Grant, who felt he could afford to be generous, said quickly:
"Dr. Ogden wrote it."

"Not only that," said Ogden, when the fan had passed on, "but all
this praise you're getting for discovering Doris is nonsense. You will remember, I hope, that you fired her. I made you take her back. Not only
have I provided you with your funniest line but I gave you your star.
How can you ever possibly pay anybody for a service like that?"

"I can't," said Grant. "I do owe Doris to you. Don't think I've forgotten it. I'll never forget it."

He squeezed Ogden's arm in gratitude.

"Moreover," said Ogden, pretending to be melancholy, "you've ruined
Doris for me. I know that from this moment on she'll be impossible.
Well, I'll have to look elsewhere."

There is nothing in the world so heady as theatrical success. It is un-
mistakable. In the upstairs private dining room at 21 there was
euphoria. The actors knew that they were in jobs for at least a year.
Doris was radiant, as indeed who should not be who has just inherited
the Kingdom of Heaven. The goddess was chewing gum. She chewed gum
on principle; she believed that it was good for her teeth. Emmeline was
enchanted with Doris; she could hardly believe that here she was right
here, pally with this magical creature. Champagne flowed. Everyone was
high. They sat at little tables but they circulated, carrying their wine
glasses. The actor who played Ogden came up. Mary introduced him to
his original.

"You're great," said Ogden. "You'll be effective for those who don't
know me."

"There must be a few such. Enough for matinees," said Ogden's im-
personator. He ambled back to his own table.

The actor who played the Catholic Communist came up. He was introduced to Ogden too.

"I have a bone to pick with you," said Ogden.

"What's that?" said the actor.

"When you introduce me to Will Dexter's father, the pure scientist, you say: 'The floating libido bumps the absolute.' I didn't care for that."

The actor pointed to Grant.

"Blame him!" he said.

"Don't worry. He'll hear from me!" said Ogden menacingly. "For your private information I'll have you know that there is nothing in the least floating about my libido. It is precise. It always has a definite objective."

"I'll say it has!" said Doris. They all laughed, including the Catholic Communist who was, of course, in the know.

At three in the morning the press agent for the company called Grant and read the *Times* notice to him. Everyone listened intently though they couldn't hear anything. When it was over Grant made a general announcement.

"Okay for the play — good for you, Ossie and Van and everybody. Rave for Doris. Never heard such a rave." He spoke directly to Doris: "He says you're the wittiest actress he's seen in years. My God, children, didn't I have something to do with it?"

This got a laugh. So it went for another hour. Grant took Emmeline home.

They sat close together in Emmeline's car. They were insulated from the chauffeur by the glass panel. They were holding hands. They sat in silence for a few minutes.

"I'm awfully glad you were there tonight," said Grant.

"It's the most wonderful evening I ever had in my life. I'll never forget it. Thank you and thank you for asking me."

"Thank you and thank you for coming. It made it for me."

"Oh Stanley! You couldn't possibly have missed me. What a genius you are! And that Doris — I've never met anyone so . . ."

She found no words to describe Doris. Again they sat in silence.

"Will you come to dinner some time? I want you to meet Mother."

"I'd love to. Any time you say."

"You'll find us very dull, I'm afraid. We *are* very dull."

"I think I can endure it. It's restful to be dull once in a while."

She smiled.

"We can give you a rest whenever you like."

She sighed.

"I could see it again, you know, tomorrow night. I'll see it and see it. I'll send everybody."

"Whenever you like — I'll take you."

"Will you? Will you really?"

"Whenever you like."

"How thrilling! To go with you!"

They had reached the mansion. He kissed her. The kiss was long and satisfying. He was really taken by her. It raced through his mind to say: "Dearest Emmeline. Lovely Emmeline. I love you. Will you marry me?" But another, cautionary voice intervened. It said:

"Better talk it over first with Ogden."

32. Failure of an Emissary

There followed a halcyon season for Grant. He was riding high. It was a bit irritating to be congratulated on all sides, not for his play, but for his clairvoyance in having discovered Doris. The play itself was sloughed aside; the critics rather dismissed it too. They said it was an agreeable light comedy but they devoted most of their space to Doris's "mischievous wit." Still, there were compensations. He met Emmeline's friends and captivated them. He employed on them the well-worn routines that had served him in the past. It was a virgin audience and he kept seducing it. Emmeline's friends agreed with her that Stanley was the most brilliant thing they had ever come across. Emmeline even had him to lunch with her mother-in-law, Mrs. Worthington Platt. This was a delicate ruse of Emmeline's. She hoped that Grant would captivate Mrs. Platt as he had her other friends. Mrs. Platt would give a rousing report to Mrs. Baer and then Emmeline could present Grant to her mother without a qualm. For Mrs. Baer, a favorable word from Mrs. Platt was the ultimate "kosher zettel" — certificate of eligibility.

Emmeline had taken her mother to see Grant's play. Mrs. Baer hated

it. She hated the constant references to the depression which did not
press upon her. She hated Dennis, the Catholic Communist, and his unemployed and rebellious friends. She did not understand how a nice
woman like Mrs. Frothingham, who was rattle-brained but might easily
have been a friend of Mrs. Platt's, could trail her living room carpets
with scum like that. She refused to meet the author of such a play.
When Emmeline, in ecstasy, described the evening of the opening night
to her mother, she got a cool reception.

"I don't care for the Bohemian way of life," said Mrs. Baer. "Your
father detested it."

Emmeline went to her room and cried. Emmeline cried easily.

Mrs. Platt's report on Grant to Mrs. Baer was tempered.

"Oh, he's very clever, very entertaining, I'm sure very talented — I
haven't seen his play yet — but rather . . ."

"Rather what?" demanded Mrs. Baer.

"Well, not to put too fine a point on it — common. Not marriage tim-
ber, I'm afraid. I should hate to see Emmeline become *too* involved with
him."

"Don't worry, darling," said Mrs. Baer, "she won't!"

Kaetchen had warned Stanley that Mrs. Baer would be a tough nut to
crack. She had strong prejudices.

"She will penetrate," Kaetchen said, "the façade of your fancy name
very quickly. Above all, don't admit your parents' Russian origin. The
existence of the Eastern immigration was an affront to the Baers. If it
comes up, say that your parents came from Germany. Dresden is nice.
Try Dresden."

"Who the hell does she think she is anyway?" said Grant. "She's just
a rich man's widow."

"She knows precisely who she is," said Kaetchen. "Her husband was
the dullest man I've ever known. He never said *anything*. He was in-
articulate. Mrs. Baer thought it was reserve. She was very proud of her
husband's reserve. And yet Baer was a man of genius."

"In what, for heaven's sake?"

"In high finance. He had a very high position in Germany. Intimate
with the Kaiser. He was a close friend of Albert Ballin, the shipping
magnate. When the Kaiser was forced to abdicate, Ballin was so upset

that he committed suicide. Baer was so devoted to the earlier mustache, that he would have done the same thing, but Clara wouldn't let him. She's very formidable, Mrs. Baer. Don't underestimate her."

"I neither under nor over. I don't give a damn about her."

"You must if you want to marry Emmeline."

"What makes you think I want to?"

"It would be advantageous," Löwe went on placidly in his light, faintly derisive tone. "It would be nice of you to emancipate Emmeline from her mother. It has to be done. I picked you because you are so gallant."

"Ogden advises me against. 'Sleep with her,' he says. 'Don't marry her.' "

Grant went on to describe the luncheon at Mrs. Platt's, how decorous and correct and just right it had been.

"She's a stuffed chemise," said Grant in summary. "Emmeline talks about her as if she were the Virgin Mary. What the hell is this anyway?"

"To Mrs. Baer and, naturally, to Emmeline, Mrs. Platt is the paragon of all women, the quintessence of dust, though she wouldn't put it that way. The day that Worthington Platt led Emmeline to the altar was the climax of Mrs. Baer's life. Subsequent events didn't really upset her — except for the loss of the jade collection, most of which she has recovered."

"But the exalted Platt walked out on Emmeline, didn't he? On the honeymoon moreover! What's become of him anyway?"

"No one knows. He hasn't been heard of since that tragic day in Paris."

Grant indulged a little flight of fancy.

"Say, Kaetchen, what do you think? Ian hasn't been heard of either. Wouldn't it be marvelous if, somehow, Ian and Worthington ran into each other and are, this very moment, sunning themselves on some beach in the South Pacific?"

"Happy endings," said the pessimist, "are for the theater."

Before they parted, Kaetchen said:

"We will have to find some way to soften Mrs. Baer. I can't trust you to do it. I will have to do it."

"And I'll soften up Emmeline," said Grant. "Fair division of labor."

Several days later Grant telephoned to Kaetchen.

"Congratulate me," he said, "it's happened. I've been invited to Buckingham Palace."

"When?"

"Tonight. Emmeline phoned in great excitement. Just the three of us. So Mother will get to know me."

"Good," said Kaetchen. "I have already sent an emissary to Clara to plead your cause."

"Who he?"

"Never mind. Better come in and let me brief you."

"Okay. Brief me so I'll know what not to do. Then I'll do it."

"I am sure you will," said Kaetchen resignedly.

Kaetchen did indeed devote a lot of thought to the problem of softening up Mrs. Baer. As a campaign document he sent her Monypenny and Buckle's six-volume life of Benjamin Disraeli. He inscribed the first volume:

For my dear Clara:

I wonder whether you will not see a resemblance, as I do, between the young man of Volume One and my young friend and Emmeline's whom you are still to meet.

Devotedly,

Kaetchen

On the afternoon of the night, Mrs. Baer sat in her drawing room plowing through Volume One of Monypenny and Buckle. Upstairs in her sitting room Emmeline was equally struggling with two volumes of Marcel Proust which Grant had sent her. Unfortunately for Proust, a new Maugham had just come out and Emmeline had that beside her as a condiment. The first two pages of Proust gave her a headache; to get through them she kept taking gobs of Maugham, like aspirins. She was irritated with herself. When a man as worldly and cultivated as Stanley Grant thought so highly of a writer she must stick with this writer no matter what distress it caused her. She tried the first two pages again. Her headache returned. She couldn't repress a heretical question: Why wasn't Proust readable, like her idol? She decided that she wouldn't be able to really concentrate on *Remembrance of Things Past* till she had finished the new Maugham. That she read through. She was spellbound with admiration. She sighed with regret when she finished the Maugham and then put on Proust again like a hair shirt. Her headache came back.

In the drawing room, Mrs. Baer, alas without an anodyne, undertook Monypenny and Buckle. She read again Kaetchen's inscription. If Stanley Grant resembled the young Disraeli, then the latter must be common too. Her husband, she knew, detested Disraeli, a mountebank he called him. Had she not heard him say once, to a business colleague, that Disraeli's budgets were laughable, a disgrace? She looked in the index to find a budget. She found one and began to read about it but it gave her a slight headache. All those Corn Laws, rates and tithes — incomprehensible jargon. What on earth was a window tax? Ah, if only her sainted husband were alive! He would have seized these disparate, morbid facts, aligned them so that they would be lying helpless there, all their fallacies showing. He could have explained it to her in a minute but she also knew that he had no penchant for elucidating the complex to the simpleminded. She gave up the budget and began to read about the young Disraeli. She read about him in mounting excitement, as she discovered, on page after page, the confirmation of all her prejudices. She hated Disraeli, his flamboyance, his foppery, his showoffishness. He had all the horrid, vulgar qualities associated with a race with which she did not wish to associate. Disraeli lacked so conspicuously her husband's reserve. All those horrible affected novels of his. All those remarks he thought so clever: "I rather like bad wine. One gets so bored with good wine." What kind of a remark was that? It showed a lack of breeding.

Ah yes, Kaetchen was right. Stanley Grant did resemble Disraeli. So much the worse for him. She would give him short shrift. She put the book away in distaste. There was no doubt about it; for once Kaetchen had miscalculated. As an emissary, to open Mrs. Baer's mind to horizons of Jewish possibility, Dizzy was a total flop. To Mrs. Baer he was like "one of those" — an epithet applied by her husband to the uncouth and menacing immigrants from the East.

Mrs. Baer looked at the ormolu clock on the mantel shelf. She must be getting herself ready to receive this young man who appeared to have fascinated her daughter. She would see to that!

Grant arrived tight and in a truculent mood. Why in hell had he accepted? He should have asked Emmeline to bring her mother to have dinner with *him*. He was shown into the drawing room by an English

butler in evening clothes. The gloomy opulence of the house depressed
him. He looked around at the paintings on the walls: portraits of distinguished English ladies and gentlemen, of well-bred dogs and horses.
Emmeline glided in: tall, lovely and unsure. She had a sense of guilt
about not having read beyond page two of *Remembrance of Things Past*.
She hoped Grant wouldn't ask her. At the sight of her, warm and smiling,
Grant's truculence vanished. Whatever her mother might be, Emmeline
was okay.

"Let's go somewhere for dinner," said Grant.

Emmeline laughed.

"You'll have to go through with it," she said, "at least once. Won't
you have a drink?"

"Scotch."

Emmeline gave it to him. Grant was staring at the knotted little figures in one of the vitrines.

"Mother's jade collection," said Emmeline. "She's very proud of it.
You might as well look at them now. It'll save you having to look at
them with Mother!"

"I have to tell you, darling, things like this mean less than nothing to
me. Don't give a damn about 'em."

"Me either," said Emmeline.

They kissed in front of the jade collection which took it in its stride.

"I love you," said Grant.

"I love you," said Emmeline.

"Why don't we go away together?"

"Where?"

"Anywhere you like. Jamaica, Bermuda, Paris."

"Not Paris. I had an unpleasant experience in Paris."

"I will efface it," said Grant, with false confidence. "This house gives
me the creeps."

"Me too," said Emmeline.

"What do you say? Let's go somewhere."

"Are you serious?"

"Perfectly serious."

"Go away? Just like that?"

"Just like that. We'll get to know each other."

"I'm afraid that Mother . . ."

"You should get away from your mother. She's stifling you. Ogden says so. You should get out of this goddamn house and begin to live like a human being — instead of like a jade collection."

Emmeline was blushing.

"I've never said more than ten words to Dr. Ogden. How does he know — to say a thing like that?"

"He *knows*. I owe him everything. I was fumbling and immature. He made a man of me. He thinks we should."

"Is that why you are suggesting it?"

Grant was stymied by this. Fortunately, Mrs. Baer sailed in. Grant was bowled over by her formidable appearance. She certainly had style; black, semidécolleté satin, a strand of pearls. Grant got an impression of tremendous vitality; her energy spun through the room in coils. She had great dignity. She was gracious. She lived up to a Xenia-bred notion of a great dowager lady.

She extended her hand to Stanley.

"It is so good of you to come, Mr. Grant. I have heard so much about you. From Emmeline, of course, and from my dearest friend, Caroline Platt. You made a very great impression on her. I thought it unfair of Emmeline to keep you all to herself. I *insisted*."

Emmeline had asked her mother not to mention that she had seen Stanley's play, and disliked it. Mrs. Baer took possession of Stanley. Emmeline seemed to disappear. Mrs. Baer's presence abolished her. As they moved into the dining room, Mrs. Baer said:

"I haven't seen your play yet, I regret to say, but I hear on all sides how delightful it is. I have to make a confession to you. I do hope you will forgive me."

"I forgive you in advance," said Grant, determined to show that he could be gracious himself.

They were seated at the table in a small dining room. Two butlers waited on them. The courses came and went in legato succession.

"What I have to confess is that I'm not really very interested in the theater. My love is opera. Especially Wagner. Especially the *Ring*. Do you know the *Ring?*"

Grant forgot to be gracious.

"Opera bores the hell out of me," he said.

Mrs. Baer received this as the revelation of unexpected but delightful idiosyncracy.

"Really! How very amusing! Perhaps you saw an inferior company."

"I saw the Metropolitan on one of its tours. I went to Cleveland and bought standing room."

"Ah! but it's not fair to judge by the Metropolitan. These operas, especially the *Ring,* must be seen in Germany and especially in Bayreuth. My husband and I never missed the *Ring* in Bayreuth: Richard Strauss and Toscanini — I heard them both. It was *sublime.* There is no other word for it."

She blew a kiss to Bayreuth.

The Wagner worship put Stanley's back up.

"I loathe Wagner. He's a bloody Nazi."

Mrs. Baer put her hand on Stanley's for a moment.

"Oh, but my dear, Wagner died in 1883."

"His spirit survives," said Stanley.

"But I think it's a great mistake, don't you, to mix art and politics?"

"It may be a mistake," said Grant, "but I can't help making it."

This idiosyncracy Mrs. Baer found somewhat less delightful. There was a tightening of the atmosphere. Emmeline felt a rising panic.

Mrs. Baer noticed that Grant hadn't touched the wine. She had ordered it especially, a rare vintage.

"But you don't drink the wine. I think you'll like it. Emmeline loves it. I ordered especially."

Grant knew he was boorish but he couldn't stop.

"The awful truth is that I don't know the difference between good wine and bad wine. I'm not a wine drinker. I like hard liquor."

"I am sure," said Mrs. Baer, forcing herself to smile at Grant, "that you will acquire a taste for it — as you will for opera."

As the resemblances to Dizzy accumulated, even to their common antipathy to good wine, Mrs. Baer was thrilled. Kaetchen was right — they *were* two of a kind!

Emmeline sat in misery. She knew that her mother's mind had long since been made up. And she had been more startled than she had permitted herself to show by Grant's bizarre proposal just before dinner. Was that all he wanted?

Cannily, Mrs. Baer began to question Grant about his origins.

"Are your parents living?" she asked.

"Unhappily not."

"What a pity! How very sad that they couldn't be alive to witness their son's triumph."

"It wouldn't have comforted them much."

"Really? Why not?"

"My success wouldn't have compensated them for my lack of religion. They were orthodox Jews and their religion meant everything to them. They lived for it."

There was a tiny silence. However, Grant observed, Mrs. Baer did not wince. She had far too much poise.

"Your parents," she went on, "were they born in Xenia too?"

Grant remembered Kaetchen's telling him that Dresden was nice, but he threw Dresden to the winds.

"Oh no. They emigrated from somewhere — I never really knew exactly from where — somewhere in Poland, Russian Poland."

"How interesting! How very interesting! Emmeline, isn't it fascinating?"

In her own mind, Mrs. Baer rested her case against Grant. She had been certain. She could have sworn. Of course! He had to be "one of those," one of that unkempt horde of Eastern immigrants who were the cross her husband and his friends had to bear, who spoiled everything, who were a perpetual reminder, who permitted no wound to heal, nothing to be forgotten, a perpetual threat to their status, an unquenchable nuisance. Grant felt a surge of joy, of exhilaration. He was on to Mrs. Baer. He knew exactly what she was doing. She had pinpointed him. By this time he and Mrs. Baer were deadly enemies. He knew it. She knew it. Well, he would bring this hostility into the open. A crusade — a crusade to emancipate Emmeline! He would show Emmeline that the standards by which her mother lived were antiquated and frivolous. In fighting Mrs. Baer he felt that he was fighting the Germans! He would vanquish Mrs. Baer, emancipate Emmeline and take her to Bermuda. Galahad!

"You know, Mrs. Baer," he said, "it has been alleged that Richard Wagner was Jewish. That equipped him to make the worst kind of anti-Semite."

Emmeline looked at him piteously. She made a gesture toward him with her hand. But the crusader, true to form, was merciless.

"What's the matter, darling?" he said to Emmeline. "You haven't opened your mouth once since we sat down to dinner. Aren't you permitted to make a remark? Go ahead. Plunge in. Make one. I'll protect you."

"Let's have our coffee in the drawing room, shall we?" said Mrs. Baer. She rose. Grant and Emmeline followed her. Mrs. Baer sat serenely by the coffee table. She felt triumphant. Grant was simmering with anger. (Who the hell does this dame think she is anyway — after all, he had a hit show on Broadway.) Mrs. Baer wasn't in the least angry. She had Grant exactly where she wanted him.

"I am sure," she said, "that Mr. Grant will want a brandy."

Grant did. Emmeline gave it to him.

Mrs. Baer, a field marshal at headquarters, began to deploy strategy.

"I wonder," she said, "whether our guest wouldn't be interested in our jade collection."

"He's seen it. I showed it to him."

"Good!"

She turned to Grant.

"You don't like opera. Are you hostile to painting also?"

"No," said Grant, "ignorant, but friendly."

"Ah! I'm so pleased. At last we have found something in common, Emmeline. Show our guest the paintings. You don't have to get up, Mr. Grant. You can see them quite well from where you're sitting."

Dutifully, like a well-behaved child, Emmeline began wandering around the room, pointing out the paintings.

"Gainsborough," she began, "*Mrs. Richard Brinsley Sheridan.*"

"That should interest you, Mr. Grant," said Mrs. Baer. "The wife of one of your predecessors."

"Cute kid," said Grant. "What a hat!"

Emmeline kept strolling and intoning:

"Reynolds — *Mother and Child*, Romney . . ."

Grant interrupted Emmeline's tour.

"I like 'em," he said, "but not as much as all that. Come and sit by me, darling."

Emmeline came and sat by him.

"Tell me, Mrs. Baer," said Grant, "are these portraits all your relatives?"

"No," said Mrs. Baer smiling. "I wish they were. They're eighteenth-century English."

"But don't you have ancestors of your own? Why don't you have their portraits?"

"Because," said Mrs. Baer sweetly, "we are not vainglorious. I have portraits of my husband and my parents in my sitting room. They are personal. We have these masterpieces for our guests."

Grant waved to the paintings.

"But all those are family portraits. They're all personal. And they're all strangers. It seems like an intrusion."

"Time and art make them friends," said Mrs. Baer smiling.

"That's the kind of remark I can't cope with," said Grant.

"Is it a contest?" Mrs. Baer asked benignly.

"You know damn well it is," said Grant.

He looked at his wristwatch and got up.

"Em," he said, "I've got to go to the theater. I've got to see a replacement. I'd like your opinion too. Come with me."

Emmeline was completely thrown off base.

"Now! You want to leave now!"

"We'll be just in time to catch the last act."

She looked at her mother in dismay.

"Genius is eccentric, darling. Sometimes it's uncomfortable. But then, we have to pay the price, don't we?"

"I'm afraid I couldn't go now," said Emmeline.

"Why not?"

Emmeline had risen. She was on the verge of tears.

"I just couldn't," she said.

"This is a test, my love."

She looked at him in agony.

"Test?"

"You remember our conversation before dinner? This is a test. Will you come or not?"

Emmeline couldn't speak. She shook her head.

Grant turned to Mrs. Baer.

"Thank you very much for your hospitality, Mrs. Baer. It has been very . . ."

"Revealing."

"Exactly. Thank you."

He left.

Emmeline sank into a chair. Her head was averted. She was crying. There was a long silence.

"What," said Mrs. Baer finally, "was your conversation with Mr. Grant before dinner?"

As poor Emmeline had never developed a technique for lying to her mother — nor to anyone else — she told her.

The confession saddened Mrs. Baer. More to herself than to Emmeline she said:

"How could a girl like you, who was, after all, married to a son of Caroline Platt's, put yourself in a position where a creature like this could make such a proposal to you?"

Emmeline did not answer. Mrs. Baer went on, musing aloud.

"What a revolting skin he has! What's the matter with his skin anyway?"

Emmeline had no dermatological theory. She ran upstairs to her room.

Mrs. Baer sat on, contented. A good cry would do her baby good. She would be all right in the morning. In the morning Mrs. Baer would lavish comfort.

Her eye caught the ponderous volumes of Monypenny and Buckle. She picked them up and dumped the three eminent Victorians one by one into a wastebasket. Then she went upstairs to bed, happy at having settled the hash of another "one of those."

When Grant telephoned the next day to apologize for his behavior, prepared to put it all on alcohol, the butler, after a wait, reported that Miss Baer was not at home. Grant was pretty sure that she was. He went to the Oak Room at the Plaza to meet Kaetchen. They were giving a farewell lunch to Ogden who was leaving that afternoon for Mexico City. He was going there to interview an important neurologist for the clinic. Mary had returned to California. They had great fun at lunch. Grant described the disaster of the night before. Kaetchen was gleeful over the failure of his emissary. Mrs. Baer had telephoned him to report that the resemblance between Grant and Dizzy was too close for comfort. Kaetchen advised Grant to go to England where he would soon be prime minister. Ogden asked Grant whether he had made it yet with Emmeline. Grant said that he didn't think he nor anyone else could make it with Emmeline while Mrs. Baer was alive. He wondered whom he could engage to kill Mrs. Baer. The logical person, Kaetchen said, was Emmeline and she lacked the resolution. Ogden said that Emmeline was a virgin. Grant said he couldn't quite believe that, since Emmeline had been married twice and at least one of her husbands must have been cooperative. Ogden said he meant virginal in the sense that Emmeline didn't really know what everything was all about. He repeated his advice to Grant, not to marry Emmeline, to hang onto his independence. Kaetchen demurred. Grant must marry Emmeline. They wouldn't be happy probably but at least they would be married. He had, he admitted, a fetish on marriage.

Kaetchen teased Ogden about being in possession of the reigning star of the season.

"You've had your revenge on me, Stanley," said Ogden. "Doris has become a pain in the neck. She's in such demand. She's so busy! She gives interviews. She speaks on the radio. She's treated like a head of state. She has views. She gives her views."

"Moreover," said Grant gloomily, "she's become a wit. She's been told she's so witty that she insists on being witty. It's painful."

"Well," said Ogden, "if things don't work with Emmeline, go back to Doris. I succeeded you. Now you succeed me."

"That's generous of you," said Grant.

When Ogden returned to his hotel to finish packing he found a telephone message from Emmeline. He called. She begged his pardon for disturbing him but she was desperate. Could she see him for a few minutes? He said that unfortunately he was just leaving for the airport. Could she drive him to the airport? Ogden said fine. He went down to the lobby, paid his hotel bill. The bellboy put his suitcases into Emmeline's limousine.

She was very pale. Ogden decided that this pallor became her. He had seen, when he met her at Kaetchen's dinner party, that she was beautiful, but had also known, as he told Stanley, that she was not his type.

"I suppose," she began, "that it's simply terrible of me to impose myself on you this way, but I just don't know which way to turn. Stanley talks so much about you. He worships you. He says you made a man of him."

"He exaggerates. To make a man of Stanley would require more time than I am able to give."

This startled her.

"He's so brilliant," she said. "So cultivated. Isn't he a genius?"

"He may be all that. He is also infantile."

Emmeline was too astonished to say anything. Ogden went on.

"Controlled by infantile ideas. Freedom. Independence. He wouldn't know what to do with them if he had them. He's not equipped for them. He's a natural dependent."

"I should think," said Emmeline sadly, "that that better describes me."

"It does," said Ogden. "That's why I encouraged him to pursue you. Psychology contradicts mathematics. Two minuses may sometimes make a plus."

"He says you told him to ask me to sleep with him."

"I did. He's ambitious, you know, to be a rake. Not equipped for that either. I thought if you consented, it would flatter him. Then, if you still wanted to, you could marry him."

"I'm not that sort."

"What sort are you?"

"That's what I don't know."

"That's what you must find out."

"How?"

He grinned.

"Too bad I'm going to Mexico."

"I wish you weren't."

"Make it up with Stanley. Like you, he is, as they say, unawakened. You both lack sexual confidence."

This puzzled her. She didn't know how to deal with it.

"He was terrible last night. I didn't know he could be so . . . brutal."

"Your mother put his back up."

"She hates Stanley."

"Nor is he enchanted by her."

"If he cared for me at all, why didn't he make an effort? He could have charmed her. Instead he did everything he could not to. He even said it in front of Mother."

"What did he say in front of Mother?"

"That he proposed to me — not to marry me, but to sleep with me."

"He was tight. When he's tight he's not himself. Maybe that's an improvement on when he's sober."

"Don't you like Stanley?"

"Very fond of him. He amuses me no end. Fascinating case history."

"I was in love with him. I wanted to marry him. Now . . ."

"Well?"

"I'm not sure I like him any more."

"Call him up. Make a date to tell him, at leisure, why you don't like him any more. Then sleep with him. It may turn the tide."

"I couldn't. I just couldn't."

"What will you lose?"

"My self-respect."

"Which is the one thing in the world you haven't got."

Her lips quivered.

"That's true," she said. "I'm nothing."

"Start from there. You can't retrogress."

They had reached the airport. Emmeline was crying.

Ogden got out.

"Don't see me off," he said. "I hate being seen off. Here . . ."

He took out a prescription pad and scribbled on it. He gave it to her.

"Have this filled at your drugstore," he said. "It's a sedative."

"It's terrible you're going," she said. "What if . . . ?"

He took another prescription blank and scribbled on that.

"Here. If things get too tough . . . my hotel in Mexico City. Call me up."

He smiled at her.

"But first call up Stanley."

He followed the porter into the terminal.

33. New Year's Eve

It was Kaetchen's fixed habit on New Year's Eve to cross out, in his meticulously kept telephone books, the names of those who had died in the preceding year. It was a little, elegiac ceremony of farewell. He had varicolored telephone books, which he kept replenishing in a shop on Bond Street: London, New York, Paris, Berlin, Vienna. The two latter had now, for some time, been in disuse, the dead outnumbered the living, but the necrology for London and New York had still to be kept up. He crossed off Varina. He crossed off Stephanie. He crossed off Vincent Edward Aldridge, the Third. At Ian's name he paused. Ian posed a dilemma. Was he alive or dead? Kaetchen did not know. No one knew. Probably, no one ever would know. Kaetchen mused on this. It was possible to disappear. It was possible to leave no trace. No one ever mentioned Ian any more. No one remembered him. And yet, while he was about, he had been amusing, attractive; he had, in men and women, inspired passion. Of course, the quartet in whom he had inspired the most voracious passion — Vincent and Vesper, Stephanie and Varina — were gone too. There must have been others, whom Kaetchen did not know. He decided to give Ian the benefit of the doubt. He did not cross him out.

But Stephanie? Varina? While he transfixed Varina he felt a special pang. Nothing could have been done for Stephanie. He did not know how she had died, whether her death had been voluntary or involuntary, but he had never been without the feeling that whatever devices he might employ to bolster her life, it was no use, it must come apart. But why Varina? They were both precious creatures. They had no malice. They wanted other people to be happy. They wished — and they succeeded — to grace their surroundings. They must, he thought, have measured the life they encountered against some idea of the life they had imagined and what it would yield them and found the reality penurious, suspicious, indifferent, withholding. They expected of life the generosity they had in themselves. They must have had visions of glory, intimations of ecstasy which, they had come to discover, would never be vouchsafed. Perhaps, had he been in New York, had he come at once when Varina wired him that she was desperate, he might have saved her. He felt pain and guilt over this. Still, as Ogden had said, when they wanted to they wanted to. You could not circumvent them. They did it. He saw Varina's gray eyes. He heard her low, drawling, caressive voice. He saw the scar on her forehead. She had given him, last Christmas, an exquisite copy of *La Princesse de Clèves* by Mme. de La Fayette. It was there, on his bookshelf. He went over to it. He read her inscription:

For Kaetchen —

That's when I should like to have lived. And of course you would have been there. Henry II would have adored you as does your loving

Varina

Kaetchen sighed and began to pace the room, his hands behind his back. He stopped to look out of the window at the dome of St. Bartholomew's Church next door. He was fond of this church with its varicolored Byzantine façade, its tessellated dome of colored tiles. It was a miniature San Marco, without the great Venetian square in front of it. It was a clear, starry night. He looked up at the tower of the General Electric Building behind the church, a guard and sentinel over it. These two buildings and the strip of Park Avenue, with its double line of traffic, constituted his New York landscape. He paused in front of one of the Czernowitz watercolors: the wooden bridge over the Pruth. That bridge was dominated by a somber triple-spired church, very different from St. Bartholomew's. The church itself was ochre-colored and like a fortress, the three onion-bellied spires a dark and hostile green. It had none of the grace, none of the beguilement of St. Bartholomew's. The trestled wooden bridge over the Pruth lay very low over the water. He remembered how terrified he was of it when, a child, he used to cross it, shivering, holding on tight to his father's hand. Later, when he was older, he would dare himself to cross it on his own and, by doing so, demonstrate his intrepidity and manhood. Later still, when the river was high, he would walk, barefoot, across the bridge and, halfway, sit on the edge of it, dangling his feet in the water. There was traffic in the water, carp and minnows. He hoped that the minnows, who traveled in schools, would touch his feet as they passed and smoothly brush them. But they never did. They always divided cleanly, made an ellipse around his feet and joined ranks directly they had passed the obstacle. He used to wonder at this, why they so sedulously avoided him, how they knew his feet were there since they looked neither to right nor left and were just blindly swimming. He remembered now how this problem had weighed on him. Standing there, in his dinner jacket, fifty years later, he chuckled. "It never occurred to me then but of course the answer is obvious: the minnows were anti-Semitic."

Smiling, he went to the desk where the letter to Monica was lying. He had already sent her a New Year's cable which she would get next morning. Should he add the fantasy of the minnows to his letter? What had he been saying? The flow of his thought was, in a sense, an unending communication to Monica, he never knew which segment he had written down. He read what he had been saying; oh yes, he had been describing his feelings about Stephanie and Varina:

Had I not known them I should not now be feeling pain for them. They would have existed and suffered nonetheless. Think of the placebos that have been invented to persuade us that the dead are not indeed lost to us, that their essences will persist: the vast theological systems, the hierarchies of faith, the eddies of seance, spiritualism. Did you ever know Sir Oliver Lodge? I met him in Salzburg. I have never known a more gracious, modest, enchanting old man. He played tennis into his eighties; I watched him once and extremely nimble he was! As you know he was a ranking physicist. He lost his son — was his name Raymond? — in the First World War. He could not reconcile himself to this fact; he set about to bend it. He investigated spiritualism, came to believe in it and found that, through it, he could communicate with his son. He addressed large meetings on the subject. As I am a frustrated littérateur, I wrote a short story about it. It told of a soldier, left for dead on the battlefield and, on his recovery, a victim of amnesia (that happy condition, solace of the amateur). Not knowing who he is he makes his way to London and blunders into a hall where he sees a distinguished old gentleman lecturing on spiritualism and describing his own communications with his son, killed in France. When the lecture is over, the young man, wandering the streets, suddenly knows that the man he has been listening to is his father. He remembers, too, where they lived and he makes at once for the family house in St. John's Wood. But at the gate he stops. He is arrested by a frightening thought. His appearance will put his father in a strenuous difficulty. He will be branded, publicly, as a liar — at the very least a victim of delusions. He turns around. He doesn't go in. He never makes his presence known. I sent this story to a friend of mine, the editor of a top magazine. He liked the story. He really did. But he advised me against publishing it. Do you know why? Because, he said, the war casualties had been so great and so many people had derived comfort from spiritualism that it would be cruel to deprive them of that comfort. I saw his point and I withdrew the story. You are the first one I have ever told about it. I just remembered it tonight when I found myself trying in some way to persuade myself that Stephanie and Varina were not to be crossed off.

But I must stop skirting the profundities and tell you of the near and tangible. Our friend Robert Sherwood has caused a great stir here with a full-page advertisement he has taken in the New York Times *urging the President to send you fifty of our overage destroyers. You have no better friend here than Bob Sherwood. His existence is a reassurance. He would be burned at the stake rather than abdicate by an iota on a question of principle. His advertisement has met with warm approbation from the anglophiles and the liberals, with searing anger from the isolationists. The anti-Semites are dubbing it a Jewish war. We, certainly, considering our numbers, displace a tremendous portion of the world's attention. I look to you, single-handed, to adjust this misproportion! Well, you are on the front; we are lolling in affluence and safety, gorging on war orders. I, for example, am waiting for your friend Stanley Grant to pick me up to take me to a glittering New Year's party. I am going to use the occasion to give Stanley a piece of my mind. I, in his behalf, have made a cardinal error. I have done what one should never do — to attempt humor with the humorless. They don't understand it; it makes them edgy and suspicious. Disraeli divided England into two nations, the rich and the poor, but there is a more universal dichotomy: the humorous and the humorless . . .*

That is where he had left it. He sat at the desk to continue:

It has, for a long time, slipped Mrs. Baer's mind that she is Jewish; to put her perhaps in a frame of mind to rejoin and to soften her antagonism to Grant, I sent her Monypenny and Buckle's Disraeli. *By doing this I violated the cardinal principle; I tried to meld the unassimilable nations. Mrs. Baer didn't see the joke; she hates Disraeli almost as much as she does poor Stanley. Isn't it funny? But, on the other hand, Stanley behaved very badly. Ogden, who appears to have a hypnotic influence over our brilliant young friend, advised him not to marry Em-*

meline but to have an affair with her. He advised Stanley to do what, doubtless, he, Ogden, would do. Poor Stanley forgets he is not Ogden. I have seen Mrs. Baer, I have seen Emmeline, in a hopeless effort to patch things up. Emmeline wept. Grant moons. He has been unable to reach Emmeline ever since. He wrote an abject letter. No answer. He wrote Mrs. Baer an apology. No answer. All he gets when he calls is the English butler who says that his mistress and Miss Baer have left town and that he doesn't know where. It may even be true. The poor girl is very conventional, unimaginative, like her mother, humorless. Grant has wounded her pride. I've talked to him about it. Will you believe that since Ogden had told him that the first thing he must do is to separate Emmeline from her mother he embarked on an orgy of rudeness thinking that he would accomplish this separation at one fell swoop? Childe Harold! That mischievous Byronic influence again! Byron plus Ogden. Not a good combination for poor Stanley. I hear him say things, utter dicta, that I know don't come from him at all. I say to him: "The voice is Jacob's voice, but the hands are the hands of Esau." Then he outs and confesses. He is, it is astonishing, incredibly naïve. As for Ogden I don't know what to say. You will ask what his motive is. I've asked myself that. I just don't know. Ogden is frank, jolly, amusing, uninhibited — about others and about himself — and, with all that, he is totally inscrutable. Maybe he is, after all, as Sally believed, an instrument of evil. I don't believe that somehow. Maybe he is just, as so many are, simply an improviser and cynical. As for Stanley, I don't know what to do with him. He is at the mercy of every wind that blows: he is amorphous. I sometimes reproach myself for bringing him into a milieu to which he doesn't belong. He would have found it anyway. He was a yokel when I met him; he is a yokel still. His sense of inferiority expresses itself in bravado. He will go to the party tonight and know to the full what Clough, I believe, calls "the horrible pleasure of pleasing the unintelligent." But there's something sad about him. He's better than that. His hollow bravado doesn't persuade him, his shallow triumphs stick ashen in his throat.

Well, my dear, I see that it is nearly 11:30. Grant will be along any minute now. I will post this in the morning. I add another year to a lifetime of applied vicariousness. You, on the other hand . . .

Air left him. It wasn't the cataclysmic pain — it was that there was no air. Beyond the door must be air. He made for it — there to recover the lost medium. He got to the door, opened it and fell across the thresh-

old. The door, closing, was impeded by his body and stuck there. So
Grant, coming blithely down the hall, found him. He knelt. He looked at
Kaetchen's face. It was not his face. He began breathing frantically into
his mouth. Then he stepped over the body and ran inside. He telephoned the manager to send up the house doctor. They came. Grant
watched the doctor kneel over Kaetchen, apply his stethoscope. But
Grant knew.

The doctor got up.

"I am afraid there's nothing to be done," he said.

The manager came up to Grant.

"I'm terribly sorry. We've never had a tenant I liked better. Will you
notify his family?"

"He had no family," said Grant. "He has friends . . ."

Grant turned away. He went to the window and looked out at the
dome of St. Bartholomew's.

"May I use the phone?" asked the doctor.

"Certainly," said the manager. "We'd better get him inside first."

The two men lifted the body and laid it just inside the hallway. Grant
watched. Kaetchen was very little.

The doctor was on the phone calling the coroner. His voice was so
low that he was scarcely audible. Grant spoke to the manager.

"Will the room be left as it is? There are many things here that his
friends . . ."

"Absolutely. As soon as he is removed, I will have it locked. No one
will disturb it. You may have the key anytime you like. Anyone else
authorized."

"Thank you."

Grant felt that he was choking up and must get out. He saw, on the
desk, the unfinished letter. He knew what it was. He had teased Kaetchen about his endless letters to Monica. There were about seven sheets
of Hotel Ambassador stationery covered with blocky, black-ink, clear
handwriting. He looked down at the last sheet. His blurred eyes caught
the words: "You, on the other hand . . ." He picked up the sheets,
folded them carefully and put them in the breast pocket of his dinner
jacket. It was the last service he could perform for his friend. He would
post it to Monica. In silence Grant shook hands with the manager and
went out. He walked out of the hotel into an irredeemably diminished

world. No more Kaetchen. He must see somebody. He must talk to somebody. He must call Lloyd McIlwaine. He remembered that the Borns were in town, staying in a hotel two blocks away, on 52nd Street. He rang them from the lobby. Frau Olga asked him to come up.

The next morning, on New Year's Day, he sent a straight cable to Monica:

DEAREST MONICA KAETCHEN IS GONE. HE WAS WRITING A LETTER TO YOU WHEN IT HAPPENED. I WILL POST IT TO YOU TODAY. BORN SAID LAST NIGHT WHEN I TOLD HIM THAT HE FELT HE HAD BEEN KILLED. THAT IS HOW I FEEL. WRITING. ALL LOVE. STANLEY

He went to the wardrobe where his dinner jacket was hanging and took out the letter. He brought it to the desk by the window, addressed an envelope to Monica and opened the letter to refold it. At the last words, there was an ink splotch. Evidently Kaetchen's pen had fallen from his hand. He decided to put the sheets in order. He saw his name. Kaetchen had been writing about him. He had been in his thoughts at the end. He read it. He read everything that was written about him. He made no further effort to put the sheets in order. He simply found the first page, with the salutation, quickly folded the sheets and put them in the envelope. He did it very quickly, as if, if he didn't do it quickly, he might not send the letter at all. He sealed and stamped it. His heart was beating fast. His hands were shaky. He put on his hat and coat, mailed the letter in the chute on his floor and went down. He must walk. He felt like walking. On the street he headed west.

"The very word," he kept saying to himself, " 'amorphous. At the mercy of every wind that blows.' Exactly the word."

Other things from the letter — words, phrases — kept beating at him: "sense of inferiority," "bravado" — what exactly had he said? . . . he couldn't remember exactly — "yokel then, yokel now," "horrible pleasure" — what was that about horrible pleasure? . . . he couldn't remember — "ashes in his throat" — what was that about ashes in his throat? All true . . . all true. And yet Kaetchen loved him. He'd said that, hadn't he, he'd said something like that. Still, to one who loved him, this is what he was. "Amorphous." It couldn't have been better put. That was the truth about him.

As if to walk out of amorphousness into definition, he strode along blindly, as if propelled. He reached 12th Avenue. The great ships were moored at their docks; the horizon was flanged with smokestacks. He liked the sight of the ships; they represented escape, on one of them he could change into the new form, register under another name, sail. But, already, he had another name. In front of the French Line pier he stopped. On the gaunt, lopsided hull, the letters smeared and mangy, he read: NORMANDIE. There she was, the great, once-proud ship, lying on her side in the dirty water, obscenely naked, peeling with rust, a gutted planet. He stopped and stared, aghast. He'd read about the fire which had done the *Normandie* in but the sight of it, to see her there, inert, helpless, disemboweled, sprawled in the water, was stupefying. He ran his eyes over the helpless creature, trying to find the verandah, the deck where Varina had stood, when she was shooting at the clay ducks. Odd bits came back to him. Ian. "Let everybody telephone everybody." Indeed there had been a great deal of telephoning on that voyage. The electrified ganglia with which the ship was threaded had been alive with messages, invitations, plans, flirtation, expectancy. René Wolfsohn had telephoned him to propose a subject. Grant had let it ring without answering. "The sign of a weak man," Wolfsohn had said. "Amorphous." The spectacle of the wallowing ship was gruesome, symbolic of the world itself lying half submerged in blood.

It was New Year's Day and bitterly cold; there was hardly anybody on the streets. Grant hailed a taxi and drove back to the hotel. When he stopped at the desk to pick up his key he was handed a cable and a message to call Mrs. Kennicott in Santa Barbara. He wondered whether she knew. He was exhausted from his walk and nerveless from the sight he had seen. In his room he sat on the sofa and opened the cable. It was from Acapulco, Mexico. He read:

KENNETH AND I WERE MARRIED THIS MORNING. YOU HAVE OUR LOVE. WE WANT YOUR BLESSING. EMMELINE. P.S. NOW WILL YOU GO AROUND SAYING I AM ANTI-SEMITIC? HAPPY NEW YEAR. KENNETH

His first impulse was to go down to show the cable to Kaetchen. That would have been a session! He wouldn't have been in the least surprised. Nothing surprised Kaetchen. From where he was sitting Grant picked up the telephone, called room service and ordered a double Scotch.

Grant realized that he had no one in the world to talk to, no one in the world to tell about this. Mary. He might telephone Mary in Santa Barbara. Did she know about Kaetchen? If she didn't it would be devastating to tell her. Doris? How would Doris feel about this? Would she be heartbroken? He looked at the large, silver-framed picture of Doris on the mantel shelf with the flourished, all-loving, all-admiring inscription. She was beautiful, certainly, but that beauty which had not so long ago preempted him seemed meaningless now. It was Emmeline he loved. He had thrown over Emmeline, preserved her for Ogden.

What should he do? He could jump out of the window. That would be fast. At least it would be an act. It would be definite. It would be conclusive. It would not be amorphous.

One thing he knew. He must get out of these rooms. He had moved here to be near Kaetchen. Now there was no reason to stay. He would find himself some human rooms, a flat. He would build bookshelves, start a library. His reading was fitful, sketchy. He would start a course of solid reading. He had had nothing to eat that day. The Scotch, on an empty stomach, gave him a sense, he used the phrase on himself, of logical insanity. He read the Ogdens' cable again. Where was Kenneth's independence, what had become of his freedom? He felt that neither would be impeded.

Then he remembered that there was a holiday matinee at his theater. He would go to see Doris. He would break the news to Doris. He would console Doris. He would propose to Doris. He ordered another double Scotch and a sandwich.

Grant arrived at the theater about the middle of the second act. The house was sold out, so he stood at the back with the standees. He hadn't been lately; he'd forgotten how marvelous Doris was. It was really extraordinary: she was so cool, so poised, so mischievous — the silvery rubato of her phrasing in the comedy arpeggios was a joy to hear. Moreover there was the abiding quality of good will toward everybody; you felt that she wanted to quicken the pace of the stragglers in life, to guide them to felicity. Grant was carried away by her. He must do another play for her. He began to think again about the play he had started in Hollywood; he hadn't looked at it since. He would get out those notes again and fit Doris into it. He would offer it to her when he went backstage. He would, he thought, offer her more. He must take a step. He had loved her before. He would love her again. They had both suffered disappointment; they would soothe each other, be companionable. Presently, in the scene between the stage-Ogden and the stage-Sally, he heard the line of the actual Ogden: "The poor have tonsils but only the rich have souls." It was unfailing; the laugh was terrific. Grant saw himself in the elegant Mirabelle in Salzburg, sitting opposite Ogden, marveling at his factitious candor. He remembered riding back to Stephanie's in the taxi, writing that line on a pad. It had cost him a hundred dollars but it was, as far as his play was concerned, beyond price. He remembered more: that was the day he saw Schwester walking with the uniformed storm trooper, the barber. What had become of Schwester? Where was she now? Had she rejoined her barber or was he at the front? She was nice, Schwester. He had been fond of Schwester.

In the interval he wandered around among the audience, picking up remarks, as is the scavenging habit of playwrights. He heard little about his play; it was all about Doris. There was praise also for some of the other actors, especially for the one who played the doctor. Grant didn't wait to see the last act; he went to a bar next door.

Doris's dressing room was crowded with fans. When he appeared she waved to him over the heads of her visitors and made her way to him. She embraced and kissed him.

"Stranger! You've neglected me. Where on earth do you keep yourself?"

She whispered to him to wait a few minutes, that she'd get rid of them. Out loud she made a mass introduction:

"This is my author," she announced. The fans permitted themselves a glance at the curiosity. Grant disappeared. He had a brief colloquy with the stage manager, who clocked the laughs.

"Great at matinees," he said. He showed Grant his chart. "Eighty-four," he said. "Six bellies."

When her visitors had gone, Doris's maid mixed Grant a drink. Doris sat in front of the mirror removing her makeup and conscientiously chewing gum.

"Now, darling," she said, "we can be cozy. Kind of expected you last night. It was terrific."

"I was busy last night," said Grant.

"But you were expected at the party. Everybody was asking for you."

"I meant to come but I couldn't make it."

"That was mean of you. Aren't you happy? Isn't it terrific?" She threw him an arch smile. "Are you sorry you engaged me? Took the old boy Kenneth to persuade you, didn't it?"

"I have news for you about Kenneth."

"Really? What?"

"He's married!"

The announcement surprised her. She turned in her chair but didn't stop rubbing.

"No kidding! Who to?"

"Miss Baer."

"Who she?"

"Tall dark girl. You met her. At 21 — the opening night party."

"Oh sure. Kenneth told me you were sweet on her."

"Well, they're married. Just got a cable from Mexico."

"He has this big thing about independence." She laughed. "That was his alibi with me!"

"You don't seem to be heartbroken."

"Who? Me? That's been over since before the play opened. That was just a quickie. And if you've still got a crush on this Miss Baer, hold your horses. It won't last long. Ken's the most conceited son-of-a-bitch I've ever known and I've known plenty. Miss Baer has my sympathy."

There was a pause. Grant was deflated. He had been prepared to initiate a mutual consolation party.

"Doris?"

"Yes, sweetie?"

"I've begun a new play. I think it would be great for you."

"Gosh, I'd love to read it. I'm sure it's wonderful. You couldn't write anything not wonderful. The thing is . . ."

"What?"

"My agent's got a terrific deal on the fire for me in Hollywood. They offer me the Pacific Ocean."

"But you've done that. Wouldn't you rather . . . ?"

"Oh, no honey. They always fobbed me off on stick parts. This, my Lord, I'll have you know is STARDOM. All the fixings. Script approval. The works."

Grant managed a smile.

"I'll give you script approval — on my play."

"I don't need it on *your* play. There's another side to it, honey."

"What's that?"

"I'm crazy in love. I'm going to get married."

She looked at him.

"Say! You look startled. Didn't you think anyone would want to marry me? Just because Ken didn't!"

"Who is it?"

"I'll show you." She spoke to her maid. "Marie, ask Terry to come in, will you?"

"Terry? Terry who?"

"Terry Shea. Our stage manager. He's going to be a director. He will be too. He's very creative."

It was the laugh clocker. He was a tall, skinny fellow, with nice blue eyes and a crewcut. Doris got up and stood beside Terry with her arm around him.

"Best stage manager in the world. Everybody knows that. From now on he's going to manage *me*. Are you up to it, darling? I'll be sweet as pie."

Terry grinned. He was embarrassed.

"Congratulations," said Grant.

Terry nodded.

"You're the first one we've told. Outside of Terry's parents, of course. Keep quiet about it for a little bit, will you, darling? Give us your blessing."

It was the second time that day that nuptial benediction had been demanded of Grant.

He rose to go. He shook hands with Shea.

"I've got a new play for Doris. Can't you talk some sense into her and keep her from going to Hollywood?"

Terry looked at him sheepishly.

"She's the boss," he said.

"So far!" said Doris.

She threw her arms around Grant and kissed him.

"When I pick my first script," she said, "you're the boy I want to write it."

Grant left.

"You sprang that on me sudden," said Terry. "In my overalls and all."

"I had to," said Doris. "In another minute he'd have proposed to me. Considering he's the author and everything it would have been embarrassing."

34. The Explorer and the General

Mr. Lloyd McIlwaine took charge of Löwe's funeral arrangements. The ceremony took place in a nondenominational chapel where the familyless and churchless, the celebrated and the notorious, the obscure, who had devoted friends like Mr. McIlwaine, were detained briefly to give the survivors a chance to offer each other public consolation. As master of ceremonies, Mr. McIlwaine arrived early and was at once faced by an emergency which he didn't quite know how to cope with. He was confronted by Selig Langfeld, the epical novelist, who carried, in his one good hand, a white rose. The novelist was distraught. He did not believe that his benefactor was dead. He insisted that McIlwaine have the coffin opened. If it was really Löwe in the coffin then he wished to place the rose in his hand. Mr. McIlwaine wiped his forehead and said that this was impossible. The novelist, not knowing that McIlwaine was the benefactor behind the benefactor in the coffin, became truculent. McIlwaine, desperate, went to the sidewalk to get help. He saw Grant get out of a taxi and enlisted him. Grant took over the skeptical mourner. He assured him that Löwe was indeed dead, he had seen him just after it happened. He persuaded the novelist to put his rose *on* the coffin and promised that there would be no other flower to compete with his.

The chapel was crowded. Mary Kennicott had flown east to attend the funeral. She sat with Grant and Katie, the chambermaid from the Ambassador who had looked after Löwe. "There never was," she whispered to Mary in her soft Irish brogue, "a kinder, quieter-spoken gentleman." She wept into her handkerchief. The Borns were there. Born found some mystical significance in the manner of Kaetchen's death, in the fact that he had died "on the threshold." There was a cabalistic symbol, he was sure, in the threshold. Dr. Binder was there and young Federn, with Dr. Binder's Irish nurse, whom he had married a few weeks earlier. There were the great, the famous, the notorious and the anonymous, refugees whom Kaetchen had helped, the persona of his other, nonopulent nation. There was nothing perfunctory in the mood of the mourners. Mrs. McIlwaine said later that she had attended many funerals of the great and the famous, and that never at any of them had she encountered the grief that throbbed at this funeral. A little string band played "Wien, Wien, nur du Allein," a syrupy melody glozing the evil of the murderous city. On the coffin was the novelist's single rose. Mr. McIlwaine spoke briefly and movingly. The speech had been written for him by his chief staff writer, but he felt the words as keenly as if they were his own. The theme was "the green thumb." Some people, he said, had psychically, in their temperament and in their sympathies, a green thumb and could make flowers grow even in the aridity of the awful present. They had a genius for friendship, unassertive, often anonymous but powerful. Their friend, he said, was often actuated by ulterior motives, always for the amelioration of the burdens of the unfortunate. Of course, he need not speak to those present, the bereaved, of their friend's charm. The night it happened, sleepless, he had been irked by the thought of how impossible it would be to convey — to his own children, for example, when they were grown, to anyone who had not known him — what their friend's personal quality had been. It was elusive, it was evanescent but for the lucky ones here, it was cherishable, unforgettable, pervasive. It bound them all together. He hoped that the bonds would not loosen, that the little society — "the friends of Kaetchen" — would meet often to remember him.

The audience stood while the pallbearers took Kaetchen away. Selig Langfeld observed, with hungry eyes, that his rose accompanied his benefactor.

Mary took the Borns, Grant and Katie downtown in her car. They sat in silence.

"We were his family," said Ludwig Born.

That night Grant took Mary to dinner. There was, Grant felt, a great change in Mary. She had an air of having given up. She was warm and interested and humorous, but Grant felt that she had resigned herself to the role of the observer. The down-droop of her mouth which Grant had noticed the first time he met her on the *Normandie* was now accentuated in a fine line. She told Grant that she was going to devote the rest of her life and her fortune to break the stubborn secret of the mystery in the brain that had divided her husband's, separating it into irreconcilable sectors of light and of darkness and that had finally separated him from the world. She had engaged a new head for her clinic, the brilliant neurologist whom Ogden had found for her in Mexico. On Ogden's marriage Mary made no comment. Grant brought it up but it was obvious that Mary had no wish to discuss it. It belonged, seemingly, to a past that was already dead for her. She permitted herself one remark about Ogden:

"With one hand he gives," she said, "with the other he takes away."

She spoke of letters she'd had from Sally. They were clear and funny; she felt that Sally was happy. In one of the letters she had described a visit of Eileen and her husband. She had greatly liked Klaus Wolff. Eileen had brought Amos to see her and this reunion was delightful. Amos plucked at her rosary and wished to own it. Sally had been sorry to deny him.

"Does she say anything about me?" Grant asked.

"She asks whether I see you and made me promise to write her about your play. I have done so. I described how Kenneth had won his bet." She permitted herself an aside. "Kenneth always wins his bets, doesn't he? But don't you ever hear from Eileen?"

"Oh, yes. Fairly often. From Klaus too. Amos is flourishing, Eileen says. 'He's almost a sabra,' she writes with great pride."

He saw Mary's questioning look.

"That means native born, in Palestine," Grant explained. "I'm going to visit them as soon as the war makes it possible."

For the rest, they reminisced about Kaetchen, laughed over his foi-

bles, his little crotchets, the acceptance and devotion to the secondary
role he had mapped out for himself in life. Mary asked Grant what his
plans were. He said that he felt quite at sea. His immediate problem
was to find a place to live. He couldn't stay on at the Ambassador now
that Kaetchen had departed from it. Mary undertook to find him an
apartment. She had intended to go back next day but she would stay
till she had found him a place to live. She did. Three days later she ushered him into a charming, agreeably furnished apartment — two floors
of a converted brownstone in the East Sixties. Mary took pleasure in
showing it to him.

"Here," she said, "you can write masterpieces."

"Anyway," said Grant, "I can read them. It's the first home I've ever
had."

He kissed her good-bye and promised, when he was depressed, to
come to stay with her in Santa Barbara, a condition, he added, into
which he would probably be plunged the moment she left.

He was. He didn't know what to do with himself. His success in the
theater was no comfort to him. It was a repetition of the first accident.
How could he go on writing these things, these comedies, with the great
cloud over the world, with the *Normandie* lying on her side, with Kaetchen gone? He was thirty. He had been married. He was a father. He
had failed as a husband, failed as a father. He was, in fact, at the core,
in the most intimate sense, isolated and a failure. Hadn't Kaetchen said
it in his letter — "ashes in his mouth"? He hadn't started out at all to
be what he had become. What had he become? That's what he didn't
precisely know, that was the question he couldn't answer. That's what
Kaetchen must have meant when he said "amorphous."

He thought of writing to Monica. He thought of going to see her.
Would she want to see him? Why should she want to see him? Had she
liked him really? What had she thought of him? She was the most entrancing woman he had ever met. She had been so kind, so humorous —
she had appeared to enjoy his jokes — she had been warm and gracious. But hadn't it been for Kaetchen's sake? She would receive so
any friend of Kaetchen's. But outside of that — for himself — what
had she really thought?

His self-hatred took a new and obsessive form — a hatred of his name. It not only was not his name, it wasn't any name, it was a name for nobody. It was a fabrication, just as he was.

He hadn't thought of it for years, he had totally forgotten it, but one evening, reading again *Remembrance of Things Past,* it came to him painfully and clearly, the exact moment when he had concocted that name, the very morning, the moment, the scene. It was a bitterly cold morning in Xenia. It was snowing hard, the windowpanes of the bedroom in his parents' squalid tenement were thickly frosted. He'd just had two rejections from pulp magazines to which he'd sent stories. He had a sudden conviction that no one would print stories under an outlandish name like his own. He decided to change the name with which he signed his stories, to acquire a new personality: heroic, remote, distinguished, a name that would obliterate everything: Xenia, the frosted windowpanes, the tenement, poverty, the epithets of hostile schoolmates. He pieced it together carefully, in a spasm of invention: an African explorer and a famous general. He was very pleased with it. You couldn't do better than that. The combination was impeccable, unassailable, obliterating. Enthroned in his new personality, he sat down to write a story called "The Waltz" which told about a romance started at a dinner dance in Newport, Rhode Island.

In his absorbed remembrance, he was interrupted by the telephone. It was Lloyd McIlwaine. Mr. McIlwaine had devoted himself to the task of settling Löwe's estate, such as it was. He had known, Löwe had told him, that he had two nieces, one in Mexico City, the other in the Argentine. McIlwaine had delegated his correspondents in those places to inform them of their uncle's death. They were both in indigent circumstances. He had decided, therefore, to hold a private sale of Löwe's effects. He thought that Grant might want to buy some of the things. Grant certainly did. The sale took place in McIlwaine's office on the thirty fifth floor of the building which he owned and which was occupied entirely by the offices of his enterprises. Grant found there the little coterie, most of whom he had met through Löwe. There were all of Löwe's effects, placed on tables and arranged around the walls. Grant felt, for a moment, as if he were back in Kaetchen's room in the Ambassador. He bought the four Czernowitz watercolors, the reversible black and white kitten which he meant to send to Eileen for Amos, and

the two little blue-and-gold-bound volumes of Montaigne, published by
Oxford, the translation of the seventeenth-century Florio edition. There
was considerable good-natured competition for the watercolors and for
the kitten but Grant was determined to have them and he got them. He
took these things himself in a taxi to his apartment. First, he looked
through the little Montaigne books. They were heavily annotated in
Kaetchen's square, clear handwriting. He decided he would go through
both the little books and list the annotations; they would give him an
insight into the workings of Kaetchen's mind. Then he removed from
the walls of his living room the excellent copies of French impressionist
masterpieces which hung there and substituted the bamboo-framed
Czernowitz watercolors. He looked at them with happiness: Kaetchen's
home town in all its aspects.

All in all, he felt there was a lot to be said for Czernowitz. It was colorful, it was lively. The square in front of the Primaria, he imagined it
was the City Hall, was crammed with men and animals: peasant women
carrying geese, their men leading cows and oxen, sheep and horses. They
stood in little groups, the women in kerchiefs, the men with round fur
hats. The Primaria itself was substantial and handsome, with two large
wings and surmounted by a clock tower. Here was the teeming center
of the town with the awful reputation, the town which, Kaetchen had
told him, was occupied entirely by hochstaplers. The impression Grant
got from the scene before him was of idyllic innocence. The children,
their parents, all of them, were obviously on affectionate terms with
their animals. And yet the collective rumor about Czernowitz was mephitic, so much so that it was an act of defiance to have your card
printed as Kaetchen had his: ALEXANDER LÖWE, *aus Czernowitz*. Were
all these people milling around before him hochstaplers? Where was the
skullduggery which was the town's principal export? Not visible here,
certainly. Maybe all these dark deeds took place inside the City Hall.
Inside were the mayor and his staff. They must be up to something inside there, surely, conniving and corrupting, extorting bribes, doing everything in their power to keep up the town's unsavory reputation.
Czernowitz must not be let down! Was it, though, Grant wondered,
more corrupt than Xenia? Was there more skullduggery there than in
New York? Certainly it was more picturesque than either Xenia or

New York, closer to the soil, closer to nature, closer to the animals, who stood around like citizens.

Grant had looked at these watercolors innumerable times, but always glancingly. Now that they were in his charge he studied them with a keener eye: the Tiermarkt, where animals were bought and sold. Here the animals overwhelmingly outnumbered the people, they were either browsing or passive while they were being inspected. Surely, they were doing nothing to enhance the town's reputation. He came then upon *Alter Jüd Friedhof,* the Jewish cemetery. He stared at it; he'd never really looked at it before. It seemed to him that the tombstones had gone mad, that they had been seized by mass hysteria. There was no order among them; they leaned away from each other, as if in aversion. The cemetery was on a hillside, the headstones climbed up the hill drunkenly, impeding each other. He brought his hand glass over, tried to decipher the flaked Hebrew lettering. He had studied Hebrew when he was a child — his father had insisted and kept him at it for as long as he could, which wasn't long. He was determined to ferret out the identity of at least one of the deceased. But he couldn't. He applied his hand glass. With a kind of painful shock he managed to decipher one word in one name: ben — the son of. But he couldn't make out anything else — he couldn't decipher who the son was the son of. He looked and looked at the sharply angled memorial of the son of somebody. It was part of his own name: ben. He had been teased about it by his schoolmates at Xenia Grammar School. "Ben isn't a middle name," they had insisted, "it's a first name. Either you're Jacob or you're Ben. Why don't you make up your mind?"

Grant went back to his armchair. He sat for a long time, lost in thought. That anonymous ben in the forgotten cemetery had stirred him in a singular way. He had, the day before, taken out the notebook in which he had written down the idea for a new play. He'd begun it after his macabre interview with Ogden. He had come to murder and remained to pray. He had thought it would be about a pure and dedicated scientist who had come to murder a sophisticated no-good who had done him in about a girl. Grant was surprised to find how many notes he had taken on it. The idea had come from his infantile ambition to kill Ogden. Spastic emotionalism! Well, he no longer wanted to kill Ogden; he was no longer a potential murderer. But it still seemed to him to be a valid, comedic idea. He was taken now by another and even more powerful idea than the homicidal one which had swept him in Hollywood. He would take his own name back. He would readmit his father. This play would be by a new and unheard of author. His dramatic agent would hit the ceiling. He had taken such trouble, poor fellow, to establish the trade name. Well, he would just plain have to do it all over again, in behalf of a more cumbersome and exotic name.

He took a sheet of paper and put it on the drawing board on which he worked. He wrote out carefully, in caps:

NO REPOSE IN BALI (TENTATIVE TITLE)

A COMEDY BY

JACOB BEN SION-TRYNIN

He didn't know quite how or why but he felt good about this. He said farewell to the shades of Sir Henry Morton Stanley and Ulysses S. Grant. Perhaps, now, he might find out who he was.